I0757322

THE DEVIL'S PROMISE

HALEY MOREAU

Copyright © 2025 by Haley Moreau

All rights reserved. Printed in the United States of America. No part of this book may be used or reproduced in any manner whatsoever without written permission except in the case of brief quotations- embodied in critical articles or reviews. This book is a work of fiction. Names, characters, businesses, organizations, places, events, and incidents either are the product of the author's imagination or are used fictitiously. Any resemblance to actual persons, living or dead, events, or locales is entirely coincidental.

ISBN: 979-8-9914247-1-4

First Edition: June 2025

10 9 8 7 6 5 4 3 2 1

To those who have ever been lost.

Spotify Playlist

To listen to the playlist, I created to go with the story, scan the QR code below.

To Hell
Armaros
Nephilim Point
Lake Lethe
Elysian Blood Bank
River Styx
Elysian Injury Clinic
Elysian Coven
Vampire Lair
Kore Gardens
Unity Center
Elysian Science Center
Apollo Arts Center
Headquarters
Shopping District
River Styx
Shifter Den
Demon District
Lake Triton
N
S
E
W
ne
nw
se
sw

The Devil's Promise

Haley Moreau

CHAPTER 1

It is done.

The invisible chains wrapped around her wrists melted from the heat. Orange and yellow flames licked from the windows, feeding off the breezy August night air. It wasn't supposed to end like this. Her freedom wasn't supposed to come at the cost of death, no matter how deserving. Sirens blared in the distance, but they would be too late. Neighbors emerged from their homes, standing on their lawns in their pajamas and robes, preparing themselves for tomorrow's gossip.

Two men dressed in identical checkered pajama pants and white t-shirts ran towards the fire. A younger man screamed her sister's and her names. She knew that voice. The drawl of her name on his lips had always felt like home.

"What did you do?" Alice Delco rasped out, staring at the fire in disbelief.

"I did what you asked me to do, Pet," her boyfriend, her savior, Lucian, drawled as he stepped towards her. She flinched at the snap of twigs on the ground as he approached. She remained frozen in her spot just behind the tree line on the side of her house. Her blue eyes were fixed on the flashing red and white lights of the now-approaching fire truck.

"No." She swallowed hard. "You never said anything about murder."

"You wanted a new life away from them. This is the cost of being able to live your life on your terms. I did what you asked me to do." He placed a hand on her shoulder. She couldn't get her body to move to shrug him off.

"When the police find out they were murdered," she whispered, her voice thick with emotion. "They'll want to know where my remains are."

"No one will find out. No one will know you survived. It's a clean slate." His breath was hot on her neck. Between the hot breath, the adrenaline coursing through her veins, and the heat of the blaze, Alice was a ticking time bomb.

"Everything I own just turned to ash."

"All are from the dust, and to dust, we shall return." Lucian quoted the Bible mockingly. The words sliced through her. He knew how important that Book was to her.

Alice inhaled deeply, only to choke on the smoky air. The coughs turned into sobs as the firemen doused the house with water, cleansing the sins from within the four walls.

This was the beginning of a new life. No longer would she be her parents' puppet. No longer would she be forced to live under anyone's rule. This was her chance to live how she wanted.

The two men from earlier came barreling out of the house, leaning on two firemen, their white shirts now gray with soot. Mason Ward and his father were taken back across the street to their front yard where Mrs. Ward and her daughter Morgan, Alice's best friend, stood in horror. Mason shook his head, and Morgan fell to the grass with a loud, earth-shattering sob. The sound was heartbreaking and shocking, like stepping into an ice bath. Mason knelt to the ground and pulled his little sister into his arms as she sobbed. Their parents held each other tight in grief.

"I need to go to Morgan. I need them to know I'm okay." She watched her best friend sob. The noises emanating from her did not sound human. Alice felt Lucian's hands on her shoulders, pressing down to keep her in place.

"That wouldn't be moving on, Pet. You'd still be holding onto the past, to your old life, and not the new one in front of you," he rasped lowly in her ear.

The Wards were the only ones who cared about her. They were her real family, and she couldn't even say goodbye. Her heart shattered at the thought of living the rest of her life without her best friend.

Morgan Ward was her best friend and true sister in every sense of the word. They were supposed to be each other's maids of honor, aunts and godmothers to their children, and the old ladies wreaking havoc in the nursing home. Now all those dreams went up in smoke. And she would never be able to tell Mason, her childhood crush, that even though he never saw her as anything more than his sister's best friend, she'd been in love with him since she was thirteen.

At half past three in the morning, her house collapsed. Everything she knew was reduced to nothing but rubble and ash. Once the smoke and dust cleared, it was eerily silent. Leaving only the shrieks of terror emanating from Morgan as she struggled against her brother. He kept a tight grip on her to keep her from running and sifting through the debris for her friend. It took everything in Alice's power to not run over and tell Morgan she was alive. Instead, she whispered her goodbye before turning to her boyfriend, if he could be called that. She didn't know what they were anymore, but he was all she had now.

Lucian sat on a broken tree trunk; boredom etched across his face. She walked over to him, her steps faltering the closer she got to him. As if on cue, he opened his arms for her, and she fell into him with a sob. She grieved for her life, for her parents and her sister. Deep down, she knew they did not deserve her grief. Had the roles been reversed, they would have sighed with relief that she would no longer be a burden to them. She never wished death on anyone but herself, and now she'd have to carry this with her forever.

"It's time, Pet. Let's go home." Lucian placed light kisses on her dark brown hair.

"My home is gone." Alice sniffled, her cries finally dying out.

"That was your house. That was never your home," he stated, pulling her into a gentle, comforting hug.

"Where do we go now? Where's home?" Her

question was muffled against the scratchy fabric of his suit jacket. She hadn't even bothered to ask where he'd been when she'd called him hysterically.

"Wherever you want. Just say where, and we'll go," he murmured in her hair.

Alice sniffled again as she wiped her eyes on her sleeve. She thought about where she could begin her new life. She would be indistinguishable in a busy city. But not here on this side of Pennsylvania. Events like tonight don't happen in their small town, and it was bound to make the news tomorrow.

Lucian said anywhere. The world was at her fingertips. She could finally go to Paris, London, or even Australia. But there was one place she loved the most. A place she felt at peace. It would be a good place to mourn and grieve until she could figure out the next steps.

"The beach." She finally lifted her eyes to meet his icy blue ones. The ice in his eyes had melted since she last looked at him. In its place, soft baby blue eyes gazed at her sympathetically. "The beach is calming. I need its peacefulness and calmness while everything sinks in."

Lucian's pearly white smile gleamed in the dark. Normally, that damned smile made her heart skip a beat, but now her heart was too heavy to notice. "Bora Bora is lovely this time of year."

Alice shook her head. "We spent the summers in Rehoboth Beach. I'd like to start there. For now."

Lucian went slacked-jawed. Ashamed, she snapped her head back the smoldering remains of her house. "Are you sure? We could go anywhere. Mexico, the Bahamas, Hawaii… And yet, you want to go to Delaware?" She frowned and pushed herself off him. He stood up with her, shaking off the tree bark that clung to his suit.

Alice nodded her head. "Please. I need something to hold onto right now. We can figure out our next moves after."

Lucian huffed but didn't argue. Instead, he picked her up bridal style. "Hold on tightly."

Alice started to wrap her hands around his neck when something feathery brushed across her fingers. She yelped as she pulled her hand to her chest. "What the hell are those?" She gasped, her face paling. Large, black, feathery wings peeked over his shoulder.

"Wings." Lucian stated coolly. He shrugged as if having wings was perfectly normal.

Alice's eyes widened and she kicked her legs violently, despite the tight, burning pain radiating from fresh cuts on her upper thigh. One hand was pressed against his chest and the other tried to pry his fingers off of her legs. It was of no use; he had her locked against him. "What the hell are you? Who the hell are you?" she asked, eyes wide with fear. Lucian met her stare. Gone were the blues she had fallen in love with. Solid crimson red eyes stared at her intensely. The red was so bright and overbearing she couldn't even find his pupils.

"I'm Lucian."

"The hell you are," Alice snapped and continued squirming fruitlessly.

"I'll explain later. Let's go before dawn comes," he said. Alice stared him up and down. He looked like her Lucian. He spoke like her Lucian. Yet her Lucian did not have wings. "Do you trust me?"

Alice looked away. Between the fire, which she knew he started, the wings that just came from out of nowhere, and those red eyes, she wasn't sure who he was. But he was all she had now. Reluctantly, she nodded her head and closed her eyes tightly as she buried her face in his chest. His familiar cinnamon, nutmeg, and clove scent wrapped around her like a blanket. It was another reminder that the man holding her was still her Lucian. His muscular arms tightened around her as they lifted into the air.

The wind roared around them. She squeezed her eyes shut and buried her head further into his chest. Immediately, her body tensed up, and her stomach began to flip flop. She tried to think of anything to get her mind off of the fact that she was airborne. For once, she ignored the thoughts about herself, about how she was too big to be carried. He held her easily and without so much as a huff of struggle. The flaps of his wings were even and steady. The wind whipped around like they were creating a rhythm to their own song. Alice squeezed his neck tightly, but he never said anything about not being able to breathe. She felt them go higher and higher into the early morning sky.

After what felt like ages, she opened her eyes and carefully turned her head to the side. She had a fear of heights, but she couldn't help but peek. She gasped at the sight. They were soaring high in the air. The roads were small, and the cars were the size of ants. Even the big trees seemed minuscule. She shut her eyes again and buried her head back into his chest as bile rose in her throat. Her body trembled with fear. Even his comforting scent was failing to do its job. She needed her feet on solid ground—now.

Alice decided she was dreaming. People do not just sprout wings and fly. Any time now, she would be waking up in bed— in her bed in her house—with Lucian by her side. This would all just be a nightmare.

Lucian repeatedly reminded her to breathe and that she was safe. No other words were spoken, leaving them both to their thoughts. Alice wasn't sure if that was a blessing or a curse. Her head was starting to hurt as the evening played through her brain like a horror film.

He landed gracefully onto bricks. He did not once stumble or falter, nor did he loosen his grip on her. Her body was still quaking with fear. Her muscles were locked tightly, and if she opened her mouth, she would vomit.

"We're here, Pet. You can let go now. You are safe," he whispered as he loosened his arms. She shook her head no and gripped onto him tighter. He didn't say anything about it. He seemed content and ready to stand there holding her for eternity. Once her shaking calmed, Alice pressed one foot onto the hard ground, then the other. Lucian slowly released her, letting her stand on her own. As soon as he withdrew his arms, her knees gave out. She hit the bricks on all fours and vomited right on the spot.

Lucian held her hair back from her face and rubbed her back soothingly. "You're okay, breathe," he whispered calmly.

Tears of embarrassment formed in her eyes. Alice heaved until nothing more would come out, then wiped her mouth and sat back on her heels. "I'm deathly afraid of heights."

Lucian did not seem fazed at all. "I'm sorry. It was the fastest way to get here," he apologized. It almost sounded genuine.

Alice inhaled deeply and shakily. Her eyes blinked open and she wiped the tears away with her sleeve. A dark mansion loomed in front of them. The distant thundering of the waves was her only clue that she was at the beach.

"Do you think you can walk? Or would you like me

to carry you?"

"Is this your place?" she asked with wide eyes and an open mouth. The building was a beautiful, rich-looking mansion. Both of her parents were doctors, but even they couldn't afford a house like this.

"More or less." He shrugged.

"I'm sorry for puking. I'll clean it up," she mumbled.

Lucian gave her a reassuring smile, "Don't worry about it. I'll handle it. Don't move." He ordered her and disappeared towards the garage. Alice sighed and tried to stand up. She barely had one foot under her before her knees gave out. Her palms splayed out on the asphalt as she braced herself. A door opened and she could hear Lucian mumbling but she could not make out what he was saying. "I got you." He gathered her into his arms and lifted her up.

He laid her down on a plush tan couch. Alice curled into a fetal position. Her face was wet and tear-stained, but she was done crying. There was nothing left in her to cry out. In its absence, a familiar numbness crept back into her bones. The same damned numbness that was the reason for the damned evening.

Lucian appeared before her with two full glasses and a bottle. The wings were gone, and his eyes were blue again. He took a seat on the coffee table and handed one glass to Alice. She gulped down the amber-colored liquid. She grimaced in pain from the burning in her throat. The drink tasted awful. The burning pain, now that she liked. It wasn't as euphoric as a razor blade, but it did the job. She snatched Lucian's glass from his hand and downed it immediately. She let the burn wash over her and bring her warmth. Little by little, the thoughts in her head quieted. Lucian refilled her glass and then his, but she threw back his glass before he could taste it.

"You know this is whiskey, right?" he asked. Amusement sparkled in his eyes and there was an easy smile on his lips. Alice shrugged and held out her glass with her right hand. Lucian filled it up. "Easy, Pet. The alcohol will go to your head." She'd take anything other than the thoughts that consumed her.

"What the hell was that?" she croaked out and took a smaller sip of the whiskey.

Lucian focused on the swirling amber liquid in his glass. "What was what?"

She sat up as she spoke. "Humans don't fly. They don't sprout wings and fly. And they certainly don't change eye color."

Lucian chuckled darkly and glanced over at her. He took a sip of his glass. "I'm surprised you haven't figured it out yet. You're very intelligent. It's one of the things I admire about you."

Alice cocked her head to the side. Damn right, she was intelligent. She got into a good college, one that she wouldn't be able to go to now. Whether that was a blessing or a curse, she wasn't sure yet. She finished the glass, her face not flinching as much now. Her body was feeling quite warm as the alcohol worked its way through her bloodstream. It was almost as blissful as using a razor blade—and certainly less bloody. She reached for the bottle, but Lucian pulled it back. She pouted; the alcohol was helping her forget. She needed to forget, just for a little bit.

Lucian walked the bottle back to the bar. "You need some sleep," he said as he put it away. Alice watched him carefully, taking note of where she could find the bottle later.

Alice laid back down on the couch, staring at the darkened fireplace. Her tired bones and her eyes grew heavy. Her eyes shut and she immediately succumbed to sleep.

CHAPTER 2

Lucian sat beside her on the bed for hours. His blood was boiling in his veins. He was just itching to get back to Hell to give her parents a taste of their own medicine. Soft snores vibrated through the room. His eyes blinked open to see the human's lax and peaceful sleeping face. This was one of the few times he ever saw anything other than pure depression and faked happiness on her face. He got up from the bed and walked to the floor-to-ceiling window. Twinkling brightly in the pre-dawn sky was the morning star. A soft smile tugged at his lips. It was beautiful, something that would take the girl's breath away.

Now she could see it whenever she wanted, and no one could stop her.

He glanced back over at the girl sleeping soundly. Something in his soul tugged at him to stay in case she woke up from a nightmare. Her parents' final act could wait since they weren't going anywhere, but he did not want to wait. Karma was due *now*.

Slowly, he tiptoed out of the room and went back downstairs. In the center of the living room, he rolled back his shoulders and let his arms drop. His fingers stretched towards the earth. He closed his eyes and envisioned his throne room. Blue flames flickered and flew out from his fingertips, hitting the wooden floor and forming a circle around him. The flames grew high above his head, engulfing him completely. Little by little, the fire began to diminish, giving way to his stone throne room. The room was dim save for a few flame-lit torches along the wall.

Thayne, the Angel of Death stood beside Don, the Angel of Hell, awaiting commands. Don's signature twisted smile stretched from ear to ear, a predator waiting to attack his prey. Don's seconds, triplets who called themselves the Furies, stood in the center, each one holding a member of the girl's family in a chokehold. At his command, the Furies kicked in their captives' knees, forcing them to kneel to the Devil—the very thing they threatened Alice with time and time again.

Lucian's black feathered wings unfurled to their full span. Her parents' eyes widened, and their faces were etched with horror and fear, just how he liked it. Her sister, however, did not look at him. Her eyes were glazed over and stared into nothing. It was like she'd already known she would end up here and had accepted it.

He prowled over to them. "Thou shalt not take the name of the Lord thy God in vain: for the Lord will not hold him guiltless that taketh His name in vain." Lucian quoted the verse he had memorized a long time ago. His deep voice echoed throughout the room. He loved using the Book against those who weaponized it. The demonic parts of him flared up to the surface begging to be let out. He also loved this part; seeing the reactions from the humans when they saw who he really was. He shut his eyes, feeling the shift into the darkness. When he opened them again, red eyes stared her parents down, and he gave them a sinister smile. "Silly Humans, did you honestly think that hurting an innocent girl in the name of our Father would get you a one-way ticket to Heaven?"

Her father, now red-faced and angry, opened his mouth. Lucian nodded once to Don in a silent order in a quick, lethal swipe of the blade, the sinner's tongue dropped to the floor. Lucian silenced her father like he had silenced Alice over and over. Her mother's terrified screams filled the air. Alice's sister didn't even flinch. The screams and torture had become standard in her life. Background noise. Had she not contributed to Alice's pain, he would have felt sorry for her.

The Devil bent down to the sorry excuse of a Human's ear, his voice a deadly whisper. "Never again will you utter such blasphemy. Never again will you silence a woman in order to fit your ideals."

At Lucian's command, Don sliced the man's right hand as if he were slicing cake. In another quick swipe, the left hand dropped to his stone floor. Blood poured from the man's mouth as he gurgled in response to the loss of his hands.

"Never again!" Lucian's deep bass-baritone voice boomed throughout the room. The echo seemed to make him bigger and taller than his six-foot-five frame. His eyes darkened with the power he held over these souls, "Never again will you pick up the Holy Book to spew such *unholy* things. Never again will you lay a hand on a woman or child, nor will you handle them like they are property."

Lucian turned his attention to her mother. The aging woman mouthed a prayer. "You willfully blinded yourself to the horrid acts of your husband. You looked away while your daughters were beaten on like punching bags. You turned a blind eye when they needed you the most. Instead of helping them, you kept your eyes on the Word of God." He stretched out his hands and looked around the room mockingly. "Where is your God now? Where is your Savior?" he taunted the woman. She sobbed in response, pleading for forgiveness.

Lucian nodded to Don with more silent orders—out went her tongue and eyes. The Devil spat on her parents and turned to Don and the Furies. "Take them to the tombs and the girl to the Pit."

The Furies dragged her family out of his throne room. Victoria had purposely been left unharmed. Although not blameless, she was also a victim and didn't warrant more pain than what she would already receive in the Pit.

The Devil took his seat on his Throne, leaning back with his hands covering his face. The joy he usually got from torture sat like a dead weight in his gut. He let his selfish urges destroy the order of the universe. The Witches and the Angels will be on his ass as soon as word gets out—and it will. The Demons gossip like rich housewives with nothing better to do with their day.

Thayne walked over to him first, sensing the heaviness. "The mother was a victim too, you know."

"I know," Lucian said curtly as his eyes slid over to him. The Angel of Death had always been more mild-tempered, more understanding, and more open-minded about people. He saw the goodness of Humans to balance the evil, whereas Lucian just saw evil. "I can't, in good conscience, allow her in the Pit. She had a choice to protect herself or her children. She chose herself and, therefore, needs to pay the price."

"It's not that easy, Lucian—"

"Like you know what it means to choose between yourself or your children." Lucian snapped. Thayne, like the majority of Fallen Angels, had handfuls of illegitimate children. Like Alice, Just about all of those children were unwanted. "I lost control, okay? Is that what you want me to tell you?" He growled. "I killed them in cold blood. She didn't ask me to kill them."

Thayne exhaled an expletive. "She really means something to you, doesn't she?"

Lucian shrugged as he took a deep breath. "Something about her..." he trailed off. There were no words to describe the Human, and he didn't know why he even cared so much about her. She was a child. "She's special."

Thayne raised his eyebrows in concern. Lucian rubbed his face in frustration. For the first time in his billions of years, the act of killing weighed on him. He'd survive, obviously, but would she forgive him?

The Angel of Death sighed and ran a hand through his copper hair. "We can handle Cate and the Witches, but pray that Micah doesn't find out what you did."

The Devil barked out a sad laugh, "Micah only pretends to care about the humans. The only person he cares about is himself. We're fine."

CHAPTER 3

Late morning sunlight streamed through the bedroom windows. Alice's head pounded as she rolled over and curled into the soft bed. Her hand splayed out beside her, sliding the length of thin sheet, and came into contact with a hard body. Her eyes flew open to see a snoring Lucian sleeping soundly beside her. He had slept over the sheets and had a light blue blanket laid over his body, ending at his knees. Fuzzy socked feet peeked out from the other end. He was fully dressed in a white shirt and black shorts. A much more casual look than the suit he had on last night. As she pulled her hand back, a black mark on her left wrist caught her eye. She lifted her wrist to her face to see a cursive 'L' in the middle of a pair of black feathery wings. It was just like the feathery wings

Lucian had sprouted last night. She licked her thumb and wiped the mark to rub it off. The mark did not fade or smudge. It was tattooed onto her ivory skin.

Alice looked away from her wrist to the ocean view. The sun glistened on the water tempting her to go for a swim. She looked back at Lucian's sleeping form, and the night before came crashing back to her.

Fire. Smoke. Screaming. Her house burned to the ground with her parents and sister inside. Alice leapt out of bed, putting as much distance between them as possible. She ran out of the bedroom and down the hall to a spiral staircase.

She came to a screeching stop at the front door. Lucian had brought her to the beach at her request. She had nowhere else to go. She had no relationship with her father's extended family, and her father had cut off all contact with her mother's family years ago. There was no way she could go to them after this. Despite the guilt gnawing in her gut, her heart felt lighter. The aloneness she felt did not feel as dark and overbearing as it did twenty-four hours ago.

She turned toward the interior of the house and walked almost hypnotically to the back door and into the warm summer day. The large deck gave her a perfect view of the Atlantic Ocean. Alice took a seat on the wicker couch immediately to the left of the door and pulled her feet up. She focused on the gentle roar and movement of the waves and the loud squawks of seagulls.

Alice wasn't sure how long she'd been staring at the waves. The noise of the sliding door jolted her into reality. Lucian stepped outside, his eyes squinting from the bright sun. "Good afternoon," he rasped. God, that voice… She could listen to it forever, and now she might. He ran a hand through his short, messy black hair. He took a seat on the other end of the couch. "How are you feeling?" he asked softly.

"My head is pounding." Her voice crackled as she rubbed the side of her head.

Lucian chuckled. "It's called a hangover."

"I know what it's called," she snapped. Lucian smirked as he stretched his legs out and leaned back. The two stared out at the vast ocean in front of them. The silence between them was deafening and the tension thick enough to cut with a steak knife. Alice finally looked over at him. "You killed my family."

"A thank you would be nice."

She ground down on her teeth. "Who are you? What are you?" The man beside her looked and sounded like her Lucian, but he wasn't. This Lucian was a psychopath. She stared at him, burning holes into the side of his face while he stared out at the ocean.

Lucian deflected the question by standing up and changing the subject. "You should eat."

Her mouth dropped open at the notion of food. She couldn't fathom how he could even think about breakfast after what he did last night. He strolled casually into the house, leaving her alone. She shot up and stormed after him. "Lucian, get back here. We're going to talk about this now!"

She had been so out of herself last night that she hadn't noticed the giant open kitchen with an island and dining room on the corner of the large room. The cabinets and drawers were a sandy color, keeping in the theme of a beach house. On the white granite countertop was pancake mix, syrup, and chocolate chips. The coffee pot in the corner roared to life as it brewed a cup.

She climbed onto an island chair with a huff and watched Lucian flit around the kitchen with ease, seeming to know where everything was. It was like he had been here or lived here before. Not that he had ever mentioned it to her. She obviously didn't know the man as well as she thought.

Alice stared at his muscled back and tight shirt. The wings she had seen last night were gone. There were no slits or holes for wings in the fabric. She didn't even see a dark color through the white shirt. The man making pancakes looked Human. But after last night, her gut was telling her he was anything but.

She silently listed off all creatures with wings in her head. None that came to mind had a human form. Her eyes scanned the house and landed on a cross on the wall above the archway.

The invisible lightbulb lit up as an icy cold shiver went down her spine. "You're an Angel," Alice whispered, astonished. There was no way she could be in the presence of an Angel. Her parents always told her she wasn't good enough to be graced with the presence of an Angel. Although, it would explain that ethereal glow he had about him and that effortless beauty that made her swoon.

Lucian placed a light blue mug in front of her filled to the brim with steaming coffee, the color a light brown. He already poured the right amount of cream in it for her. He remembered how she liked her coffee. An *Angel* remembered something about her. She was tempted to push it away, but the smell of freshly brewed coffee was too enticing to her pounding head. She brought the mug to her lips and took a sip. "A Fallen Angel, technically." His voice was even, like they were discussing the weather.

Alice choked on her coffee, the liquid almost coming out her nose. She set the mug down and grabbed a napkin from the holder at the end of the island. She believed in Angels. She spent every Sunday morning at the Lutheran church near her house. But Angels, fallen or not, were spiritual, not realistic. She took another small sip of her coffee. God, he even added vanilla syrup, he made her favorite coffee without having to ask. Her muscles began to loosen up. "Angels have white wings."

"Correct. But Fallen Angels' wings turn black when they fall." He plated the pancakes onto two plates and brought them over. He set her plate in front of her.

Despite her emotional protest, her stomach growled loudly. "What did you do? To be forced out of Heaven?"

"Just a little teenage rebellion." He chuckled, laughing at a joke she didn't understand. He slid his knife into the tub of butter.

The realization washed over her like an ocean wave in January. She felt the hair on the back of her neck stand up. He wasn't just any Fallen Angel. He was *the* Fallen Angel. She had fallen in love with the Devil himself. She was a God-fearing, Jesus loving girl who went to church every Sunday. She prayed to God and spoke to Him daily and still managed to let her guard down long enough to let the Devil in. Everything she had been raised to do, she failed. If her parents had still been alive, they would kill her and tell her she really was going to Hell.

Yet, there he stood. The Devil she had been taught to fear was a far cry from the messy haired, slightly bearded, kind, blue-eyed man who stood before her. He had been so nice to her ever since they'd met. They joked, laughed, played soccer, and watched movies together. The man before her never showed an ounce of evil towards her. He was the kindest person she knew, aside from Morgan and Mason. Although she was told the Devil was a sneaky bastard and he would do anything he could to pull her away from God.

Lucian slid a copper coin across the island to her. "Penny for your thoughts?" In the beginning, the two quickly learned that they were both heavily introspective people. One day, Alice gave him a penny she found and jokingly offered him a penny for his thoughts. The two now had a collection of pennies to swap between themselves.

She bit her lip and picked up the coin. All the memories from the last few months played in her head as she twirled the coin between her fingers. "You're Satan."

"I prefer King of Hell or the Devil," he said proudly, albeit a bit dryly, as well. He cut a piece of the pancake and put it into his mouth.

Alice's eyes traveled down her left arm to the tattoo. She held out her arm for him to see. Lucian's eyes drifted to the tattoo, and he gently rubbed a thumb against it, admiring the work. Her skin unfortunately tingled at his touch. "Why do I have that?"

"Because you are mine now," he rasped darkly. There was no mistaking the additional possessiveness in him that terrified her. His eyes frosted again into that iciness she hated. She preferred the soft baby blues that looked at her like she was important.

Her eyes narrowed. "I thought that fire last night gave me freedom. Freedom means I don't belong to anyone."

"Freedom also comes with a price."

She pulled her arm into her chest. "What do you mean?"

"Do you remember what you said to me before the fire?" he asked coolly.

Alice pushed her breakfast and coffee away from her. She thought back to the haze that was last night. Her face fell, and her muscles tensed at the memory. "Oh, my God." Shock and anger flooded her bloodstream. "No." She couldn't have, yet she did. "Give it back," she demanded as her vision turned red.

"I can't. It's binding. Your soul is now mine to collect when I see fit." Lucian's tone was dark and final.

"You tricked me!" Alice growled through clenched teeth, slamming her fist on the counter. The silverware rattling. "You led me to believe you liked me. I let you into my life. I fell in love with you! And not once did you feel the need to mention that you were the fucking Devil?" She got up from the island and stomped to the back door. Not only had he lied to her, he had condemned her to a life on his terms. Her life was done when he said it was. That was not any more freeing than being forced to become a doctor and live a life she despised.

"Alice, come back." Lucian followed behind her. "We're not done discussing this."

"The hell we aren't!" Alice roared. Her right hand wrapped around the door handle. Lucian grabbed her left hand and tugged her back towards him. In a fit of rage, she pivoted to face him and swung.

As fast as lightning, Lucian caught her fist with his hand before it contacted his annoyingly handsome face. Smirking, he lowered her arm. "Easy, tiger."

"You bastard." Alice tried to flail her arms to hit *something*. It was futile to think she could injure an Angel anyway. Her arms barely moved from the pressure he had on them. Lucian bound her wrists together against her chest. His long fingers circled her wrists, squeezing them tightly. He pushed her back, pinning her to the door. His eyes darkened, and his lips quirked into a twisted smile. The Devil, in all his Demonic glory, leaned down to her, his lips almost touching her ear. "Keep that up and see what happens," he warned before letting go and stepping away.

Her heart thumped hard against her chest. He was no better than her father. He had tricked her, made her feel safe and then hurt her. "Fuck you," she panted. No matter how much air she gulped down, it wasn't enough to steady her. Alice remained pressed against the cool glass. Whatever she thought was between them had just been a figment of her imagination. She was just a toy to him.

"How much time do I have left?" she asked once she felt her lungs and heart steadied, her voice small and shaky. Her face scrunched up as she braced for the answer.

The Devil had wandered back to the kitchen table to finish breakfast. He shrugged his shoulders and swallowed his bite of pancake, "The rest of your natural life, which is considerably more than what the rest get. Unless you do something unsavory that puts your life in danger."

"Is that supposed to make me feel better?" she asked sarcastically. She knew what would happen if she kept her attitude up, but she couldn't bring herself to care. She was already dead.

"Yes, you can be happy now. Your life is now fully your own. The world is yours for the taking. Don't let your family win," he tells her softly. They already won.

They had told her many times that she was going to Hell, and now she was.

"Don't think for a second that I forgive you for hiding what you are from me. I would have never uttered those words if I knew who you were," she hissed.

Lucian barked out a cold laugh. "Of course, you wouldn't have! You were too afraid to stand up for yourself. If you had not sold your soul, they would have been on track to kill you—or you would have done it yourself."

Alice's face flushed hot with anger. She knew deep in her soul that he was right, but that did not allow him to throw her suicidal thoughts back into her face. Alice swallowed expletives she wanted to throw at him and stormed out of the house. She walked down to the deserted beach and sat on the damp, densely packed sand. The icy cold water ebbed and flowed by her feet, but it didn't cool the fire raging inside her.

CHAPTER 4

Lucian watched her walk out the door with her name dying on his lips. He exhaled instead and ran a hand through his messy hair. She was not like the other Humans he had dealt with, and it infuriated him. Typical Humans reveled in the idea of power, money, and love. Normal Humans were quick to shed their earthly ties. Husbands and fathers giving up a good and average life with their wives and children without a second thought for a new life that held very little meaning. Very few gave it up for freedom or in exchange for another life. This girl had the world at her fingertips now and was squandering it with grief over people who never loved her.

Nothing about her lined up with his normal interactions with Humans. Then again, there was something about her that *wasn't* normal. He shook his head as if trying to shake her from his thoughts. Yet, here he was, playing house for an ungrateful Human. He didn't have to do anything for the stupid girl, but there was something about her that he could not stay away from. He didn't *want* to stay away from her. She was made for something bigger than this stupid little Human world.

He wrapped her plate of uneaten pancakes in tinfoil, muttering under his breath. "I constantly go out of my way for her. I got her out of her house when she asked. He spent weekends playing soccer with her when she asked. I learned to cook for her, for Hade's sake!"

Lucian finished his breakfast alone, not bothering to wait for her. If he had learned anything from the women in his life, it's that it's better to stay away when they're fuming.

His back was to the sliding doors when they opened. He turned his head to see the girl walk towards the stairs, bypassing the kitchen completely. "Your breakfast is getting cold."

"I'm not hungry," she snapped.

"Eat. Now," he demanded. The girl stopped in her tracks, and he could see the fear creep into her skin. She only responded to anger and violence, and it hurt him to know that. It *pained* him to use it against her to get her to act. He hated to see her upset. He'd spent one too many nights holding her, comforting her after she had gone around and around with her family. The number of times he spent wiping the blood off her face from their fists or from the self-inflicted wounds on her body was one too damn many.

She crossed her arms like the insolent teenager she was. Her back was pressed against the stair railing. "I do not have to listen to you. My life is my own now, right? That's what you told me."

Lucian glanced down at her tattooed wrist. She covered it with her other hand, rubbing it as if it burned her. It probably did. He could control any soul of his when he was near them. It would burn incredibly hot with the rather aggressive souls. He sent a little bit of fiery heat in her direction, then lifted the coffee mug to hide his smile of satisfaction. "You belong to me now. If I say jump, you say how high. Now, eat."

The girl glared at him for a moment. "One." He warned her like he was scolding one of the Nephilim toddlers or his nieces when they were younger. She stood her ground. "Two. You don't want me to get to three," he threatened. The girl huffed as she walked back towards the kitchen and took a seat at the dining table. Lucian unwrapped the tin foil and set the plate in front of her. He played dirty, but someone had to try and keep her alive, and it sure as hell wasn't going to be her.

"I'm not a child," she fought weakly as she cut the pancake.

He leaned against the counter with his cup of coffee as he watched her. "Then stop acting like one."

She raised her middle finger at him with one hand. The other held the fork as it stabbed mini holes into the pancake. It was pathetic and almost painful. He would rather spend a few hours in the Pit than watch this.

"Are you ready to talk yet?" he asked her softly once she finished.

"There's nothing to talk about."

Lucian's nostrils flared. "Yes, there is. You need a new identity. You can't remain Alice Delco. I need to get your new license and the other important documents you'll need." She could finally be the wonderful person she was. Not the clone her parents wanted her to be.

The girl didn't bother lifting her head. He didn't even know why he bothered helping her start her new life. He never helped any of his souls. He didn't have the time, nor did he want to. He should have just left while she was outside, but something in his gut kept him near her. Something about that damn aura she had framing her body like a halo. She must have been a Saint in her previous life.

She stayed silent.

He exhaled loudly and slammed his mug on the counter. Hot coffee sloshed onto his hand. The hot liquid felt like ice compared to the heat of his anger. "You know what? Fine. I don't have to help you, I *wanted* to help you. I know you can be so much more than what they wanted you to be. I'm sorry you can't see that. If you want to waste this second chance, fine. I can take you down to Hell right now. It makes no fucking difference to me." After more silence, he turned his back on the childish Human and started walking out of the kitchen.

He got to the doorway when she whispered, "What do you need to know?"

Lucian halted and slowly turned around to face her. He leaned against the archway. "Well, for starters, what do you want to be called?"

The girl set her silverware down and leaned against the back of the chair. Her hand went to her mouth, and she picked at her lip, a nervous habit of hers. She did it unconsciously every time she was deep in thought.

He leaned against the doorway and watched her struggle for a name. "May I make a suggestion?" She considered letting him speak, then nodded once.

"Celeste," he suggested hesitantly. Her ocean blue eyes lit up with the reference to Cosmos. She loved the night sky. He had been there when the sky was created, but she knew more than he ever cared to. Now she was free to explore the unknown, both on Earth and in the sky.

She slowly pieced together a middle and last name. Alice Jane Delco was now dead. Celeste Mae Ride rose from the ashes of her old life. Her middle and last name in honor of her two role models. Her new middle name in honor of the first African American woman in space and her new last name in honor of the first American woman in space. The woman in front of him was a new person. One her parents could never maim. One her sister could never critique.

CHAPTER 5

Summer faded into autumn. Time went on yet she remained trapped in grief and blame. The blood on her hands kept her tossing and turning at night.

Lucian seemed content to stay here with her. He spent his days stealing souls, making deals and ruining lives. Celeste spent her days on the beach. Not tanning or swimming in the ocean, just sitting on the sand and staring at the waves. The movements calmed her and distracted her from her grief.

Their nights were spent in separate rooms under the same roof. Much like how she lived with her family. Celeste spent her nights in the master bedroom watching reruns of her favorite television show. Lucian spent his nights downstairs in the basement den where the previous owners had their entertainment room. The only time they were ever in the same room at the same time was at dinner.

Every night well after the sun went down, she'd trudge up the deck stairs to see Lucian waiting for her at the outdoor dining table with dinner. He tried to get her to eat other meals, but she conveniently left for the beach before he could order her to eat. Any food left out or in the fridge for her went untouched to spite him.

"I need to leave," Celeste blurted out one Mid-October night while drying their dishes from dinner.

The soapy dish in Lucian's hand slipped back into the sink with a clang and his head snapped to her. His eyebrows furrowed with confusion. "As I said before, you can stay here as long as you like. This is your home now."

"This was only supposed to be temporary," Celeste reminded him. "A place to be while I grieved."

"Okay," Lucian agreed and nodded slowly as he picked up the dish he had dropped and handed it to her. His face was void of emotions. "Where should we go next? If you still want to be warm, we could go to Australia or New Zealand. South America would be lovely."

Lucian was so calm about her request to move. He was ready to pack up and go with her on her command. A heavy weight dropped into her stomach. He may have her soul, but if she ordered him around, he'd probably do it with a smile. She set the now dry dish and the towel on the counter and stared at the tile backsplash in front of her. "I..." Celeste sighed nervously, unsure how he was going to react to what she was about to say. Her hands flattened on the counter to support the heavy weight she now became. "I'm going alone. The ID and the documents are in my possession. I don't want you to come with me." Celeste's voice got smaller like it did whenever she tried to take up for herself.

Her body tensed and froze with anticipation of being grabbed or having her hair pulled. She closed her eyes and winced, ready for the pain. None came. "You need me, Pet," Lucian's voice darkened in a whisper.

Celeste didn't dare look at him. *You won't survive without us;* her father would tell her often at the dinner table. "You are the King of Hell. Don't you have souls to torture and people to deceive?" Celeste held in a breath as she waited for the hit that never came.

"Where do you think I go when I'm not here with you?"

"No. You aren't getting it." Celeste shook her head and finally faced him, her eyes focusing on the wooden cabinet behind him. "I don't know you anymore! You look like Lucian, and you sound like Lucian, but you're not the Lucian I met at the beginning of the year. That Lucian was sweet, thoughtful, and kind. And you—" Each word louder and thicker than the last. "You steal souls and torture people in this giant pit of fire. You have black wings and red eyes. And most importantly, you lied to me."

Lucian leaned against the counter next to her. His arms crossed over his chest. "Yes, I lied to you, but it was for your safety."

Celeste's eyes rolled into the back of her head. "The Lucian I knew understood how much I value honesty and trust. This Lucian broke it the minute you tricked me into selling my soul! Now, I have to spend the rest of my life trying to forget what you took from me and what's waiting for me on the other side." She crossed her arms and looked away from him.

Lucian took her head in his hands and forced her to meet him eye to eye. His held that icy rage that she'd only seen when she spoke about her father. "What I took from you? You mean what I saved you from!"

Celeste scoffed as she pulled his hands away from her face. She took a step back to put distance between them. "You took away my chance to go to Heaven, and the Lucian I fell in love with knew how religious I was and how serious I was about my faith!" Out of all the things her parents forced her into, her faith was the one thing she loved. It made her feel less alone in the world.

"I haven't forgotten. You have to understand—"

She ignored him and continued, "And when I see you, I don't see the freedom you have supposedly given me. I see a life of servitude!"

The Devil's jaw ticked. He bit his lip as he shook his head in disbelief. "You have another eighty or ninety years to do everything you could ever want. Most only get ten years at most. I am allowing you a full life! How many times do I have to say it? Do you need to hear it in another language?" he snapped. "You are an ungrateful bitch, you know that?"

Celeste grimaced. She knew. Her parents told her that at least once a month. Especially when she told them she didn't want to play any sport other than soccer, and when she fought them when they enrolled her into academic summer camps she'd never agreed to go to. She crossed her arms and tried to steel herself. "And you're a cold-blooded killer!"

The Devil growled, turning and stomping away. Suddenly, he whirled around again and stalked to where she stood. His face was inches from hers. Red eyes bore into her blue ones. Her heart fluttered. She needed to get away from him, but her feet glued her to the ground. With teeth bared, he snarled, "I didn't have to bring you here and take care of you while you sat around and moped and felt sorry for yourself. I didn't have to help create a new identity for you. I didn't have to do shit! I could have left you there in Pennsylvania with nothing but the shirt on your back and let you figure out what to do from there. So, tell me again how I'm not the same person you met earlier this year! You think you know me based on my title, but you are so wrong."

His breath was hot on her face, but she didn't flinch; she knew better than to give a reaction. He stormed away from her, creating space between them. He roared loudly in frustration. The demonic undertone had her jumping back towards the archway. Lucian slammed his hands onto the granite island top. His fingertips began turning red, and she could see a small stream of smoke from under his hands. Lucian inhaled and quickly released his hands off the counter, his handprints now burned into the granite. He gently shook out his hands to calm himself down.

Her eyes widened as she watched him. Lucian had never lost his temper in front of her before, and this shook her to her core. Another piece of evidence that the man in front of her was not the same man she fell in love with. This Lucian could easily burn, choke, or strangle her after one more quick remark. He was more lethal than her parents.

"Did you even love me?" Celeste asked bluntly. She did her best to keep her breathing even. Lucian's face softened, but he did not say anything back to her. His silence was a knife to her heart. "I loved you, Lucian. But I guess the Devil is incapable of love."

He blinked and stood there as if she caught him off guard for once. Lucian broke out into another dark roar of frustration that reverberated throughout the room. His arm swung, hitting the napkin holder on the island and sent it flying across the room. It hit the wall, leaving a small dent and clattered to the ground. He pinched the bridge of his nose, and a dark chuckle rose from within him. "They were right! They told me it was a bad idea." He paused and stared at her, stared into her soul. "You are just a stupid, silly Human. You think because you go to church every Sunday and worship my Father that you know everything about me, who I am, and what I'm capable of." He shook his head and paused for a moment before speaking with an icy evenness that cut right into her. "I'm sorry I let it get this far. This was a mistake. *You* were a mistake."

The invisible knife in her chest twisted. She blinked back the tears and rolled her shoulders back, keeping her composure. He continued, "Maybe you wanted to be a doctor more than you let on. Maybe you secretly wanted that life, because you don't seem grateful for getting out. They aren't here to make your life worse or to cause you pain. You no longer have them blocking you from your dreams, and you are acting like I sentenced you to life in prison! Or maybe you just liked having a reason to slice your skin open, for people to see you and give you attention."

The knife twisted more, ripping her heart as it turned. Tears welled up in her eyes and threatened to fall over. Lucian knew the line and had passed it in spite. The scars on her wrist were tingling, calling her. Going upstairs and cutting would stop her crying and would numb her. It would numb her enough to forget. Although there would be no forgetting the words *You were a mistake.* She knew that. She heard it enough that she believed it. Her mind told her that every day of the week. Hell, she had the word carved into her hip after a particularly bad night a few years ago.

He tossed his key onto the island in her direction. "As I said, this mansion is yours. I *inherited* it from a soul I took years ago." He stepped away from the island, arms at his sides and fingers pointing to the ground. Blue fire spurted out from his fingertips and enveloped him in a circle of blue flames. The flames grew tall and touched the ceiling. When the fire rescinded, the Devil was gone. The fire left no trace or burn marks on the wood or ceiling.

The beach house was eerily quiet. She could barely even hear the roar of the ocean waves. Celeste was truly alone now.

CHAPTER 6

Lucian appeared on his friend's lawn. He did not want to go back to his empty house. If he was lucky and the Witches weren't ready to murder him, they would have some kind of calming brew on standby.

As he stomped to the door, it swung open before he could knock. All the lights were on inside. He found his friends at the younger Witch's kitchen table. An open box sat in the center with black and white cards scattered around.

"What are you doing here, Lucian?" the homeowner asked without enthusiasm. She was still pissed. Lucian ignored her as he stalked over to the kitchen in search of her bourbon.

"Trouble in paradise?" the Angel of Death smirked, earning a whack on the back of his head from the younger woman. "Ow, what the hell, Cate?" He rubbed the back of his head.

Lucian gave the young Witch an amused look. Served him right. The Devil found an open bottle of bourbon and a shot glass. He threw the shot back and set the glass in the sink before carrying the bottle of bourbon to the table. He took a seat between the young woman and Thayne. The older Witch, Hester, got up and went to the stove.

"Did she break up with you?" Thayne continued, holding the back of his head for protection.

"I was not dating her, Thayne," Lucian hissed at his friend. A hand ran through his hair and tugged at the ends. "She's barely older than Bea. Not to mention she's Human." He had no desire to date. Abby, his former lover when he was still in Heaven, betrayed him and crushed him into pieces. Lily, the woman he thought he'd spend the rest of his life with had been good for him until she tasted power. Not to mention Micah and his Father cursed him, making it clear that no soul in the universe would ever fall in love with him.

"What happened?" Hester asked as she put on another pot of tea. He could smell the lavender from his seat.

Lucian took a swig from the bottle, ignoring the burn in his throat. "I'm worried her mind will end her second chance before it's her time. She's a danger to herself. Not to mention she's alone in that world." He hated himself for being concerned about her. He hated the effect she had on him.

"You did kill her parents," Don added in. "Not that they didn't deserve it."

"She did not sell her soul to kill her parents. Just to get away from them. Lucian went rogue," Cate reminded them with a cold look in the Devil's direction.

"They were abusing her and making her live a life she would not survive. Now that she has her freedom, she acts like I just sentenced her to death!" Lucian exclaimed loudly as he ran a hand through his hair again. He hated abusers just as much as he hated his Father. He had no qualms about what he did to Celeste's parents.

"Her whole life turned upside down. Cut her some slack, Luce," Cate defended the Human.

Lucian tilted his head back and took a larger swig of the alcohol. "Normal Humans are glad to get out of their shitty lives for something greater."

"But she's not a normal Human, Lucian." Hester reminded him as the tea kettle squealed. She poured him a cup and walked back to the table. She set the mug in front of him and gave his shoulder a comforting squeeze.

"Humans are Humans," Don commented. "They don't care about others. They only care about themselves. It's not until they're standing in that line outside the Pit that they start wishing they can turn back time."

"Don, that's only the bad ones. There are good ones too. She's clearly one of them," Cate scolded the Angel of Hell. "Lucian even said her aura—"

Don cut her off. "It doesn't matter, Cate. They are all the same no matter what. There's evil inside everyone. It just depends on how deep they shove it down or how much they let it out."

Lucian slammed the bottle on the table. Tea from the other mugs sloshed out onto the cards, staining them brown. "This is why I don't get involved in their affairs. It's not worth my time or energy to help them."

"I told you that in the beginning, you idiot," Don said, running a hand through his short dark hair. "That's why you just fuck 'em and leave 'em."

"You only do that because you have a fear of attachment." Cate gritted her teeth.

"Pot. Kettle," Don shot with a look and pointed his finger at her. Cate raised her middle finger at him in return.

"Enough," Lucian scolded them. Mother, give him strength. He did not want to deal with them today.

Cate turned her attention back to Lucian. "What she needs is a friend. I should go up there. We'd be fantastic friends."

Lucian shook his head. "Absolutely not, Cate. I offered her everything I could, and she refused. If she wants to waste the next eighty years, so be it. If she wants to be alone in this world, so be it. We do not need to get mixed up in her life anymore."

Cate stood up from the table. "No one should be alone in this world. She might think she wants to be alone, but I can tell you she doesn't. The spirits said things were going to start changing, and I think this is it."

"You do realize this place is crawling with spirits, right?" Thayne asked her, amusement shining in his chocolate brown eyes. The corner of Lucian's mouth tugged upwards. Thayne was the only person that could get a smile out of him in a time like this.

Cate's turquoise eyes narrowed at the Angel and began to glow. Thayne's chair slowly but steadily lifted in the air, lifting him. A heartbeat later, the chair was yanked out from under him, letting him fall on his ass. She turned back to Lucian with a satisfied smirk. "It's a good idea,

Lucian. We become friends, and when it's time, she'll have a friendly face here."

The idea was compelling. Cate would be the most sympathetic to Celeste's past. Not to mention the two girls were more alike than he cared to admit. "What about Hester and Bea? That's a long time away from them." Lucian asked her. Cate had not been separated from Bea since the day she learned she was pregnant.

"I'll still be able to come down here from time to time. And it's not forever. It'll be awkward when she's forty, and I still look like this." Cate saw no fault in her plan.

"What about your position?"

"Mother is my number two. She'll stand in for me." She glanced quickly at Hester who nodded her approval. Cate then looked back to him, her turquoise eyes pleading with him. He stared back, seeing the shy girl she used to be and how she struggled to make friends. She still didn't have many friends. She had Gabby, but it had been ten years since they saw each other last. Lucian opened his mouth to tell her no, but she took off and left them without another word. He may be the King of Hell, but the young Witch answered to no one but herself.

EIGHT YEARS LATER

CHAPTER 7

The Marlin Bar and Grille was packed with drunk, sweaty bodies. It was a usual Saturday night at the beach. Celeste ran up and down the bar, taking orders and making drinks. She had a love-hate relationship with the bar during the warmer months and special event weekends throughout the year. A vast majority of the customers had an attitude with her when she asked them to get off the bar after getting their drinks, while others constantly spilled their drinks, making her bar top sticky. The racket the DJ called music boomed so loud she couldn't even hear herself think. The only thing she liked about it was the over-generous tips from drunken customers. She needed those tips to get her through the winter months living in the tourist town.

Regardless, she would not want to be anywhere else. Eight years later, she still couldn't get over the fact that she woke up to the sound of the waves every morning and went to bed with them, lulling her to sleep. And every morning she was convinced it was all a dream, and she'd wake up in her parents' house in Pennsylvania. The icing on the cake was the fact that Ocean City, Maryland was a short drive to Assateague Island for nights when she could stargaze with her telescope.

Working the bar with her was her roommate and best friend in this new life, Cate. The two girls met shortly after Lucian left, and they quickly became inseparable. Very rarely did one work a shift without the other. They served the last of the customers for the moment and took a reprieve together.

"Purple tank," Cate muttered to her friend, nodding towards a beautiful, curvy blonde girl by the corner of the bar, sipping some fruity drink Cate had just made for her. Cate even went so far as to put a paper umbrella in it. Cate only puts umbrellas in bar drinks when she finds the person attractive. It was her fourth umbrella tonight.

Celeste loved her best friend dearly and admired her confidence. "Whore," she teased, her lips curved upwards into a wide smile. The five-foot-three woman playfully stuck her tongue out. Her best friend was so free with her heart and her love. She dated just to date, which is something Celeste envied. Dating and developing feelings and emotions would only complicate the deal she was tricked into when the Devil came for her soul. She did not want to put someone through the pain of loving her and then grieving her. She saw to her needs through short summer flings and one-night stands. She broke men's hearts without a second thought. It was easier than letting someone in to break hers.

Not to mention, whenever she caught herself falling for someone, or when she was mid-fuck with her flavor of the night, Lucian's mark burned white-hot against her skin. It was like a hot iron rod telling her she was with the wrong person. Sometimes, it came in handy when she missed the red flags and the person eventually showed their true colors. Most of the time, it just pissed her off to no end. It was like he was watching her, taunting her. It was a constant reminder that this second chance was finite. There was no promise or hope of growing old with someone. Not that someone would want to fall in love with her anyway.

Her eye caught a tall blonde patron waving at her, his face flushed from the heat and green eyes that silently undressed her. Blinking back an eye roll, she pulled her work tee shirt up higher over her breasts and took his order. She placed the drink in front of him and cashed him out. He leaned on the counter, head close to her ear. "What's a hot thing like you doing later?"

Celeste raised her pierced eyebrow. "Going home." She wasn't sure how drunk he was, but he wasn't slurring his words at least.

"Alone? You shouldn't be alone." He grinned at her, making the hair on the back of her neck stand up. "I'll keep you company."

"I won't be alone. I'll have my vibrator," she spat, crossing her arms over her chest. His face slackened at the mental image. His eyes darkened with lust as he leaned in more; any further and he'd be behind the counter. She shuddered with disgust at the look and took a step backwards.

"C'mon, babe. Give me a chance. What time do you get off?" he asked her again. She shook her head and scanned the room for a bouncer to get him out. He was quickly becoming a problem.

"Say one more thing, and I'll throw your ass out," she snapped as she took his drink back behind the counter, emptying it out. Of course, the bouncers were looking in every other direction but hers. She looked to her left for Cate, who had conveniently disappeared.

"C'mon," he whined. "I just want to find out the reason Lucian's defensive of you. I can be—I am—a better lover than he is." Celeste froze at the mention of the Devil. The breath in her lungs caught in her throat. She hadn't heard his name spoken aloud in eight years.

"What did you say?" she demanded.

The man looked her up and down again. "Lucian hates Humans. The Fallens want to know what is so special about you, but he won't say a damn thing. He doesn't take Human lovers, so I want to know what is so damn special about you."

Celeste's blood turned to ice, and her stomach flipped as nausea settled in. Rehoboth Beach was not that far away, but she thought she was safe. Safe from that house and the bad memories that haunt her—and most importantly, safe from him. She was going to be sick. "Fallen? How—did he send you here?" she asked, warm adrenaline coursing through her. She glanced at the clock to see if it was worth faking an illness and running home.

"Doesn't matter. He didn't do you justice, sweetheart. You really are much prettier in person." He grinned. "He's so old-fashioned. You, on the other hand, you look like you need a real man—"

"Hey, can I get a rum and coke?" A gruff male voice interrupted the blonde. Celeste's eyes glanced over him. His dirty blonde hair and hazel eyes looked familiar, but the bar was too dark to make out the details. He wasn't a regular, but she could swear she had seen him before. Celeste nodded in thanks and fixed his drink.

"Crazy night tonight?" he asked as the Fallen Angel made a noise to speak. Celeste made a noise of agreement and handed him his made drink. "Is it always like this?"

"In the summer. Do you want to start a tab?" His dreamy hazel eyes smiled at her. She glanced around for Cate's paper umbrellas; the damn girl probably gave them all out. He shook his head and handed her the cash.

"The music is nice," he commented as she handed him back his change. He waved it off. "Keep it."

Celeste gave him a small smile as she put the change in her apron pocket. He returned the smile, and she nearly fell over. Beautiful eyes, nice smile, tall; she was sold.

The Fallen Angel opened his mouth, annoyed. "Excuse me. I was speaking to her."

Her dirty-blonde hero looked the other man up and down with distaste and stood up to full height—he was easily six feet—and hissed, "Looked like you were bothering her. I suggest you leave her alone, or else you won't be going home with anyone tonight."

The Fallen Angel looked between Celeste and the dirty blonde. His eyes darkened as he stood up a little straighter. He matched her hero's height with an added couple of inches. Cate finally reappeared next to her, glaring at the creep.

"Remi, you're a little far from home, aren't you?" Cate asked, hands on her hips. His eyes widened in shock and fear.

"Your Highness, I—" Remi stuttered, bowing his head slightly. Celeste's head snapped to the side at her friend.

Cate cut him off and then spoke to him in a tone too quiet to hear over the music. His face relaxed immediately, and his eyes glazed over, almost hypnotized. She coughed and spoke louder, "My goodness, you're drunk. Time for you to go home, but first, you're going to apologize to my friend here."

The man did not miss a beat. His eyes met Celeste's, and he bowed his head with his apologies before stepping away from the bar and out of sight.

Celeste's lips parted slightly in shock. Her eyes met her hero's. He shrugged his shoulders and took a sip of his drink. Her eyes then traveled over to Cate, who looked furious. "You know him?" Celeste asked.

"Unfortunately." Cate didn't divulge any more information. He was a Fallen Angel. Cate had never mentioned knowing Fallen Angels. Then again, she hadn't either.

"He addressed you as 'Your Highness.' What the hell was that about?" She didn't dare mention the Angel thing in this crowded bar.

Cate shrugged her shoulders. "He was drunk. I'll be right back." Her voice was tense but distant as she walked away from the bar. Celeste stared at the space her friend had just vacated. In the last seven and a half years, she'd never seen Cate act so strange.

"You okay?" asked her hero.

Celeste rolled her shoulders back, shoving her emotions down for the time being. She couldn't do anything until her shift was over. She plastered a fake smile on her face, hoping it would fool him. "Yes. He was not the first creepy guy and certainly won't be the last. Thanks for stepping in..." Her words trailed off when she realized she didn't get his name.

He opened his mouth to introduce himself but was cut off by another customer a little way down the bar asking her for a mixed drink. When she returned minutes later, the man had disappeared into the crowd.

Time ticked by slower than normal. Every new person she interacted with terrified her and had her worrying that they were going to sprout wings and take her away. That Fallen Angel had found her which meant it would be too easy for Lucian to find her or to send more of his people out to mess with her. Lucian probably sent that bastard to fuck with her head. It had been eight years since she saw or heard from him. Maybe he thought she was comfortable now and needed to be reminded of her fate. Celeste and Cate walked home in a comfortable yet tense silence; her head was swimming, and her body was on high alert, lying in wait for danger to strike.

It wasn't until she heard the click of her deadbolt and door lock that she breathed a deep sigh of relief. She was safe here. No one or nothing could get inside her rundown, two-story cottage. At least that's what she told herself. The image of Lucian leaving the mansion in that circle of fire occasionally haunted her dreams.

Cate went straight for the kitchen to grab a snack. The pads of her dog's feet echoed through the quiet home. The morning after Lucian vanished into thin air, she went to a local rescue and adopted a chocolate Labrador puppy, Chocolate Chip. Celeste had always wanted a dog, but her parents did not. She wasn't even allowed to have a goldfish. Chip barked his greeting to her as he rubbed against her leg.

She knelt down to pet him, her head pressed against his soft fur as she grounded herself. He was here. She was alive. She was home. "Hi, Chippy boy! I missed you! Wanna go outside? Outside?" she chirped. Chip barked in agreement and ran toward the deck door.

"Can you let him out?" Celeste asked Cate who had stuffed her face full of deli ham. She nodded her head and followed the dog outside.

Celeste rummaged around the refrigerator and pulled out a bowl of grapes and a bag of shredded mozzarella cheese. Walking out to the far corner of the family room that had turned into their dining room, she took a seat on the old wicker chair. Remi had found her, which meant her location had been blown. She'd have to leave everything she had– again and hide somewhere else. The thought of packing up her things and her dog was unfathomable. Ocean City was her home. Her life was here. She found freedom here. Her mental health had improved drastically since moving here. It had been six years since she'd needed a razor blade to regulate her emotions. For once in her life, she was truly happy.

The deck door alarm chimed as the door slid open. The Lab ran straight for his water bowl, lapping it up loudly. Cate followed behind him and shoved a few more pieces of deli ham into her mouth.

"Hey, Cate?" she asked. Cate made a noise of acknowledgment as she put the carton of lunch meat back into the fridge.

"Why did that guy at the bar call you Your Highness?" Celeste asked again. Working at a popular bar in a tourist town meant she had heard just about everything from the mouths of drunkards, but never 'your highness.'

Cate's turquoise eyes looked everywhere but at Celeste. Her shoulders lifted slightly, shrugging the question off. "You know how drunk people get. You literally got called princess by that one guy last week. It's late, Celly. I'm going to bed," Cate said with some finality as she trudged to the stairs. Celeste watched her friend go upstairs. The two shared most things about each other. Her body felt leaden. Did she know Lucian? Were they both hiding a similar secret?

CHAPTER 8

Sleep didn't come easy that night. Celeste spent the majority of the night tossing and turning. Half the night was spent playing the conversation with the man over in her head, and the other half was spent weighing her options. She felt like she was eighteen again, trying to figure out her next steps the night Lucian left. Chip hopped down from his spot at the end of her bed, growing tired of her constant movement.

The morning sun peeked through her blinds. Celeste threw the covers off in frustration and got up for the day. She changed into lounging shorts, a long sleeve tee, and a pair of flip-flops. With her phone in her pocket, a mug of hot coffee in one hand, and a dog leash in the other, she set off for the beach for her morning walk with Chip. Chip loved the beach as much as she did, so much so that he often tried to rush her across the busy streets to the Atlantic.

Once she crossed over the boardwalk and onto the sand, she let Chip off his leash and watched him bound for the water. She followed him to the edge of the tide and sat down. Normally, she'd get knee-deep in the water and play with him, but today, she didn't have the energy to play. She sat on the dense sand and let the water lap around her ankles. The soft pounding of the waves calmed her system. The salty air brought a small smile to her face. This was Heaven. This was home.

That Fallen Angel wanted her for whatever God-forsaken reason, he'd said that Lucian was *defensive* about her, which was a blatant lie. She was nothing but a mistake to him. He told her so. She ruminated on how the man had discovered her. In the last eight years, she had found herself. When Lucian last saw her, she had been eighteen years old, Now, she neared twenty-six, and the numerous tattoos and piercings made her nearly unrecognizable from her old self. The prick must be keeping tabs on her.

The rational voice in her head told her running was not going to make a difference and wouldn't be worth it. The Devil had his ways. If he was keeping tabs, he would find her.

He took her away from her home once, the next time, it will be on her terms.

When she and Chip returned from their walk, Cate was pacing around the living room with her phone pressed to her ear. "You need to do a better job of keeping them in line. Not only did he try to fuck her, he mentioned *your kind,* and almost outed me! She's finally happy, and if you fuck this up, I swear—" Cate whisper-threatened to the poor soul on the other end. Chip barked a hello and ran towards the kitchen for fresh water. Celeste tuned her ear to focus on Cate's conversation and took a painfully long time to lock the front door. Cate ended the call without another word. Celeste turned around to see her best friend set her phone on the dining room table. Cate's eyes met hers, and her face shifted. She blinked and plastered on a fake smile. "Good morning!" Cate said a bit too enthusiastically for the morning after a late night.

"Who were you talking to?" Celeste asked and leaned against the door, unsure if she wanted to know the answer.

She shrugged the question off. "No one important. Do you wanna get breakfast since we're up? I could go for some crepes."

Celeste's eyebrow arched, and she crossed her arms. "You were talking to another Fallen Angel," she pushed.

Cate's mouth thinned into a line. "Fallen Angels aren't real, Celle."

"Remi admitted it last night, Cate." Celeste bit her lip, hesitant to reveal her deep dark secrets. "But I knew of them before that. I had gotten close to one in another life." *The One.*

Cate sucked on her lip and stared at the floor. After a moment of silence, her shoulders dropped as she sighed. "Yes, I know some Fallen Angels. I know Remi. He's an perv, but he should not be a problem anymore."

Celeste nodded her head slowly as she took in the information. She didn't want to ask Cate how she knew of them. It would open the doors to her own story, to

Lucian, and she didn't want to talk about him. Lucky for her, Cate didn't ask either. She never really asked about her past. It was another reason on a long list of why she loved her best friend. Cate just accepted her as she was and never judged or questioned unless it was vital to her health and survival. God saw Celeste needed someone after losing Morgan and sent Cate. That's all she needed to know.

True to Cate's word, Remi never showed his face again. With every passing day, Celeste's shoulders relaxed a little more. Two weeks had passed since the incident, and with every passing day, her shoulders dropped an inch from her ears.

Cate threw a French fry at their television as the main character in their favorite cheesy romantic drama movie leaned in to kiss the villain as if the fry could stop them. Chip happily jumped up to eat the discarded food. "No! Fuck him—not literally, he's a douche!" Cate yelled, her ivory face flushed pink from her second extra-strong frozen strawberry daiquiri.

Celeste laughed as she took a bite of fried shrimp. "We know she'll dump his ass later."

"Still," Cate retorted as she munched on another fry.

The couple on the screen engaged in a loving passionate kiss, not realizing the good guy had come in. His face dropped, and Celeste could hear the crack as his heart snapped in two. "I wish I could have a guy like the other love interest." Celeste hummed despondently. Due to Cate's influence, she developed a love of cheesy romantic dramas, romantic comedies, and romance novels. In each piece of fiction, she got to live vicariously through the main character and experience a love she would never have. Getting attached wasn't worth the pain of losing them.

"You could. You just said that's what you wanted. Go after what you want," Cate encouraged her.

As if on cue, the damn brand on her arm started to heat up. A mild burn this time, reminding her she belonged to someone else, although he was not someone she wanted to take to her bed. It was another reminder that she'd made her bed, now she had to lie in it. *Alone.* "It's a long story," Celeste mumbled.

"Is it about the guy from eight years ago?" Cate asked. Celeste nodded. In one of their brief conversations into Celeste's past she had given her friend a vague background story. Cate knew her parents had passed in an accident and she lived briefly with a boyfriend and when that ended badly, she moved to Ocean City. "It's been eight years, Celle. You deserve to be happy with someone."

Celeste ran her foot on Chip's furry back, who curled himself back up into a ball in front of the couch. He always laid by her, protecting her. "I don't need a man. I got a man, right, Chip?" she asked the dog. Chip yelped in agreement, earning a laugh from the two girls.

Celeste looked back up at the television. The main character and the good guy were now intertwined in a kiss. "What about you? You dated that one girl for what, six months?" Celeste deflected the attention back to her friend. She had her own reasons for not engaging in any long-term dating, but her best friend did not. Cate was stunningly beautiful, with her uniquely colored eyes and perfectly curled mahogany red hair. Her makeup was always flawless. She was the picture definition of old Hollywood glamour.

Cate's eyes glazed over like she was thinking about someone, and her posture shifted inward. Her eyes tilted downward. "It's complicated," she murmured as she increased the volume on the television, effectively ending their conversation.

They went into the second movie with another glass, feeling buzzed and content. Chip stirred halfway through the movie. A beat later, he was on all fours, growling as he faced the back door. Cate and Celeste shared a concerned look before turning towards the back door.

"What's wrong, bud?" Celeste asked the dog. Chip ignored her, continuing to growl, and took off down the short hallway for the back door. Cate got off the couch first and unsteadily followed him. Her hands stretched out in front to keep her from running into the walls.

"Do you see anything?" Celeste whispered to her friend.

With her back pressed against the wall, Cate peered down the hallway and shook her head. "Kill the lights."

Celeste reached for the floor lamp in the corner beside the couch and switched it off. She turned off the television, enveloping them all in darkness.

Cate snuck down the hall, holding onto the wall for dear life. The three alcoholic beverages had her stumbling. She opened the hall door where a baseball bat was kept for security. Celeste stumbled off the couch to follow in Cate's footsteps. Her top half was a heavy weight, ready to tip over. She braced a hand on the wall to keep herself upright.

"The deck light isn't coming on, and I don't see anything outside," Cate whispered. Chip growled in disagreement. It was a wonder he wasn't foaming at the mouth. Cate picked up the bat in a swinging position. She took one step towards the back door, paused, then brought her other foot to meet her. She repeated the movement slowly and wobbly until she got to the door.

Celeste's eyes traveled past Cate to the deck. Moonlight glistened on the darkened Isle of Wright Bay just past their small backyard. Like Cate said, there was nothing sitting on the deck or on their furniture. Everything was as it should be. Chip's paws clawed at the door; he wanted out badly.

"We should call the police," Celeste whisper-hissed. "We're too drunk for this."

Cate ignored her and slid the back door open a couple of inches. The door alarm failed to chime. The silence was sobering; whatever was outside did not want to be announced. Chip squeezed his way out into the backyard as Cate peeked her head out. Celeste held her breath while she waited for the mass murderer to cut off her best friend's head with an axe.

The door slid open farther, and Cate tiptoed onto the deck. She made a slow circle around herself slowly, mumbling incoherently. She came to a halt a quarter of the way through her second turn facing the side of the house, still mumbling. She took a few steps and was out of Celeste's line of sight. The mumbling faded into dead silence. It was eerily quiet both in the house and out in the yard. Chip had stopped his barking and the crickets had even paused their nightly song to watch them.

A violent gust of icy cold wind blew in as Cate called for Chip and rushed back inside. Whatever she saw outside had sobered her up completely. Chip ignored her, frozen on the lawn. Cate yelled for him again in a dark and powerful voice, totally unrecognizable from her normal cheery voice. Almost robotically, Chip turned and ran inside.

Chip barely cleared the door before Cate slammed it shut and locked it. She pressed her palm on the glass and began chanting incoherently. A pale blue light shined out from her palm and onto the door. Light rippled along the door and faded as it reached the edges.

"What the hell was that?" Celeste asked. She had never seen light glow from her friend's hand. Cate ignored her as she hurried into the kitchen then ran to their back door with their salt shaker, the bat tucked firmly under her arm. "What the hell are you doing?"

"Warding the house," Cate said, void of all emotions as she opened the shaker and poured salt along the floor in front of the door. Cate's turquoise eyes began to glow, a shiny beacon in the dark.

"Why?"

"I'll explain later."

Chip prowled over to his owner and brushed up against her before taking his spot in front of her, protecting her. Cate pressed her palm to the front door and began chanting again, louder than before. Celeste still couldn't make out the words, Latin maybe. Cate repeated the chant and the salt line on all the windows of the cottage.

Celeste's back was still pressed against the wall, frozen. Her best friend's hands and eyes just glowed, and her voice was different, darker, more menacing. Cate became someone else right before her eyes. She was hiding more than just knowing Fallen Angels. A cold sweat broke out on her forehead, and dread filled her stomach like it did whenever she'd heard her parents come home angry.

"What the hell was that?" Celeste asked again.

It was too dark to see her friend's expression. Cate didn't say anything at first, as if she was debating on what she would tell Celeste. Cate sighed out a curse. "I haven't been honest with you. Just promise me you won't flip out."

Whatever she had to tell her was not going to top her deal with the fucking devil. "Believe me, what you're about to tell me would not be the craziest thing I've heard."

Cate's weak laugh turned into a blood-curdling scream.

CHAPTER 9

A flash of firelight illuminated the living room. A circle of red flames, similar to the blue circle Lucian disappeared into, appeared in the center of the living room accompanied by black smoke that grew thicker by the moment. As the fire and smoke receded, a tall figure shrouded in black emerged. Large dark-colored feather wings flapped slowly before coming to a complete stop. Adrenaline pulsed through Celeste's veins. Lucian had lied to her, again. He came for her early. He had told her she would have the rest of her life. It's been eight fucking years. God, maybe she should have left when that Fallen

Angel found her. She managed to duck into the kitchen before frozen terror sunk into her muscles.

She peeked over the kitchen counter. The man in her living room was not Lucian; it was that Fallen Angel from the bar-Remi. He looked bigger and taller now than he did weeks ago. Cate's left hand shot out towards him. Her palm turned red as a small ball of red light formed from it.

Remi closed her hand, red light extinguishing. He bared his teeth at her. "I'm not here for you, you stupid Witch," he hissed. His dark and menacing voice filled up the room. "Where is she? Where is Lucian's pet Human?"

Chip charged towards him, growling and ready to attack. Remi didn't bother to look down as he kicked the dog. Chip howled as he went flying across the room. His back hit the hallway wall. Her face winced as her dog whined in agony. Celeste broke through the ice surrounding her muscles and ran to Chip. She wrapped herself around him in a comforting hold.

"There she is," Remi said gruffly.

"You have direct orders; you're forbidden to touch her! " Cate screamed as she swung the metal bat into his stomach. Remi held his stomach and doubled over in pain. Cate made a beeline for Celeste. She yanked Celeste off of Chip and threw the bat into her hands. Her glowing eyes were wide with worry. "Take the bat and go upstairs. Lock the door and do not open it under any circumstances. I will knock on it three times. Then you can open the door." A loud bang followed by the shattering of glass echoed through the first floor. "*Go,*" her friend repeated.

Celeste didn't question it and screamed for Chip as she ran for the stairs. Halfway up the steps, she collided with something hard. The top half of her tilted backward.

Chip was on the step beneath her keeping her supported, but she couldn't stop falling backwards. Her free hand waved wildly for the railing. She screamed in terror. This was it; she'd fall backwards down the steps and die and Lucian wouldn't even need to break a sweat for her soul. Large, rough hands grasped her sides and yanked her forward, slamming her into his brick-like chest. The man's smelly, hot breath beat down on her, circling her throat like a collar, constricting her breathing. A heartbeat later her feet lost contact with the stairs, and she was thrown over a hard shoulder. Her nose hit the hard bone of his wings.

Celeste thrashed her legs violently trying to hit him, but his free hand locked her legs in place. One hand pressed against her nose while the other gripped the feathers and pulled them hard enough for a few to fall out.

"You little bitch!" The man howled in pain and quickened his pace. He brought her into the first bedroom on the left, her room. The door slammed shut with supernatural force that shook the walls. The sound of the door locking reverberated through her. She swallowed hard. She was going to die, and no one would be able to save her. Celeste gripped his wings tightly and pulled out a fistful of black feathers. With a howl of pure agony, he threw her onto her bed with a snarl. Her eyes locked onto her captor. Remi's eyes were bright red—the face of evil incarnate. His sleazy smile told her everything she needed to know.

"Lucian!" She screamed his name without a second thought. If this was it, if Remi was going to rape and kill her, he had to be near to claim her soul. If he was as decent as he claimed, then he would put a stop to this now.

Remi laughed, a sick and twisted sound. "You honestly think he's gonna help you? Not even God could help you now." He sauntered towards the bed, unbuckling his pants.

She was not tied to the bed, thank God for small mercies. *Move you idiot! Use your fucking legs!* Celeste's mind screamed. An invisible weight pressed on her chest keeping her in a frozen, helpless place. God, she was a failure. Eight years later and she slipped into her old self like it was nothing. Maybe she deserved it since her body refused to move.

A loud explosion sounded from the outside of her door that had the décor on her wall rattling and falling. Her head turned towards the door, hoping someone would come in and help her. The edge of her bed dipped. Remi's fingers wrapped around chin and jerked her head towards him. His red eyes stared into her soul; he could see she belonged to Lucian. The sinister smile on his face told her he'd kill her before he'd let Lucian save her. "Look at me while I'm fucking you," he demanded gruffly. In her last act of defiance, she squeezed her eyes shut. His ringed hand collided with her cheek, leaving a stinging pain. She held in her whimper and kept her eyes closed. God, she wished he would kill her first. Death would have been better than this. "You better be a quick learner. Next time, there will be no warning." Remi's rough hands pulled her to the edge of the bed and separated her legs. With a dark, animalistic growl, he ripped her shirt off, exposing her to the cold air. Calloused hands roamed her body, making her skin crawl every time he made contact with bare flesh.

Remi cupped her breast and thumbed over her nipple. She prayed it would be over soon. Prayed for someone to save her, for Lucian or for God. Heaven or Hell. Someone save her.

But her shorts stayed on.

Blue firelight lit up the room and extinguished immediately. Violent wind gusted throughout the room despite her memory of having her window closed. The sound of grunting and wings flapping assaulted her ears. The mattress rose as Remi was pulled off the bed. There was a guttural scream and then red firelight. The howling wind came to a sudden stop, and everything was eerily quiet. Her heart pounded in her ears. Celeste gulped air, filling her lungs with as much as she could.

CHAPTER 10

Lucian's throne room was a frenzy of activity. Don held Remi in a chokehold, his glowing blue knife pressed into Remi's throat, cutting off his airway. Small streams of red blood trailed down his neck. Thayne held another rogue Fallen, one of Remi's co-conspirators, in the same hold with his blue glowing scythe circling the man's neck. The smallest movement would sever the head. Meg, one of Don's Furies, held tightly to the other rebel. Blood pooled in large puddles all over the newly polished stone floor. Feathers ripped from wings were strewn about. Cate did a hell of a job on her attackers. Lucian would've been beaming with pride if he hadn't been seething with rage. The rage he just unlocked made God's wrath look like child's play. Not only did these rogue Angels attack his family, they defied orders and almost defiled Celeste after he promised her no harm would ever come to her. Blue fire erupted from his fingertips.

All of them squirmed as they begged for forgiveness. Lucian let out a dark, rough laugh. He marched up to the rebel Fallen Angels. "You disobey direct orders and then have the audacity to ask for forgiveness. Please! Forgive us for we do not know what we do, right?" He mocked the Bible verse with a sick and twisted smile. "I think you forgot I am not in the business of forgiveness." The Devil gave a slight nod to Thayne. "You are all sentenced to death and torture for defying orders and attacking Cate, Queen of the Witches and Elysian's coven leader. And my servant, Celeste Ride."

Thayne dragged the tip of his scythe across the rogue Angel's throat. Blood squirted out, spraying Lucian and everyone around him. The Fallen Angel gurgled and dropped to the ground. The Angel of Death never really enjoyed the act of murder. But there was no mistaking the grotesque smile on his face as he dug the scythe deeper, effectively severing the Fallen's head. The head rolled far from its body. Blood, light, and shadows poured from his neck and dematerialized, now nothing but negative energy floating in hell. Lucian shot hellfire from his fingertips and set the body ablaze.

"And you." Lucian moved to the rebel in Meg's arms. "You are no Angel." He placed fiery fingertips on the other rebel's feathers. The blue flames spread like a wildfire. The rebel wailed in misery as his feathers shriveled up, burnt to a crisp, leaving only charred bone. Without having to give orders, Meg began sawing off the bone. The Fallen screamed again in agony as he lost the two limbs. The bone hit the ground with a thud. Blood poured out of his back from the two gaping wounds.

Thayne sauntered over and brought the scythe down on his neck. Lucian set his body ablaze.

Remi was pale and green from the sight of his co-conspirators being tortured. Don dropped Remi, letting him hit the floor. Lucian stalked over and picked him up off the ground by his throat. "That'll be all. I'll handle this one."

Remi's eyes widened in fear as Don, Thayne, and Meg walked out; there would be no witnesses to this execution. Lucian's red eyes glinted mercilessly in the torchlight on the wall.

Lucian slammed Remi into the obsidian stone wall. Remi's skull hit the stone, leaving a large crater. Lucian's eyes darkened as he leaned into Remi's ear and hissed, "I believe I made myself quite clear. The Human was not to be harmed. As your king, I do not have to explain myself to you. My word is law." The Devil took his own ringed hand and slapped the man in the face, a taste of his own medicine.

"Her aura, that power… She could produce a powerful Nephilim. The child would be powerful enough to take you down. She would be stronger than Lily. I can wait until you bring her down here. A Demon-Fallen Angel child could take over Heaven, Earth, and Hell." Remi suffocated on his words.

Lucian pulled Remi off the wall and slammed him into it again. Bits of rock clinked to the ground. No one spoke ill of Celeste. No one spoke of Lily either unless they were asking for death. "You must be sadly mistaken. I'm the fucking Devil. No one will be able to overpower me. Aura or not, she will not be the one to carry on your disgusting legacy," Lucian hissed.

The Devil pulled out his Angel Killer from his back pocket, and sliced Remi's throat. Blood, light, and shadows leaked out of him. His open eyes were lightless and frozen. Lucian released him, and Remi collapsed onto the ground. Just like the others, Lucian set him ablaze. He watched Remi's body burn. When the last of him had turned to ash, he marched out of his throne room doors. "Clean this up. And fix the wall," he barked at the closest Demon and stalked off.

Three hard knocks rapped at Celeste's door. She turned her head to look and almost cried with relief. She wasn't sure how long she had been lying on top of her bed. There had been no sound from inside or out. She couldn't bring herself to leave the room to see the bodies of her best friend and dog. Celeste bolted out of bed and threw on a not-quite-dirty shirt off the chair at her desk. She raced over, unlocked the door, and threw it open. Cate's normally perfect hair was a mess, there was dried blood around her nose, and her lip was cut. She looked how Celeste felt. Chip practically tackled his owner. The feel of his fur in between her fingers grounded her back to the present. She was alive. By the grace of God, she was alive.

"Thank Creation." Cate sighed with relief as she embraced her friend tightly. Cate sniffled; she had been crying too. "Are you okay? Did he touch you?"

Celeste shook her head. "Well, he slapped me, and he...uh...he...cupped my chest, but he never got..."

Cate nodded, somewhat relieved. "Remi brought two friends. They ruined the cottage. I have a feeling it will crumble by morning." The stress and panic in her voice was unfamiliar. Cate was always the calm one of the two, the one who had all the plans and always knew what to do. Now, she sounded lost and unsure of herself.

Celeste's eyes widened. "What do you mean? What happened?"

Cate brought her out into the hallway. There was a giant crater in between the girls' rooms. Looking through the hole, what remained of the hallway to the backyard had blown to bits. They walked to the stairs to assess the damage in the main room. The furniture was either ripped or burnt to a crisp. Intermittent holes down the walls exposed drywall and support beams.

Celeste let out a string of curse words. Their home was gone. No hotel would take her dog for the night. She exhaled slowly and turned to her friend. She had a perfectly good house. She just never wanted to go back. This little cottage had been hers. It was the only home she knew. "I have a house in Rehoboth Beach. We can go there tonight." She bit her lip, waiting for any negative reaction from her friend.

Any anger or frustration that she expected from her friend for hiding a much nicer house never showed. Cate gave a slight nod of her head. "Let's go."

They piled everything they could into Celeste's fiery red sports car. The car had belonged to whoever owned the mansion before Lucian took them to Hell. She dreaded going back, but there was no other choice. From the back seat, Chip put his head on her shoulder. She smiled sadly as she leaned into her dog, breathing him in as she steadied herself.

"It'll be okay, my love," she whispered to him weakly, unsure if she believed the words out of her mouth

CHAPTER 11

Every mile northward made her sick to her stomach.

The mansion brought back too many bad memories: the death of her family, the death of her old self, and Lucian. Not that she missed her family; she certainly didn't miss the abuse. If they had still been alive, she would have been forced to go to medical school and would probably be preparing to work for her parents at their family practice with Vicky. Her parents would have set her up with some pretentious doctor because that was the only type of guy her family would accept. Or she would have been dead, one cut too deep or beaten to death.

As she pulled up to the mansion, it was like she never left. The grass was still short despite her never coming here to cut it. The porch light was on, but inside, the mansion was dark.

From the corner of her eye, she saw Cate's jaw drop open. "Why haven't we been living here? Holy moly, how can you afford this place and split the rent on that shabby cottage?"

"It belongs to him," she mumbled. She had Cate dig out the visor clip for the garage door that she had buried in the bottom of the glove compartment years ago and said a short prayer that the battery inside still worked. Miraculously, the garage door rattled and lifted. Celeste cleared the door and coasted into the dark garage. She threw the car in park and leaned back into her seat as if it would swallow her up.

She squeezed her eyes closed, telling herself when she opened her eyes, she would be back at the cottage eating junk food and sipping from their fruity drinks.

"But he gave you the house though, didn't he? Who cares if it belonged to him? It's yours." Cate got out of the car and called for Chip. The dog hopped out and investigated his new surroundings.

Celeste sighed as she pressed the close button on the clip and got out of the car. "After he left... after everything I went through, I couldn't stay. So, I left and never looked back."

They grabbed all their important items from the car, saving the rest for later that morning. She turned the doorknob, but it didn't move. She pushed inwards, but the door still didn't budge. Cate pointed to a keypad with a slow blinking red light next to the door. She stared blankly at the keypad, wracking her brain for the code Lucian told her once in passing.

It wasn't her birthday...or was it? She entered the date.

The keypad flashed red.

Lucian's birthday? She didn't even know if he had a birthday and never bothered to ask. Was it the day her family was killed? She entered that unforgettable date.

Red again.

She had one more try before it alerted police, and she'd have to explain she's breaking into her own house. She entered in the day they met all those winters ago.

The keypad flashed green, and the door clicked, unlocking itself. The sentimental son of a bitch. She rolled her eyes and inhaled deeply before walking into the mansion. She hit the light switch next to the door, and the basement came to life. It was a big storage area that was mostly empty, save for a water heater, furnace, washer, and dryer. Boxes lined the wall with masking tape labels that had to be from the previous owners. She led Cate further inside, opening the door to the next room—the den. They climbed the steps to the main floor and switched on the lights. Everything was the same as she left it but with an added layer of dust.

"It's beautiful in here," Cate said in awe.

"The bedrooms are upstairs. Mine is the farthest on the right and the rest are up for grabs."

Cate immediately went up the spiral staircase. Chip inspected the main floor, sniffing at everything. For a moment Celeste wondered if he remembered the place. Celeste beelined over to the bar area near the couches. Unsurprisingly, it was still well stocked. She grabbed an upside-down glass from the shelf and reached for a bottle. She pulled out an almost empty bottle of whiskey. She exhaled quickly through her nose in a quiet huff, the corner of her mouth twitched in remembrance. Lucian had given her that whiskey her first night. She set the whiskey on the counter to throw away. The older the alcohol, the better, she was told, but she imagined she would regret drinking eight-year-old-opened alcohol. She inspected the other bottles in the bar, gathering any other open bottles she could find. As she dumped the alcohol down the kitchen sink, she made a mental note to go to the liquor store tomorrow. They would need a lot of it to process the last few hours.

Celeste cleaned the kitchen. She tossed the moldy food she had stupidly left when she abandoned the house. The smell was enough to make her want to die. As she dusted off the kitchen counter and island, a black smudge caught her eye. Immortalized on the counter was the ashen imprint of Lucian's hands from their last argument. A cold chill brushed against her arm causing goosebumps to form on her skin.

You were a mistake.

She was. Her life was a mistake. She made the mistake of staying after Remi found her and it almost got her best friend killed.

She turned her head towards where she last saw him. Unlike the counter, the wood floor never blackened to ash from the blue fire that had engulfed him and sent him back to Hell. Hesitantly, she walked over to the spot, knelt down and pressed a hand to the cold, dusty wood. It was almost as if he had never been here. Celeste wiped away newly formed tears as she stood up and made her way to the couch where he had laid her down that first night.

Celeste tiredly plopped down onto the plush couch. The memories of that night played in her head so vividly, as if it happened yesterday. Her throat burned as if it remembered all the whiskey she drank that night. Lucian was perched on the oak coffee table, watching her carefully as he refilled her glass with a plea to slow down.

She could make out everything from that night; his red buttoned-up shirt with multiple dark stains caused by her tears as he held her and the haunted look in his icy eyes and the five o'clock shadow along his jaw.

The familiar cinnamon, clove, and nutmeg scent of him wafted through her nose. He was there, he was right there. She could see his chest rise and fall with breath. She kicked her foot out to touch him. Her foot whacked the wooden table and Lucian disappeared. The bastard was just a hallucination, nothing more.

Chip climbed up on the couch and placed his head in her lap. She threaded her fingers through his fur and petted him. Even as a puppy, Chip had seemed to understand Human emotion. The first time they'd met at the shelter, he had come right up to the gate that separated them like they were long-lost friends. He had looked at her with those wide, deep brown eyes of his. She could tell he had been through some stuff in his short life. She didn't need the shelter worker to tell her that the pup's mother abandoned him because he had been a runt. Celeste just knew he was hers. The first night she brought him home and every night since, he would curl up at the foot of the bed. Always there, always watching out for her.

The dog was part of the reason she'd tried to stop the self-harm. In the brief weeks before she met Cate, if she had gone too deep, no one would be there to take care of Chip, and she could not bear the thought of him winding up back in a shelter cage, crying because he didn't know where she went and why they weren't at home. The guilt of that ate her alive most nights in the beginning.

"You don't remember this place, do you, Chippy? You were just a baby when we lived here," she asked the dog as she calmly smoothed the fur on top of his head. "Mommy isn't much of a fan. The view is beautiful, but the memories are not." Chip let out a whine and shook out the fur on his head.

Celeste closed her eyes and tilted her head back. Remi's beady eyes appeared. Lucian might be the head Devil, but Remi had all the makings of a true Demon. Her blood boiled with anger towards him and towards herself for freezing. She had strong arms and legs from her near constant swimming in the ocean and from her years playing soccer. She should have fought back; she could have fought back. She had no problem letting her smart mouth fight her battles for her at the bar, but she couldn't understand why she froze.

She had not felt that defenseless since the night her parents died. She had *refused* to let herself feel that helpless since that night. There was no excuse for her to act the way she did. Alice was weak and powerless, not Celeste.

The clanking in the kitchen brought her back to earth. She glanced towards the kitchen, but the wall blocked her vision.

"I wouldn't trust anything in the cabinets. It's eight years past the best by date," Celeste yelled from her spot on the couch. Chip's ears perked up thinking he could get a midnight snack.

"Oh, trust me, I'm not. I brought what I could salvage from our kitchen," she called out as she clanked around some more.

"What are you doing?"

"I'm making tea. We need it. Where are your fucking mugs?" Cate yelled back.

"I'd rather have whiskey, but to each their own."

Cate laughed and mumbled something under her breath. Celeste laid her head back on the couch and closed her eyes, ruminating over the attack again. Suddenly, a strong stench of lavender had her eyes bulging out.

Cate, now standing directly in front of her, held her chipped sage green mug in her face. "Drink," her friend gently demanded.

"Thanks, mom," Celeste joked as she took the mug and took a sip. The lavender overpowered the slight hint of chamomile and some other earthy taste. She coughed a little but managed to swallow it. It was clearly not from the tea bags from their cabinet. Cate had a small garden in the back of the cottage where she grew all kinds of herbs and used them in teas and meals. She tolerated it fine in food but Celeste cherished her store-bought tea. "Is this from the garden?"

Cate nodded and took a seat next to her, sipping her tea. "Lavender, chamomile, and valerian root. It's supposed to calm you and help you sleep. Knowing you, you won't sleep tonight."

Celeste made a face. "I hate that you know me so well. We're like an old married couple."

Cate laughed. The first happy sound since they were watching that cheesy chick flick mere hours ago. "We're best friends. It comes with the territory." She took a seat next to Celeste and sipped on her own mug of tea. For a moment, she wondered if this was what she and Morgan would have been like had they got to be adults in the world together. Best friends, maybe roommates who spent their nights with tea and silly movies. Maybe Cate and Morgan would have become friends and it would have been the three of them against the world.

CHAPTER 12

The lavender worked like charm. It slowed her heart rate, but her mind ran a million miles an hour. "What was that back there? It's like you were doing magic," she asked as she took a sip.

Cate shifted uncomfortably in her seat. She stared at her light blue mug for a long while before she set it on the table. "I was."

Celeste spit out her tea back into the mug. "I'm sorry. What?" she asked, her voice raising an octave like it did when she was shocked.

Her normally confident best friend sunk into the couch and fiddled with her fingers. Cate was much shorter than Celeste, but her big personality made it seem like she was ten feet tall. Now, she looked smaller than Celeste had ever seen her. "I'm a Witch."

Celeste blinked. "I know you're into witchcraft. I bought you a new set of tarot cards for Christmas. You have a collection of crystals, and everything that happens is because I'm a Cancer sun and Gemini moon or whatever. But back there, your hands and eyes *glowed*. Not to mention you spoke a different language."

Her friend let out a tense laugh and reached for her tea. Her shoulders relaxed slightly, and she grew a little taller. "Yes, yes, that's witchcraft too. But I'm much more than that. I can do spells, I can make potions, curse, hex, you name it."

The realization hit Celeste like a tidal wave.

'… and almost outed me!' Cate had yelled at the man on the phone a while back.

'I'm not here for you, you stupid Witch!'

Cate *knew* Fallen Angels. She *knew* Remi. Celeste had been so determined to keep everything 'Lucian' away from her new life she refused to put the pieces together.

"Why didn't you tell me the full truth?" Celeste asked.

"I really don't like people to know."

"I'm your best friend."

"Witches get a bad rap," Cate said and looked down at her mug. There was more to the story, but Celeste was not going to press her, not tonight.

Celeste couldn't find it in herself to be mad at Cate. Unlike Lucian, Cate had been open with some aspects of herself and hid what she needed to survive.

Just like she did.

"I'm sorry, Celly," Cate apologized.

Celeste inhaled deeply; eight years was a long time to keep the cat in the bag. "I haven't been completely honest with you either," Celeste admitted as she set down her mug on the coffee table and came clean about her own shady past. She told Cate about Lucian, how they met, and how she fell in love with him. She told her best friend all about the deal and the fire that killed her family. She talked about Mason and Morgan and how much she wished she could let them know she was alive.

"Holy shit," Cate gasped once her story had reached present day and wrapped her arms around her. A small weight lifted off Celeste's chest. Now, her truth and guilt no longer had to fester inside of her and wait to die. She was no longer completely alone.

Celeste let go of her friend and exhaled. "I've made my peace with it. I'm not even mad that he got me out of there—although I'm furious he killed them after he promised he wouldn't. I'm angry that I let him in, *trusted him*, and he lied to me about who he was. I am *livid* that he forced me into a deal that I agreed to under duress. I had no idea what I was saying. My life literally went up in smoke in a matter of *minutes*, and I couldn't process it. There was no closure. He thought I was being ridiculous, but it was all I ever knew. At times, I miss who I was, but I don't think I could be her again. Celeste healed in a way Alice was never going to." Tears threatened to spill over. With every uttered word, her shoulders lowered away from her neck and her back began to straighten.

Cate rubbed her friend's back in an effort to help calm her down. "Maybe it had to happen, to allow yourself to grow."

She wiped her eyes. "I still feel stuck. I never lived this grand second life he said I could. I've been too riddled with fear and anxiety. The bastard could call in my debt whenever he pleases, and that keeps me up at night. He gave me freedom, but I'm constantly looking over my shoulder. And Remi *terrified* me. Not just because he was a creep, but because I thought it meant Lucian sent him, or it was Lucian sending someone to collect me because he didn't actually care about me. I'm so scared of him coming back that I feel like I can't even breathe. I can only live in the moment. I can't even consider a future. I had a shitty future in my old life and no future in this life. I don't know what's better."

"Then the attack tonight! God, I hate him. He probably sent them." She accused Lucian, though she knew he would never send someone to rape her. He was the Devil, but deep in her heart, she knew he wasn't that evil.

A defensive look flashed in Cate's eyes. "He didn't send them. They came of their own volition. There are some Fallen Angels, like Remi, who have no regard for Human life and will hurt them, especially women, because it brings them joy."

"You don't know Lucian. But neither do I, apparently," Celeste mumbled. There was a slight uptake of Cate's shoulders. "You knew Remi, do you know Lucian too?"

"All Witches know of the King of Hell. We know of both Fallen Angels and Heavenly Angels. Some we only know by name. Lucian, I've heard, stays to himself mostly; He doesn't come up to earth much. I knew Remi and his goons as they frequent earth. They have a thing for human women, and they love to take what is not theirs. I think they get off on it," Cate tells her.

"There were more of them?" Celeste's heart stopped beating for a moment. Cate fought off two Fallen Angels on her own, and she couldn't fight off one.

You're pathetic.

"His two friends. They will not be bothering us again."

"Are you okay?"

"I'm fine." Cate gave her friend a reassuring smile.

"Are all Fallen Angels like Remi?"

"Ehh…" Cate's head tilted back and forth, trying to think of the best way to word her answer. "Not all, Majority of the males are like him, and there's a handful of females. But not many are violent and forceful like Remi. Drunken one-night stands are usually preferred." She spat with a heavy dose of venom.

Celeste's eyebrow arched up her forehead, "Who broke your heart?"

Cate sighed deeply, sinking back into the couch. A look of longing washed over her face. "It's complicated."

"I'll beat her up for you." Celeste smiled weakly. A small joke, she was going to be okay. A large grin cracked Cate's face, then a small laugh. She was going to be okay too.

The girls fell into a comfortable silence. Chip began to snore softly beside his owner.

It was a while before anyone spoke. "When Lucian left here, he left in a circle of blue flames. Tonight, I swear I saw those same blue flames. It was like he was there," Celeste said quietly.

Cate stiffened and bit down on her bottom lip. "It's been a long night. Why don't you head up to bed?"

"I can't. Too many bad memories," Celeste admitted. She looked back at her mug on the coffee table and stood up. As if on command, Chip woke and got up too, ready to follow Celeste to the ends of the earth. "I'm going to sit on the deck." She grabbed a blanket from the love seat to the right of the couch and made her way outside. The salty air hit her nerves like ice, but it instantly soothed her. She shook off the dust on the blanket and wrapped herself in it. She curled up on the wicker couch and stared blankly at the ocean. In the sky, the morning star glistened and shone. She was alive for another day.

CHAPTER 13

Lucian bounded up the front stairs of the mansion, skipping every other step. It'd been eight years since he'd last been here. He knew she had abandoned it. He came back once to check up on her, but she had been long gone by then. He continued to pay the bills and care for the empty house in the event she would come back. At the top of the steps, he let out a slow breath and slowed into a fast walk into the mansion. It didn't even occur to him what he would do if Celeste saw him, but he couldn't breathe until he saw with his own eyes that they were safe.

"Cate!" Lucian whisper-yelled, not wanting to wake up Celeste or scare her even more.

"In here!" Cate yelled in the same hushed but broken tone. Lucian hurried into the main living room.

Cate was sitting on the couch with her head in her hands, her body heaving in quiet sobs.

He knelt in front of her, gently tugging her hands away from her face. It broke his heart and infuriated him to see her crying. Cate was his family, and no one messed with his family and lived to tell the tale, except his brother. "It's okay," he assured her. Cate flung her arms around him and pressed her head into his shoulder. Lucian held her close like he used to when she was a little girl. "It's okay, Cate. He won't hurt the two of you again."

"Is he dead?"

"Yes. He has been destroyed." He rubbed her back soothingly.

It was a while before her heaving subsided and she could talk. "I failed, I'm so sorry. Luce I—"

Lucian shushed her, tucking her dark auburn hair behind her ear like he did when she was younger. Her turquoise eyes held the same guilt he had seen before, a guilt he was unable to shoulder for her. "You two are both safe. That's all that matters to me."

The sobs came back with a vengeance. Her attempts at calming deep breaths turned into short, shallow ones as the sobs kept coming. Like many times before, he held her until she ran out of tears.

"Where is she?" he whispered once she was quiet.

"Outside. Lucian, do not go out there. I don't know if she's awake or not. If she's asleep, do not wake her up. It's been a long night for both of us."

"I'm not going to wake her up. I just need to see she's okay. Remi almost raped her," Lucian hissed, purposely omitting the rest of what he'd said.

"What are you going to do if she sees you?"

"She won't," Lucian insisted. He didn't wait for another word from her and went outside. When he was born, he could yield both light and darkness with the swipe of his hands. After the Fall, the light burned into flames. Tendrils of darkness fell from his palm and wrapped around him, shrouding him from view. He found Celeste curled up in a ball on the outdoor couch. Her head was cranked awkwardly between the back of the couch and the armrest. Her feet were pressed against the back of a sleeping brown dog.

An old grey blanket lay in a pile on the ground. Her face was slack and relaxed. She was at peace and, most importantly, safe. He let out a sigh of relief. The girl was physically okay. Time would tell with her mental state, but it was enough for him for now. Lucian reached down and grabbed the blanket when he heard a soft growl. He froze, eyes shifting to the dog and held in a breath. The dog lifted his head up and began to bark. Lucian glanced over to Celeste; she was stirring. The damn dog. His shadows made his appearance invisible, not his being. He dropped the blanket and backed away from the couch quietly.

Celeste shot up from the couch, her blue eyes wild and scared. His breath caught in his throat as he froze in place. He said a silent thank you that his shadows made it easy to blend in with the early morning light. She was stunning, and a far cry from the teenager she had been. She had grown into her features, her face rounder and softer. She lowered a hand to her dog, assuring him that there was no one out there with him, although she was not too convinced herself. Once she deemed herself safe, she picked the blanket off the ground and laid back down. When her breathing slowed, Lucian went back inside.

"Yeah, she won't see me," Cate mocked in deep voice. "You woke up the fucking dog. Good going."

"She didn't see me. Why is she sleeping outside?"

The young Witch shrugged, "She put herself there. She never wanted to come back here, Lucian," Cate said as she turned on the television. The noise drowned out the loud silence.

"What does that have to do with her sleeping outside?" he repeated as he took a seat on the couch next to her.

The side-eye dirty look she shot him had him shifting further away from her on the couch. "She's traumatized. She told me her side of the story. Lucian, you traumatized her!"

Lucian returned the glare. He went above and beyond for her. "She was being abused! I saved her."

She let out an exasperated sigh. "You killed her family and burnt her house down!"

"So? They didn't love her. They acted like they were better than others and acted like they were rich. The house was cheap looking. I did her a favor, really."

Cate pinched the bridge of her nose, the same thing her mother would do when she was irritated with him. "She's *Human*. She went face to face with her mortality, she watched her family turn to ash, and her neighbors almost burn to death trying to save them. And then, in the process of coming to terms with that, you tell her she sold her soul! Honestly, Lucian, are you dense?"

Hot fire bubbled at the surface of his fingertips. He did what needed to be done. Hades, he had reined himself in that night. "You do realize whom you are speaking to, correct?" He took a deep breath trying to cool the growing anger. He rarely exploded at the other women in his life. The Witches had no problem hexing him and his sister Gabby would explode right back at him and the two would go around and around until one of them gave in. Guilt still ate at him from when he exploded at Celeste.

Cate flung her hands in the air. "Don't get all high and mighty on me, asshole. Just because you're best friends with my mother doesn't mean I can't curse you." He sunk into the soft couch. The last time the two of them went head-to-head, he had plucked neon yellow feathers out of his wings for the next six months. Cate sighed and turned her eyes to him. "She told me you called her a mistake. The same word her family used to call her."

Lucian flinched. He had instantly regretted his words the moment they came out of his mouth. "I wish I could take it back." Although the two sat in silence, his last words to Celeste screaming back at him. He finally broke the silence, "How is she otherwise? Is she happy?"

"For the most part," Cate answered curtly.

"You are so insightful," he bit out sarcastically.

Cate huffed and crossed her arms. "She's my best friend."

"What am I? Chopped liver?" he quipped with a smile.

The corner of her mouth turned upwards. "She trusts me. And unlike you, I don't intend on breaking that trust."

Lucian winced. He would never forgive himself for hurting her, and it seems like she wouldn't either. "She belongs to me. I think I'm entitled to know how she's doing."

"Pig," Cate narrowed her eyes at him, her turquoise eyes glowing.

Despite his earlier convictions, this had been good for them. They had gotten very close, and it seemed the friendship would transcend beyond this life. Cate was a rock; she helped people and took care of others constantly and always put on a strong front. Celeste was water, taking the shape of whatever someone else needed her to be. But water smoothed rocks after some time, and Cate hopefully helped Celeste solidify herself.

Lucian raised his hands in defeat. She blinked her eyes, and the glow faded away.

"She knows most of the truth about me. She's okay with it, I think."

"She took it well?"

"I think. I told her about Fallen Angels and Heavenly Angels. She seemed okay with it."

"Well, she believes in Angels. That's to be expected. The poor girl still believes in my Father."

"She thought she saw you tonight." Cate looked over at him. "I had to tell her I didn't know you; she's going to kill me when you bring her down."

"That's like seventy years away. She'll have forgotten by then." He shrugged. "How is she?" She was still alive, so at least he had that.

"She's Fine." Cate clipped and moved on, "Can you get my things from my room at the cottage? Remi's friends put a giant hole in the floor and I can't get to my room. I don't have wings like the rest of you."

"Of course. I'll be back shortly." He stood up and kissed the top of her head. "Call Hester, Bea, and Don. They're worried."

"Gee, Don's worried? That's a first," she murmured.

"Cate," Lucian gently scolded the girl. He bid her farewell and walked out of the house onto the deck. He took a final look at Celeste's sleeping form and walked down the steps toward the ocean, disappearing into the night.

CHAPTER 14

Settling into the mansion was easier the second time.
Almost overnight, the house went from an empty shell to
a cozy seaside oasis. Even the master bedroom felt more
like hers now. Every trace of Lucian had been erased, and
she found herself loving the mansion. Chip loved the
bigger space; there was more room for him to run around
and play. He especially loved the on-demand access to the
ocean. Now, he could spend his days on the deck
watching the waves and not risk his or her life by crossing
a busy highway.

A couple weeks after the attack, the Marlin's dinner
rush was in full swing. Celeste hurried from one end of
the restaurant to the other taking orders, running food
and zig-zagging between families coming and going to

their tables. The only thing that kept her from screaming out any frustrations was the hope for big tips and the beach concert she and Cate were attending that night.

She passed by a table when a familiar gruff voice shocked her system. "Vicky?"

Celeste skidded to a halt and closed her eyes tightly. She had not heard that name in years. Her breath hitched as she braced herself for whoever recognized her as her dead sister. She opened her eyes and turned towards the table. Sitting there was her hot, dirty blonde hero who saved her from Remi at the bar. Upon further examination of his features, all air left her lungs.

Her neighbor and childhood crush, Mason Ward, stared back at her. The man had aged like fine wine. The dirty blonde hair complemented his sun-kissed skin. His hazel eyes studied her as he tried to place Vicky's features on her.

She opened her mouth to deny the name when he coughed, side-eyed the woman across from him, and spoke again. "I'm sorry. You, uh, you just look a lot like a person I once knew."

Celeste glanced at the rest of the table. Across from him was Morgan. Unlike her, Morgan looked relatively the same as she did eight years ago. She had gained some weight and filled out more. Her once curly, long dirty blonde hair now reached her shoulders. Next to her was a dark-skinned man around their age. He was holding a toddler in his lap, coloring the kid's menu with her. Her heart ached at the sight of her old friends. The little girl was the niece and goddaughter she never got to know. Next to Mason was another child, around six or seven, face contorted in concentration—Morgan's concentration face—as she colored on her own kid's menu. Anger and grief overwhelmed her system. *This* was the life she was supposed to have.

Celeste's returning smile barely reached her eyes. "It's okay. Have you been helped?"

Mason denied it, and Celeste took their orders, keeping her countenance neutral. She fast-walked to the drink fountain, inhaling deeply and then once more in an effort to keep her composure.

Cate walked over to her. "He's hot. You should get it." She winked and grinned. The smile fell immediately upon seeing Celeste's face. "What's wrong?"

"Remember I told you about Mason and Morgan from my past? That's them." Celeste's voice wavered as she set the drinks on a tray. Cate looked back at the table. "I didn't realize it till now that it was Mason who saved me from Remi that night at the bar."

Cate gave her an apologetic smile. "Do you want me to cover the table for you?"

Having Cate take over the table would save her the hurt, but this might be her only chance to get the closure she never had. She wanted one moment with the people she had loved so dearly and the nieces she was deprived of knowing. "I need to do it. They were the only ones that cared about me," Celeste sighed and went back over to the Wards. Mason's head was turned down to the older girl's menu. They were playing one of the games on the menu.

Morgan thanked her for the drinks and ordered for the table: steamed crabs.

As she put her notepad away, Mason spoke to her again, beautiful hazel eyes stared into her soul.

Please see me. It's me, it's Alice!

"Are you from Elizabethtown, by any chance?" Morgan hissed Mason's name lowly, followed by a small *thunk*. She probably kicked him in the shin. There was a brief flash of darkness in his eyes.

A sense of relief flooded over her. He *saw* her. Celeste wanted to scream to the Heavens that she was and that she was their long-lost friend. Her lips began to form the words when her mark started to overheat, reminding her where she was headed. She gave them a sad, small, smile, "No."

Mason's face fell into a dejected look that broke her heart. She excused herself before she could change her answer. After entering in their order, she marched straight into the walk-in freezer. The cold air was a welcome shock to her heated system. She pressed her forehead on the icy metal shelf. Tears pricked at the corners of her eyes. Damn Lucian and the damn deal he forced her into. It was her own fault. She let herself be vulnerable and let her guard down. She knew better than that. Every time she did, she got hurt.

The freezer door opened moments later. A feminine arm rested around her shoulders. The floodgates opened and Celeste wrapped her best friend into a hug. "Celly, It's just a part of grief. Everyone goes through it." Cate tried to comfort her.

Celeste let go and wiped her eyes. "I should be eating crabs with them, not serving them. She was my best friend, Cate. She was *you* before you."

"Just because you and Morgan were friends in childhood doesn't necessarily mean you two would have been friends now." Cate tried to reason with Celeste, always the logical one.

Celeste shook her head feverously. "Yes, we would have. We had been best friends since we were born. We had all these dreams and plans, and Lucian took it all away!" Celeste ran a hand through her curls. "Morgan and I were basically sisters. We dreamt of living together once we hit our twenties and having our kids be best friends. Hell, I was so in love with her brother, I used to daydream in class and my notebooks were covered in 'Mrs. Mason Ward' scribbles." She leaned against the shelf. The metal was cool against her hot cheek.

"That doesn't mean you would have ended up together. He's what? Ten years older than you? He would have found someone else. He would not have waited for his little sister's best friend," Cate argued.

Regardless of if he *did* wait, her parents would have never approved of him. Back then, he was just an average soldier in the Army. He wasn't a military doctor or some yuppy doctor, which is all her parents cared about.

"He's six years older than me." She crossed her arms with silent annoyance. "There was always hope."

"Hope is fleeting, Celle. You can talk all you want about the what-ifs and the hopes but at the end of the day, hope destroys people. It lets them believe in the impossible. Hope hurts more than the truth. Trust me on that."

Celeste huffed, patience thinning. "You don't get it, Cate! You weren't there! You don't understand. They were the only family I had. They were the only ones who loved me for who I was."

Cate sighed loudly through her nose. "I get that, Celle. What I'm saying is people change. They may not be the same people you knew. You're not the same person you were eight years ago."

Celeste laughed bitterly. "I didn't have a choice but to become a different person!" She rubbed her eyes and smoothed out her shirt. She needed to make her rounds.

"I'm not talking about Lucian and the deal. I'm talking about your mental health. You had to become a different person because your whole existence depended on it! You are a different person and that's okay. Humans are allowed to grow and change."

"I had a soul back then—When I knew them. When Lucian comes for my soul, I'll be a demon without a heart. They are the last remaining part of my humanity. They remind me that I used to be human." Celeste grounded her teeth and stalked out of the walk-in without another word.

She wasn't fully human anymore. She had turned into someone else entirely. She was kind to those kept at arm's length, and she loved her best friend, but she was a bitch to everyone else and proud of it. She knew firsthand the power words held, yet easily and without remorse, she'd let her words cut her dates like knives. She never meant the mean words she'd spit out, but it made her smile, knowing it hurt them. Alice would have been ashamed of Celeste. But since she was destined for Hell...

The Wards took forever to leave. She felt like a ticking timebomb. Every minute they were there, another inch of her fuse was burned away. She attempted to busy herself with other tables, running food for other waiters, doing anything she could to stay away from that table and confess. When they finally left, she had to restrained herself from writing her number down for Mason on the check. She snuck some final glances at her past as they walked out the door, etching their faces in her mind so she can remember them as they are. Even after they left, her fuse still burned hotly, and finally exploded with regret.

After their shift, she and Cate were supposed to go to a concert on the beach. It was an early 2000s punk rock band that she and Morgan used to listen to all the time at Morgan's house. Cate promised her months ago that she would go, but after the argument in the walk-in, Cate made an excuse and backed out. Her clipped words told Celeste all she needed to know—Cate was furious with her.

She changed into black jean shorts and a ruffled purple top to hide her stomach. The ruffled short sleeve hid the tops of her arms but showed off the tattoos on her arms. On her left arm, to hide Lucian's brand, a half sleeve stretched from her wrist to the crook of her elbow. The constellations Cancer, Draco, Chamaeleon and Microscopium danced across an indigo sky. It had taken hours and majority of what was left of her paycheck after rent and bills, but it was worth every cent. Not only did it hide Lucian's mark. It was effective at covering the dozens of lines that curved along the inside of her wrist and forearm. Along her right wrist was a key with a crescent moon on top. Cate had an identical one on her right wrist.

As she fixed her hair, she took a good look at herself in the mirror. A small silver barbell in her right eyebrow glinted in the lamp light, along with a thin silver hoop in her nose. Two sets of purple studs and one set of purple teardrop earrings adorned her ears with a single silver barbell in the cartilage of her left ear.

Unlike Mason, she didn't see her sister staring back at her. She didn't even see Alice staring back at her. Her parents permitted one piercing in each ear that she wasn't allowed to get until she turned 16. They would roll over in their graves if they saw her now. Knowing them, they would call her a heathen and ship her off to the nunnery.

The Atlantic Ocean back dropped the constructed stage. Loud rock music thumped from the speakers, and colorful lights shined every which way. To the side was a pop-up beach bar, now crowded with concert goers ready to get absolutely wasted. Celeste immediately hit the dance floor, ready to dance the night away. Anything she could do to forget about Mason and Morgan.

During a dance break, she walked over to the bar and ordered a third frozen strawberry daiquiri and her third shot of cinnamon whiskey.

"Rough shift?" She turned her head to see Mason Ward standing beside her, his hazel eyes intently staring at her. All the alcohol she had consumed drained from her completely and she felt as sober as she did when she first got to the concert.

"Complicated," she tells him as she pulls out her debit card.

"Hopefully, it wasn't on my account." Mason gave her a boyish smile that set her heart thumping erratically. It was the same smile that solidified her crush over ten years ago. He waved her card away and ordered a beer. "I got it."

"Oh, thank you." Her cheeks felt even hotter for a moment. Mason had paid for the dinner earlier today, giving her a considerable tip. Way more than other tables who had spent as much as they did. "No, you guys were great. The kids were really well-behaved. And neither kid had a tablet glued to their face! I was shocked."

Mason paid for their drinks and took a sip. "They're good kids." He smiled proudly.

"Are they yours?" she asked and threw her head back, downing the shot immediately. The whiskey a calming burn down her throat.

Mason shook his head, and she relaxed her shoulders slightly in relief. "No. My nieces. I don't have any kids. I'm Mason, by the way." He held out his hand for her. His hand was strong, warm, and slightly bigger than hers. She debated on whether to tell him the truth or just let herself have this night to live out her old dreams. Tomorrow he would be gone, and it would be like it never happened.

"Celeste." She put on her most seductive smile. "What are you doing here?"

"Vacationing with my family. My sister and her best friend used to listen to this band all the time growing up. So, I bought tickets for her birthday. The girls are with their grandparents tonight."

She quickly scanned the crowd looking for her best friend. Many a night growing up, she and Morgan would be blaring the band's music until the early morning hours when Morgan's father came in, unplugged the CD player, and left the room with it, ordering them to go to bed. Celeste's parents did not approve of rock music or most secular music for that matter; they claimed it was Devil's music.

"Having fun?" she asked.

"As much as I can third wheeling an engaged couple kid-less for the first time in years." Mason winced, not wanting to think of his sister and her fiancé.

She suddenly felt inadequate with her measly little life here at the beach. Morgan had moved on, gotten engaged, and started a family while Celeste waited tables and bided her time.

"They deserve it," she said and took a sip of her daiquiri, praying she reached her earlier level of drunkenness, anything to forget the other choices Lucian took from her.

Mason took a swig of his beer; hazel eyes trailed her head to toe. "What about you?"

"I also loved this band growing up. However, my friend bailed on me tonight." The band played the opening chords of one of their more energetic songs. Mason and Celeste snuck off to the back where some tables were placed to continue their conversation.

"Do you live here?" Mason asked loudly over the music. They stood mere inches from each other. The sun had set hours ago but she was growing hotter with every moment spent beside him.

"I did. My best friend and I just moved to Rehoboth Beach. Do you come here often? I haven't seen you around here before."

"It's been a while. I was here earlier in the summer with some friends from the Army. I don't know if you remembered, but I was the one who interrupted the other guy who was creeping on you when you were working the bar a few months ago."

Celeste nodded. "You left before I could thank you."

He tilted his head downward in a small nod. "No need. I'd do it for anyone in need. But seeing you there gave me a reason to come back to the place this evening." He winked.

Celeste blushed and looked down at her drink. Heat pooled between her legs. The band began another fast tempo song. "Let's dance!" she grabbed his hand and pulled him to the dance floor.

Never in her wildest dreams could she have imagined dancing with Mason. An electric shock coursed through her as his hands gripped onto her hips, and his front pressed into her back as they swayed to the music. She could kick herself for drinking as much as she did. Of all damn nights. Her head fell back into his chest. She wanted to remember the feel of him against her, the feel of his growing erection, and the feel of his lips as he placed small kisses on her neck and behind her ear.

Her eyes focused on the clear, starry night. A shooting star soared southward; she squeezed her eyes tightly and made a wish.

CHAPTER 15

The band wrapped up their set to her displeasure. Celeste didn't want to leave his arms. Her tattoo burned hotly; it felt like a punch in the gut. Not him, not tonight. Anyone but him.

"We don't have to go home, but we can't stay here, sexy," Mason whispered lustfully in her ear and nipped it as his hand wrapped around her middle.

"Can you drive?" she asked. Celeste was three sheets to the wind had taken a rideshare down to the concert. She said a silent prayer for Cate to not be home. "We'll go to my house."

They left the beach together. Mason slid a protective arm around her after she almost took a nose dive into the boardwalk as they crossed it. He all but carried her to his silver sports car. The sleek car looked and smelled new. Mason helped her into the seat. A moan escaped her lips as soon as she got off her feet. She could stay here all night.

Mason smirked as he buckled her up, pausing to look at her. The remnants of his cedar and bergamot cologne filled her nose. She had never cared for the scent before, but now she couldn't get enough. His eyes darkened with lust. "Such a pretty moan, and we haven't even gotten to the best part." He whispered huskily to her before moving and shutting the door. Celeste's cheeks flushed a deep red and heat pooled in between her thighs. The black leather seats were cool to the touch but did little to cool the inferno burning inside her.

Mason climbed into the driver's side and took off. "Rehoboth Beach, right?"

Celeste slurred the address to him then closed her eyes and pressed her head against the headrest. She was convinced that it was all a dream, and once she opened her eyes, she'd be back dancing with some random person who thought they could get lucky with a drunk girl.

When her eyes opened, she was still in Mason's car. One hand was on her left upper thigh, lightly tapping to the beat of whatever music played softly from the radio. She turned her head over to study him. God, she felt like a teenager again, stealing glances of him from the back seat whenever Morgan's mom forced him to drive the girls to the mall, the store, to Scouts, or to soccer practice. He always complained but did it anyway.

"See something you like?" He chuckled and glanced at her. He gave her a wink that made her cheeks heat up again and her core burn with need. Celeste gave him a flirty smile and giggled. "Definitely."

Grinning, Mason pulled into the parking lot of an all-night convenience store. "Stay here." He kissed the top of her hand before running inside. He was back before she had time to miss him. The tires squealed as he sped away, his hand found its home on her thigh.

The feathery touch of his fingers had sent a flood of heat and electricity downward. The coil in her lower stomach tightened with every stroke. With each mile closer, his fingers moved closer to her center, occasionally brushing against the hem of her shorts. God, his hands. She had spent an ungodly amount of time dreaming of how his hands would feel on her.

He pulled up to the mansion and let out a slow breath. "Holy shit. You live here?"

"Yes, with my best friend. I don't know if she's home or not. But I do have a dog, he's just a love bug," Celeste slurred as she climbed out of the car, tripping over her own two feet.

The house was silent and pitch black as she stumbled in. There was no sign of Cate or of the dog. Hopefully, Cate was fast asleep in her room.

On autopilot, she went into her kitchen and grabbed two plastic cups from the cabinets. "Do you want something?" she asked as she went to the sink and poured herself a cup of cold water.

"Just you," he said huskily from behind her. Celeste choked on her words, and her cup of water clanged in the sink.

One hand wrapped around her waist and the other gathered her hair and pushed it aside. His lips pressed against her neck, kissing her favorite spot. A small moan escaped her lips as she leaned backwards into his chest, tilting her head to the side to give him more access. The hand on her waist slipped under the hem of her shirt. The needy touch sent an electric shock through her body. Celeste helped him shed her shirt and turned to face him.

"Get on the island," he ordered her, his voice deeper and darker than she had ever heard. With a little help, Celeste hopped onto the counter top. Mason spread her legs apart and stood in between them. Her core screamed with never ending need. His hands cupped her breast through her black bra as he leaned into her, his lips capturing hers. Their tongues danced for dominance over the other. His lips tasted of cedar and bergamot and alcohol. Celeste's hands found home in his hair, tugging at it with a need for more closeness. Mason obliged; grabbing her thighs and pulling her to the edge of the island counter. Her legs automatically wrapped around his hips.

His hands immediately went to her bra, and fiddled with the clasps. He unhooked it on the third try and tossed it to the side. An animalistic noise erupted from him as he took in her large breasts. His hands cupped them again with a squeeze, and they spilled over his palms. A purely male smile danced on his lips as he leaned down to kiss her jaw. With each kiss, he worked his way down her neck, shoulder, collarbone, then the top of her breast. His fingers lightly twisted and pinched one nipple. The other, Mason took in his mouth, his tongue making deft work of the peaked nub.

She was getting antsy from the foreplay. She *needed* him. She'd dreamt of this moment for years. Mason switched, giving the other the same care and attention, bringing the nipple taut against his fingers. Celeste brought her hands down from his hair to the button on her jean shorts.

"Someone's needy." He smirked and reached up to kiss her lips once. His hands gently pushed her to lay back on the island. He unbuttoned her jeans and slid them off her, tossing them by her shirt.

Celeste rested on her forearms. Mason's eyes were black as midnight as he traced his knuckle against her opening through her soaked underwear. Electricity shocked through her. He cussed under his breath and looked back at her face with that boyish grin she loved. "Damn, is all that for me, sweetheart?" he asked huskily. He slid her underwear off and tossed them. Celeste shivered from the cold air hitting her center and closed her eyes. She wanted him so bad she didn't even consider if her weight was a problem for him.

Mason's hands gripped the outer parts of her thighs as he bent down to place light, breathy kisses on her inner thighs. Every kiss was closer to her core than the last. When he got to her center, he paused for a moment. "Eyes on me, sweetheart," he demanded. Submitting completely, Celeste opened her eyes. His face had a devilish grin on it as he inserted a finger. Celeste gasped as he added a second finger.

"More," she breathed. Mason grinned and pumped his fingers in an even rhythm. Celeste moaned his name loudly as the back of her head hit the island. His pumps quickened, but she needed more and needed it *now*. Mason cupped one of her breasts in his free hand and squeezed it.

"You like that? Just wait until you see what my mouth can do." He smirked. Celeste moaned; her lower stomach was coiling tightly. Just when she felt she would explode, Mason removed his fingers. A small whine escaped her lips at the loss of him.

"Patience, baby girl." Mason smirked as he put a leg on each shoulder and pulled her body toward the edge of the island.

His mouth paused at her entrance; his warm breath teased her endlessly. She opened her mouth to tell him what she wanted when she felt his tongue slid in her. Celeste moaned in pleasure as her back arched off the counter. Each flick of his tongue tightened the coil in her lower stomach. She moaned his name again along with other shouts and pants. Mason squeezed her legs, urging her on.

The feel of his tongue was overwhelming. The coil let loose, and she climaxed, screaming his name as she came. Mason stayed between her legs, licking up every last drop of her orgasm. When her release subsided, Mason lifted himself and pulled her up to a sitting position, an animalistic grin on his face.

"You taste sinful," he told her in between kisses

"I want you," she whispers against his lips.

"Oh yeah? How much?" he asked lustfully. Her fingers immediately began unbuttoning his beige shorts. The shorts dropped to the ground, and the boxers pulled off easily. His erection sprung out of its cage. Her hand wrapped around him and pumped him a few times.

Mason braced his hands on each side of her on the counter as she stroked him. His head buried in the crook of her neck. He moaned her name as his body shuddered in pleasure. He lifted her hand off of him and gently pushed her back down on the island. Mason bent down to his shorts, pulling out a small, wrapped square. He slid the condom on quickly. Without a moment to waste, his hands gripped her hips as he positioned himself in front of her opening and slid into her, all the way to the hilt.

Celeste gasped at the feel of him inside her. The pumps into her quickened their pace, and Celeste splayed out her hands across the island, knocking over a plastic decorative vase.

"You take me so well, sweetheart," Mason grunted as he picked up speed. Celeste's pants quickened, and her moans became shorter and louder, louder than the slapping of their skin coming together. They came to their climax together, and she rode Mason out until he came to a stop.

Panting and blissful, she closed her eyes, drinking in the heavenly moment. He was everything she had dreamt about and then some. "Am I dreaming?" she asked breathlessly with a huge smile across her face.

"This is better than any dream."

Bright, early morning sun streamed through the bedroom windows. She had forgotten to close the blinds when she left last night. Celeste opened her eyes only to immediately shut them again, groaning from the pain of the light. Her head was pounding, and she felt ready to vomit. Her head ached when she tried to remember what all she drank. As she rolled over to go back to sleep, she bumped into something hard and muscular. Her eyes popped open to see Mason snoring beside her. Flashes of bodies, lips, and teeth pounded through her head. Grinning, she lay her head on his chest and closed her eyes again. God, what she would do to wake up beside him every day. Within seconds, Mason's arms were around her and he squeezed her tightly against him.

Mason pressed a soft kiss to her head, "Good morning, beautiful," he rasped. She could listen to him talk like that for the rest of her life.

Celeste murmured her own sleepy good morning as she lifted her head and kissed him. Her mind was cussing out the sky for the bright reminder that their night was over, and he had to leave.

His hazel eyes, bright but glazed with sleep, gazed at her lovingly. "Last night was amazing." He kissed her again before letting her go and climbing out of bed. Celeste's head hit the pillow again and pulled the blankets further up her chest.

"We should do it again sometime," she teased with a smirk although she was dead serious. She would do anything to remain in his orbit. Mason laughed as he walked to the private bathroom in her room.

Celeste put a hand on her throbbing forehead. She needed medicine badly, but any attempt to sit up, and she would vomit. "Can you bring me some water and the bottle of painkillers in the cabinet?" she called out to him and rolled over, closing her eyes.

She must have fallen asleep again because she woke up to someone shaking her shoulder and calling her name. She opened her eyes to see Mason standing beside the bed holding a picture in one hand. His whole demeanor had shifted into something dark. His jaw was set and his eyes held an angry darkness.

"Why the *hell* do you have a picture of my sister and her dead best friend in your room?"

CHAPTER 16

She took the simple silver frame from his hands.

Teenage Morgan and Alice smiled happily at her with their arms around each other. It had been from their senior prom. Her parents insisted they do the pictures in their backyard under their own delusion they were richer than Morgan's family and had a better garden. Morgan wore a navy-blue gown with glittering sparkles from top to bottom. It was strapless, showing off her breasts. Celeste's parents had talked shit about the dress for *weeks* afterward. Celeste's mother chose a soft pink dress with lace detail in the bodice. Her shoulders and the tops of her arms were covered by a small pink cotton shrug. *The problem areas,* her mother had called them. Her mother made fun of her appearance in tank tops constantly, even forbid her from wearing them altogether. Even to this day, the only time Celeste will wear a sleeveless garment is when she's in her bathing suit. The only good that came out of it was more surface area for her to mark up with her razor blade.

The girls had matching hairstyles—waterfall braids. Morgan had done Celeste's makeup, which her mother disproved of but allowed with strict rules: brown eyeshadow only, no eyeliner, and certainly no lipstick. Morgan, ever the rebel, had used pink eyeshadow, black eyeliner and mascara, and a soft pink lip. Celeste's mother bit her tongue that night but the next day grounded her for disobeying orders. Their nails matched their respective dresses. Pink or nude nails were all her mother allowed. Everything else was deemed gothic or slutty.

Nice men don't like that goth stuff. They want a lady.

To get the pictures, Celeste had gone through her old social media page and downloaded her three favorite pictures onto her new laptop and phone that Lucian had given her. The one in her hands typically sat on her dresser. There was another one on her nightstand—the two of them at the beach as children—but he hadn't noticed that one. The last one was in the corner of her room on the wall, a picture from their eighth-grade graduation. They were at Morgan's house lounging on her bean bag chair watching TV.

She swallowed hard and looked up at Mason. His eyebrow arched, waiting for an answer. The moment she had waited years for was here, and she couldn't get a sound out. She set the photo on the bed and slowly sat up, trying to keep her composure and to keep from getting sick.

Mason picked up the photo again. "I'm going to ask you one more time—why do you have a picture of my sister and her friend in your room?"

Celeste glanced back down at the picture and heaved a sigh. "Because that's a picture of me." He doesn't move. "I am—I was Alice Delco." The name cracked on her tongue like it had been covered in cement for years. It sounded foreign to her now.

"Bullshit. She died in a house fire when she was eighteen."

Celeste shook her head, inhaled deeply and bit her lip. "I survived." Her eyes focused on a spot on her blanket. She couldn't bear to look at him as she confessed her sins.

"There were no survivors. I went into that house, and I couldn't save Vicky or Alice. The house collapsed," Mason said thickly. That night must have been a sore part of his life too. Celeste reached out for his hand, but he pulled back. "We had a funeral for Alice. My parents funded a gravestone for her specifically because of her friendship with Morgan. If you really are Alice, did you not think for one second to reach out to her? Your death fucked her up for years!" Mason raised his voice and threw the photo. It flew across the room, hit the wall, and clattered to the ground, leaving a little nick in the sandy colored wall. She flinched; her mother was famous for throwing stuff when she was angry.

"There's a lot more to the story, but you have to believe me. I am… I was Alice." Her voice waivered. This was not going the way she had always hoped.

"No, I don't know who the hell you are. Alice is dead. Vicky is dead!" Mason raised his voice.

"How many bodies did they find in the rubble? Who were they?" Celeste snapped. In the days following the fire, Lucian went back to Elizabethtown and brought her newspapers. He'd protested at first but finally gave in, thinking it would give her some closure. She also followed the news stories on social media. Hell, it even made the local news in Rehoboth. Seeing herself and her family plastered all over the media made her sick and had her body visibly shaking. Her sister and parents were made out to look like saints. She wanted to go to the press and tell them everything they did to her.

Mason ran a hand over his face and exhaled loudly. "Three. They found three bodies. Both Dr. Delcos and Vicky. Fire investigators and police assumed you were nothing but ash since your bedroom was in the basement. Between the fire and the rubble of the collapsed house, there would have been no way Alice would have survived or hadn't been turned to dust." He studied Celeste as if he was trying to find Alice under the piercings and last night's smeary makeup.

"You called me Vicky at the restaurant yesterday, and you said I looked like someone you used to know," Celeste reminded him.

"That was a mistake. *This* was a mistake." He gestured to the two of them. "I should have never come here," Mason snarled as he turned on his heel and marched out of the room.

"Mason!" Celeste yelled. She jumped out of bed and grabbed a shirt that was on the floor. She slid it on as she chased after him.

Mason flew down the steps. He found his clothes folded on a bench by the front door. Mason dressed quickly and threw the front door wide open. He ran out without another look back. Celeste skidded to a stop in the doorway. Her shirt barely covered her bottom half, and she had been in such a rush, she didn't grab shorts. She slammed the door and watched Mason get in his car and speed away.

Celeste pressed her palms to the cool stained glass, and stared solemnly out as she blinked away the hot tears threatening to spill over. *Mistake.* Her parents and her sister told her that. Lucian called her a mistake and now, Mason. She was a mistake and had been her whole life. But she was so tired of everyone telling her that. Her forehead pressed against the glass. She *was* a fuck-up.

"Celly?" Cate called softly and peered from behind the kitchen wall. Celeste didn't turn around, didn't want to see her friend with a smug 'I told you so' look.

"Go away," Celeste murmured.

"Was that *the* Mason?" her friend asked calmly. Celeste mumbled a noise of agreement. "What happened?"

"A mistake. A fat, ugly, no-good mistake." Celeste wiped the now-shedding tears from her eyes, talking more about herself than him.

"Go put some shorts on. I'll make pancakes," Cate told her friend. Pancakes were a comfort food in their house. It was something they always did after a bad day or break up. No matter what time of day it was, if one was having a moment, the other made pancakes. Despondently, Celeste trudged up the stairs, keeping her eyes on the ground.

Chocolate chip pancakes were ready on a plate when Celeste made her way back downstairs. Next to the pancakes were a cup of iced coffee and two acetaminophens for her pounding headache. Cate had unknowingly perched herself at the island where Celeste and Mason had sex the night before. Celeste winced as she grabbed her plate and moved to the dining table. Last night was such a blur, she couldn't remember if they cleaned it afterward. Cate unquestioningly followed her. Chip padded towards them and laid at Celeste's feet. Her toes dug into his soft fur. The feel of him kept her mind from spiraling.

The two ate in comfortable silence. Cate didn't initiate any conversation, which was probably Celeste's favorite thing about her. She was always just there. Until Celeste was ready to talk about something, just the mere presence alone was company enough.

"Was the sex good at least?" Cate finally asked as she finished her breakfast.

Leave it to Cate to force her to laugh. She thought as she exhaled through her nose and laughed once. "Oh, my God. Best I've ever had. I thought I saw Jesus." Cate threw her head back, laughing from an inside joke they shared.

"But I'm assuming that wasn't the reason he ran out of here?" Cate asked once she could catch her breath.

Celeste's shoulders dropped as she took a sip of her iced coffee. She shook her head before rehashing the morning's events. Cate listened intently. Not once did she twist her face or make a comment saying she was right and that she told her so. Celeste really lucked out on a friend as good as Cate. Especially after losing Morgan.

"What are you going to do now?" Cate asked her calmly.

She ran a hand through her hair and shrugged. "I doubt I'll ever see him again. You should have seen his reaction, Cate. He was so angry; he threw the photo across the room! If that is how he reacted, Morgan's reaction will be a thousand times worse. Their parents paid for my fucking gravestone. They wasted money on nothing! Maybe it's about time I give up hoping and praying. You were right; hope destroys people." Celeste rubs her face with both hands. "Not to mention he said I was a mistake. My parents and sister told me that daily. Lucian told me that before he left."

"You're not a mistake, Celle. I'm sure Mason—and Lucian—didn't mean it." Cate tried to rationalize. "You are not a *mistake*. Not in the 'God's plan' or 'you were here for a reason' way. They were not good enough for you. If they can't accept you for who you are, then fuck them. Not literally."

"Everything has been a mistake. Yes, I know I was a mistake child, but I also made the mistake of getting to know Lucian. I made the mistake of selling my soul to him, and now I'm stuck here in this limbo. Morgan has two kids and a fiancé. She moved on, and I haven't. I'm stuck here."

"Well, if you would stop looking for one-night stands, that could be you too."

Celeste leaned back in her chair and crossed her arms in defiance. "You know why I can't do that. It wouldn't be fair to them." The words came out a little harsher than she wanted them to.

"Death comes for everyone," Cate said absentmindedly. Celeste flinched. She knew he was coming for her soul, but it never registered in her brain that she would have to *die*. "Sorry, but from what you told me, Lucian won't come for you until you're old and wrinkly anyway."

His words meant nothing to her now. "Fuck Lucian." Celeste said as she let out a breath.

"Yeah, fuck him." Cate replied in solidarity. Celeste gave her best friend a small smile. "Fuck men. Not literally, they're trash. Get a girlfriend. They're less trash, and you'll be more satisfied after sex."

Celeste barked out a laugh. She didn't need Mason. She told herself she just needed to fuck him out of her system, and she had. Now she can close that chapter in Alice's book. It was still open with just one unfinished chapter left, but maybe she could find peace with that.

CHAPTER 17

Cate and Celeste's annual Independence Day cookout was in full swing. For the last five years, they hosted a cookout at the cottage for their co-workers and any other friends who had come and gone. This year was even better with the addition of the mansion's hot tub, pool, and oceanfront accessibility.

The sun was dipping into the horizon, and the citronella candles they had placed around the deck illuminated the area. Chip was having the time of his life swimming in the pool with their co-workers and their dogs. A young hostess threw a beach ball from one end of the pool to the other, the dogs chasing after it. Some of their coworkers were seated on the outdoor couches and recliners with their significant others, while another group sat at the outdoor table, playing a card game and laughing hysterically.

Celeste relaxed on a step leading into the pool. Her neck was starting to ache from constantly sneaking glances at Cate and her new friend, Don. The two were currently in the hot tub. The Asian man's skin was pale despite today's hot sun. His shoulder length inky black hair was shiny and wet. He was devastatingly good looking with a jawline that could cut glass and deep, black eyes. He did not look too thrilled to be here with a permanent sneer on his face which all but faded whenever he looked at Cate. The man was absolutely in love with her. Cate claimed they were only friends since he lived far away, but between the little movements and light touches, there was more to the story. She made a mental note to pester Cate later. In the last seven years, she had never seen Cate look at a man like that. Women, yes, but never men. Don had his head tilted towards her. He had one arm around the edge of the hot tub, fingers intertwined in her hair. Cate leaned against his muscled chest and the two stared at each other like they were the only ones in the room. Her smile widened as she laughed at something he said. Even Cate's smile was different. Celeste longed to have someone look at her like that; like she was wanted. She turned her head away; she had invaded their privacy long enough.

The stars had just emerged when the doorbell chimed. Her eyebrows knitted together. At this hour, guests were leaving, not coming. She glanced over at Cate. The girls locked eyes, and Cate shrugged before turning her attention back to Don.

Celeste climbed out of the water, grabbed her red towel, and wrapped it around her midsection as she walked to the door. She peered through the stained glass windows. Her breath caught in her throat, and her heart dropped into her stomach as she unlocked the door with haste and threw it open.

"Mason?" she questioned breathlessly. After the way they left things last month, she figured she would never see him again.

Mason stood there nervously with one hand in his hair and the other shoved into his shorts pocket. "Alice."

She blinked, and her breath hitched again when he called her by her old name. She had forgotten what it was like to respond to that name. Words struggled to form. "Wha-What are you doing here?"

"I needed to talk to you. About what you said. If you really are Alice."

Celeste moved out of the way to let him in the house. He stepped inside and took another long look at her. "There's a party on the deck. But we'll have space on the beach. Do you want something to drink?"

"A beer if you have it," he said.

Celeste led him to the deck. She grabbed a beer for him and a whiskey neat for herself—she was going to need it. The two walked side by side to the beach, the sand cool on the soles of her feet. They took a seat at the edge of the tide and sat in a comfortable silence as the water lapped up their heels.

The alcohol did nothing to soothe her nerves. She was going to tell him everything—she owed him that. She owed Morgan that much. Hell, she needed it for her own closure. Her finger traced swirls and whorls in the sand to keep her in the present and to keep her from going off the deep end. She inhaled deeply to prepare herself and broke the silence. "Winter break of senior year, Morgan, her boyfriend at the time, and I went to Harrisburg for New Year's. My parents thought I was at your house. Her boyfriend made fake IDs for us so we could get into bars. The line at this outdoor bar was long and slow. It was a clear night, and as we waited, I showed Morgan the constellations that were visible that night. The man in front of us, Lucian butted in our conversation and we all got to talking. Lucian and I became fast friends. He would come over when my parents and Vicky were gone for the night, or we'd go out somewhere."

Mason's eyebrows furrowed as he thought back to eight and a half years ago. "Morgan never said you had a boyfriend."

Celeste shook her head. "I couldn't officially date anyone back then. For starters, my parents had forbidden Vicky and me from dating. Vicky got caught a few times, and the aftermath wasn't pretty. But Lucian never treated me in a romantic way, we were just friends. He'd get me out of the city. We'd go to Harrisburg and go get dinner. Sometimes, we'd go to the planetarium there."

"He took you on dates," Mason growled lowly and protectively, causing something within her to stir.

"I wished we'd dated," she admitted. A knot formed in her stomach. Lucian had been her venting board, a safe place to complain about her family, and a good shoulder to cry on. "It was just a schoolyard crush." She could feel the fondness she once had for Lucian slip through whatever cracks had opened in her. She closed her eyes and shoved them back down.

"What does this guy have to do with anything?" Mason asked, bringing her back to the present. His eyes had slid over to lock on hers.

Everything. "Lucian is the *actual* Devil; I didn't know that at first. The night of the fire, I was crying and ranting and unknowingly sold my soul to him. I didn't know until the morning after."

Mason was silent for a moment. She was convinced he thought she was insane. "The Devil. Like Satan?"

"Yes. Ruler of Hell."

"The Devil isn't real, Alice." He leaned back on his hands.

Celeste sighed; she knew he wouldn't believe her. "He's real, Mase. Lucian *is* the Devil. He admitted it himself. I have a tattoo to prove it. It's just covered up." She held up her left arm.

His eyes traveled to her night sky tattoo. His Adam's apple bobbed as the muscles in his jaw ticked. "You sold your soul to kill your parents and Vicky?" he asked slowly, as if trying to understand.

"No, not kill. It's complicated." She sighed and closed her eyes.

"Murder is not complicated," he snapped.

"You know my parents abused me, right?" She snapped right back.

"Morgan claimed they did. Vicky mentioned it a few times. I never believed them. Your parents were good people."

Her eyes rolled into the back of her head, as much as she wanted to be surprised, she wasn't. Her parents fooled everyone. "The night of the fire, my father got a hold of my college schedule. To this day, I'm still not sure how they got access to my university email. I had gone behind their backs and declared Astronomy and Physics as my majors. They were *fuming*. They said because they were paying for it, they got to choose my major, just as they did with Vicky, which meant I was to major in biology and pre-med. I told them I didn't need them to pay for it, and that I could take out a loan. But I had no bank account, no job, or anything so that wouldn't have panned out well. He said I needed to get my head out of the stars as my life was already planned out. I was to get good grades, go to med school, then work with him, Mom, and Vicky. Once they retired, Vicky and I would take over the practice. My dream of studying space was a silly little dream."

"A doctor is a great career to go into," Mason commented softly. Celeste shot him a dirty look. "Sorry, continue."

Celeste took a deep breath, that night playing in her head like a horror film. "They reminded me of how great Vicky was. How she graduated *summa cum laude* in her undergrad and how she got into med school at Johns Hopkins. They told me again how I needed to be more like her. So, I ratted on her; she was dating her professor."

Mason's eyes shot to hers, a brief look of betrayal sliced through them. "She was dating her professor?"

Celeste nodded her head. "I only knew because Lucian and I went on a day trip to Philly, and we ran into them. Vicky, in turn, lied and told them she caught us having sex, which wasn't true. Lucian and I *never* had sex. The man never did more than hug me when I was upset or crying. My father went off on a tirade. He hit and screamed at us while Mom just sat and watched. He called us all kinds of names too: 'good for nothing whores' and 'heathens' and said that we were going to Hell." She smiled slightly. God, the irony.

Mason grabbed her hand and gave it a comforting squeeze. "You and Vicky were not any of those things." His hazel eyes looked her over. Hurt swam in his eyes. He was just as upset about it as she had been so many years ago.

The corner of her mouth turned upward briefly. "After that, he reminded me that not only was I a mistake and should have never been born, but I was also a disgrace to the Delco name. Afterwards, I went back to my room and started to cut myself. I knew I couldn't be alone, so I called Lucian and asked him to come over. He got there after I sliced my thigh open. He forced me to stop, cleaned me up, and sat me on the bed. He asked me to explain what had happened." Celeste sighed and wiped her eyes. She had not shed a tear for that night in seven and a half years. Adrenaline coursed through her veins, and a heavy guilt settled into her stomach.

Mason called her name softly, having lost herself in her thoughts. He dusted off the sand on his hand. His thumb wiped away a tear. "What happened next?"

Celeste shuddered.

"I hate them. I hate all of them. I'm eighteen, I'm an adult. I need to live my own life. I don't want to be a doctor. I want to go to space, see the universe. I can't do that if I'm elbow deep into some stranger's body." She vented to Lucian as she hobbled-paced around her room, her thigh yelling at her to stop.

"Then do it, Pet. They don't own you. You can walk away. The only thing stopping you from walking away from all of this is you," Lucian told her from his spot on the corner of the bed.

Her hand rubbed her forehead furiously. "I can't! I don't have any money. I don't have a car. I don't have anything. At this point, I would sell my soul to get away from them."

Lucian stiffened, icy eyes locking on hers, "You don't mean that."

It took her less than a second to answer: "Yes, I do."

"Are you sure you would give up your soul to get away from them? Really think about it."

She thought for a moment and stopped pacing, then turned to face him. "If the Devil showed up in my bedroom, I would give him my soul on a silver platter."

Immediately, Lucian stood up. "It will be done. I will get rid of them."

The murderous look in his eyes made her stomach roll. She took a step towards the door to keep him in. "What do you mean? You aren't going to kill them, right? Their death won't solve anything. I just want them to be upset they lost me. I want them to burn with the anger they festered in me. I want them to feel the pain of losing me. I want them to be sorry." Her chest lifted slightly. Just telling him these feelings that she harbored in the pits of her caused her to feel lighter.

He walked to her and lifted her chin with his finger. "No one is going to die by my hands, Pet," Lucian promised her and walked out to the hallway...

"When he came back, I smelled smoke. He took my hand and led me to the tree line on the side of the house. I watched you and your dad go inside the house and get carried out by firefighters. I saw Morgan crumble in your arms, I heard her screams of terror. I wanted to go over to you guys so badly to let you all know that I was okay. Lucian said it wouldn't be moving on. In fact, it was probably better if everyone thought I was dead."

"Alice, the fire was due to a candle your sister lit and some faulty wiring that had gone unnoticed," Mason countered.

Celeste's hands flung out in exasperation. "Mason, if that had been it, I would have just booked it across the street to your family the moment I smelt smoke. Why the fuck would I have changed my identity for a fucking candle fire?"

"He wanted to kidnap you?" Mason theorized.

"I was eighteen. Lucian brought me here at my request. It wasn't until the following day that I found out what I had done. Who he really was," she told him honestly.

"How did you not know he was the Devil?"

"Growing up, we're taught through images that the Devil is red skinned, has horns and a tail, and carries a red pitchfork. Lucian was incredibly hot. He had thick shiny black slightly curly hair and these bright blue eyes. The icy color you only see looking at pictures of Antarctica." Celeste sighed, remembering the way the ice would soften and melt whenever he looked at her. Something stirred deep in her stomach thinking about him.

She shoved the feeling down and continued, "Church taught me the Devil was evil and would lead us away from God. Lucian was kind, sweet, and caring. He was there for me when my parents would get physical or scream at me. He'd come over when I asked. Sometimes, he'd get there before I could cut myself, or he'd get me to stop if I was already slashing away at my body. He'd stay with me until I no longer felt the urge to hurt myself. Sure, we'd talk about religion, but he never spoke negatively of God or Christianity. I was in love with him. I thought he was my boyfriend." Celeste sighed, her hand absentmindedly rubbing her scarred right thigh. The raised scars were a stark reminder of her own evil and of her own survival.

The silence that followed was unbearable for her. Mason's eyes drifted down to her thigh, staring at her cuts. At the pure hatred she had for herself. He stared at her like the others did when they first noticed her cuts. The pity in their eyes was unbearable and only fueled her with anger. She didn't need their pity. No one cared about her back then, she didn't need them to care about her now.

Mason caught her staring at him. He quickly looked down at his beer bottle and coughed. "We would have kept your secret. We would have done anything you needed. We would have helped you."

We. Plural. No *Morgan would have*, no *I would have*. *We.* Her heart beat a little louder as the thread of hope she had cut mere weeks ago started to reconnect.

Celeste stretched her legs out, digging her feet into the cold sand. "I need you to keep the secret now. You can tell Morgan, of course, but no one else. I'm not Alice anymore. She still died in that fire."

His eyes lifted to her face. "You can't change your personality, no matter how hard you try to change your appearance or go by a different name," he commented, eyeing all of her piercings with a hint of displeasure.

"This is who Alice would have been if I'd had different parents," she tells him.

"Maybe." Mason shrugs, "Maybe not. What do we do now?"

Her heart skipped a beat. She had no idea. She never thought she would get this far. She shrugged. "I always dreamt of this day, but I never imagined what happened next."

"Come home." Mason turned his head to look at her. His face was flat and humorless. He was dead serious.

Celeste's eyes blinked in disbelief. "Didn't you hear a single word I just said? This is my home. I can't have you mixed up in my life. I don't know when, but Lucian will come for me, and I don't want to spend eternity knowing I hurt you and Morgan more than I already have."

"Everyone dies eventually. No day is promised to us."

Her hands waved wildly in frustration. "I'm already dead, Mase! Alice is dead, and Celeste is just living on borrowed time." Her voice raised an octave.

"You said it yourself; you didn't know you were making a deal. There's got to be a loophole. I'll help you fix this," Mason said with a tone of finality. A glimmer of hope shined in his warm hazel eyes. He meant every word he said.

Her face softened. Her old feelings crashed down on her like a large wave from the Atlantic. She wanted to collapse into his arms and thank him, for being her knight in shining armor again.

Waves of pain snaked up her arm suddenly. Her tattoo burned hotly—a reminder. Reality set back in, and she turned her head away. "This cannot be fixed. I've accepted my fate."

He tucked a piece of hair behind her ear, the touch sending shockwaves through her system. "You don't have to be alone, Alice. We can get through this."

"Why do you want to help me? You ran away when I told you who I used to be."

His fingers hooked around her chin, and he gently turned her head back to him. "Because you're important to us. Morgan struggled after the fire. According to her fiancé, she still has nightmares about that night."

Celeste winced and turned her head away. Many nights she would wake up with a start, screaming Morgan's name, tears staining her cheeks. "Don't get me wrong, I like this you. I saw you at the bar and I thought you were the hottest woman in the room, I knew then I needed to come back to see you. I was so surprised to see you at the concert. And then we talked, and I got to know you. And now that I know who you really are, I'm not letting you slip through my fingers again."

She thanked the darkness of the beach for hiding her now heated red face. His words were sweeter than honey. She truly wanted to believe him. She wanted to believe he liked her as much as she loved him, but the sight of him speeding away was still clear in her head. "Then why did you leave after I told you the truth? Why did you tell me I was a mistake? Do you know how hurt I was? I used to dream about you and me. I have been in love with you since I was thirteen! I had the night of my life, and the next day you told me I was a mistake. Was the sex we had was a mistake?"

Guilt washed over his hazel eyes. He quickly looked away to the ocean. He downed the rest of his beer before speaking, "I was in shock, Alice. For the last eight years, I thought you were a pile of ash. I truly believed I failed you and Vicky because I went into that house and came out of there without either of you! The fire department announced they didn't recover your body, assuming you completely burnt up. After I stormed out, I went back through the articles of the fire and of my memories for any sign that you had made it out that night. I couldn't find anything. So, I came back to talk to you. To hear your side of the story."

Like an echo, she could hear Mason screaming Vicky's and her names as he ran into the burning house; the desperation in his voice clear as day. The movie of that night replayed in her head like it has time after time; Mason going in and coming out soot-covered, leaning on a fireman. She could see every detail on his heart broken face and every wrinkle in his clothes. It was as if she was watching it in real time again. A sob escaped her lips, tears now clouding her vision. "I'm sorry. I'm so sorry. I wish I could take it all back, but I can't. I wish I could change the past."

He put his arm around her and pulled her into him. She sobbed into his chest. Mason rested his head on hers and rocked her gently. He didn't speak again until the only noise was the sound of the ocean. "I will do everything I can to save your soul from damnation," he vowed.

A sad, broken laugh escaped her. "It's a done deal, Mase. It's probably best if you leave. You got closure. I'm sure explaining it to Morgan will bring her closure. Just tell her I'm okay, and I love her."

Mason's lips pressed into a tight line, and he looked down at her. "Do you want me to leave?"

She wiped more tears away from her cheeks. "Of course not, but I'm not leaving you and Morgan a second time. It's better this way for both of you to grieve me as I was. Not the soulless girl I've become." She quickly stood up and grabbed her towel, bits of caked sand falling to the ground.

Mason got up and grabbed her face, halting her movement. His fingers pressed into the side of her neck as his thumb stroked her cheek. Bright hazel eyes bore into hers. A look so full of hope and determination, a promise. "No day is promised to us, Alice. But I want as many days with you as I can get."

Her cheeks and body heated at his words and touch. Her heart melted into those words. The idea of seeing him day in and day out filled her with a warmth she had never felt before. "I want that too," she whispered. His thumb traced over her bottom lip as she said it. The moment she finished talking, his lips captured her in a kiss full of promise and desire.

She wasn't sure how long they stood there kissing. But shouts and laughter from behind them broke them apart. A group of people walked down past the dunes carrying boxes of what looked like fireworks. "We should go back before we lose a limb," Mason joked as he took her hand.

The moment her foot touched the flat surface of the deck, one of the waitresses yelled out from the hot tub, "Cate, she's back!" Celeste's head snapped to the side door. She opened her mouth to speak when Cate appeared holding a white icing cake with twenty-six lit candles. A chorus of Happy Birthday erupted as Cate walked to the table with a giant grin on her face.

Celeste always hated her birthday. She never minded the getting older part— It was a reminder of another year she would have missed had she taken her life so many years ago. A new birthday meant another year closer to Lucian coming for her, but most importantly, she hated the fact that she shared a birthday with a day associated with freedom when she had never tasted freedom once in her life.

Celeste plastered a fake smile on her face like she did for each and every birthday. If she didn't, everyone would call her an ungrateful bitch. Mason lowered his head and sang quietly in her ear. When they were done, Celeste looked around the deck; everyone was smiling at her. Cate did this every year, and every year, Celeste always forgot and was surprised that people actually cared about her. Or, at least they made a good show of it.

"Make a wish," Mason murmured in her ear. She thought for a moment and trudged over to the table, never letting go of Mason's hand.

As she blew out the candles, she made the same wish, a plea she had made every year for the last seven years. *I wish I could save my soul.* As soon as the candles went out, fireworks boomed from the beach, illuminating the night sky in reds, whites, blues, greens, and yellows as if they were also celebrating her birthday. Everyone around her cheered for the display. Mason put a hand around her waist and gave it a light squeeze. His lips placed a soft kiss on her cheek and for the first time in years, she was excited for her next trip around the sun.

CHAPTER 18

The other side of her bed was empty when she woke up.

The clothes she had tossed onto the floor last night had vanished into thin air. He must have woken up and realized trying to beat the Devil at his own game was more than he could handle, and he wanted nothing to do with her. With a heavy sigh, she dressed quickly and ambled toward the staircase. A strong scent of freshly brewed coffee greeted her as she descended the stairs. She made a pit stop to greet Chip good morning at his spot on the couch.

She entered the kitchen to see a glowing Cate sitting on the bar stool at the island, nursing her coffee. Don was beside her with one hand on her upper thigh and the other holding his mug. "…And that's why Heath Ledger's Joker is the best Supervillain," he said to thin air looking towards the stove.

A glance at the stove jolted her awake. Mason's back was to her as he made breakfast. A wide smile broke across her lips as she practically ran over and wrapped her arms around his waist. Her face pressed into his back, inhaling his cedar bergamot scent. He was *real*. He was *here*.

Mason chuckled. "Good morning, sweetheart."

"You're here," she whispered. Mason lifted his arm up to allow her to snake around into his side, his arm wrapped around her as he continued cooking.

"Am I not supposed to be?" he asked curiously.

"You weren't upstairs. I was convinced I dreamt you," Celeste admitted quietly.

"Last night was better than any dream." Mason placed a kiss on the top of her head. "I'm not letting you go again," he promised. "Go make yourself a cup of coffee. Breakfast is almost ready." He pointed to the coffee pot with his head. Celeste kissed his cheek before walking to the coffee pot. She poured her coffee into her sage green mug before taking her seat on Cate's other side.

Celeste eyed multiple little bruises on Cate's collarbone. "Have fun last night?" Celeste whispered, smirking.

Cate glanced down at her chest where more bruises colored her ivory skin, then smirk-winked at Celeste. "Right back at ya." Celeste cocked her head and looked down. Small bruises decorated her own tanned chest. All color drained from her face. Mason had marked her like she was *his*. She couldn't tell if she was turned on or horrified.

The four made light conversation, and Mason seemed to get along with the other two, especially Cate, which thrilled her. Don and Cate excused themselves after breakfast to wrap up any loose ends before he left and

Cate went to work her rare shift without Celeste, leaving her and Mason to clean up the kitchen.

Mason dried a plate and set it down on his other side. "I'll probably go home tonight. I didn't bring a change of clothes. I wasn't sure how last night was going to go; I came here on a whim."

Celeste stayed silent, focusing her attention on scrubbing the plate. "Am I going to see you again?" She handed him the wet, newly clean plate. The thought of him leaving sent new waves of anxiety through her. He'd leave and never come back, never to hear from him again.

"Of course. I meant what I said, Alice." He set the now dry plate down on the counter and turned his body and attention to her. He placed a gentle hand on her cheek and carefully pulled her face towards him. The sponge and dish slipped from her hands back into the sink as she met his eyes. In the daylight, golden flecks sparkled like the sun on the ocean water. "I was thinking about your…situation. I want to see if we can talk to a priest. An exorcism or something."

Celeste's eyebrows furrowed and pulled away from him. The other shoe had finally dropped; he thought she was delusional. "Mase, first off, I'm not possessed. I'm soulless. Second, I'm Lutheran. I've never heard of a Lutheran exorcism."

"Both are caused by the Devil. Don't demons take over the soul when their possessing someone? I mean, look at you." Mason studied her face. His eyes glazed over her facial piercings.

Her head tilted in confusion as she stared at him in shock. "I'm not possessed, Mason. Besides, I like the way I look. I've always wanted these piercings." She still struggled with body image issues, but she was in a better place now than before.

"You are beautiful Alice," Mason backtracked. "I meant you don't look like you. The Devil could have possessed you to change you."

She exhaled as she turned off the kitchen sink and leaned against the counter, her arms crossing over her chest. "Back then, I was what my parents wanted me to be, not what I wanted to be. Not to mention it's been eight years. Are you the same person you were when you were eighteen?" She flicked the water back on and went back to washing dishes, scrubbing them a little too hard.

"No," he whispered, considering her words. "The Army, having to take care of Morgan and my nieces, and my failed marriage…"

Celeste's heart stopped and dropped into her stomach as her eyes bulged out. "What?" Of course, he had been married— he was a catch. Cate was right. It was silly of her to think he would have held out; she had been declared dead. They had both moved on from that night. First, Morgan with her fiancé and her children, now Mason. The world kept moving for them, and she had stood still.

Her parents voice rang in her head. Voices she hadn't heard in eight years;

You're a failure. You'll never amount to anything.

Mason went back to drying the dishes and continued like he was having a conversation about the weather. "I'm officially divorced as of the beginning of summer. Maybe it's fate or something. I get divorced, and right after, I find you."

Maybe it was fate, or maybe God finally answered her prayers. She opened her mouth to say something, but the words turned into a screech. Her left wrist burned hotter than ever, worse than anything she had ever experienced. The pain seeped into her bloodstream; she was being burned alive from the inside. She shifted the faucet to cold and stretched out her left arm, letting the cold water rain down on it, but the icy water was futile as her arm burned even hotter. Tears pricked her eyes. Cutting it off would be the only way to stop the pain.

"Alice?" Mason asked beside her. His eyes were wild with worry. "What's wrong?"

She shook her head. The pain was so unbearable, the only sounds she could make were sobs. An eternity passed before the hot pain ebbed. Just as quickly as the fire ignited under her skin, it extinguished. Her knees gave out and she dropped to the floor with her arm pulled tightly into her chest. Sobs escaped her lips.

Mason stared down at her, unsure of what to do. "What just happened?" he asked once her sobs quieted enough that words could be heard.

"Mason, I think you need to go. It's better that way," she panted, the pain starting to subside.

"I told you; I'm not going anywhere."

She didn't speak again until she stopped gasping for air and the tears dried. She held out her left arm to inspect it. Her skin was not red like she had expected, just tan from a summer at the beach. Her night sky tattoo looked perfect and untouched. "Under this tattoo is another tattoo. It's the mark of people who belong to Lucian. It burns me when I get too close to someone. It's a reminder that I belong to him and only him."

Mason's eyes darkened with anger. Not at her, he was angry with the Devil. "We'll go to a church and see if we can get holy water. Isn't God's grace supposed to save everything?"

"I can't be saved, Mason. God turned his back on me that night. I never tried holy water, but what's the point? I already sinned against God. So, even if we break this promise to the Devil, my soul is already fucked. God's not going to want me."

He would never want a heathen like you.

Mason set down the towel and held out a hand for her. She placed her hand into his cool one and got off the ground. He led her to the living room and took a seat on the couch. He pulled her into his lap, wrapping his arms around her tightly. For the first time in years, she felt safe in the arms of a man. She had nothing to worry about with him.

"Don't say that. I'm sure He adores you. You were the most religious person I knew, aside from your parents."

"And Vicky."

"Vicky was an atheist. She hated God," Mason told her. That was news to her. Vicky apparently made a good show about being pious. Their parents used to rub it in Celeste's face, time and time again.

Vicky acted like she believed in God. Their parents acted like they were in a loving marriage and loved their daughters. And she acted like she hadn't been waiting for the sweet embrace of death and now, she was still acting. Maybe Mason was right, maybe she was pretending to be someone she wasn't.

"Come home with me," he muttered softly, his lips brushing against her temple.

Celeste jumped out of his arms like they just gave her an electric shock. She *was* home. The beach was her home. "Are you insane? After everything I told you! I can't go back to Elizabethtown."

"We live in Philadelphia now. I haven't lived in E-Town in years. You should come visit at least. You need to see Morgan again. You need to meet AJ and Breanna and Derrick. After that, we'll try the churches there see what they can do to help break the deal. We'll go to the fucking Vatican if we have to. But first, Morgan deserves to see you. You owe her that much."

She needed to see Morgan, too, even if it was only to say goodbye. It would give her the closure she desperately sought.

Celeste rubbed her face in frustration. He was either not understanding her or choosing to ignore her. "Mason, I can't just pack up my life here and go with you. I have a job here, bills, and a dog," she argued. Mason gave her a look of determination. It was a face she knew well; Morgan had the same look. He was going to get her to Philly or die trying.

"You work in a tourist town and live at the beach. You're living like you're on vacation. This is not the life Alice planned out," Mason retorted.

Celeste glared at him. "Alice's parents had a life planned out for her. Alice would have been a family doctor and been set up with and forced to marry some other doctor. Alice didn't have a say in what she did. Celeste does!"

"Was this your plan? Tell me, when you made that deal, was this the life you imagined?" Mason bit back.

"Of course not. I told you I was extremely upset when I made that deal. I didn't even know I made the deal until the day after. Until then, I wanted to go to college and become an astronomer. That's all I ever wanted."

"And how did that go?" His eyebrow arched as he threw the invisible knife at her. She knew she'd failed at life again and did not need the reminder. "You picked up and left once. You can do it again."

Celeste's eyes rolled into the back of her head as she let out a groan of frustration. "Have you not been listening to me? This is my home. *This* is who I am! I'm more myself now than I ever was before. You didn't have a problem with who I was at the concert and most certainly not when you fucked me in the kitchen!" Celeste pointed to the island they had eaten breakfast on earlier.

Mason's eyes followed her hand. A muscle in his jaw ticked. "I like the new you, I do, but I also remember who you used to be. It's like night and day. And if what your saying is true about the Devil, he could have possessed you to change, to be someone you're not. Life was really bad for Morgan in the months and years after the fire. If anything, come back for her."

Guilt tugged at her heart. She didn't have to know how bad it was for Morgan because it was worse for her. The only reason she didn't take her own life right after Lucian left was because she didn't want to see him again so soon. She was content with her life here. She had a job she enjoyed. She had friends. She liked where she lived. Philadelphia also had a lot of light pollution. She'd have to travel who knows how far to be able to stargaze. "I have nothing in Philly."

Mason's eyes softened, almost hurt. "Your family is in Philly." He spoke the words she'd been longing to hear for years. It was kryptonite to her heart. She sighed, giving in. A visit was temporary. The restaurant would be slowing down in a couple of months, and she could use a week away.

"Fine," she agreed with a sigh.

"Fine," she agreed with a sigh.

CHAPTER 19

Lucian let out a low whistle as he walked around the shiny black Ferrari in the run-down parking garage in some city he didn't care to note. There were no dents or scratches he could see. It was the newest model, which was fortunate as he already had a plethora of older models stashed away in various locations around the world for he or his friends to use.

Humans were so predictable. Almost every soul he'd taken in exchange for power or money always made the same purchases. Fancy sports car here, penthouse there, nothing they could take with them to Hell. Well, they did take their high-end technology jobs with them. Technology fascinated Lucian. Rightfully so, he had been a child before the creation of the written word. Each time something new came out, the newly minted Demons who had sold their soul to become the biggest inventor of that new technology were then ordered to bring that technology to Elysian.

Footsteps charged down the parking garage. "Hey! Get away from my car!" A man's voice shouted at the Devil. Lucian looked over the car's glossy roof. The man came screeching to a halt. His eyes widened in fear as he recognized Lucian.

An evil grin spread across the Devil's face. "It *was* yours. It's a nice car too. Pity you'll never see it again." He strode to the back of the car. "All you Humans are so ridiculously materialistic. You all are so quick to trade your life for material things," Lucian commented as he strolled towards his newest demon, a CEO of some corporation he didn't care to know. He stuffed his hands casually in his pockets; looking ever the disinterested villain. The middle-aged man dropped to his knees begging. Mother, he was so tired of the begging. Lucian stood just before the man. "And what was it that you gave up? Hmm, oh yes, 'my mediocre life with that broad of a housewife.'" Lucian used the man's words against him. Lucian never forgets those who mistreat the ones they are supposed to care for. "How is she doing, by the way?" He already knew the answer. She was fine. After the man struck his bargain, Lucian looked into the man's past and made sure his wife and child would be financially okay. The last he heard; the son had gotten into college on a track scholarship.

"You have no right to bring her into this," the man argued. The L tattoo on the man's skin turned bright red. The man groaned in agony. His other hand splayed over it to rub it, attempting to cool the stinging pain.

Lucian smirked devilishly and looked down at the man, then pressed his foot into the man's chest, sending the man flat onto his back. The crack of his head onto the oil-stained concrete echoed through the mostly empty level. "Oh, I have every right. Unlike you, I have a conscience and morals. I was an Angel once, remember? That *mediocre* wife and child of yours would have ended up on the streets had I not given them the means to support themselves because her good-for-nothing husband and father of her child was tired of his wife holding him back from his career and was tired of supporting his child. And unlike you, they will live a much longer, happier, and more fulfilling life."

Red fire erupted from the tattoo, burning up his arm and towards his heart. The man screamed bloody murder, but it was no use. Lucian lifted his foot off the man's chest and pointed at the ground. Blue sparks came out of his fingertips and encased them into a circle, swallowing them whole. The red fire from the man's wrist spread down his arm and across his body, burning him alive.

Lucian looked at his new, extremely expensive watch, one he took from another soul a few months back. He'd be back in time for a night on the Block, a section of road that was filled with various strip clubs and nightclubs, with Thayne and Don.

The blue hellfire dissipated, giving way to the dimly lit stone hallway. Other newly minted demons stood pressed tightly into the person in front of them, waiting to enter Hell and Elysian for an eternity of servitude. Red fire receded back into the man's tattoo leaving a pale, translucent soul with eyes now black as midnight. Lucian grabbed the keys to the Ferrari from the ground and pocketed them. Anything else of importance he would get after the Demons stripped him.

"Welcome to Hell. Hope it was worth it." Lucian spun the keys around on his finger as he sauntered off into the dark stone castle.

This medievalesque castle, jokingly referred to by Angels and Fallen Angels, as Hell's Welcome Center, was where souls, both evil Humans and the Supernatural, came upon death. It was also where his throne room resided for when the Angels, most notably, his twin brother, Micah, decided to schlep down to annoy him.

Lucian walked up to the roof of the castle. The roof was the gateway to Elysian. The two floors immediately below the roof were dedicated to the supernatural and the start of their afterlife. His back muscles shifted as he hurried over to the edge of the launching pad, letting his wings unfurl. He hated hiding his wings. Every time he tucked them in and pulled them out again it was as painful as when an arm or a leg falls asleep. He beat his wings several times to wake up the muscles and shot into the air.

The kiss of the wind on his face was euphoric. Being in the sky was his favorite place to be. Flying allowed him to feel free and unbound by the world. Thirty thousand feet in the air also gave him some perspective. Seeing how small the world looked made even his biggest problems seem manageable.

He touched down on the roof of his office building. The seven-story building was in the heart of Elysian and housed the main offices for leaders of each of the five sections of Elysian and their seconds, with a main conference floor that was only used in extreme emergencies. He hopped down the flight of steps from the roof to his office, whistling a tune, ready to finish the paperwork on his newest demon. As he entered his office, his whistling came to an abrupt stop. The Queen of the

Witches sat in the chair in front of his desk and the Angel of Hell leaned against the floor-to-ceiling window that overlooked Elysian. Both of their faces were tight-lipped and grim.

"What's wrong?" he asked worriedly as he shut the door to the office. It had been years since she last came to visit him. He knew she'd entered Elysian from time to time throughout the last eight years, but only to visit her mother and daughter. The hair on his neck began to stand up as a cold chill swept over him. Worry sunk into the pit of his stomach. "Is Celeste okay?"

"She's fine," Cate said glumly. Lucian sighed in relief. Celeste was fine and there was no need to come to her aid and freak her out. He looked between Don and Cate, both looking like they couldn't stand to breathe the same air as the other. For Hades' sake, he was not in the mood to play couples counselor. Soul recovery exhausted him mentally. All he wanted to was finish the paperwork, get drunk with his best friend, and maybe find a pretty Fallen Angel to share her bed with tonight.

Lucian plopped down in his desk chair with a thud. "At this point, you two—"

"It's about Celeste," Cate interrupted him.

A cold chill settled over his bones, freezing him in place. His hands braced the desk to keep him from running out of the office to the Human. "You just said she was fine. What is going on? Is she cutting? Did she attempt to kill herself?" His mind raced with any and every possible scenario.

The Witch shook her head. "She's fine. She reconnected with her childhood crush, which was all fine and dandy, except we met him the other day..." She trailed off.

Lucian exhaled and muttered a curse under his breath. His hands scrubbed his face. Celeste was allowed to do whatever she wanted in her new life. He promised her that. He has her soul for that. "Are you fucking kidding me, Cate? You are over three hundred years old. Just talk to her. No need to bring me into this."

"She had a crush on him for years. She is so excited to see him again, but I think he's dangerous."

Mother help him. "Okay, I'll bite." Lucian sighed, sinking back into his chair. He ran a hand through his black waves. "Why do you think he's dangerous?"

"For starters, Chip kept growling at him. And he doesn't growl at people. Remi and company aside."

Lucian rolled his eyes. "He's a *dog*. He barked at me when that night and almost blew my cover. Hades, my dog growls when she sees a fucking squirrel in the backyard! That doesn't prove this man is dangerous."

Cate huffed through her nose and turned to Don, silently pleading for him to back her up. Don's black eyes glanced at the woman and then at Lucian. "His aura is pitch black, like looking into an abyss. I have never seen an aura around a Human this dark before."

The Devil's ears perked up a little. He and Don dealt with the darkest of humanity on a daily basis. Handling dark auras came with the territory. If Don was startled, then maybe this human *was* worth looking into. For Celeste's safety, of course.

"No wonder you got along with him," Cate quipped, turning her body to face him. Her eyes narrowed at him.

The Angel of Hell rolled eyes and snapped, "It is called being civil. You and your mother should try it one day."

"Don," The Devil warned as he pinched the bridge of his nose. "What do you want me to do about it? Do you have concrete evidence that her life is in danger? I promised her a full life, and it's only been eight years."

"For the last eight years, she has been so afraid of you. She won't move on. She won't go get the degree she wants; she won't get a decent job. She won't even let herself fall in love because she thinks you're lurking around every damn corner. The one time she decides to say 'fuck you' to you, she decides to see a man who I think will kill her one day. I can't do anything about it without showing my cards," Cate admitted.

Lucian flung his hands out exasperatedly. As if he didn't almost have a Witch uprising when he killed Celeste's family when the deal she made was only to get away from them. "That's not concrete evidence, Cate. And you know that. I can't just kill a man for no reason. Not only will your Witches be on my ass about it, but Micah would also stick his big ass head into it. I haven't seen Micah in over a hundred years. I prefer another millennium before seeing him again." The two went quiet, knowing the exact reason for the last Micah sighting. They were constantly avoiding the elephant in the room. Dancing around it like it was a game and it drove Lucian to drink.

Don spoke up first. "Bargain or no Bargain, *I* believe the girl's life is in danger."

Lucian's eyebrow arched as he studied the Angel. Just like him, Don never cared about Humans. The only difference between them was that Lucian felt for the humans who had been mistreated and Don saw all Humans as torture objects. "Why do you care?"

"Not only did we kill three of our kind for her, she's important to Cate, and for some Angel-forsaken reason, you," Don said.

"There are other people who are important to me and should be important to you; More important than *anything*," Cate bit. Lucian sighed deeply. He opened his mouth to cut off the conversation but Don talked over him.

"Don't bring her into this," Don argued, his nostrils flaring. "We were doing so good…"

"Yeah, because I was horny," Cate turned to face him.

"Mother, have mercy!" Lucian interjected and exhaled loudly through his nose. Mother save him, for a couple who hated being together, they can't keep away from each other. "Can we focus, please? Just because you don't trust him doesn't mean I can intervene. Unless she is in immediate danger, I can't do jack shit. Even then, I shouldn't intervene. I'm the king of the dead, not the king of the living. That's my father's job." He pinched the bridge of his nose, "What is his name?"

Cate huffed and crossed her arms. "Mason Ward."

It took him a few minutes to place the name. "As her house was burning, she wanted to tell the Wards she was alive and I told her no. It broke her heart." He sighed deeply and scrubbed his face, "Let her work through her shit, and maybe she can finally do something with her second life instead of working at that damn restaurant." Celeste had the talent, ability, and resources to become an astronomer or astrophysicist, whatever the hell it was she wanted to do. He knew Celeste's dreams and fears like he knew his own. She was made for much more than waiting tables at the beach for sixty more years. He had offered her the world on a string, and she cut the string out of spite.

165

CHAPTER 20

Finding coverage for her shifts was much easier than Celeste had anticipated. The college kids here for the summer constantly jumped on the chance to take as many shifts as possible to have extra money to take back to campus. Their eagerness allowed her to take a long weekend off to visit the Wards in Philly. Nerves rattled her bones the closer she got to her estimated arrival time. This weekend would be her first time back to Pennsylvania in eight years. Celeste didn't remember half of the drive to Mason's place as her mind ran through fake scenarios about how the conversation with Morgan would go down. Dread filled her stomach where excitement should be.

The GPS led her to a dark red brick townhouse with white steps and a black metal railing. She pulled behind Mason's silver car and cut the engine, taking a deep breath.

Mason appeared behind the glass storm door. He saw her, it was too late to leave now. *This is what you wanted,* she reminded herself.

She grabbed her duffel bag from her back seat. Celeste got out of her car and inhaled deeply. *There's no going back now;* she reminded herself. Her feet dragged with every step towards him. A whole new life was waiting for her on the other side of his front door if she chose Mason over the fear of the Devil.

Mason's smile reached his ears as he opened the door for her. "You made it!" He extended his hand out for her duffle bag. She handed it to him and walked inside.

The living room was sparse, with beige walls and limited décor. An old faded couch faced the television, and a gaming system rested against the wall underneath. As teenagers, she and Morgan would sneak into his bedroom in the early years of his deployment to play the violent action games on his gaming system that her parents had forbidden her from playing.

Against the back wall under a window were a small loveseat, a coffee table and a small bookcase with children's books. She looked to her right where three trunks lined the walls. Two of the three trunks were so stuffed with toys that they did not shut all the way. She heard music playing faintly from a speaker, but she couldn't make out where it was coming from. Despite the soft music and the trunks of children's toys, the house felt cold and devoid of life. Already she missed Chip and his loud barks filling the walls of her home. "Where is Morgan?"

"I made her go on a fool's errand," he said as the corner of his mouth pulled upward on one side. Mason had sent the two girls on many wild goose chases, especially when he was forced to take them to the mall on his leave from the Army.

"Remember when you made Morgan and me run all over the mall because you said our favorite celebrity was there filming a movie, and if we were there, we could be extras? We looked all over the mall for him. Meanwhile, you were at a movie with a date." Celeste laughed at the memory, although unbeknownst to both Mason and Morgan, she had been *insanely* jealous of his date.

Mason laughed at his own memory of those days as he led her upstairs to his bedroom. "I needed you two out of my hair. I was not about to have my kid sister and her equally annoying friend crash my dates."

Celeste slapped his arm playfully. "We were not annoying!"

He gave her a boyish grin, "Probably not anymore."

"Obviously. We all grew up." She murmured as she walked into his bedroom.

Mason leaned against the door frame and stuffed his hands into the pockets of his jeans. He paused and looked her up and down. "Yeah, we did."

The bedroom was just as plain as the living room. Beige walls and dark hardwood floors, a couple of scattered rugs were placed haphazardly on the floor. There was nothing on the walls except for a Philadelphia football flag. The dark blue bedding looked soft. He set her duffel by the bed. "It's very boring in here," Celeste blurted out. She and Cate had gone overboard decorating the beach house, but it was fun to be able to make it their own, something Lucian never touched.

"My ex-wife took almost everything in the divorce. I haven't had the time to make it a bachelor pad." Mason shrugged.

Celeste slowly walked over to the bed and sat down, sinking into the softness. "What's the story?"

He walked in and set her bag on the floor by his dresser. "We met in the army, not long after Vicky and you…er, when Vicky died and got married soon after that."

"Why did you get divorced?" Her eyes darted around the room, anything to attempt to hide her jealousy.

Mason shrugged again; he didn't seem torn up about it. "We wanted different things out of life that weren't evident when we got married."

She scanned the empty room, void of all his old personality from when she knew him. Then again, her current self was new to Mason too. "God, I still can't believe you were married."

He wandered over to her and cupped her cheek. His thumb grazed the side of her face. Her head leaned into his hand. "Time doesn't stop for anyone."

Celeste clamped down on her lip. Time did stop. Yes, she let herself do what made her happy, but she was always *stuck*. Always thinking Lucian was lurking around every corner. Always keeping everyone at arm's length. Only Cate was stubborn enough to be let in. Celeste was always stuck wishing to see Mason and Morgan again, waiting for that closure. The closure that was now in front of her.

"What about you?" he asked, stroking her cheek gently.

"No point in dating anyone long term. I could not, in good conscience, let someone love me and then hurt them because Lucian could come for me at any time. It's been all one-night stands or casual summer flings. Besides, I don't deserve that kind of love."

Mason bit the inside of his cheek. "You deserve love and happiness. We'll save your soul. I promise."

Celeste smiled weakly. She loved her friends, and they loved her back, but she did not deserve romantic love. Hell, her parents had told her multiple times she wasn't worth their love or even God's love, for that matter.

Mason's thumb ran across her bottom lip. "Talk to me, Alice."

Celeste pulled away from him upon hearing her old name. Hearing herself be addressed as Alice was foreign to her now. Alice was a stage name, a persona she had to live with to survive. "Alice Delco died in that fire."

"Alice Delco is who you are. You don't need to pretend you are someone else anymore. You don't need to hide who you are." Mason's fingers lightly brushed over the metal bar in her eyebrow as he tucked a strand of hair behind her ear, his fingers caught on the green metal bar in her cartilage. "I like you for who you are." He leaned down, placing feather-soft kisses down her forehead, nose, cheek, jaw, and lips.

Everything she had wished for since that night was within reach. A small moan escaped her lips after he bit down on her bottom lip and tugged. A coil in her lower abdomen began to tighten. Her hands quickly found purchase in his hair, giving it a gentle pull. A low growl reverberated in Mason's throat. She laid back down on the bed, pulling Mason down with her. His hands pressed against the bed on either side of her as he leaned into the crook of her neck, teeth lightly dragging on her skin. The quick pain of the love bites he gave her paled in comparison to the sudden blinding, white-hot pain under her wrist tattoo.

"Fuck!" she yelped as she shoved him off. Mason quickly got off her like she had electrocuted him. The pain was excruciating and all she could do was cradle her arm into her chest and curl up into a ball. Death would be a better alternative than this. Tears welled in her eyes as she fiercely rubbed her tattooed arm. "Damn you, Mother F—"

This was a mistake. She let Mason in and had planned on letting Morgan in, but for what? A couple of good years? It was only a matter of time before Lucian stole her away from them.

After what felt like an eternity, the pain ebbed slowly, leaving her panting, and crying. "I can't do this," she told him, sitting up.

"Can't do what? Are you okay?" Mason asked her, placing her a hand on her shoulder. His hazel eyes were filled with concern.

Celeste smacked his hand away and flung herself off the bed. She needed to get out. *Now*. "I made a mistake." She admitted, grabbing her duffel bag. Like a bat out of Hell, she dashed down the hall leaving Mason behind, confused.

"Alice!" Mason called after her, his footsteps loud and quick. "Alice. Stop."

"I can't do this, Mason. I can't hurt you and Morgan again," she said, not bothering to look back. She bounded down the stairs two steps at a time and jumped over the last steps.

"Alice. Stop," he repeated in a voice so demanding it did not even sound like him. It was loud, stern, and rough; like her father after she talked back to him. Celeste skidded to a stop, her hand on the doorknob.

A moment later she felt Mason's chest against her back. One arm wrapped around her middle. His other hand covered her fist, forcing it open. The duffle bag dropped with a heavy thump. Slowly, he guided her away from the door and closer to the sofa. "It will be okay. Everything will be okay. I promise you; we will save you. But *please*, do not walk out that door. Please do *not* walk out on our lives again," He pleaded into her hair. His baritone voice was soft and genuine. Butterflies began to flutter low into her stomach. He *wanted* her around.

This was a mistake. He had told her that once before too.

"You walked out on me once," Celeste muttered, wiping a runaway tear from her eyes.

"And I wish I could take it back, but I can't. I don't regret that night. I only regret how it ended," Mason whispered softly. The hand still on her waist gave her a light squeeze. He meant every word he said. It was the first time someone apologized for calling her a mistake. Her heart fluttered and tugged at the strings. "Our crossing paths again was not a mistake. We were meant to find each other again, but you need to let me in."

Celeste inhaled deeply and exhaled slowly. "What if we don't figure it out in time? What if everything we do ends up a waste of time and I'm still sent to Hell?"

Mason kissed her ear gently. "Then I'll go to Heaven and Hell to save you. I couldn't save you from the fire, but I will this time. I promise."

She turned in his arms to face him. His hazel eyes bore so much guilt and remorse. For eight years, he blamed himself for not getting her out. A burden he never was supposed to carry. Celeste cupped his face in her hands and pressed her lips to his. He kissed her with a passion and longing that had her heart melting and her body growing warmer. She tasted the bergamot scent on his breath that was beginning to feel like home.

His front door swung open with force. "Mason Alexander Ward! I'm going to kill you! I've been trying to call you, and you didn't—" a shrill female voice paused. "Oh. I didn't know you had company. Why the hell would you invite me over if you have company?" The voice lowered in shock and embarrassment. The couple jumped away from each other with a gasp. Celeste spun around and came face to face with her old best friend.

Morgan's long wavy light brown hair was pulled back in a half up-half down hairdo. She was a little taller than Celeste remembered, but time aged her well. She still looked like her best friend from the days of yore. Morgan studied her intensely as if trying to figure out who she was. There was no light of recognition in her eyes. "Who are you?"

Celeste opened her mouth to speak, but Mason answered for her. "It's Alice, Morg." His voice soft.

Morgan's hazel eyes, almost identical to her brothers, studied her again in disbelief. Various emotions flashed on her face—pain, anger, and grief—as she shook her head fervently. "That's not funny, Mason. Alice is dead." Morgan's face twisted in anger as she snarled, "How *dare* you say that to me." Morgan shot Celeste a dirty look. If looks could kill, Lucian would have appeared to drag her to Hell now. "And how dare *you* come in here pretending to be a dead girl! Do you have no self-respect?" Morgan yelled, arms crossing over her chest.

Celeste rolled back her shoulders. She wasn't surprised by the outburst; she hadn't been expecting happiness and excitement. "Morgan, I know what you're thinking, but it's really me. I'm Alice. I swear to you. I did not die in that fire."

"No." Morgan shook her head again in disbelief and took a step back towards the door. Her eyes welled with tears. "No. W-we watched the house go down in flames." Morgan pointed at Mason accusingly. "You went in there with Dad and didn't come back with her!"

"I know. But it's her." Mason reiterated.

"Dead people don't come back!"

"I know but let her prove it to you," Mason pleaded with his sister.

Morgan eyes narrowed at Celeste. She felt small and getting smaller with every second of the glare. It was like she was a specimen on the stage of a microscope. "I don't need to hear it, and I don't want to hear it. Alice would have sent something. She knew our address; she could have at least mailed something to us!" Morgan was screaming now, acting like Celeste wasn't in the room with her.

"Morgan, I'm right here!" Celeste shrieked. Morgan wiped her eyes and looked away, disgusted with Celeste. It was obvious that this was not going well, not that she expected anything less. She had been right all along and should not have come. Seeing Morgan only made things worse. Her eyes traveled to the duffle bag beside the door. She could tell Morgan everything she wanted to hear, leave, and never come back. She'd let Mason go once and for all. Mason nudged her and the two exchanged a glance. His head tilted towards Morgan, urging her to continue. In a low voice she continued, "I wanted to tell you I was alive, but I couldn't. *Please*, just let me explain."

Morgan wiped her eyes and then looked at her brother. He gave her a nod of agreement, nudging her to listen. "Fine," she muttered, moving towards the worn loveseat by the window.

Mason and Celeste took the couch. He placed a comforting hand on Celeste's knee and gave it a reassuring squeezed. Celeste gave him a quick look, took a deep breath, and told her story. Morgan listened intently, hanging on to every word her friend had to say. At the end of the story, Morgan was silent, but her red face was loud with emotions, ranging from grief to disbelief.

"My God," Morgan whispered as she leaned back into the loveseat, her elbow propped on the arm as her fingers massaged her temple. Celeste couldn't get a read on if Morgan believed her or not. "This is outrageous. Mase, please tell me you aren't stupid enough to believe this?"

Celeste flinched. It was the answer she'd expected, yet deep down, there was a kernel of hope that Morgan would believe the wild story. Hell, Celeste probably wouldn't have believed it if she'd been in Morgan's shoes.

Mason's eyes shifted from his sister to Celeste, unsure if he should say something or not. Eventually, he spoke. "She had a picture of the two of you in her house. It freaked me out as well, but there was no other reason for her to have that picture if she wasn't Alice."

"Then she's a stalker," Morgan snapped as she narrowed her eyes.

"For God's sake, Morgan, *look* at me. I still look similar to how I did when we were eighteen!" Morgan shook her head and crossed her arms across her chest. In a last-ditch effort, Celeste walked over to Morgan and shoved her right wrist in her friend's face. Morgan stared at the multitude of faded white lines. She knew what they meant. Alice had been very open with her about her struggles with self-harm. Before and during Lucian, Celeste would sneak over to Morgan's house and spend the night to keep herself from swallowing pills. When she couldn't sneak over to Morgan's, Morgan snuck over and stayed up with Celeste to keep her from making a suicide attempt and kept sharp objects away. Morgan's eyes snapped between Celeste's cut-up wrist and her face.

Fresh tears soon welled up in Morgan's eyes. "Ali." Morgan whispered, stunned. Within moments, she shot out of her seat and enveloped Celeste into a tight hug, almost knocking them to the floor.

Relief washed over her and dragged the heavy weight off her shoulders into the ocean. Eight years without her best friend was too damn long.

CHAPTER 21

The girl's friendship picked up right where it had left off.

After the dinner Mason prepared for them, the girls curled up next to one another on the couch, drinking straight from the same bottle of Moscato as they'd done as teenagers. Only this time, it lacked the adrenaline rush of Morgan's parents walking into Morgan's room and catching them.

"These are my girls." Morgan flipped through her phone's camera roll to a picture of her daughters. "This is AJ. I named her after you, Alice Jane. She's seven and the light of my life." AJ grinned back at them with a toothless smile that stretched from ear to ear posing with her sister and a boardwalk costume character performer. The toddler resembled the dark-skinned man she saw at the restaurant. AJ's smile and complexion resembled Morgan but that is where the similarities ended.

"She's beautiful, and looks just like you!" Celeste gushed to her friend, not wanting to bring up the elephant that had entered the room.

Morgan detected the lie immediately. Her smile fell sharply and her bottom lip curled inwards. Her body shifted uncomfortably. Morgan had always been easy to read, and Celeste could see through any mask her best friend tried to put on. Celeste handed Morgan the bottle but she lightly pushed it away. "No, she doesn't." Morgan took a deep breath, her tone shifting from their previously jovial tones to extreme seriousness. "She looks like the man that raped me."

Celeste froze, her lips pursed around the opening of the bottle. A heavy weight settled into her stomach as she placed the bottle on the faded coffee table. "What? Oh my God. When?"

Morgan set her phone face down on the arm of the couch. "I snuck into a bar with my fake ID freshman year of college. I was three sheets to the wind, and the next thing I remember was waking up on some frat's couch. I was told that a girl, Dani, and her boyfriend found me drunkenly walking around looking like a mess. They took me to the boyfriend's frat house where he lived and laid me on the couch, and she stayed with me all night. A month later, I was pregnant."

"Jesus, Morg. That's awful, I'm so sorry. I'm sorry I wasn't there."

Morgan sniffled and shrugged, "I made the decision to get raging drunk."

"Because you were grieving, and you hadn't made any friends yet," Mason cut in venomously from his seat by the bookshelf and window. Celeste whipped her head towards him, the angry look on his face added more fire to the guilt that had started to seep into her bones and settle in her stomach. If she hadn't met Lucian, hadn't listened to him and walked across the street that night, then maybe Morgan wouldn't have gone to that bar.

You're a terrible friend. Her thoughts told her. *You don't deserve them and certainly don't deserve to come back to their life.*

"Even if Ali never disappeared, we wouldn't have even been at the same school. I went to school in Maryland; she was supposed to go to a state school." Morgan shot at her brother. At the time of the infamous fire, Morgan had been weeks away from starting her degree at a teacher's college in Maryland. Alice's father had preferred that she get into an Ivy League like her sister, or even Johns Hopkins University, but settled for a state school after she received rejection after rejection from the Ivy Leagues. Because of that failure, she was expected to graduate at the top of her class and get into med school at Johns Hopkins.

"This is all my fault, I'm so sorry," Celeste whispered, more tears brimmed around her eyes.

Morgan shook her head. "It's not your fault, Alice. It's mine. I should have argued harder with my parents. I told them repeatedly that your parents were abusing you. They didn't believe me! They didn't believe me until after the funeral. It's my fault that you made that deal with the Devil. If I had just done more to make them believe me, you would have never made that deal."

The fucking irony. Each of them blamed themselves for the other's misfortunes. Celeste took her friend's hand and gave it a soft squeeze. "It's not your fault that your parents didn't listen to you. It was never on you."

"Yes, it is! I knew what was going on and I didn't do shit."

"You were a child! You did your best. I've begrudgingly accepted my fate." Her words hung in the air between them like a heavy weight. The silence that laid in its wake was thick and made it hard to breathe.

Morgan sniffled and asked her best friend softly, "Do you regret it?"

She opened her mouth to answer but clamped it shut immediately. Without a doubt she regretted it in the beginning. But as the years went by and her mental health improved, she stopped feeling sorry about that night. She'd do it again if she had the chance. Differently, but she would still find a way to get out of her parent's control. "Certain parts, but no. Do you regret keeping AJ?"

The ghost of a smile danced across Morgan's face at the mention of her daughter's name. "I regret how she came into existence. I hate that she's not Derrick's, Not a day goes by where I don't wish she had Derrick's eyes, nose, or smile. But I don't regret having her. Having AJ led me to find the love of my life, and the chance to have a family with him." The somber look in her eyes immediately lifted at the mention of Derrick. Now she was practically glowing.

"Tell me about Breanna and Derrick." Celeste redirected the subject.

The love that shone in Morgan's eyes made her briefly jealous. A completely foreign look to her. Anytime her mother looked at her, it had been with disdain. "Breanna is two. AJ absolutely adores her and loves being a big sister. Remember that girl and her boyfriend I mentioned? Derrick was a frat brother and roommate of the boyfriend. During the next nine months, we got close.

He adored AJ from the beginning. We moved up here three years ago to be closer to Mason and Tori."

"Tori?" Celeste's head whipped over to Mason. He sat with arms crossed in the seat with a nasty glare in Morgan's direction.

Mason rolled his eyes and murmured, "The ex."

"She was *interesting*," Morgan commented. Mason made a throaty noise, a not-so-obvious hint to change the subject, "Well, she was! I mean you could do better."

"Morgan," Mason said in that demanding voice from earlier—a warning.

Morgan's eyes rolled into the back of her head as she grabbed the bottle of wine from the coffee table. "I'm serious. Alice is a billion times better than Tori." Celeste's face heated and she looked down into her lap, sneaking a glance at her boyfriend. His eyes were focused on a spot on his shorts. He must have sensed their eyes on him because he looked up after a moment and agreed with a smile. "How did you find her?" Morgan asked.

The couple exchanged a glance. She did not want to be the person who told her best friend she slept with her brother. Fortunately, Mason explained everything except the sex and the morning after.

Morgan clapped as her eyes lit up knowingly. "That's why you kept asking her questions at the restaurant! Wait, is that why you weren't at breakfast the following morning?" Morgan's eyes cut right back to Celeste. "Why didn't *you* say something when you were our waitress?" Her voice raised an octave as it had always done when Morgan was angry.

Celeste opened her mouth but Mason answered for her again, "I wanted to make sure she was really Alice. I didn't want to hurt you again if she wasn't. You were suicidal after Alice's death. You still have nightmares about it, according to Derrick."

"I'm not a kid anymore, Mason," she chastised him. "I've been through a lot."

"I know you have." Mason leaned back in his chair and shrugged. "You're still my kid sister. I'm always going to protect you."

"I don't need your protection, except from seeing you two swap spit," Morgan remarked with a fake gag.

"I'm sorry." Celeste felt her face go hot with embarrassment. "Are you mad? You have every right to be mad."

A range of emotions scanned over Morgan's face. She chewed her bottom lip as she searched for the right words. The quiet ate Celeste alive, afraid of what her best friend would say. "I don't know." Morgan's voice wavered. "I want to be. I want to scream at you and be furious because you left. You let us think you were dead. I want to be angry with you for not letting me know you were okay." Celeste nodded her head; she had expected as much. She would have been furious if the roles had been reversed. "Now, I understand why you left. I just need time to get used to you being back."

Celeste nodded slightly. It was probably the best answer she would get from Morgan and that was enough.

How long are you here for?" Morgan continued; eyes wary.

"Just a long weekend-"

Mason cut Celeste off. "Hopefully for a long time. My hope is after this weekend, she'll want to move here permanently. In order for her to come live with me, we need to find a way to save her soul from damnation.

Tomorrow, we have a meeting with a Pastor at the nearby Lutheran Church."

The brand on her wrist started to prickle and itch at the mention of visiting a Church. Her lips flattened into a line. Not once had he mentioned that to her during their nightly phone call in the last few weeks. She wasn't meant to be saved. The plan was to give them the weekend and get the closure she ached for. Then she'd say goodbye and finally close Alice's book.

CHAPTER 22

The enormous oak front doors of Grace Lutheran Church loomed over Celeste like a parent about to scold a misbehaving child. Nerves sent electric shivers through her as she balled up fistfuls of Morgan's pastel pink dress. Because Mason dropped that bomb on her, she had not packed any church-appropriate clothing. Morgan, being the reliable best friend she had always been, dropped off a dress for her this morning. The dress was full of frills and lace; it was exactly the kind of dress her mother would force her to wear.

Mason advised that it might be a good idea to ditch her eyebrow and nose piercing. She initially balked at the idea; the piercings were a security blanket. She'd never had the piercings out for more than a few minutes. Not only did they help her feel more confident, but they also helped her discover who Celeste is and would become. She eventually obliged and took them out, leaving her feeling exposed and vulnerable.

In addition to the lack of piercings, her normally heavy eyeliner and dark lids had been replaced with light brown eyeshadow and a swipe of mascara. Her dark brown hair was neatly brushed and pulled back into a half-up, half-down hairstyle, also courtesy of Morgan.

When she looked in the mirror, the only remnants of Celeste were the tattoos. Alice Delco had risen back to the surface, and with her, the sadness, depression, and self-hatred she had shoved deep into the darkest pits of herself.

"Ready?" Mason asked quietly from beside her. His light blue button-down was tight across his biceps and chest. Her heart skipped a beat at the sight of him. She'd rather just go home and undress him. She placed a hand over his bicep and gave it a light squeeze. Touching him reminded her she was on Earth and not spiraling somewhere else.

No, she was not ready. She hadn't been in a Church since the morning she killed her family. In the early days of her deal, she scoured the Bible. One, for grounding; two, to see if the Bible held any answers on how to break the deal Lucian forced upon her. Time and time again, the Bible failed her. Deep down, she knew God had given up on her a long time ago; she reluctantly gave up on him. Her church became the ocean. There was something spiritual about floating between the waves and letting the current drift her.

Celeste eyed the church doors, then her boyfriend. "I don't know if I can go inside. I might spontaneously combust." Her fingers raised to her lip and she began to pick at the skin.

Mason broke out into a joyful laugh like she made a hilarious joke, but she wasn't joking. "It'll probably be more like an exorcism."

"I told you, I'm not fucking possessed!" Celeste hissed. Mason continued to laugh as he lifted her chin with his hand, her head tilting up. The warmth in his hazel eyes seemed to settle her shaking bones. "Stop being so dramatic. It's just a joke." Mason tried to calm her down with a brief kiss.

"It's not just a joke to me, Mase. This is my life," Celeste mumbled against his lips.

"Everything will work out. Have faith." He took her hand and led her into the church.

Mason breezed through the main doors and dragged her behind him. They stopped just before the sanctuary. She peered over Mason's shoulders and stiffened. The door to the sanctuary had been left open, inviting her in. Maybe it was God, welcoming her back to the church. Mason moved beside her, his hand on the small of her back. "Why don't you go in?"

Celeste shook her head. It had to be a trick. Lucian was fucking with her. One slight nod turned into more and soon she was shaking violently. Her chest tightened. No matter how much air she gulped down, it wasn't enough. "No. No. Mason, I can't." Her feet started to backpedal the way they had entered.

"Alice, you have to do this. Mason turned and followed after her. His long strides had made it easy to get a hold of her arm and stop her in her tracks. "We are going in there; you will talk to the Priest and we will figure out how to get your soul back."

She paused, her breath coming in short pants as if she had been running a marathon. "What if it doesn't work?"

"You're already in a church. I'd say that's half the battle." He reminded her and yanked her back towards the sanctuary. Celeste tried to wrangle herself free of him but his hold on her was tight. He could easily overpower her, and get hurt if she tested his limits too much.

Inside the sanctuary, her hands gripped the back pew tight enough to turn her knuckles white. Mason stood behind her, effectively keeping her from running. Her heart thumped wildly in her chest as she stared at the altar. An icy cold breeze caressed her cheek. Her eyes turned to the linoleum floor, waiting for it to open up and expose the fiery Hell that awaited her. Nudging Mason away, she walked into the aisle of the sanctuary. Squeezing her eyes shut, and exhaling slowly, she took one achingly slow step towards the altar. Her muscles locked up in preparation for the hellfire to engulf her

Nothing.

Another slow step and still nothing happened. A grin spread across her face as relief washed through her. As she took another step, euphoria filled her lungs and bloodstream. A joyous laugh escaped her after the third step. Happy tears welled up in her eyes for the first time in her life. She turned to Mason who was a few paces behind her, a soft loving smile on his face. Celeste took a few more steps and came to a stop beside a pew. She looked ahead towards the altar.

On the altar's ceiling, colorful painted pictures of Jesus and cherubs stared back at her judgingly. Celeste's face fell. She had no right to be in here; deep down, she knew it. This was a place for the holy and she had disobeyed God. She rubbed her arms feverishly, checking for red spots or goosebumps. Her fingertips only found the slight bumps where her white scars lay. She took another deep breath and walked farther into the sanctuary. Her hand lightly dragged along the light-colored wood of the pew.

Growing up, Sunday school and Sunday morning service were the only time her parents left her alone. Sometimes, to avoid punishment she would make sure her parents saw her reading the Bible because they wouldn't hurt her while reading the 'Good Book.' Sunday School had been her favorite. Not only was she away from her overbearing parents, but she got to ask all kinds of questions, no matter how silly, dumb, or 'unchristian' they sounded, and her teachers never went to her parents about what she had asked. They just smiled and either gave her an answer or some semblance of an answer to her more philosophical questions. What those teachers taught differed greatly from her parents' ideas, but Celeste never said a thing. Had her parents known, they would have immediately pulled her out of Sunday school. The thought of being pulled away from her only solace was unfathomable. It was in those classes and in that morning service, she prayed for Jesus or God to take her away from them. Never in a million years would she have anticipated an Angel coming to her aid.

Lucian had been her saving grace until the truth came out. Looking back, she should have known better. He was too good to her to be true. How stupid she felt when she remembered the Devil had once been an Angel. God's favorite, for that matter.

Her eye caught the golden cross behind the altar. Not once in her walk down the aisle did her skin melt off the bone or bubble up. Her eyes lifted back to the painting on the curved ceiling. She breathed out another shaky laugh of relief. The self-imposed excommunication had been for nothing. The church had not abandoned her-God had not abandoned her.

Her triumph did not last long. Guilt and anger overpowered the elation that had just filled her. The anger came so quickly that it shook her to her core. The cold, hard metal of the altar rail bit into the palm of her hands as she braced herself to stay on her own two feet. God, she could have done this earlier had she not been so terrified. So much God damned time wasted. Her knees finally gave out and she sank into the leather-padded step in front of the rail, mumbling a soft, shaky prayer.

As a child, the warmth of a summer sunset would settle deep into her bones whenever she prayed. That warm comfort always caused a few tears to slip down her face.

There was no warmth to stave off the icy cold air of the sanctuary. *You're mine.* Lucian's words echoed in her ear. She belonged to the Devil now. God wouldn't want to save her anyway.

The sanctuary was silent save for her mumbled prayers. She didn't even hear Mason approach until his hands clasped down on her shoulders. A small gasp escaped her lips and her shoulders tensed upwards. "Calm down, it's just me…Are you okay?" He asked, giving her a reassuring squeeze. Her shoulders relaxed as she nodded in response. Her words and heart were stuck in her throat.

Another set of eyes bore holes into her back, and they weren't from the painted Jesus. "You must be Mason Ward," a gentle, older man's voice called out to her boyfriend. The two turned their heads to see an older man dressed in the pastor's uniform of slacks, a black shirt with a white collar, and dress shoes. His graying brown hair, kind face, and nice smile reminded her of her grandfather.

Mason gave the Pastor one of his charming smiles as they shook hands. "Yes. And this is my girlfriend, Alice Delco."

The world and her bones went still. *Absolutely* no one could know who she used to be. The Pastor would assume she was crazy and call the cops. She could already hear the detective's questions about how she survived the fire. They wouldn't believe a word and she'd be thrown into jail immediately.

"Mason!" Celeste hissed as she stood up and marched over to him. There went the rest of her weekend. God, this whole trip had been a bad idea. She'd have to leave Philly *now*. Mason remained silent, lightly knocking into her. The two exchanged a quick glare. A strange darkness flashed in her boyfriend's eyes.

The pastor, unfazed, held out his hand to Celeste. Her left hand extended to shake his. The pastor's warm hands clasped over hers. The brand on her wrist burned hotly while he held it. "It's nice to meet you both. Mason said you got yourself into some trouble." There was no sense of mockery or anger in his voice, just calmness. He motioned for them to take a seat at the first pew. Mason made the short walk over with him. Neither of them realized she had turned into a statue.

It took Mason sidestepping, letting her take a seat first before he realized she hadn't followed them. "Alice," he breathed her name like a sigh. His voice was a million miles away from where she stood mere feet from them.

All words failed her. This was a bad idea; she wouldn't put it past Lucian to know what she was up to and be waiting for her either outside the church's perimeter or at her house. If he was there…

God, Cate. She would be okay. Cate was a Witch and had handled herself quite well against Remi. She could handle Lucian. But Chip…

"I…" she trailed off, her voice hoarse and meek. A sudden wave of nausea sat in her stomach. She needed to get the hell out of there. Her eyes darted around the room and landed on the back of the sanctuary. She willed her feet to run but even they failed her.

Mason walked back over to her, cupping her face in her hands. "Hey, he can't help if you don't tell him what's going on." His voice was low but soft, caressing her nerves.

She shut her eyes tightly and shook her head, "I can't."

"Yes, you can." He encouraged her, "I'll be right here with you. You're not doing this alone. Whatever happens, we'll get through it together." He sealed his promise with a chaste kiss to her forehead, effectively calming her down.

"Together." Celeste breathed, trying to calm the nausea. She opened her eyes to her boyfriend smiling warmly at her.

The promise was reflected in the green flecks of his hazel eyes. "Together."

An icy shiver went down her spine as she joined the pastor in the first pew. Her fingers fidgeted with the pink cotton of her dress. Mason placed a warm hand on her knee, giving it a reassuring squeeze that he was still with her.

"I didn't…I would have never…had I known…" Her stuttering voice barely above a whisper. Thoughts raced around her brain in an attempt to find a decent place to begin her story.

"Start at the beginning," he advised. His kind eyes patiently waiting until she was ready.

With a deep breath, her past came tumbling out, "I come from a very religious family. On the outside, we were the epitome of a good Christian family. Inside, it was hell on earth. My father hit us almost daily in addition to yelling and screaming at us when we didn't do what he wanted us to do. My mother also yelled and screamed at me and my sister. She would guilt me into taking the blame for her mistakes so my father wouldn't lash out at her. My sister also had no problem throwing me under the bus for a rule she broke.

"I was expected to wait on my parents' hand and foot, and I had to do exactly as they said and live how they wanted me to be. Being a teenager, you're supposed to find yourself, and when I started to display my individuality, I was told I was ungrateful. If I had a belief that differed from their own, I was the enemy and a heathen." As she laid out the truth, a tremendous weight lifted off her chest. The rush of telling someone all that she had endured was euphoric.

Mason's fingers brushed against her tear-stained cheek. She didn't dare look at him. Seeing the pain on his face would send her into a tailspin.

When she told Morgan, Morgan looked at her with pity and an uncomfortable silence had settled between them. Morgan begged her to tell Ms. Ward but she couldn't do it. No one would believe her since her family was so popular, rich and loved. She'd be labeled an ungrateful bitch. Silence was safer.

There were no pitying looks from Lucian the day she came clean about why she self-harmed. murderous rage in his icy eyes had been the first time she felt validated, *felt seen*. Finally, someone felt the anger she'd been carrying for years. That had been the catalyst for her love of him. He vowed that she would be safe with him. Never in a million years did she think safe meant being his slave in Hell.

Then she opened up about the self-harm and her suicide attempt. "I regained consciousness at the hospital. They were *pissed* and embarrassed that they had to bring me there. They almost let me die by taking me to a hospital *miles* away from home so word wouldn't reach back. The doctors told my parents to put me in therapy, but they refused. They had to fight to keep me from being admitted into the psych ward.

"Their idea of therapy was to put me into more bible study classes. I had weekly meetings with a pastor friend of my father to do an even deeper study of the Bible. All those meetings were just a way to shame me and tell me how upset God was with me. They faulted me, saying I gave into the Devil and if I just prayed more, all my problems would be solved." She paused, waiting for the pastor to agree with her parents, but he remained quiet.

He's too quiet. He agrees with them. God hates you.

Tears flowed down her face. Her eyes squeezed tight; her mother glared at her with that damned disapproving look of hers. Her father, red-faced and ready to burst into his famous rants.

A soft and slow movement traced over the top of her hand. The harder she focused on the movement the more her family disappeared from view. Once everything went black, she opened her eyes again and saw she was in the sanctuary with Mason beside her.

"Tell me about this deal Mason mentioned." The pastor asked solemnly.

She opened her mouth and then clamped it shut. Lucian was a topic she avoided like the plague. She kept their story so close to her heart that he was almost imaginary.

"He can't hurt you here, Alice." Mason reminded her, nudging her.

Celeste hesitantly glanced at both men before she told them about Lucian and the night everything changed. Goosebumps pebbled on her arms as another icy chill kissed her skin. As she finished the story, the first person she laid eyes on was the pastor. His previously neutral face became contorted. "The Devil can trick people and presents himself as anything or anyone."

"So, you believe me?" she asked breathlessly, relief teetering on the edge.

"I think…" The pastor hesitated. "I think based on your religious upbringing, you wanted to find a way to walk away from God. What better excuse than to bring the Devil into the narrative. Also, I think you have some survivor's guilt from being the only one to walk away from that fire. You needed someone to blame, and that young man was there."

The relief that had started to emerge, fell back into her stomach as a dead weight and rolled into a knot of nausea. He didn't believe her. "You think I made this all up?" her voice rose an octave.

"Everyone reacts differently to trauma, Alice. You had a very traumatic childhood, there's no denying that.

But people lie all the time. Especially one claiming to be the Devil. Evil people like that love to take advantage of vulnerable people. The Devil strives to take people away from God and lead them into a life of sin. You were at the precipice and became an easy target," the pastor explained.

Red-hot anger heated her blood. That heaviness that had been lifted off her shoulders slammed back down with double the weight. He didn't believe her. "No. That's not... I'm very religious," Celeste said defensively.

"The Devil tempted you, and you gave in. Have you been to a church since that night? Jesus can help you, but you need to allow him in."

Her face twisted in anger as she jumped from her seat. "I may have not been physically in a church, but I prayed. I've read the Bible in the years since! I *am* a Lutheran. I love God and Jesus, and I believe!"

A realization slammed into her like a forceful wind. "They abandoned me that night." Her voice soft and breaking, "Why weren't They there to stop him? Where are They?" Her muscles tensed as she stared back at the painted Jesus on the altar. The nausea crawled up her throat, and she took off in the direction of the church hallway and into the bathroom before she could ruin the dress and the floor.

When she emerged from the ladies' room, Mason was leaning against the wall in the narthex. "Better?"

The nausea had faded but, in its place, a numb feeling overtook her. She hadn't felt this numbness in seven years. It was a state she would get into right before she would cut herself. The numbness was her mind's attempt at protecting her from exploding with emotions. "I want to go home," she mumbled weakly.

"Are you sure? You look like you need to talk to him." His eyebrow arched up. Celeste shook her head. This had been a mistake.

CHAPTER 23

Celeste's face planted into a throw pillow on Mason's faded sofa. A few tears slipped from her eyes.

"It's not the end of the world, Ali, " he reminded her as he lifted her legs to sit beside her. A gentle hand ran down the backs of her legs.

She lifted her head and wiped her eyes. "The only constant in my life abandoned me. I believed in God and Jesus and they *left*."

"There's other things to believe in," he mentioned. Her leg lifted to kick him, but he gripped it tightly and forced it back down. My soul was going to be damned to Hell with or without Lucian's intervention." She swung her legs away from him and sat up on the couch.

"He's only one pastor. There are others here in Philly. They might give you a different answer."

She gulped down air in an attempt to calm her nerves. Her fingers found her lips and began picking at the skin. "That pastor didn't seem to believe me. What makes you think other ones will?"

The silence echoed loudly.

"You believe me, right?"

There was more silence before he spoke. "I believe something happened. You and Morgan were attached at the hip. I don't think you would have left her without good reason. But as he said, you had a more troubled life than any of us knew. The fire was ruled an accident, and you were the only survivor. No one would have blamed you for running away," Mason said, his fingers finding a home in her dark brown locks.

Celeste scoffed and crossed her arms. "I was so unhappy with my life that death felt like a better option. They controlled every part of my and Vicky's lives. The only reason Morgan and I became friends was because we lived across the street, and they could keep tabs on me. Luckily, Morgan and I really caught on and became best friends. The only normalcy I got was because of her. I was only allowed to go on vacations with your family because my parents knew yours. I was only allowed in Scouts because Morgan was in it. Your parents raved about it to mine, and my parents vetted the troop. I was so exhausted and tired that if the fire had truly been accidental, I would have just let myself get consumed by it. Dying would have been easier than starting over with absolutely nothing. The only reason I'm not homeless is because of Lucian. He got me everything I needed to get started."

She never told anyone about the afterthought of just letting herself get consumed by the fire. Sometimes, she still entertained the idea. Other days, she looked at her dog, Cate, and the ocean, and she was glad she was still alive.

Mason pulled her into his chest and kissed her temple. "I'm so sorry, Alice. I'm sorry we weren't there for you. But like Morgan said last night, it does sound completely out there."

"I wouldn't lie to you, Mase." Her heart sank into her stomach. No one believed a word she said. She started to wonder if she was making all of it up. But Cate believed her; she had admitted to knowing of Lucian.

"I'm not saying you are. I'm just saying there are holes."

"If there were holes, you shouldn't have introduced me by my old name.

"Your name is Alice. I called you by your name." Mason clipped.

"What if he reports me to the police?"

Mason's eyebrow arched. "Why would he? The fire report said it was a candle. Vicky loved candles."

Fucking Vicky. He's constantly mentioning her sister. Celeste's eyes narrowed on him and she leaned away. "Why do you know so much about my sister?"

Her boyfriend was quick with a response. "We were closer in age. We saw each other at school, ate lunch together, and we were both on the school newspaper together. She took me to her senior prom, remember?"

Vicky's senior prom was a night she could never forget. She was thirteen and had been so jealous that everyone had been treating Vicky like royalty. Meanwhile, she was the ugly stepchild hidden away in her room. Mason was in his second year of the army and the moment he walked through her front door was the moment her world stopped. The teenager she knew had turned into a well-defined man. Mason looked sharp in his tuxedo and light pink bowtie. His wavy hair was slicked down, and his dreamy smile was fully displayed. That night, she dreamt of going to her prom with him, and every day since, her heart fluttered with even the smallest glance in her direction.

"Right," she muttered with a sigh, her back pressing into the couch. "In the future, I would appreciate it if you would stop introducing me as Alice Delco. She's dead. My name is Celeste Ride."

"You're always going to be Alice to me," Mason protested.

"In private." Celeste compromised.

"I have other names for you in private." He smirked.

Her cheeks flushed as she stared at his lips. Leave it to him to make a dirty comment to distract her from her thoughts. His free hand had found its place on her thigh, toying with the fabric of the dress before slipping underneath. A small smile danced at her lips as heat flooded between her legs. She reveled in how good Mason's hands felt on her. With her many flings over the years, their touches had been driven purely by lust. With Mason, desire filled every caress.

Celeste leaned into his body and captured his lips in a passionate kiss. His tongue was eager for admission into her mouth. Her lips parted with a whimpering noise of want. His fingers slid up the inside of her thigh and brushed lightly against her panties. She shivered from the touch, craving more.

In a moment of unfamiliar dominance, she swung her leg around Mason and sat in his lap. Her fingers made deft work of unbuttoning his shirt. She didn't even bother to push the sleeves down his arms, instead, her hands traced over his chiseled abs. Mason's hand wrapped around her bottom and pulled her closer, his hard member lightly brushed against her, sending another wave of heat to her lower abdomen. A shit-eating grin stretched along Mason's face as he pushed the dress upwards, exposing her thin lacy pink underwear.

He kissed and tugged at her lips with a hunger she hadn't seen from him yet. His name fell off her lips in a moan.

"Lay down for me, baby." Mason orders huskily. Immediately and robotically, she slid off him and laid back on the couch. Mason pushed her dress up past her stomach and tugged the pink underwear off and tossed it aside. Her legs automatically opened for him, sending a shock of cold air through her. She needed warmth, she *needed* him. Mason chuckled and inserted a finger into her. "You're already soaked for me. How convenient."

Celeste moaned with pleasure from the curling movement. The addition of another finger sent her back arching off the couch. One hand found snaked through his hair and she tugged his head down towards her center. A low chuckle vibrated from his chest.

"You look delicious," he said, his voice full of lust. His fingers were immediately replaced by his tongue. A moaned expletive escaped her lips.

His tongue darted into her, curling up and hitting her bundle of nerves while his fingers rubbed the sensitive nub right above his mouth.

The coil in her lower abdomen was tightened. "More," she breathed.

Mason removed his tongue, his lips placing light kisses along her inner thigh. A desperate whine fell from her lips "More? Your wish is my command." He excused himself and ran upstairs.

Celeste's mouth dropped open. "Mase?" She sat up and looked towards the stairs. None of the guys she had been with before just *ran away*.

"Sorry. These were upstairs." Mason bounded down the stairs shirtless and shaking a box of condoms. He quickly shed his pants and boxers, his erection popping out.

"You could have said something..." She trailed off. All thoughts evaporated from her brain at the sight of him. Celeste hungrily reached out to him; not wanting to wait another minute. He slid on the condom as quickly as he could. She opened her mouth to urge him back, but the words turned into a moan as he slid himself in her. He rocked them both easily at first to get the rhythm and then worked up to faster movements. Her hips bucked upwards as she gripped the arm of the couch for dear life.

Celeste climaxed first, yelling his name as she came. A few thrusts later, Mason followed moaning her old name. His hands caught himself above her head on the arm of the couch. Their faces were mere inches from each other. Celeste cupped his face in her hands and kissed him sweetly. Slowly, he lowered himself onto her, resting his head on her chest. Celeste ran a hand through his wavy hair. A calming, woodsy scent filled her nose. No matter what, she was not truly alone. Mason was always going to be there.

They laid in silence for a while, enjoying each other's company.

"What time is it?" Mason asked, lifting his head up as he reached for his pants. The sun was still high in the sky, giving them a few more summer hours A soft curse fell from his swollen lips as he slid off of her. He discarded the condom in a nearby trash can and hurried back upstairs. Celeste watched him leave curiously but got up, fixed her dress, and floated to the hall bathroom to clean herself up. Being with him was almost everything she imagined it would be.

"Ali, you ready?" she heard Mason yell from upstairs.

"For what? Round two? Hell yeah, I am," she yelled as she exited the bathroom.

A deep joyful laugh floated from the stairs. "Later, sweetheart. We need to go to dinner. I didn't realize the time. We're gonna be late," he yelled out as he rounded the corner from the stairwell, now dressed in a simple yellow shirt and jeans.

Her head cocked to the side as she looked him over. "We have plans?" they hadn't spoken of doing anything else today. She'd imagined more sex and takeout.

Mason kissed her cheek. "We're getting dinner with Derrick and the girls."

Celeste's jaw hit the floor. She wanted to meet her nieces, and had *dreamt* of it. Meeting her nieces would make it even harder for her to leave for good on Sunday. She crossed her arms across her chest. "When was this decided? And by whom?"

"Earlier today by Morgan and me. You need to meet the rest of your family."

"Where was I?"

"Getting dressed."

"Do the girls even know about me?" Celeste asked.

"Yes, the girls know about you. AJ might be a little confused, but it'll be fine." Mason kissed her cheek again and walked past her, grabbing the keys from the bowl next to the door. He turned to her and flashed that damned beautiful smile. "It's everything you wanted, right?"

Her feet cemented into the hardwood floor. This trip was to get closure, not to open another chapter.

CHAPTER 24

Loud Mariachi music flooded her eardrums as she passed by a table. The aisles were crowded with filled chairs, people walking around and waiters and waitresses trying not to spill the drinks on their trays. It reminded her of summertime at the Marlin and she was thrilled she didn't have to work a dinner rush for once. The patio was teeming with people ready to kick back and enjoy their Saturday night. Celeste gripped Mason's hand as they snaked around the chairs looking for her best friend.

"Mason! Alice!" Morgan shouted to get their attention. She was grinning ear to ear while she waved wildly at them with one hand, holding the toddler in her lap with the other. Derrick sat beside her; eyes glued to his cell phone. The older girl sat at the head of the table, studying the kid's menu. Mason let go of her hand and walked up to the older girl. He ruffled her hair, earning a whine from the child.

"About time! We're starving! I ordered some taquitos and a pitcher of strawberry margaritas. I hope that's okay." Morgan stood up with her daughter and hurried over to Celeste.

"Uh, yeah, sounds great." Celeste embraced her friend and the child.

Morgan bounced the two-year-old on her hip. "This is Breanna." Although Breanna had her mother's hair, she was clearly her father's daughter with matching dark skin and dark eyes. Her brown eyes were large and doe-eyed with long lashes. "Bri, this is your Aunt Alice. Can you say 'Hi, Aunt Ali'?"

"Hi, Aunt Ali." The little girl smiled widely and waved. Immediately, an undying love filled Celeste's heart. She was so consumed by this immediate love for her youngest niece that she did not even bother to correct the name. Celeste smiled brightly as she greeted the baby.

Morgan grabbed Celeste's hand and led her to the end of the table where AJ sat. She let go of Celeste to run a hand through her daughter's coppery curls. "AJ, this is your Aunt Alice. She and Mommy have been best friends since we were younger than you. Can you say hello to Aunt Ali?"

AJ lifted her head and brushed some flyaway strands from her face. The two Alices looked at each other. "My name is Alice! But I like AJ," the younger Alice exclaimed.

"I like that too. It's a beautiful nickname." Celeste smiled as she took the remaining seat between AJ and Mason.

"You are named after her, silly. I've told you that," Morgan reminded her daughter. Mason eagerly snatched Bri from his sister's arms and blew a raspberry on the girl's cheek. Bri shrieked with laughter. Across from Celeste, Derrick kept his attention on his phone. "This is Derrick. My fiancé. Derrick, this is Alice, my best friend growing up. She's basically my sister."

Derrick only bothered to look up when he felt Morgan's hand on his back "The dead one?" Venom spewed from his mouth as his dark eyes skeptically looked Celeste up and down.

"It's complicated," Celeste mumbled as she leaned back in her chair, finding the menu suddenly interesting.

"I'm sure," he bit, annoyed, like her presence was bothering him. She glanced up to see Morgan nudge him and shoot him a *'we talked about this'* look before leaning into his ear, whispering about something.

They talking about you and how you ruined Morgan's life.

God, it was so hot. The warm night air was stagnant. She missed the breezy ocean nights when she and Cate would go out with their friends from work, or regulars who had become friends, on their off nights. Celeste did not waste a single second once the margarita pitcher was brought to the table. Immediately Celeste filled her glass to the brim and took large gulps. She had poured her second glass as soon as the other adults finished pouring their first.

"Thirsty?" Derrick raised a judgmental brow at her.

"Bad day." Mason apologized for her.

"When's the wedding?" Celeste changed the subject; anything to get the attention off of her. She picked up a taquito to give her fingers something to do.

Morgan turned to her fiancé. Her eyes held so much love for him. She could only hope Mason looked at her that way. "Next May. Speaking of, I'm going dress shopping tomorrow with my friend Dani, Derrick's mom, and his sister. You're coming too. I'll pick you up at ten."

Celeste choked on the shredded beef. "Are you sure that's a good idea? I-I mean, it's the first time I've seen you since..." She picked up her margarita and drained the rest of the glass. A small groan escaped her as her brain started to freeze. This trip was slowly turning into a disaster.

"It's like divine intervention or something, Ali. You were—are—my best friend. I still haven't picked a maid of honor yet. Dani was going to be it, but you're back now, and we dreamt of this moment for years. It wouldn't be right if you didn't come to help me pick out my dress. I mean, I was already fretting about how I was going to do this without you," Morgan pleaded with her friend. Celeste smiled weakly. They had spent hours growing up designing their fake weddings with their celebrity crushes. When they were looking for prom dresses, the two spent at least thirty minutes looking at the wedding dresses, pointing out what they would want to wear. They were twelve when they called dibs on being each other's maids of honor.

"But Danielle knows...right? You must have told her about..." Celeste hinted at her 'death'.

Her best friend leaned back into her chair; shoulder hunched defeatedly. "Of course she does. And so does Derrick's family. We'll have to come up with something."

Although conversation flowed easily between Mason, Morgan, and Celeste, it was obvious Derrick was only here because Morgan forced him to be. He was civil but made it clear he didn't like her. Every question from him was an interrogation. She crafted a delicate lie, darting between the truth, and vague answers to purposefully avoid the whole truth. Fortunately for her, Morgan and Mason did not contradict her or call her out on her lies. Her history was for another day after the two warmed up to each other. AJ, however, warmed up to her aunt very quickly.

"What is this?" AJ asked, pointing to her forearm tattoo.

"It's a tattoo of the night sky and a couple of constellations."

"It's real?"

"Yes, it's permanent."

"Do you have others?" AJ asked her, eyes wide with amazement.

"Yeah. I have butterflies. See?" She pointed to her collarbone and shoulder. "And one here." She pointed to her other wrist and her forearm. "This is a key." The vintage style key was a matching tattoo with Cate.

AJ grinned. "That's so cool! I want one!"

"Absolutely not," the other three adults said with complete disdain.

"Tattoos are trashy, and you're not trash," Derrick told the child.

"Like Aunt Alice said, they're permanent. Meaning they will never go away," Mason added.

Celeste flinched and sank into her seat; she'd heard her parents spit the same excuses. AJ huffed and went back to eating her rice mumbling something under her breath about not getting her ears pierced either. Celeste remained quiet and waited with bated breath, thinking they'd get into a conversation about piercings. Her hand brushed across her brow waiting for the feel of the metal, but all she felt was the holes. She had forgotten she had taken them out this morning. As much as she loved her piercings, she sighed with relief for once that she wasn't wearing them.

AJ and Bri had taken off with Derrick as they left the restaurant, leaving Celeste, Mason, and Morgan hanging back.

"I'm so glad you got to meet your nieces," Morgan said as they watched her daughters race with their father to their car.

The corner of Celeste's mouth turned upward. A knot twisted in her stomach. She loved her nieces already and knew she could not be in their lives and then get ripped away. "I am too, but I don't want the girls to get attached. With Lucian and the deal… It's probably best if I stay at arm's length; I'll be the fun aunt who lives at the beach." Although it would have been better if she just remained a story.

Morgan's eyebrows knitted together in confusion. "You guys said you were going to break the deal. How did the meeting go today?"

"Not good." Celeste sighed and scrubbed her face in frustration. "It was awful."

Mason whispered something into Morgan's ear. A quick rundown of what happened earlier.

Morgan gave her friend a sympathetic look, that look of pity she wore so well when Celeste opened up about her struggles and Morgan didn't know how to respond. "He's one pastor. There are other churches." Derrick honked the car horn. They all turned to look at the minivan. "I'll see you tomorrow." Morgan hugged them both, bidding them farewell before running over to her family.

The drive home was silent. Mason placed a comforting hand on her thigh. The kind touch did little to calm her down. She couldn't help but feel that she was digging herself a hole she would be unable to crawl out of later.

CHAPTER 25

Of course, Celeste, Morgan, and her kids were the last to arrive at the small bridal boutique. AJ broke into a run towards the four women standing by a small platform. They all greeted her with a smile and a hug. Morgan greeted them all the same, smiling brightly and oozing the charisma that she had been lucky enough to be born with. Celeste hung back, twirling a strand of hair around her finger, feeling like a fish out of water. She was a long way away from her bubbly persona at the beach-one she had modeled after Morgan.

Morgan had always been the popular one of the two. Her outgoing personality and good soul allowed her to make friends easily. Although more reserved, Celeste had been generally liked by her peers. She was funny, smart, and always willing to help them with homework or classwork. Like Morgan, she'd been invited to parties but hardly went. She purposefully kept everyone at arm's length, mostly due to her parents' erratic nature. But also, because she had an air of uneasiness around people. Her mind taught her that her peers were constantly judging her because of how strict her parents were or were comparing her to Vicky. There was also the continuously running thought that her parents would find out what she was doing behind their backs.

Morgan turned to see Celeste still hovering at the front door and waved her over. "This is my best friend, Alice."

Celeste groaned internally as she trudged towards them. Like brother, like sister she guessed. She'd specifically asked Morgan to use her new name around outside people; fearing old friends from high school would be attending the wedding and would start asking questions.

"My name is Celeste," Celeste whisper-hissed, reminding her friend.

A tall bottle blonde girl Celeste assumed was Dani, eyed her up and down then crossed her arms defensively. "I thought she was dead."

"Yeah, we all thought that. Turns out we were wrong." Morgan jumped to an excuse

"Then where has she been all these years?" An older dark-skinned woman asked. It had to be Derrick's mother.

"Witness protection," Celeste blurted without thinking and chomped down on her lip to suppress the growing smile on her face. Everything she had endured almost felt like witness protection.

Morgan coughed through a laugh. The blonde raised an eyebrow at the two of them, not believing a word out of their mouths.

"Why would an accidental candle fire trigger you to go into the witness protection program?" the younger dark-skinned girl asked; Derrick's sister.

"Her family was killed, and by the grace of God, she escaped the fire. The police took care of her. Can we please move on?" Morgan linked arms with her. Like always, Morgan came to her defense because she couldn't do it herself. The grace of God; what a joke. More like the grace of the Devil. Morgan huffed and began to introduce everyone to her and set them off with their instructions.

Celeste wandered down every aisle, slowly and intently looking over each dress. The pads of her fingertips grazed over lace and embroidery. She tried to picture Morgan in each dress, but all she saw was herself. Her in the dress at the end of the aisle with Mason in a tux smiling broadly at her.

As a kid, she dreamt about her wedding more than most as she thought it was the only way she was going to be free from her family. Now, it was just one of the many dreams she was forced to let go of. There was no point in spending hundreds and thousands of dollars on a wedding to not be able to live a full life with her future husband.

Her hands glided across silky fabric, giving her pause to study the dress. A slow, wide, smile stretched over her face as she looked it over and took it off the rack. The dress was exactly the type young Morgan had dreamt about. Celeste hurried over to the group and laid the dress down in the growing pile.

Around a small circular platform were two velvet couches. Derrick's family and Dani, were equally spread out between the two to keep her from joining them. She perched herself on the edge of a bench further away; In that moment, she realized Mrs. Ward was absent. Mrs. Ward was a warm and inviting woman who loved her children and Celeste more than life itself. She couldn't fathom the idea of Mrs. Ward not being here to help Morgan pick out a wedding dress. Hell, if the fire had never happened and Celeste been lucky enough to fall in love and gotten married, she would have wanted Mrs. Ward there and not her mother. Her mother would have decided on the dress, venue, and officiant without asking Celeste or her fiancé, taking Celeste's choice away yet again.

Having a moment of free time, she unlocked her cell phone to text Cate for an update on Chip. Her phone dinged immediately with a response. AJ took a seat next to her on the bench. "Is that your dog?" the little girl asked as Celeste looked down at her phone. Cate had sent her a picture of Chip happily gnawing on a piece of driftwood.

"Yeah. His name is Chip. Short for Chocolate Chip." Celeste beamed and opened her camera roll to show the girl more pictures of the chocolate Lab.

AJ giggled as she rested her head on Celeste's arm, turning her heart into a puddle in her chest. "That's a silly name."

"Well, he's a silly dog." Celeste swiped through photos of Chip. AJ giggled and looked on with awe. The child was more accepting and receptive of Celeste than the adults, even acknowledging her as her aunt when her family demanded AJ come over to the other couch with them. Celeste saw Derrick's mother mumble something under her breath. Although she didn't hear the words, she knew what the woman said. Celeste was not one of them and didn't belong here.

Her reprieve lasted only as long as Morgan was in the dressing room changing into each dress. Each new dress she tried on made her look more and more like a princess, yet there was something off with each one. Some were overly frilly or extremely lacy. Others had an open back or a plunging neckline that did not seem *right*. Derrick's family and Danielle gave their loving opinions on all of them.

The next dress she tried on was the one Celeste picked out. The silky A-line dress had floral lace sleeves caressing her shoulders. The floral lace outlined the chest bodice area and led to a small v-neckline then slowly faded down the dress. Morgan's tan complexion and light brown hair seemed to accentuate the dress. She looked more beautiful than any princess. Her best friend was absolutely glowing.

"You look beautiful, Morg," Celeste spoke up for the first time all day.

Morgan's smile reached her ears as she looked at herself in the mirror, twisting to see all angles. The woman was practically giddy, and it lifted Celeste's spirit. She still knew her friend well, despite the long gap. "It's perfect. It's like something I imagined when we were teenagers."

"I don't know, M," Dani cut in. "You've been looking at mermaid-style dresses. Remember all those dresses we pinned online when we were in college? Besides, you had two kids and bounced back like nothing happened. You deserve to show off!" Danielle gave Celeste a smug look, throwing it back in her face that she wasn't around during their college years. "And it'll be a summer wedding, go strapless. He'll enjoy the view."

Every thought in that room was about Derrick and what would be easy on his eyes. To her, it was as if she was the only one who cared more about the person wearing the dress. Morgan had defended Celeste time and time again, and now it was her turn to repay the favor. Celeste shook her head and looked at Danielle with disgust. "It's Morgan's wedding too. She should pick out a dress *she* likes. What makes *her* feel beautiful; not what Derrick would want to fuck her in." There was a small, sharp, collective gasp. Morgan's eyes shifted from Celeste to Derrick's mother and sister. The mother and daughter glared back at Celeste.

"I do like this one the best so far," Morgan commented, not drawing any more attention to Celeste's comment as she ran a hand through her hair. She turned to face her daughter. AJ had pulled out a book from somewhere. Celeste smiled softly. She remembered trying to hide behind a book when she was forced on errands with her parents. They always snatched it away from her because it was a fantasy book from the school library. "What do you think, Ali Jay?"

AJ looked her mom up and down and tilted her head. She made a noise like she was deep in thought. "You look like a princess."

Celeste returned the smug look at Danielle. Danielle clicked her tongue and rolled her eyes. "If that dress makes you feel beautiful and you love it, get it."

Morgan poured over the dress again, examining it from every angle. Her eyebrows furrowed and her earlier smile faded with doubt, a look Celeste knew all too well. They were forcing Morgan to make decisions that they wanted, not what Morgan wanted. "I really do love it." She sighed and did another turn in the dress. "You're right, Ali. I'm the one buying it, I should go with what I like."

"You have one more dress to try on." Danielle protested; another dress picked by Danielle.

Morgan rolled her shoulders back and steeled her face. "This is the one," she announced loudly. Her eye caught Celeste and the two exchanged a small nod. The ghost of a smile danced on her lips.

While the seamstress set to work on getting the measurements, Morgan directed the others to look for bridesmaids' dresses, giving instructions for a specific pattern or styles to look for. "And Alice is going to be the Maid of Honor."

All of the women's faces went slack. The growing tension in the room was suffocating. The regret she had felt earlier about coming to Philly solidified into a heavy rock in her stomach. It had been barely 48 hours, and life as she knew it had flipped on its head. Even before her nasty outburst, she knew they hated her.

Celeste went off alone, searching through colorful bridesmaid dresses, pulling out ones that matched the description she was given. Her ears detected whispers in the next aisle over. She leaned into the dresses, straining her ear to hear what was being said.

"It's complete bullshit! I helped her through college, the rape, and AJ. It's because of *me* that she met Derrick while that girl's been God knows where." Danielle's voice was gravelly.

"Do you think she started that fire?" Derrick's sister whispered.

Celeste gripped a dress. This was a mistake.

"Maybe. Do you see those thick lines on her arm? Maybe she's just been institutionalized this whole time. Maybe she escaped the nut house?" Danielle theorized. "She's a danger to herself and to Morgan and AJ. I wouldn't want her around my kid. We need to keep AJ away from her."

She glanced down at her arm, regretting wearing the short-sleeved shirt. The occasional customer would stare at her arms, but no one ever said anything about the dozens of thick and thin white faded lines across her upper arm and elbow. Celeste wiped her eyes, wanting to go home. Too much time had passed in her friend's life, and it was becoming obvious she had meant to become nothing more than a memory. Celeste rested her head on the cool fabric of the dress hanging up in front of her. She was leaving once she got back to Mason's apartment. God, Lucian *was* right; it was a bad idea to try to cling to the past. The reunion of her dreams did not match the reality. So much time was wasted on hope. Cate was right too— all hope did was disappoint her.

She took extra time examining each dress she came across, purposefully delaying having to see them again. When she couldn't avoid them any longer, she trudged back to where AJ was spinning on the podium in a light pink, poofy, princess-style dress. Morgan turned to Celeste and looked through the pile of dresses she was holding in her arms. She tugged out the third one from the top. Morgan's eyes glittered, and her face broke out into a wicked grin. "This one."

Celeste chuckled; Morgan seemed to know her style better than she did. She changed into the dress in the dressing room with her back to the mirror. Even now, she could not look at herself in front of a full-body mirror.

Her eyes would immediately fall right to her scars and her weight. In the days following even the smallest of glances, thoughts would swirl in her brain about how much she hated her body. How much she hated herself.

When she emerged from the dressing room, a hush ended a side conversation. Three pairs of Judgmental eyes stared at her. The silence was only broken by Morgan's joyful clapping and waving her over to the platform. "You're beautiful. This is the one! Just look at yourself!"

Each step to the platform was heavy and slow, like bricks had replaced her feet. She kept her head down as she stepped up onto the platform. Celeste inhaled deeply and lifted her head and gasped. Her hair was pulled back and half up just like Morgan's. As teenagers, they tended to style their hair the same way. Her face was still naked as it was last night, since she hadn't put her piercings back in after dinner.

All of her tattoos were on full display in the dress. From her forearm tattoos to the flying butterflies trailing from her left breast to her upper shoulder, flying away from her past. She barely recognized herself. Aside from the tattoos, *Alice* looked back at her and Morgan.

"What do you think, Ali?"

Celeste blinked, pulling herself out of her mind just as the negative thoughts about her body started to swarm her brain and focused on the dusty blue dress. The neckline was square cut and gave ample view of her full chest. Small gems sparkled throughout the bodice and skirt. The skirt part of the dress flared out a little. The neckline was fantastic, but she could not stop staring at her arms. The sleeves capped off at the top of her shoulders, leaving her arms exposed. Her arms felt too wide for the dress and too noticeable.

"My mother is rolling in her grave." Celeste's voice wavered.

Morgan bit her lip as she touched the side of the dress, her fingers rubbing on the tulle. "How do *you* feel?"

Celeste examined herself from top to bottom. Her damned arms were too big for the dress and her self-harm scars were just as noticeable as her tattoos. "It's your wedding, Morgan. It's not up to me."

"I think you look beautiful. As long as it's comfortable and *you* like it, you should go with this one." Morgan made a motion to the seamstress. "Who knows, maybe next year, we'll be here picking out your wedding dress," Morgan said absentmindedly, standing beside her friend. Celeste slouched and then straightened when the seamstress made a fuss.

"When's the wedding again?"

"May 18th."

Heat prickled at Celeste's wrist. It wasn't as hot as it had been, but warm, like she had been by a fire too long. Her body stiffened. May was just under a year from now. If she and Mason prove to be unsuccessful, there's a chance Lucian will have come for her. She shut her eyes to keep the tears in. "Can we talk?"

Morgan nodded her head and waited for the seamstress to finish the measurements. The two girls walked into the dressing room Celeste had changed in earlier. "What's up?"

Celeste shut the door and then faced her friend. Her hands balled up the dress as she willed herself to speak. "I think you're making a mistake making me your maid of honor. You and I are best friends, always and forever, but I don't know if I'll be here next May. If Lucian drags me to Hell before then, you'll be without a maid of honor.

That's not fair to you. If I'm still around…I'll be content to sit in a pew. I just think Danielle should be your maid of honor. She's the reason you met Derrick." However, if Celeste had never caused the fire and remained in Morgan's life, then Morgan would have never gotten drunk.

Morgan was silent, but her face showed everything she needed to say. She was hurt, and now Celeste felt even worse. She should have never said anything. "But what if you are here?"

"I can't make any promises."

Morgan looked down at her hands, as if trying to hide her face. She swallowed hard and looked back up at her friend. "Is that what you want?"

"Of course it's not! But I'm trying to be realistic. Danielle deserves it more than I do."

Morgan shook her head, "It's my wedding. *You* are the one I want to be up there with me." The tone in her voice effectively shut down any further conversation.

Celeste exhaled deeply. How many ways could one trip go so wrong?

CHAPTER 26

"**H**ow was dress shopping?" Mason asked over their Italian dinner later that night. He'd taken her out to a fancy restaurant that she was way too underdressed for. A bottle of pinot grigio sat in a small bucket on the table. She preferred Merlot, but Mason was paying for the meal and she knew better than to complain.

"It was okay. She found a dress she liked," she said as she twirled pasta onto her fork.

Mason took a sip of the wine and raised an eyebrow. "Just okay?"

"I'm the Maid of Honor." Her flat voice had Mason's eyebrow arching.

"And that's a problem? You two are thick as thieves."

"*Were*," Celeste reminded him. "It's been eight years. That one girl, Danielle or whatever was crying because

Morgan made me her Maid of Honor. I didn't ask for it. Danielle deserves it more; she was here when I wasn't."

"Did you talk to Morgan about it?"

"Yeah. She insisted I stay her maid of honor. I can't do it. Mase, this is too much too fast. Two days ago, she thought I was dead. Now, I'm the Maid of Honor in her wedding. Two days ago, I was worried about how she was going to react to me showing back up. And today she bought me a dress that I might not even be able to wear if Lucian comes for me by May!" she hissed and dropped her fork with a clatter. The table next to them turned their heads towards them. Celeste sneered at the couple, who quickly turned their attention back to each other.

Mason quietly set his fork down and stretched his hand out for her. Almost upon instinct, her hand slid into his. "You *will* be here in May," he said with a sense of finality that made her want to believe him. His lips pressed a small kiss to the top of her hand. "We have a meeting tomorrow with another Lutheran church after their service. We should probably go to the services as well."

Celeste yanked her hand out of his as if he had shocked her. "No. Absolutely not, Mason, we're done with that. God and Jesus, they abandoned me. They left me. I'm not savable." Her hand wrapped around the stem of the wine glass and chugged the rest, trying to keep her face from scrunching up as she swallowed the dry white.

"That's not true—"

"*You* don't even believe in God," she cut him off, "so why is it a problem when I say He left me?" There was no point in going to another church. She got her hopes up only to have them get stepped on and broken. As Cate said; hope really was deceiving.

Mason leaned into the table, his voice a low, even, hiss. "You believe in God, and you claim you sold your soul to the Devil. That's a job for the church to look into." A dark shadow clouded Mason's eyes for a brief moment before he sat upright, picked up the bottle and refilled her glass. "Look, Alice, I made you a promise that I would help you and that I wouldn't let you walk away from us again. I don't intend to break that promise."

She took another gulp of the wine in her glass and eyed the bottle. It was almost empty, and she probably drank most of it. "It's pointless Mase. I'm sorry I brought you into this. It's my cross to bear, and I'm not getting out of this deal. Coming back was a mistake. I will always treasure finally seeing Morgan again and meeting my nieces, but I don't belong here. Derrick's family and Danielle made it *very* clear that I don't know Morgan anymore." She shifted her gaze to the uneaten pasta on her plate. Her defiance only lasted as long as she did not get a reaction from him. One disappointed look would send her backtracking and giving in to him to make him happy.

"You do belong here, Alice. It's been two and a half days. Give it more time. They just need to warm up to you. They'll love you, just as we do."

Her eyes glanced towards him. *She belonged.* The affection and want that shined in his hazel eyes caused a warmth to settle in her bones. She was *wanted* here with him. He was fighting *for her*, keeping that shred of hope alive *for her*. And with that, the brick wall around her heart crumbled.

✶

Gentle organ music floated down into the pews. Celeste sat straight-backed in the last pew in the very back of the church. Nerves wracked her body. Her knee bounced rapidly and her hands shook violently. Mason encased her hand in his, gently rubbing the top of it in an attempt to comfort her. The last service she attended had been with her family the morning of their murder. Despite his efforts, she could not shake the eerie feeling that enveloped her.

Then there was the stained-glass window above the altar. Jesus stared at her, mocking her. *You're wasting your time* his painted eyes seemed to tell her. Deep in her gut, she knew it was the truth.

Being here was eerie. Here she was listening and mumbling the same hymns and prayers she had spoken mere hours before she sold her soul. Muscle memory had her speaking the prayers and hymns as if no time had passed since she last sat through a service. Other prayers however, had her stumbling through with a wince. Her family would have scolded her for forgetting and then forced her to sit and studying them for hours every day after school.

Mason mumbled his way through the service. His family had been indifferent to religion, never caring if Morgan attended a church event with Celeste whenever she needed a friend.

Her arm burned hotly, but it was tolerable. It was nothing like the excruciating pain she felt when it flared up in the middle of sex with Mason. She skipped communion in fear of it causing her to roll on the floor writhing in pain in front of all of the parishioners.

At the end of the service, they stood in the atrium, his hand around her waist as they waited until the pastor could see them. Older ladies and men, amazed that a young couple was there, kept inviting them to coffee with the other older members. Celeste declined politely, despite the enticing thought of coffee.

After the last of the parishioners departed, the pastor introduced himself and took them back into his office. He poured them a cup of coffee from his coffee machine. The smell of freshly brewed coffee instantly stopped the shaking once and for all and the first sip caused her shoulders to drop from her ears. After a brief moment of pleasantries, Celeste jumped into her story.

The pastor listened intently, showing no hint of emotion. He was quiet for a few moments after she finished her story. The silence was loud and caused her shoulders to inch back up towards her ears.

"Like you said, you are not possessed," he finally stated. The breath in her lungs wanted to sigh out in relief, but the inflection in his voice made her pause. "But you clearly did something wrong. You lost your faith and let temptation sweep in and take control. It seems like you are making a good start by coming in today. Even though we don't deserve it, Jesus died for our sins and was sent to love and bring light to the non-believers."

Celeste's head cocked to the side. Unease tugged at her gut. She set the cup on the desk and shot out of the chair. The chair tipped backwards and fell with a heavy *thunk*. Rage over took her and she let her emotions get the best of her. "No shit, I'm not possessed! The Devil is a real person. His name is Lucian. He's six foot five with curly black hair and ice-blue eyes that can turn red. He has neatly trimmed dark facial hair. He's the epitome of tall, dark, and handsome! He has large, black feathery wings. But they aren't always out. He can shoot fire out of his fingertips. He disappeared in a ball of blue fire in my kitchen, and it didn't leave a burn mark on my floor!

"He killed my family, burned my house down, and he left a mark on my wrist." Celeste's voice raised vehemently. This was a disaster. A hopeless disaster.

The pastor kept his face neutral, ignoring her outburst. "It sounds like you had a troubled childhood. You met an older man, one you thought would save you and things got ugly quickly, it sounds like you planned a murder."

There it was. The sole reason she didn't try to find a way out of the deal in the first place. She was screwed, it was only a matter of time before the cops find her. She couldn't stay here; she'd go back to Ocean City and tell Cate what happened. From there the two could go back into hiding. She'd changed her name once and could do it again.

Mason leaned forward, setting his cup down. "Her parents died in a fire caused by an untended candle her sister had lit. It was late at night and everyone had been asleep. The investigation revealed the smoke detectors in the house had not been installed properly. Alice lived in the basement of her house. By the time she woke up, the upstairs had been blocked off by smoke and flames, so she couldn't get to her family. Therefore, she ran out the house through the basement door. Believe me when I tell you Alice had nothing to do with her family's death." He lied through his teeth defending her. Not only did she get herself into trouble, but now Mason would get in trouble for aiding and abetting a criminal.

Uneasiness was all over the pastor's face. Nausea washed over Celeste's stomach. "If that is truly the case, then she probably has a mental disorder." He talked to Mason like she wasn't in the room. "She should see a professional."

Her hands slammed onto the desk, startling both men. "The Devil is real. Fallen Angels are *real*. I was attacked by one back in June. I wouldn't make this up to get attention. I don't want attention." *I just want God to love me again.*

"Ali, sit down," Mason pleaded.

Celeste stood her ground.

"I think you should seek professional help and bring prayer back into your life. Prayer does wonders for the lost," the pastor said, leaning forward.

Celeste growled in frustration. He was no different than her parents. "I'm done here." She turned on her heel and walked hurriedly out of the room, breaking into a run as soon as they disappeared from view. She didn't slow her pace until she came up to Mason's car. Celeste tugged hard at the passenger side door. It was locked, and Mason had the key. She cursed and kicked the tire in frustration; another failed attempt. There was no saving her soul. Hell, she wasn't even worth being saved. Lucian should just take her now.

Mason came out minutes later, making a beeline toward her. He was upon her instantly, pinning her to the car with his hands on either side of her head. His eyes held a scary darkness within them. It was a look he might have used in his military days. "What the hell was that about? Mason demanded.

"He thinks I murdered my family. It's only a matter of time before he calls the police in Elizabethtown and they come knocking on my door and I get arrested!"

"Well, you did in a way. You claim you sold your soul for it." Mason snapped angrily at her.

Celeste bared her teeth at him, all the earlier rage coming back tenfold. "Fuck you, Mason. I never wanted them dead. All I wanted was to get away from them. Death was never on the table. Lucian tricked me." She pressed her arms to his chest and shoved him hard. He took a few step backs to regain his footing. Mason never believed her; he lied to get her to come to Philly.

"Maybe he was right." Mason said with teeth clenched. "Maybe I was looking at this wrong. Instead of pastors, let's get you to a doctor."

The words were a blow to the chest. "I'm not crazy," she snarled.

"But you're acting crazy! A Fallen Angel attacked you? Someone just broke in. People don't grow wings," Mason argued.

"They weren't just people, Mase! They were *Angels*."

Mason rubbed his face in frustration. "Do you hear yourself? What? Now are you gonna tell me witches exist too?" Celeste opened her mouth and closed it. It wasn't her place to say what Cate was. Mason continued, "I think he's got a point, Ali."

Her hands flung wildly in exasperation. "What point? If I prayed more, it would break the deal? Or was it the part that I strayed away from God and gave into temptation?" Mason opened his mouth to answer. Her eyes narrowed at him and snapped, "Don't. Answer. That." Tears rimmed her eyes. God she was an idiot. Smartly, he shut his mouth again, his jaw ticked in anger. "You say you believe me when I tell you something happened. You promised me you'd help me but now you just want to dump me at the hands of a *doctor*. What do I have to gain by lying to you?"

"Alice, you need to calm-."

"*Don't* tell me to calm down," she snarled. "I'm leaving. This was a mistake."

"We aren't done with this conversation."

"The hell we are!"

"I have the keys," Mason reminded her. A challenge.

Celeste sized him up. He was taller than her, but he didn't tower over her like Lucian did. Her eyes drifted down to his pants, looking for the outline of the keys. His left pocket looked bigger than the right. She quickly reached for his left pocket. Mason, faster than the speed of light, caught her hand. He twisted her around so her back and arm pressed into his chest. Her front pressed hard into the passenger side door. It was so sudden she didn't have time to yelp. Panic filled her stomach, and her heart raced. She had been in this position many times years ago. For a moment, she was thirteen years old and back in Elizabethtown.

Mason's head tilted towards her and whispered darkly in her ear. "Don't. Do. That. *Again*." His voice was cold, deadly and promising.

Celeste whimpered; her gut was telling her to obey. Alice would have obeyed and played it safe to make the other person happy, but that was not Celeste. Celeste could handle herself. She lifted her foot and came down, *hard* onto his. Grunting, he let go of her. "Fuck you. I'll walk."

"You don't know how to get home," he growled.

"Cell phones have maps," she seethed. Celeste pulled her arm close to her chest, rubbing it carefully as she made her way to the sidewalk, not bothering to look back.

She marched down the sidewalk, following the directions her phone's GPS had given her. Her hands were quaking, and she could not still them. A part of her now dreaded going back to Mason's. He told her she would be safe with him, but right now, she was not sure. Deep down, she knew she wouldn't be safe with someone who did the same shit her father did. She thanked God she was leaving today to go back home to Cate and Chip.

She was a quarter of the way to Mason's house when his silver car pulled over and the window rolled down. "Ali, get in, please," Mason pleaded.

"The walk is good for me. It helps clear my mind," she lied and wiped the sweat off her face. She was absolutely miserable. Her sheer blouse was glued to her skin from the stagnant city heat.

"It's ninety-three degrees, Alice."

"I'm fine," she snapped and kept walking. Mason inched the car forward, keeping pace.

"Alice, please. I don't want to fight with you," Mason pleaded with her. Celeste peered into the car to see Mason leaning over the center console, staring at her with guilt-clouded eyes.

"We already fought." She skidded to a stop and walked to the car window, standing beside it with arms crossed, not leaning in. "Not to mention, you twisted my fucking arm!" she hissed.

Mason hung his head for a moment before meeting her eyes. "I'm very, *very* sorry about that. Military training."

Her eyes rolled into the back of her head. "I'm not your enemy, Mase. I'm your fucking girlfriend," Celeste spat.

"I know. It won't happen again," Mason apologized sincerely, something she never got from her family. "Please, get in."

She studied his face, seeing the remorse there. Her eyes softened looking at him. "My father used to twist my arm," she spoke in a soft voice.

Mason's eyes softened; she saw the guilt in them. "I'm sorry for twisting your arm and I'm sorry for implying you are crazy; you are not and I never want to hurt you. I am not your father, and I will never be like him. I'll do better."

Celeste watched him for a moment. With a sigh, she opened the passenger side door and got in. The blast of icy air felt good on her skin. Mason held out his hand through the rest of the drive back to his townhouse but she kept hers to herself.

The two entered the house silently. Celeste kept a healthy distance behind as they stepped inside.

"I'll get a spare key for the house for when you move in." He told her as he put the keys on a hook beside the door.

Celeste shut the front door and shot him a disgruntled look. She was not in the mood to have another argument. "I'm not moving in Mason. After this weekend, I've gotten way too involved in your lives again. I'm not getting out of the Deal, and it's only a matter of time until Lucian comes looking for me. Hell, he probably knows we've been visiting churches."

"You let him control your life. It's time for you to live your life the way you want. I want you here. Morgan wants you here. Your family wants you here. You belong here," Mason said kindly as he strolled over to her. Celeste's heart melted at the thought. She wanted to belong with them, she dreamt of it. But she also belonged at home, with Cate and Chip and the friends she made in Ocean City. "Look, I get it, it's been an overwhelming

weekend. Just take some time and think about it. Please."
He asked her and placed a soft kiss to her temple.

The weekend had been a roller coaster. She came here on Friday with the intent of reconnecting with Morgan and just spending time with her friends and instead it was a whirlwind of meeting new people and watching the rise and fall of newfound hope. It was a lot to process for one weekend, and decisions were better thought out by the sea.

CHAPTER 27

The salty air did wonders for her spiraling thoughts and cleansed her body of the tight Philadelphia air. The air, sand, and waves had become her therapy program, one she wouldn't know if she could survive without.

Cate wasn't home when she arrived. The house was too big and empty for her thoughts so she took Chip down to the water's edge and set up her telescope. Pluto was at opposition with the Sun, making it the best time she could gaze at her favorite planet. She had been a child when the planet was downgraded to a dwarf planet, and she could still feel the anger in deep in her being, thinking it unfair that they made it a lesser planet because it was so small. Pluto didn't ask to be small, just like she never asked to be so unlike her family. They both were just made that way.

Yet, the stars that she tracked along the way kept pulling her attention away from the dwarf planet. Each twinkle reminded her of the sparkle in Mason's eyes every time he reminded her that he wanted her in Philly with them and that she belonged with them.

"There you are. I saw your car in the garage but you and Chip weren't inside." Cate spoke loudly as she walked across the sand.

Celeste pulled away from her telescope and ran towards her best friend, enveloping her into a hug. "I missed you so much!"

"I missed you too! I want to hear about your trip. Are you hungry?" Cate held up a plastic bag full of takeout food. Celeste grinned and took the other towel from Cate and laid it on the sand. The two sat and immediately opened the containers. Chinese food, their favorite.

The two girls sat on the blankets and caught each other up on their respective weekend events. Celeste gushed about her nieces and reconnecting with her old friend before settling into the more serious theme of the weekend.

Cate's eyebrow shot sky-high up on her forehead. "Are you sure you want to do this?" the skepticism in her voice had Celeste second-guessing herself.

"I don't know." Celeste's voice wavered. "A part of me wants to keep trying to get out of the deal because I never asked for Lucian to murder my family. I never consented for him to *own* me. But the other part realized that God and Jesus gave up on me. I don't think any amount of church and prayer will let me back into their good graces. I mean, I royally fucked up by getting attached to Lucian. I'm not savable anymore."

"Has this life really been *that* miserable for you?" Cate asked. Despite her neutral face, Celeste could see the hurt hidden behind the mask. This life had been good to her, but it had never been her own.

"No, it hasn't." She sighed loudly, setting down her now empty carton of orange chicken. "But Lucian took my freedom. I'm going to be spending an eternity in Hell as a Demon. I never wanted that. I believed in Heaven and God and Jesus and salvation. He completely disregarded that."

"Heaven and Hell are…" Cate trailed off and tilted her head side to side, trying to find the right words. "The Church is not everything. A lot of it is just stories—fables, really," her friend said. Her eyes held a sadness in them like there was more to what she said out loud.

"It's all I had, besides soccer and cutting," Celeste murmured. As a child, she dreamed of Heaven, of a life better than she had. "The only things that made me feel good were soccer, church, and cutting. I don't want to cut anymore, I haven't played soccer since high school, and now I lost the church."

The silence between them was palpable, only the soft roar of the waves and Chip splashing around could be heard.

Cate broke the silence first. "I'm sorry, Celle. I know it was important to you. Maybe you can create something that works for you. I hate the church, but I don't hate religion. I find salvation and hope in magic and Mother Earth. Sometimes, you just have to find a new way, even if it's not in a building."

"I doubt He would listen anyway."

"Probably not. I've never been too fond of the Big Guy anyway."

A comfortable silence fell on them again. Cate's words rang in her ears over and over again. Her friend was always so rational and level-headed to the point Celeste would jokingly call her *mom*. Sometimes, it was helpful. Other times, it drove her insane.

An uneasy feeling began to settle in Celeste's stomach. The outdoors was not big enough to hide the elephant that pressed on her heart and gut. "Mason asked me to move in with him."

Cate froze mid-bite of her sweet and sour chicken, her eyes locked on her best friend. "What?"

"Mason wants me to move to Philly." she repeated slowly, as if as soon as she spoke the words, the offer would be rescinded. "To be closer to the family." She turned her attention away and focused on Chip, feeling like she was telling her friend that she was about to marry the first guy she met and move across the country.

"You can't be serious. You can't be considering it, especially not after what he did this morning."

Celeste chewed on her bottom lip. She could still feel the hot metal of the car door on her skin. "I told him I'd think about it," Her voice was low like a child about to get in trouble. "Even if it's just to shut him up."

"And you're going to wait a few days and tell him no, right?" Her words were clipped and dripped with obvious disgust.

"I don't know." Her voice was barely above a whisper. Her fingers dug into the sand. The cold, densely packed sand was a welcome shock to cool the heat rising in her body. "I wanted to break up with him today, because of what he did. I don't belong there, I've been gone too long, and my place is here. Yes, my life here hasn't been miserable, but I also haven't been living. I've been going through the motions for eight years. I've just been surviving. But after meeting AJ and Bri, I feel like I have something to live for aside from Chip. Lucian said I wouldn't be moving on if I held on to them. But my life hasn't moved on without them either. I've been here partying, living every day like it was my last, and I'm tired of it.

"They want me there. He said I belong with them. Morgan wants me to be her Maid of Honor, and Mason really cares about me. Do you know how long I've waited to hear that?

"On the other hand, I know I can't go. I can't knowingly abandon them again. Not to mention, you are my best friend and I don't want to leave you. But we're getting older. You're going to find a girl to settle down and move in with, and then I'll be left alone waiting for Lucian with bated breath."

Cate's lips thinned, and her turquoise eyes practically glowing with hurt and anger. Leaving here would mean abandoning Cate. No matter what choice she made, she would be hurting someone. Anger surged through her; she should have just died in that fire. She couldn't hurt anyone if she was dead.

"I see," Cate said, with a voice clipped with emotion. They were both treading on thin ice.

"Morgan was raped because she decided to get raging drunk at a bar to handle her grief of losing me. If I had reached out and told them I wasn't dead then maybe she wouldn't have gone out with the intent of getting blacked out. Maybe she wouldn't have been raped."

Cate put a hand on Celeste's shoulder. "Do *not* blame yourself for someone else's misfortune. You had nothing to do with that. That was the man who raped her."

"Yes, it was, but if—"

Cate cut in, loudly talking over her. "No ifs, ands, ors, or buts. That is *not* on you. You are not obligated to do anything out of pity. Personally, I think you're rushing into this, Celeste. I don't want to hear you've had a crush on Mason since you were thirteen. Have you forgotten he ran out of the house after he found out who you were?"

Why did you open your mouth, you dumb bitch? The voices in her head yelled at her. *You upset her. Now you can't leave even if you wanted to.*

The anger she'd tried to keep at bay exploded, "His family bought me a fucking headstone! Everything is different now!"

"Yes, everything *is* different now! You are different, and they are different. Hell, I'm not even the same person I was eight years ago!" Cate yelled.

Mason twisting her arm flashed through her mind. Then Morgan flashed through her mind with her two kids and a fiancé—things that became impossible for her the day she met Lucian.

Cate pinched her nose with her finger and thumb in an attempt to stifle a scream. "I love you. You are my best friend. But uprooting your whole life for a guy you used to know? Even I wouldn't do that, and I've been around the block a few times. You need to do what makes *you* happy, not what makes other people happy. We spent a lot of time working on your mental health and the trauma from your past. Like Hades if I'm going to sit here and watch you spiral backward."

It had been seven years since she last let a razor blade regulate her emotions. "I'm not going to spiral. I've healed."

"Clearly you haven't." Cate snapped harshly, then flung her hands exasperatedly "Celeste, there's more to life than them."

"I'm aware," Celeste said curtly as she stood up. "There's more to life than this." She gestured to the ocean, their house, and finally to them.

"I'm aware," Cate said, her tone slightly mocking.

Celeste narrowed her eyes. The anger from earlier found its way back to the surface. Her blood was boiling and her skin felt hot. Her words spewed out like hot lava, "You're just jealous that I have a boyfriend and that guy you were with lives in London!" There was no denying the love in her eyes as she looked at Don at their party.

Cate scoffed and narrowed her glowing turquoise eyes. The words sliced through Cate right where she knew it would. "I can get any man or woman I want." Her eyes lit with her next words. "He's a perfect example. Don is someone from my past, and you don't see me packing up everything and moving in with him because he asked."

"With Mason, I have a family. A family I dreamt about. You don't have a family with Don," Celeste shot.

Cate went still as a statute, unblinking. The woman rarely ever cried, yet there was no mistaking the glassy look in her eyes. "You don't know anything about Don and me." Her voice wavered and she finally blinked and looked towards the ocean to hide escaped tears.

"And you don't know anything about Mason and me," Celeste shot back, venom laced every word.

Cate placed two fingers at her temple and rubbed them. Memories flashed through Celeste's head of her mother sitting at the kitchen table, doing the same motion, begging Celeste to keep her mouth shut when Vicky threw her under the bus for something she didn't do. "For fucks sake Celeste, I don't like Mason, okay? When he was here that morning... Something about him is off. Don didn't like him at all. I wanted to give him the benefit of the doubt because you are my best friend and you've dealt with enough shitty people to see the kind of person they are. But how can I give him the benefit of the doubt when he pushed you against his fucking car, twisted your arm, and called you crazy?"

Each word was a knife to her chest. Mason apologized sincerely. They were not there to see how sorry he was. The two previously had made no mention of their dislike Mason. "Don barely knows him. Why should his opinion matter?" she sneered.

"His opinion matters because I care about him and I care about you," Cate said. The twinge of darkness that laced the words said everything Cate would not; she was going to protect him, hell or high water.

"Just because you care about him doesn't mean I have to," Celeste argued.

Cate shook her head in disbelief. "There's so much you don't know, Celeste. Don has dealt with a lot of bad people; he can pick them out anywhere."

"I thought this was about what makes me happy. Not what makes Don happy," Celeste bit back.

"It's also about your safety," Cate argued, her voice low and cool as steel.

"Mason is a good man. He was in the military, for God's sake. I know him."

"Do you? Do you really?" Cate cocked her head to the side, a threat and a challenge.

He had changed so much in the intervening years. They all had. "Enough."

"That's not good enough." Cate clicked her tongue.

Celeste raised her hands in the air in frustration. "Cate. My soul was taken from me at eighteen years old. I never asked for that. I don't know how much longer I have, and I have let Lucian dictate my life. I can't do the things I used to dream about because he could come at any moment and whisk me away, and everything would be for nothing. I want out of this deal, and Mason agreed to help me. That's been his concern since the moment we reconnected. His concern has been *me*. Giving me *my* life back."

Cate pinched the bridge of her nose again and yelled, "Why are you so adamant about breaking the deal?"

"Have you not heard a word I said?" Celeste's voice raised a frustrated octave. "Why are you defending Lucian?"

"I'm not defending him. You're assuming things and rushing into territory you know nothing about. The two of you are going to be messing with things you shouldn't. From what I can tell, he did it to help you. It seems like he only cared about your well-being."

A bitter laugh escaped her lips. "If he cared, he would have rescinded the bargain when I asked. Aside from that, I accepted my fate because I had no choice. I didn't think it could be done. I tried and gave up. Mason offered to help me. He wants what's best for me, and I'm ready to start living. You have never once offered to help me break the deal. I told you what Lucian did and you just took it as a fact of life. You just want to hold me back!"

Cate's eyes narrowed and her jaw ticked. Celeste hit a nerve again, but she didn't care right now. Cate picked up her towel, letting the empty food cartons scatter around them. "Oh, for Creation's sake! *I* held you back? Go look in the fucking mirror, and you'll see who held you back. Who was there for you when you were suicidal seven years ago? Who helped you out of your depression and kept you distracted so you wouldn't cut yourself? It wasn't them. Who encouraged you to find yourself? Not him. But go on, go play house with him. But when you're on the floor and thinking about slicing up your thigh again, *do not* call me crying." Cate turned her back on her friend and disappeared into the night.

CHAPTER 28

Sleep failed her again. Hours ticked by as she tossed and turned restlessly. Her mind replayed the fight over and over again. The two never fought like this; petty squabbles about dishes or house cleaning sure, but never to this caliber.

Regret ate at her insides. The vitriol had been uncalled for. Celeste could not have asked for a better friend the last few years. Cate had locked up the knives and razors when asked, held her when she cried in the middle of the night as she relived the fire over and over again that first year, and by the grace of God, Cate had even walked in on her mere moments before she swallowed a handful of pills.

The hours after fights were always the worst. The tension afterwards caused the hairs on her arms to stand up straight and her heart would race for hours after the fact. Growing up, it was best to make herself invisible. Her bedroom had become her safe haven and prison. The space under her bed had become a small pantry to keep her safe in her room and away from her family's torment. Going to the kitchen for food would leave her vulnerable to screaming, yelling, and the basis for another fight.

So she made herself scarce for the majority of the day. First escaping to the beach to let Chip out and then to the Rehoboth Beach boardwalk with a coffee and a book. Maybe working their typical shift tonight would get them back on track.

The Marlin's patrons seemed livelier than the staff. Conversation only seemed to flow from the dining rooms. Walking into the back felt like walking into her old home after school the day after a fight.

The Marlin's manager made a beeline for her as she clocked in. The two started around the same time and had become fast friends. Celeste had quickly become her number two in keeping the bar afloat. The older woman's lips thinned, making her grave face look even older. Someone got fired and her night just got more difficult. "Celle, is everything okay with Cate?"

She arched a brow and gave the manager a quizzical look. "I think so, why?" Pangs of anxiety rose in her chest. Something was wrong and Cate was in trouble.

"She called as soon as we opened and quit," the manager told her.

Celeste's racing heart stopped mid-beat as if she had just been told the Queen of England was dining with them tonight. She spun to face the manager, stunned. "I'm sorry, what do you mean she quit? Did she say why?"

The woman shook her head. "That's why I asked you. Is she okay?"

Celeste pulled out her cell phone and looked down at a blank lock screen. Chip dressed in last year's Halloween costume happily stared back at her. "We got into a fight last night. I haven't seen her since." The words ran together in a panicked slur. Her fingers flew as she swiped for Cate's number. Immediately after tapping on Cate's name, the three beeps and an automated voice told her the number was no longer in service. She called the number a few more times with the same result. Her thoughts started to spiral.

"I, uh, I gotta go. Something is wrong." Celeste clocked back out and ran to her car. Dread filled her stomach; Cate was in trouble or dead and the last time they saw each other, they fought.

After searching their usual spots in Ocean City to no avail, Celeste speeded home. Her cracking voice screamed Cate's name as she ran around both the exterior and interior of the house, Chip glued to her side. There was no response from Cate. The house was freezing despite the humid weather and completely silent aside from the grating noise of Chip's nails against the floor and her nerves. The inside was hollow and empty, just as it was in the days following Lucian's departure. The upstairs hallway was growing dark from the setting sun, and there was no sound coming from her room and no light or movement from under the door. It was an eerie silence again; the same eerie silence she felt the night they were attacked. Oh God, Remi or his friends came back and took Cate. That or her best friend was dead, and now she would have to spend eternity knowing their last interaction was a negative one.

Celeste banged on Cate's door, calling her name. No response, *again*. Her hand slid to the doorknob and twisted it open. She flicked on the light to reveal an empty room devoid of all life; like Cate never even existed.

Everything was gone. The drawers were open and empty as well as the closet. The only thing left was the bedding. Chip slowly canvased the room, sniffing every corner and under every piece of furniture. He went so far as to go inside the closet, thinking Cate was hiding. He slowly sauntered out and sat in front of Celeste with a head tilt and a whimper, as if asking her where his friend was.

"I don't know where she is, buddy," Celeste called him out of the room and shut Cate's door. The shakiness from earlier returned with a vengeance, and her heart seemed to thump erratically against her chest. She rushed back downstairs to the kitchen hoping she missed a note or something to indicate where Cate went. Nothing. No mark of Cate remained in the house; it was as if she disappeared into thin air.

Her first call was to the police. The man on the phone laughed at her as she tried to make a statement. Cate voluntarily took her things and left, which wasn't against the law.

The next call was to Mason and Morgan. Sobs wracked through her body as she spoke to them. A slow, choppy, rocking movement inched up her body from the balls of her feet, then crept up her body to her shoulders.

The floodgates opened at the sound of Morgan's voice on the other end.

When the line disconnected, Celeste fell onto the couch and rooted herself to the soft, velvety fabric. She couldn't pull herself off to turn on the lamps.

As darkness settled into the house an unfamiliar broken laugh escaped her lips. It was so unrecognizable that it took a while to realize the pathetic sound was emanating from *her*.

Better to laugh than to cry. Cate had told her once, after a long night shortly after she moved in.

History had repeated itself. Cate had left without a trace just like she had; just like she could have done at eighteen without losing her soul in the process. If only she had been strong enough to leave, then maybe guilt wouldn't eat at her insides.

The weak laughter faded into nothing as a numbness settled into her bones. Growing up, becoming numb was a way for her body and mind to protect her; it regulated her emotions when she could not. *The shutdown*, she called it—the middle ground she used to find sanctuary in. From there, she'd either come out okay, or she would slice up some body part to wake herself back up.

The numbing would start slow, encroaching like a dark shadow, ready to swallow her whole. First, the depression would go away, along with any contentment or peacefulness she may have felt mere hours before hand. Then her mind would still, but not in the meditative way. Then she'd stare, her eyes not focusing on any one thing in particular, just staring into the nothingness. The world around her kept going and she physically followed, but no memories would form and conservations would be instantly forgotten.

Although she hadn't cut herself in years, she still tended to fall into this numbness when the world became too much. Only now, she could survive it. The corner of her mouth turned upwards; *the shutdown* had been and will always be, the only constant in her life.

A hazy yellow light lit up the room causing Chip to stiffen beside her, but Celeste continued to stare, her eyes softening and her vision blurred. Muffled voices broke the heavy silence. She couldn't tell who they belonged to; everything felt a thousand miles away. Soft arms enveloped her stiff body. It could be Lucian to carry her to Hell for all she knew.

The next morning, she woke up in her bed, sandwiched between Mason and Morgan. Mason's arm was draped over Celeste's stomach and her back was tightly pressed into his chest. His soft breaths and soft snores in her ear sent her heart fluttering. The soles of her feet touched the warm, furry back of her dog. Her eyes opened to Morgan sleeping peacefully beside her.

They came for her, just like they promised on the phone. Before Lucian, after a bad night or when she would have a panic attack and being left alone with her thoughts would be deadly, Celeste would call Morgan to come over and stay the night with her. Fortunately, her basement bedroom made it easy for Morgan to sneak in and out.

Cate had done the same thing many a night; staying with her in her room or having 'sleepovers' in the den, watching cheesy movies as a distraction— and she took it for granted. And now that Cate was in the wind, there would be no way to make amends with her. But Morgan was here, despite having every reason not to and there was no way she'd take it for granted this time. Without thinking, she silently thanked God, forgetting he was no longer there to listen.

Morgan must have felt eyes on her. She made a low noise and opened up her eyes to see Celeste staring at her. "Creep."

The girls giggled softly. "You're here," Celeste whispered.

"Of course, I'm here. It's what sisters do," Morgan replied and reached behind her for her phone on the nightstand. *Sisters.* They had always said that about each other. But the word felt different now, new and permanent. Celeste finally had a sister who loved her, no matter how many times she would screw up.

As Morgan reached for her phone, her eye caught the framed photo from their prom. The same one that Mason confronted her about. She grabbed it and brought it closer to her face. Her eyes glazed over, whether from sleep or impending tears, Celeste didn't know.

"God, we were babies," Morgan commented, in awe of the picture—The complete opposite of her brother's reaction to the photo.

"It feels like a lifetime ago. Hell, it was another life." A hint of a smile danced on Celeste's lips.

"Yes, definitely another life," Morgan agreed softly. "We're a long way from E-town aren't we?" She exhaled slowly as she put the photo back on the nightstand. "C'mon, I need coffee."

The scent of roasting coffee seeped into her bloodstream, fully waking her up. They took their mugs and two beach chairs to the water so Chip could have his morning rendezvous with the Atlantic. The two slipped into an easy, comfortable silence. The low roar of the waves was enough to dim the noise in her head, but her thoughts kept pushing their way to the forefront.

Seven summers she could have sat here with Morgan and Cate, drinking their morning coffee or nightly wine or tea and watching Morgan's kids play in the sandy backyard with Chip. Hell, maybe Mason wouldn't have married his first wife, and they would have married and had kids of their own. The thought cracked at her heart. It was a thought she couldn't afford to think about. Not now or ever.

Celeste stared down the waves as they rolled in. They were a calming presence she cherished. Being able to see the water and feel the warm sand between her toes daily would have never happened had it not been for the damn Devil. Another wave of guilt overcame her as she thought about how her disappearance had affected Morgan.

"I'm sorry," she whispered thickly.

Morgan's sleepy eyes met her own. "For what?"

"For leaving you. For not being there for you when you were attacked."

Morgan finger traced around the top of the mug and shrugged her shoulders. "It's in the past. You were busy rebuilding your life. I was rebuilding mine. We can't go back and change it."

Celeste turned towards Morgan. Her shirt clung to the scratchy material of the beach chair. "I could have just left. I was eighteen. I could have just packed everything up and left. We could have stayed in touch, maybe you wouldn't have been raped." Tears pricked her eyes.

"Alice, listen to me." Morgan's lips thinned into a straight line as she set her mug down in the sand. She grasped her friend's shoulder and gave it a soft squeeze. Her eyes bore down onto Celeste, her face sympathetic but strong. Celeste didn't even want to think about all the times Morgan had to be strong without her best friend. A small part of her felt envious of Morgan's ability to appear strong when she could barely get through a day without hating herself and feeling weak. "Alice, I forgive you."

Celeste blinked. Forgiveness was a foreign concept to her. She didn't have it in her to forgive at all. The constant white-hot anger that took up residence in her being fueled her, and destroyed her. It festered within her like a time bomb, ready to explode at anyone who tried to calm it. Most of the time, it exploded on her. That was when she would cut because feeling physical pain was better than feeling the onslaught of emotions she buried deep within her.

She learned at an early age to apologize to her parents for mistakes she didn't make, but they were always hollow. She could fake the sincerity to keep the peace in the house, but she could never shake the anger she felt when she had to own up to the mistakes of her sister, mother, or, father. Her apologies were never accepted. Her family never truly forgave her for something she never did. Instead, the actions hung over her like a dark cloud full of blackmail.

You don't deserve it. You are not worth forgiving. Her parents' voices snarled in her mind.

"I don't deserve it," she said immediately, her voice hoarse.

Morgan gave her friend a small smile. "I didn't blame you then and I never will. You wouldn't have been able to stop the rape even if you had been there. Yeah, I got drunk because it was easier than grieving, but even if you lived, we would have been in two separate schools in two separate states. It's the bastard's fault for overpowering a drunk girl who didn't have the ability to say no or to comprehend what was going on. None of that is on you. I don't blame you for any of it."

Tears spilled down Celeste's cheeks. Morgan was telling the truth. She stretched out her pinky finger towards her childhood friend. "Promise?" Like most children, they had taken up the pinky swear law. Even until their teenage years, promises had been bound to the pinky swear.

Amusement danced in Morgan's hazel eyes. With a grin and a slight shake of her head, she wrapped her finger around Celeste's. "Promise."

Celeste wiped her eyes and let out a shaky laugh as they shook on it. She sat up a little higher, feeling like a weight had been lifted, and a small amount of anger dissipated with each tear falling from her eyes. For the first time in her life, she truly apologized and in turn, was truly forgiven. It was euphoric.

CHAPTER 29

Warm yellow-orange lights glowed from the windows in the currently abandoned home next to Lucian's mansion. Lucian changed his course and landed on his neighbor's front lawn. The front door of the ivy-covered house was wide open and welcoming, just like it always was when the owner was home. Lucian's eyes rolled into the back of his head. He had told that Witch countless times to keep the door shut for her safety, but she never listened. Not every soul in Elysian was as kind and civilized as their family was.

Relaxing his wings, he walked up to the house and knocked against the open door. "Cate?" he bellowed. Noises floated down from the second level.

Cate's house was much smaller than his mansion and the other homes on the street, but she did not mind it. She purposely had it built that way. And, not to his surprise, the smallest house in the neighborhood was also the coziest of them all. He, Don, and Thayne tended to spend more time here than their dwellings. He entered the square foyer and walked up the stairs.

He followed the noise to her master bedroom. Large moving boxes lined the walls and formed narrow walkways to the bed, the closet, and the bathroom. Cate was by her closet, hanging up clothes. A teenage version of her with black wings was sprawled out on the bed with her head propped on a pillow, eyes focused on her handheld video game system. Lucian leaned against the door frame; eyebrows furrowed with confusion. The younger girl was supposed to be living with her grandmother and Cate was supposed to be earthside.

Feeling his eyes staring at them, the teenager glanced towards the door and dropped her game system beside her. "Luce!" she called as she all but flew off the bed and threw her arms around him. Over a hundred years and she still ran to him like a kid seeing her dad after a day of work.

Lucian wrapped her into a fatherly hug, "Hey, bumble Bea." He pressed a gentle kiss on top of her head and let go. He crossed into the room. "Aren't you supposed to be on Earth?" Lucian asked cautiously as Cate bent over a box marked clothes.

"I'm not needed there anymore." Cate said curtly. Every word was laced with venom and jealousy.

With a sigh, he sat on the corner of the bed, "What happened?"

As if ignited by a spark, Cate rehashed her argument with Celeste last night, her hands failingly around in half-American sign language and half-large non-sensical movement. Cate constantly talked with her hands to the point her mother had her study sign language back in the 19th century. Although fluent, she only signed when she was extremely volatile.

Bea shot her uncle a deathly glare and a mouthed *thank you*. When Cate got started, she would be a short fuse for hours after the fact and was absolutely miserable to be around. Lucian exhaled as he ran a hand through his hair; this was above his pay grade. He should call Don since he is the only person that can calm her down. "Celeste is an adult. And she sold her soul for freedom. Freedom to do what she wants, when she wants, and *who* she wants," he reminded the Witch.

Cate made a noise of frustration. "No, she can't! She's so damned worried you're going to pop out of nowhere and drag her to Hell, and I can't say shit because she doesn't know that I know you! And I can't say anything bad about the Wards because then I'm the bad guy."

"How is that my problem?" Lucian asked.

"Because you're a man," the young girl added in cheekily.

He nudged the girl playfully. "Thanks, *Bee-yaa*." Lucian rolled his eyes, adding emphasis on the 'a'. "You sound just like your mother."

Cate threw the jacket she just grabbed back into the box. "She thinks Mason can help her break the deal for her soul."

Lucian snorted. There was only one way for the deal to be revoked-by his hand alone. "She can try all she wants, but she is still mine."

"They've already been to two churches. It's only a matter of time before Micah gets wind of it. Of what *you* did."

Bea stiffened at the name. None of them liked to mention the Head Winged Pain-in-the-Ass up in Heaven. Fortunately, Micah was so busy feeding his own ego and lies, it would be a while before he heard Celeste's prayers.

"I think it's time to collect your debt *before* Micah can find her," Cate said, her face tight. The request came from Cate's selfish reasons—losing another person in Cate's life might kill her.

"No, that is out of the question." He shook his head. "I'm sorry, Cate but I promised Celeste a life, which I will give her. If she wants to waste it, fine. That is not my problem. Besides, Micah does not care about a little human like her," Lucian reminded Cate.

Cate moved onto another box with 'bedroom' written in permanent marker. "Celle is convinced they can break it and she's more determined now than when I met her. She will not let go of her past, even if it kills her. And it *will* kill her."

"What's so bad about him?"

"He's a man." Bea commented slyly. Earning a snort from him and a levitating pillow to the face from her mother.

"What's his name again?"

"Mason Ward. He was married once to a Victoria Green-Ward, no children. They met in the military and were married for five years. Their divorce was finalized this past June on the grounds of irreconcilable differences. Victoria alleges that he abused her."

Lucian's head snapped up. "Does she know?"

Cate bit the inside of her cheek and rolled her shoulders back, trying to shake an uncomfortable feeling. "I don't think so. And I doubt she would believe me if I told her. There was clear evidence of abusive behaviors and she just forgave him! He and his sister are the last pieces of the life *you* tore from her. She visited them for closure and came back thinking she could beat you. When she fails, she'll die and she'll be just as soulless as those in the Demon District." The Witch's eyes bore into his intensely, just like her mother did when she was pissed at him. "Call in your debt. *Now.*"

Lucian swore as he exhaled. History was about to repeat itself, and *all* of this would have been for nothing. "She will hate the two of us for eternity if I collect her now. She'll never forgive u—forgive me, for separating them again. She needs to see him for what he is. I'll keep an eye on her for now." The reassurance rolled off his tongue like a death sentence. He'd be breaking one of his promises to the human girl, and would pay for it for eternity once she learned of it.

The following weekend, Celeste, Morgan, and Mason sat on the wall separating the beach from the boardwalk, eating ice cream after Celeste's shift that evening. A chaotic sea of families, couples, and friends walked up and down without a care in the world. In the distance, various music swelled towards them from the vast number of street performers.

Celeste stabbed her spoon into her cup of peanut butter fudge. "I put in my two weeks today." There was no mistaking the hope gleaming in the Ward's eyes as they stared at her, mouths agape.

"Not that I'm not excited, but why?" Morgan asked.

Celeste shrugged, staring at the cup. "I moved to Ocean City to get away from the beach house. It was too big for me and Chip. Then the cottage Cate and I lived in was destroyed so we moved back and it felt less empty. Now she's gone, the house is as empty and cold as it was eight years ago. Besides, you both have been begging me to 'come home,' so I am."

Morgan squealed and threw her arms around Celeste. "Oh, this is going to be great! I can come back next weekend to help you pack up. AJ still has a little bit of summer left before school starts. Could we stay the final week and all leave together?"

A family vacation, just like the one she had dreamed about. "I'd like that a lot."

Mason kissed the top of her head and put a comforting arm around her shoulders. "I'll stay here with you so you won't be alone," he promised her.

Morgan left the following day. Although Mason stayed behind; both she and Chip could still feel the coldness from the hole his best friend left behind.

Two weeks later, her things were distributed between Mason's car, Celeste's car, and part of Morgan's. Morgan and her family had headed back home an hour ago. Like Cate, Celeste took her personal effects and packed some non-beach-themed décor for Mason's plain walls.

Celeste entered the garage, locking the door behind her without another thought of staying. Chip sat by her sports car with his head tilted in confusion. "I know, we're moving again, but it'll be okay. It's not the beach, but it'll be nice." She opened the back door. Chip grudgingly climbed in after a bit of coaxing with the promise of a treat and new toy.

She backed out of the garage onto the road and pulled up next to Mason's car This time it was bittersweet to watch the garage door shut for the last time. Mason walked over to her already-down window and leaned in to kiss her. "You ready?"

Celeste closed her eyes and took a final, deep inhale of salty air. "I'll miss the beach, but I'm ready to enjoy what little time I have left with you and Morgan."

His thumb gently caressed her cheek. Her head immediately leaned into his hand. "We will have the rest of our lives, I promise."

An icy cold breeze blew between them, and a shiver ran down her spine as she pulled away. She threw her car back into drive. "Let's go before I change my mind and live in the dunes."

Mason laughed and kissed her goodbye before getting into his car. He took off first, leading her home.

Celeste glanced at the rearview mirror. The view of the now shrinking house sent a pang of regret. They hadn't gone that far yet, there was still time to turn around. Chip seemed to sense her moment of doubt and brushed his head against her shoulder. She gave him a couple of scratches and a brief kiss. "This is it, baby. Pray to God things will work out the way we want them to."

CHAPTER 30

Settling into the townhouse was easier said than done.

Both she and Chip were untrained to handle the hustle and bustle of major city life. Chip whined constantly at the lack of blue in his scenery. The backyard was smaller than what he was used to, although he loved the addition of squirrels to run and chase after. The constant din of Philadelphia kept Celeste up night after night. Ocean City was busy during the summer months but this was more than she was used to.

Mason did his best to make the transition easy on them but even that was proving to be a challenge. Mason was a high school history teacher, and now that mid-August was upon them, he was gone most of the day, preparing his classroom for the upcoming school year.

Instead of waitressing during the day, Celeste's days were now spent either babysitting her nieces or browsing employment websites for a *better job* as Mason put it. He claimed that waitressing was not going to get her anywhere in life, and that she was destined for better things. Lucian had said that many a time but there wasn't much she could do without a college degree. Her nights that once consisted of bartending were now spent in Mason's bed usually naked and curled up in his arms.

Any moment of free time was spent trying to break the deal. Since the faith route had blown up her spirituality, she tried the academic approach; splitting her time between the local library or online researching the Devil and the various ways he had been dealt with in all the Christian religions. She even went so far as to look into the requirements to audit a religious study class at a nearby community college this fall. Yet with every flip of the page and new web search, she was getting nowhere fast, and was losing patience and hope. She needed a break; one that did not involve calling Cate's cell phone, only to hear the line had been disconnected, again.

After another day with no results, she kicked the front door closed and trudged over to the loveseat. Chip padded over to her with a whine. "Hi, baby," She cooed. The Lab put his front two paws on her, signaling either its playtime or cuddle time. "Come on." Patting her lap, the large dog immediately climbed into her chair. The dog was too large to be a lap dog but he didn't care and neither did Celeste. If she was going to go out cuddling a giant dog like a puppy, then that was the best way to go.

The two stared at her cell phone screen, scrolling through social media. Celeste made comments about celebrities and people she knew as if Chip was equally invested in what was on the small screen. Then across her screen came a post from one of her astronomy groups about Saturn being at opposition tonight, making it a good night to see its rings. There was also a meteor shower that had just passed its peak. It was good a time as ever to find astronomy groups in Philly. Nothing, however, would beat the feeling of camping at Assateague Island with the wild horses and having an unrestricted view of the sky. Already feeling out of place in the big city, if she could find one place where she could continue her hobby, then Philly could finally start feeling like home.

After looking up a decent stargazing area nearby, she quickly gathered her astronomy logbook stuffed with graph paper and drawings and her pencil case full of pens, pencils, markers, and erasers and put them into her backpack. Upon move in, she marked the end table and loveseat as hers. It was the only window in the house with a somewhat decent view of the sky. The rest of the windows had a view marred by buildings and trees.

Climbing into her bed, she set her alarm opting for a quick nap. The alarm never went off, instead, she was woken up by chilly fingertips brushing her hair aside and a light kiss on her forehead.

Celeste squeezed her eyes tightly and made a noise in protest, pulling the blankets further up her body. Her eyes slowly blinked open to the soft yellow light of the lamp on the nightstand and Mason sitting beside her on the bed. "You're early," she murmured sleepily, rolling onto her side and facing him.

"It's seven pm, sweetheart." Mason nodded his head towards the clock on the nightstand. "Isn't it too early for you to be asleep?"

"I'm going stargazing tonight. I need a break from finding a way out of the deal. I'm getting nowhere with the research, and I think the librarian wants to burn me at the stake." Celeste giggled a little as she sat up. Every time she went to the library, the elderly woman had a permanent scowl plastered on her face and always kept Celeste was in her line of view.

"I know, sweetheart," he sighed, the hint of a sad smile on his lips. He picked up her hand and placed a chaste kiss to the top of her hand. "Since tomorrow is Saturday, I was planning on taking you on a little road trip." Mason surprised her as he tucked more of her now blonde highlighted hair behind her ear, her waves no longer catching on her barbell piercing. It had been taken out the day after she moved in.

Her spirit lifted slightly. "Oh? Where are we going?"

"You'll find out tomorrow." He smirked.

"You're no fun," Celeste groaned as she swung her legs over the bed and stood up. She walked over to one of the drawers Mason had cleaned for her and grabbed a long sleeve shirt to change into. "Do you want to come with me?"

"Where are you going?"

"The internet said Fairmount Park is a good place."

Mason stiffened. "It's really not safe to be out that late at night. Besides, most parks close at sundown."

Celeste rolled her eyes and changed her shirt. Mason's eyes trailed the outline of her chest and bra, his eyes darkening with a need. "Then come with me. It'll be a good date night." She walked back to him. Mason's hands immediately went around her hips, fingers gripping her ass.

"By the time we get out there, you won't have that much time to look through your telescope."

"Good thing I know how to hide," Celeste joked. A wry smile danced on her lips.

"That's not funny, Alice." His voice was stern. Her eyebrow arched up. "Philly is not Ocean City, it's dangerous no matter the time of year."

"Relax, Mase. It'll be fine. It will be a fun date." Her hands clasped over his, her eyes pleading with him. "We'll pick up some pizza, snacks, and a bottle of wine. Then we'll go to the park and have a picnic under the stars. It'll be so romantic."

Mason still wasn't convinced. Celeste gave him a sultry grin and tangled her fingers into his hair.

"I don't think you can drink in the park. But we can get drunk here, and we don't even have to change clothes." Mason squeezed her ass, pulling her into him.

"You can as long as you don't get caught." She broke into a laugh. Her fingers danced in his dirty blonde strands.

Smirking, Mason raised his head, a playful look shined in his eyes. The look had her heart melting. She could die happy knowing she got to look into those beautiful eyes all day every day. "You little devil."

Celeste's smile faltered. Her hands dropped, and she pushed herself away. She was never and would never be like that bastard.

Mason's smile fell as he realized the severity of his words. His eyes softened apologetically. "Alice, I… I didn't mean it like that." His hands reached for hers, but took another step back, purposefully being just out of his reach. His long stride had him matching her pace. Mason pinned her between the dresser and him. His finger hooked under her chin and tilted her head up, forcing her to look at him. Unlike the last time he had her pinned, the look in his hazel eyes was apologetic and sincere. "You aren't a devil. You're just…different than you used to be, braver. You would have never said that years ago."

"I wasn't me back then." She couldn't do what she wanted or say what she wanted. If she did, it would come around to her parents and bite her on the ass. Her growth and bravery were mostly because of Cate. Cate had been there for her when she didn't want to show up for herself. Regardless, she was proud of her growth and her independence. Something she would have never gotten had Lucian not done what he did.

Mason sighed, seeming to give in to make her happy. "I'll go with you tonight. We could use a proper date night."

The August air had cooled off just enough to make it comfortable. Celeste found the perfect space in the park far enough away from any remaining city lights. An empty pizza box from their late-night picnic was tossed aside. A bottle of half-finished wine sat in an open cooler Mason had packed. Celeste's telescope was set up a few feet away with her camera ready for pictures. It was long past midnight when she saw the first streak of silver fly across the night sky. Celeste squealed with delight, jumping on the balls of her feet. No matter how many times she'd seen this meteor shower, it was like she was a kid again.

"What is this again?" Mason asked tiredly, lying on a blanket, halfway to a deep sleep.

"Earlier, we saw Saturn and its rings. This is the Perseid meteor shower," Celeste told him for the sixth time that night. "It's debris from comet Swift-Tuttle. It's called Perseids because it looks like it comes from Perseus."

Mason's eyebrows furrowed in confusion. "What's a Perseus?"

Her eyes rolled into the back of her head again. She had explained this in the car. "A constellation named after Perseus from Greek Mythology. He slayed Medusa and saved Andromeda from a sea monster." She lifted her head from the telescope, slightly annoyed. It was like he didn't listen to a word she'd said. "Just come here." She waved him over.

Mason got up from the blanket with a groan and walked over to the telescope. He bent down to peer through the viewer. Celeste put a hand on his back, guiding him and telling him what to look for. "Isn't it beautiful?"

"Very nice." Mason straightened up and smiled at her; his sarcasm coated in honey. "Are you ready to go, sweetheart?"

She shook her head and scrunched up her nose like a rabbit. "No way! I gotta take pictures, sketch it, and journal it." She bent down to grab her journal which was sitting on the grass.

Mason's eyes widened in disbelief. "It's after midnight, Alice. The park closed hours ago. Every minute we're here, we could get into trouble!"

Her eyebrows furrowed. "You didn't have to come with me." She didn't need him here. She *wanted* him here. She wanted to share her hobby with him. Lucian always faked interest when she went on her space tangents. Mason could at least feign an interest. "You agreed to come with me."

Mason scoffed, "I agreed because I cannot in good conscience, let you be here by yourself late at night. *A,* you could be kidnapped, murdered, or raped and *B,* you just moved here, you barely know your way around!"

Remi's disgusting face flashed in her mind, and a cold chill ran down her body. "I can handle myself. I've spent plenty of nights camping at Assateague Island by myself."

"This is a park in Philadelphia, not a beach filled with wild horses. We don't know who lives in these woods." Mason scrubbed at his face with irritation. Something dark flashed in his eyes. "Alice, I'm not going to lose you again because you stayed out in the park hours after closing; I *cannot* lose you."

His voice was so sincere. All trace of irritation had left his face, replaced by a look of worry and concern. She cupped his face in her hands and lightly brushed her thumbs under his hazel eyes. Mason *worried* about her, was *concerned* about her. That was more than she could say for any other man that had been in her life.

"Go sleep on the blankets. I'll wake you up when I'm done. Okay?" Celeste kissed him quickly on the lips before letting him go. Mason bit his bottom lip, weighing his options. Then he silently went back to the blanket and busied himself with his cell phone.

She snuck glances at Mason as she sketched and logged what she saw through her telescope. For a while, he was scrolling on his phone. The blue light painted a heavenly outline of his chiseled square jaw. God may not be around or even exist now, but her boyfriend surely was created by one.

Later, she found him lying on the blanket snoring softly. His golden face was relaxed, peaceful, and beautiful.

Butterflies fluttered in her stomach. It was Vicky's prom night all over again. But now it went much further, what was once a schoolyard crush has turned into something deeper. Mason had only improved her life in the short time they'd been reunited. He reunited her with her real family when everyone else told her to stay away. Mason had become the first person to promise to fight to save her soul. He even told her he *wanted* her. She was *wanted* before, but that didn't compare to the way Mason made her feel. He wouldn't have done any of that had he not felt something for her as well.

Celeste set her journal down and joined him on the large blanket. She stretched out, resting her head on his chest, and looked towards the night sky. Sleeping under the stars was a common occurrence for her back at the beach. The beauty of the twinkling lights still had her in awe. Mason's body tensed under her from the sudden pressure on him. She lifted her head and jumped away from him, remembering the last time she touched him without him anticipating it. He bolted up, now wide awake as he assessed the area for any signs of danger.

"I'm sorry. I-I forgot." She bit her lip and held her breath, waiting for him to yell. Her hands began to shake violently.

Mason's eyes traveled from her face to her shaking hands. His muscles relaxed and his eyes softened as laid back down, motioning for her to come closer. "It's fine. Come back," his voice was low and gentle. Celeste hesitated, waiting for him to change his mind, but he only called her name again. Slow, she laid back on his shoulder with her hand on his chest. Mason enveloped her tightly against his chest and tilted his head down to press a kiss to hers. With every breath, she willed herself to stop shaking. She focused on the feel of Mason's arms around her, his head pressed to hers, and trained herself to focus on the sweet nothings he whispered to help cease the trembling.

Once the shaking stopped, she tilted her head up to see Mason's moonlit sparkling eyes. There was so much love in those hazel eyes. *Too much.* It overwhelmed and terrified her. She had never been loved by anyone before. She wasn't worthy of romantic love.

You aren't worth loving, her mother used to remind her.

"Hey," Mason softly pulled her from her thoughts, a finger gently brushing her cheek as she focused back on him. His lips captured hers in a sweet, yet passionate kiss. Following his lead, Celeste immediately opened her mouth to let him in while throwing her leg over his hips. His hands held her sides steady as she swung herself onto him to straddle him.

A mischievous smirk danced upon her lips as she began to rock her body to an easy rhythm. Mason moaned her old name as his fingers dug into her sides. Celeste leaned forward to kiss his lips, jaw, and neck, hungry for every part of him. She was never one to take control, but things were different now. She was no longer going to sit on the sidelines.

Her tattoo burned hot, but she tried to ignore it— willed herself to ignore it. His hands traveled from her sides to her backside. He cupped her bottom with a playful squeeze. Celeste yelped from the unsuspecting touch.

"Hey! Who's there?" A powerful, authoritative, disembodied voice shouted into the night. Celeste straightened up to see a small flash of light.

"Shit," the two whispered in unison.

Celeste jumped off Mason and scrambled to her telescope. The swinging white light grew bigger and brighter by the second. A dark shadow ran past her on four legs. Her heart dropped into her stomach as she worked to break down her telescope. An icy cold wind blew past her as she got the tube off the stand.

Mason shoved the blanket into a bag and grabbed the cooler. "Come on!" he whisper-yelled.

"My telescope—it's stuck," she hissed as she twisted the bolts that would not come loose. The light of the flashlight swung within mere inches of her. Her heart thumped like a jackhammer against her chest, she had mere minutes before the flashlight landed on her. Mason's hand wrapped around her arm tightly and dragged her away from her things. Her heels dug into the grass to fight him. A trail of torn grass and dirt followed them towards the car. "My telescope! My sketches! Let me go!"

"We'll come back and get it. I'm not trying to go to jail tonight, Alice," he hissed through his teeth. "We need to leave. *Now.*"

"No, not without my journal. I can't lose it."

"For the love of God, Alice! You won't risk the cops finding out about the fire when talking to Pastors but you'll risk it for damn journal?"

The light landed squarely on her telescope laying on the ground. Had she gone back, she would have been caught by whoever was looking for them. Begrudgingly, Celeste snapped her open mouth shut and stopped resisting. Dark shadows surrounded her things. Angry tears slipped down her cheeks as she let him lead her to the car.

That telescope was the first thing she bought once she no longer had to worry about choosing between rent and food. She'd asked for a telescope every Christmas and birthday and was constantly told no. The day it finally landed on her doorstep, she called out sick for three days and went camping on Assateague Island with Chip. Every moment on that trip from sunset to sunrise was spent tracking the stars and planets. Her sketchbook was a gift from Cate, a journal she had bought when they visited the Maryland Renaissance Festival one weekend the previous October. The cover was dark blue with the phases of the moon hand-painted on it. Inside, the handbound journal held six years of sketches and data. Everything that made her who she was, was now at the mercy of a stranger.

The rest was a blur. Mason shoved her into the back seat of his car and threw the cooler and blanket into her lap. She heard her door slam and his open. He tore off into the night, wheels squealing. Out the side mirror, she watched the flashlight scan her telescope. The telescope stared at her longingly. She squeezed her eyes shut to keep herself from crying.

Hours later, in the first light of day, Mason went back, but her telescope and sketchbook was long gone. First Cate, and now her telescope. Celeste seemed to have disappeared along with them.

CHAPTER 31

Celeste wanted to do nothing but crawl under the covers and mourn the loss of her telescope. She could afford to buy a new one, but that one was *hers*. It helped her find her new self; it made her dreams somewhat of a reality. Hell, it was an extension of Celeste. Now, she was just another loser who had sold her soul to the Devil.

Mason was not exactly comforting or sympathetic to her pain. He refused to cancel the surprise road trip, ignoring her multiple pleas. The passenger seat of Mason's car was not as comfortable as it was after dancing the night away in Ocean City or their bed, but she still managed to curl up in the seat with a blanket. The car was freezing despite the warm day.

Mason drove with one hand on the wheel and the other on her thigh despite her shoving his hand off, over and over again. Eventually, she had fallen asleep, and it remained on her leg.

A tight squeeze on her upper thigh jolted her from her light sleep. She gasped loudly and her heart hammered, ready to break through her chest. Her soul would have jumped out of her body if she still had one. Her legs jerked upwards, and her head snapped to each side, trying to remember where she was.

"Hey, easy, easy," Mason told her gently. "You're okay. We're here."

Celeste descended back into her body; curse words tumbled out of her mouth breathlessly. She pressed the back of her head into the headrest and an eyebrow arched. "Where is here?" she asked, still scared half to death.

He pointed out the passenger side window. She snapped her head to the right to see the grey stone building of another church. A sigh escaped her lips; a road trip for another failed conversation with a pastor. Then her eye caught a small red and white sign with a red outlined cross. She scanned the road in front of her. The familiar street was teeming with life. People were going about their lives like it was just another day. The realization hit her as an unfamiliar coldness seeped into her bones. This was not any church.

This was *her* church.

The church her parents belonged to. The church where she spent the last morning of her old life.

"No." Her voice was faint. "No."

"Surprise." Mason's voice was lighter than she felt.

"What did you do?" she rasped out, throat drying out by the second. She couldn't be here. Lucian took away any and all chances for her to go back to Elizabethtown.

"I figured we'd try to go back to where it all started."

"Take me home."

"Alice, we have a meeting with Pastor Louis."

Dread entered her heart, there was no way she could look her old pastor in the eye. "I can't be here." If the pastors in Philly thought she was making everything up, then her former Pastor who knew her and had a close relationship with her family would think she was absolutely insane. "He thinks I'm dead! Or I'm the real-life Lazarus."

Mason huffed and shut off the engine. "Stop being dramatic, Alice. You need to come back here. You need to remember who you are."

Who you were. A familiar deep voice sounded in her head.

"I know who I am and I'm not going in there," she snapped.

Her boyfriend got out of the car and slammed his door shut. Immediately she pressed the lock button to keep him out of the car and crossed her arms. Mason pulled at her door and banged on the window.

"Alice, stop acting like a fucking child," his muffled voice scolded her from the other side of the car.

"No!" she yelled.

"I'm not fucking around, Victoria," Mason reached into his pocket for his keys, and manually unlocked the car. The door swung open and he leaned in, unbuckling her. "I'll carry you if I have to."

He called her by her sister's name. *Again.* The name only ignited a fiery anger within her. "I'm not Vicky!" she yelled loudly into his ear. "You're an ass, Mason Ward. An absolute ass." She put her hand on his shoulder and shoved him away.

"You'll thank me later." Mason let up, but he still had a hand firmly around her wrist as he forced her out of the car.

She stumbled out and pulled her hand towards her. Mason didn't let her go until he locked the doors to the car. The beep and the click of the lock felt like a death sentence. As they walked to the front of the church, she lagged behind him, shooting daggers with her eyes in his direction. Mason didn't seem to feel it or hear it.

Pastor Louis seemed to sense their presence. The giant wooden door swung open as the approached the front steps. Celeste stopped in her tracks when she saw her former pastor. He had aged of course, greyer than he had been. Pastor Louis had watched her grow up. He was the one who baptized her and Vicky. He also led her confirmation classes. She saw him every Sunday for eighteen years straight. Sometimes, all day long. In middle school, the Delco's would go to the early service, then she would go to Sunday School. After that, she and her classmates were expected by the heads of the church to attend the late service since most of her peers would sleep in as long as possible on the weekends. Her parents would pick her up afterward for a quick lunch. Then she would be dropped back off an hour later for choir practice and confirmation classes.

She had admired Pastor Louis. Unlike the rest of her family, he patiently entertained all of her wild questions and answered them in a way she could understand. Each answer started with 'That's a good question' or 'What a fantastic question, Alice!'

His eyes fell on them, and he gave them a warm smile. A sense of home and belonging washed over her. He was one of a handful of people in her life who smiled at her and genuinely seemed to care about her. "Alice Delco! As I live and breathe! I didn't believe Mason when he called me. But after they didn't pull your body from the fire, I just knew you were alive. You do not know how happy I am to see you." Pastor Louis raised his hands in joy. Mason shot her a smug look which she wanted to smack right off his face.

"Hi, Pastor Lou," she said weakly, forcing a smile. "I'm surprised you recognize me."

"You look just like your mother. God rest her soul," he told her. Her eyebrows furrowed, and then she remembered her newly blonde highlighted hair and piercing-less face. Still, the compliment was foreign. Her parents and Vicky told her she looked nothing like them. Hell, her mother had to wear blue-colored contacts and darkened her blonde hair just so no one would question why Celeste had blue eyes and brown hair when she came from a family of brown-eyed blondes.

When she was five or six, some bully Mason and Vicky's age would get in her face on the playground or at the park and tell her she was *the milkman's kid*. She hadn't known what it meant at the time. The day after she asked her parents what that meant, her mother started dying her hair brown and wearing blue contacts.

The three of them grabbed coffee from a nearby coffee shop and gathered around a table in the shop's outdoor garden. An array of colorful flowers were in full bloom and the trees were holding tight to their green leaves for a little bit longer. Butterflies fluttered by them on their way to sit on the petals. It wasn't the beach, but peace still wrapped around her in a tight embrace.

"The loss of your family is still felt here. We even renamed some of our meeting rooms after you and your family. The high school renamed the soccer field after you and Vicky. You were never forgotten here. Although it seems like you have forgotten us."

The words were an invisible knife to her heart. She wanted to be forgotten about here. She wanted her evil parents to be forgotten about.

"What happened that night, Alice? Where did you go?" the pastor asked her softly. Unlike the other two, he sounded genuinely curious. There was no real reason to fear the man as he had always been so nice to her. Then again, her parents had been big donors to the church, and they dedicated all of their free time there. The Delco's were the epitome of a 'good Christian family'.' He would never believe her. The pastor called her name. Mason gave her knee a light, comforting squeeze. She inhaled deeply and started at the beginning. What she should have done over fifteen years ago.

Her body was shaking with sobs by the time she finished her story. Her cheeks were hot and blotchy, and her head pounded from all the crying. Her whole body ached from reliving over twenty years of trauma.

Mason, put a comforting arm around her shoulders and pulled her towards him. Even the feel of him beside her was not enough to calm her.

The pastor was speechless. The silence was endless and a part of her wanted to run, but there was nowhere for her to go. She'd be recognized anywhere in this God forsaken town.

You idiot, he'll never believe you.

This was a mistake. Just. Like. You.

The tears glistening in the pastor's eyes though, that was genuine.

Celeste wiped her face. "I'm sorry, I shouldn't have told you this. This was a mistake." She apologized and stood to leave.

"Don't go," the pastor asked softly. Despite her convictions, she slowly sat back down. The pity in his eyes was so unbearable that she had to stare past him, watching a black dog run down the sidewalk. "Alice…Why didn't you tell me about the abuse when you were younger?"

Celeste's head snapped up. Every muscle in her body froze. "You believe me?"

He nodded solemnly, and a new wave of tears flooded her eyes. Someone *believed* her. Of all people, it was her childhood pastor. "There were…accusations after the fire."

A cold breeze caused her to shiver. "Who made the accusations?"

"Morgan," Mason stated, "She was the most vocal about it."

"And another man came to me and Pastor Micah. You remember Pastor Micah, right?" Pastor Louis asked. Of course she remembered Pastor Micah.

When she was a child, her church had a fill-in pastor for Pastor Louis occasionally. Micah would be the one to preach when Pastor Louis couldn't. He had been a powerful orator with a lot of influence. The congregation held on to his every word. Her father adored his sermons, and the two got to talking after service one Sunday. A friendship had bloomed between Micah and her father, so much so that Micah was a regular at the Delco family dinners whenever he was in town. She'd loved it when Micah came to town. He would always bring her and Vicky a toy from wherever he went. He'd pick her and Vicky up from school and take them for ice cream. He even came to a few of her soccer games. He would listen to her talk about anything and everything under the sun and would play games with her. It was the only quality time she had with her sister or anyone other than Morgan. It was the only time she felt important and valued. Instead of his attention turning to Vicky like everyone else's did, it was on her, and she had basked in it. Her life was better when he was there. Sometimes she would pray that Micah would finally see the abuse she suffered and take her away and be her new father. Then, one day, when she was twelve or so, he stopped coming to visit and stopped filling in for Pastor Louis.

She nodded and he continued. "The man said he was a doctor and used to work with your mother and claimed he saw bruises on you a decade earlier, but your mother talked him out of contacting the police. Funny enough, he looked a lot like how you used to look."

The chill in her bones turned red hot. Anger boiled under her skin at that man who listened to her mother all those years ago. "If he had said something earlier, I wouldn't have sold my soul to the Devil. I wouldn't have started cutting, I wouldn't have wanted to kill myself." Celeste said a short prayer to never cross paths with the bastard.

Pastor Louis acknowledged her statement but kept going. "Pastor Micah said he knew your father very well and denied the allegations. You and Vicky weren't here to confirm or deny. So, it just…went away."

"Pastor Micah and my father were best friends. He would want anything negative about my father to be swept under the rug."

"Pastors in the State of Pennsylvania are mandated reporters. He could be in serious trouble if he swept it under the rug."

"That hasn't stopped anyone before," Celeste said a little too harshly.

The pastor remained quiet, his eye twitched and he looked away for a moment. "You are right. I am so sorry about everything you endured growing up."

"Sorry doesn't bring my soul back." Celeste sniffled. "But do you believe me about Lucian? About me selling my soul?"

Pastor Louis nodded very slowly, "Alice, if you had come to me after the fire, no one would have blamed you for it. Everyone would have been relieved just to know you survived. The death of your family was a devastating blow to the community. The high school hosted a wonderful memorial for you. The football stands at the high school were filled to the brim with your classmates. The school still puts on a memorial soccer game in your honor every summer on your birthday as part of the Independence Day festivities."

Celeste swallowed and brought her gaze down to her hands. That was not the reaction she expected. Vicky was the beloved one. She was a part of the homecoming court all four years and was homecoming queen and prom queen her senior year. Meanwhile, Celeste never won a superlative in her life. She had been liked by most of her acquaintances, but her only claims to popularity were her starting position on the Varsity soccer team all four years of school and her friendship to Morgan.

You aren't worth missing.

"That's not what I asked," Celeste stated thickly. The pastor sunk into himself a little. She fixed her posture, pulling up a wall for when he tells her that he doesn't believe her.

"I'm not saying that it didn't happen, but I'm also not saying that it did happen. There are no true accounts of someone selling their soul to the Devil. However, I do not think I am equipped to answer the question either. Pastor Micah deals with a lot of dark subjects and is knowledgeable in demonology. I have heard him mention a Demon named Lucian. But I don't want to give you any wrong information. I will give him a call and have him come here for a visit. Or I can see about him coming to you."

Hope. There was hope. She grabbed Mason's hand from under the table and squeezed it. Maybe their luck would start to change. They bid Pastor Louis goodbye, full of hope for the first time in a long time.

The two walked towards the car, hand in hand. Celeste was walking on air. Pastor Micah would help her. He had been a friend; he would want to help her. But how would he take to knowing she'd been alive all this time? Would he ask her why she never went to him when Lucian came into the picture.

"You're welcome," Mason said as he led her back to the car.

Celeste raised her eyebrow and slowed her movement. "Yes, Pastor Louis might be the first one to give us any hope, but don't think for one second you're forgiven for lying to me about where we were going."

"I didn't lie…I just hid the truth," Mason admitted shyly.

She came to a full stop and poked a finger into his chest. "Exactly my point, you kept it from me. You know I had issues coming here."

"But it's our first glimmer of true hope. The end justifies the means, Alice." He walked past her to the car and got in.

Another cold breeze blew past Celeste. Her head turned, following it, into the direction of her old house. If she was facing her past, she might as well go all the way.

CHAPTER 32

It was as if she never left her small street. Life had continued for her neighbors. People jogged, neighborhood kids, ones that had been toddlers when she lived there, were shooting hoops in their driveway. Unlike earlier, she was wide awake during the drive to where her house once stood. Her knee bounced uncontrollably as the various houses passed by. Mason approached the end of the street and pulled over in front of her old front yard. She looked out her window and gasped.

A community park had replaced the rubble of her house. The trees that she had stood behind had been chopped down to make room for a soccer field and a playground. "Delco Memorial Park" was carved into a brown wooden sign.

"Do you want to get out?" Mason asked her softly.

Celeste inhaled, watching the various kids swing on the swing set, ride the spring toys, and climb monkey bars. Slowly, she exhaled and shook her head. "The fire cleansed the property. It's better that it stays pure." Her head turned to the house across the street—Mason and Morgan's. The front looked different. The whole house had a new coat of paint, and the front door was now a different color. It was oddly familiar yet foreign. Mason looked at the house too, eyes glistening. "Let's go see your parents. It's probably better they see me now than at Morgan's wedding."

Mason's lips flattened into a straight line, and turned the car off. "Alice…they're dead."

Time came to a halt. Much like when she watched her house collapse. "What? What do you mean your parents are dead?" It would explain Mrs. Ward's absence at the dress fitting and why Mason and Morgan never talked about them.

Mason's eyes glazed over, and his hands gripped the steering wheel so hard his knuckles turned white. "They passed away two years ago in a car accident." The grief in his voice was painful, even two years later.

Celeste sank into the seat. "You said that night at the beach party that the girls were being watched by their grandparents."

"Derrick's parents."

Mr. and Mrs. Ward loved her more than her own parents did. Mr. Ward went into her burning house to save her. His parents bought a headstone for her. Yet, they stood by while she was getting beaten within an inch of her life. She brushed away a tear. "I'm so sorry. I didn't know. Oh, my God. Mason…I…" she stuttered in shock.

He gave her the slightest of nods. "We buried them next to your headstone. Morgan said it helped her to know you were there with them."

"Where are my parents and Vicky?" she asked, never giving their final resting place a thought until just then. She never really cared either. Lucian said they were in Hell and that had been good enough for her.

"There was nothing to bury and any cremains had been mixed in with the ash of your house. Because of that, there was a community memorial service for your whole family, and then one just for you at the high school since you had just graduated months before."

"Vicky graduated from there too."

"Yeah, I guess they figured four years removed from their school was long enough to not do anything," Mason said bitterly. "It was like she was forgotten about."

"That's not possible, Vicky was popular. I was the forgotten one."

"Maybe in life, but not in death," he grumbled and started the car. The engine roared to life.

Her head whipped towards him, and a fire ignited in her belly. "What the hell is your deal with my sister? Why do you keep confusing us? You called me Victoria again."

Mason's jaw ticked, and his hand gripped the steering wheel tighter as he turned the car around. "I wasn't thinking about your sister today. My ex's name is also Victoria. She would do the same shit, and it was like I was back taking her to the loony bin for the umpteenth time."

Celeste's breath hitched in her throat as she took in his words. Her muscles froze as she stared at his profile. Nothing on his face indicated he even realized what he said. "That's incredibly rude of you to say about your ex, and from my limited knowledge of her, we are not the same."

"It was an accident," he replied, darkened eyes sliding over to her.

"Regardless, how can you say that about someone you used to love?"

"Because she wasn't the girl that I married!" Mason raised his voice and increased his speed down the long stretch of road.

Celeste was quiet for a while, silently fuming. She didn't speak until he merged onto the highway. "What happened with your ex?"

"I met her while we were in Afghanistan. She was beautiful, fun, caring, proud. We got married in between our two tours. After the second tour, she became someone I didn't recognize. She wouldn't do anything to help herself. No job, couldn't get out of bed, but also didn't sleep at all. She kept pushing for kids. I didn't want kids, and there was no way she could take care of kids when she couldn't take care of herself. She tried to off herself once," Mason said casually, like it was no big deal. "The doctors said she had PTSD and depression."

"PTSD is very common in vets," she reminded him.

He just shrugged and looked over at her, his eyes cool and neutral. "I came back fine. It's been years, and not once have I acted like she did. I got out, wrapped up my education, and got a job teaching high school history. I got up every day and did what I needed to do to earn a living. I couldn't afford to lay around like she did even if I wanted to."

"War affects everyone, whether it's physical war or the war inside your head—"

"I'm fine," he snapped immediately, cutting her off with a disgruntled look on his face. Celeste winced at the tone of his voice. "She was looking for attention."

Celeste felt heat rise up under her scars. She slid as far as she could away from him in the passenger seat, shocked. Not only at how cruelly he spoke of his former lover as a person, but also about her mental health struggles. "Mase, I suffered with depression, and I still deal with anxiety. I tried to 'off' myself twice. God, look at my arm!" Celeste pushed her right arm in his direction and turned it over, palm up. Dozens upon dozens of white lines in various sizes were clearly noticeable. "Am I looking for attention?"

Mason bit down on his lower lip as his eyes quickly raked over her arm. There were more. He knew them, and he saw them every night when he undressed her. A mix of thick and thin white lines marred her right shoulder, right hip, right thigh, and right leg. She had words etched into her hip. He had never said anything about them during sex, which surprised her. It was like they didn't exist to him. Mason gently pushed her arm out of view. "I need to focus on the road."

She breathed a huge sigh of relief when she saw the exterior of the townhouse. As soon as Mason parked the car, she was out and running to the tune of Chip's barking. The rest of the ride back home was quiet and tense. Being in a confined space with him as pissed off as he was felt like the hundreds of tense car rides with her family. She hurried inside to greet her dog, the one man who understood her.

Mason walked in slowly behind her. "Vicky—"

An exasperated scream erupted from her as she shook her head and held her hand up to stop him. Heated, instigative words were pushing to come out, to lash out and cut him where he stood. "Don't. Just don't. I don't want to look at you right now. I'm going outside with Chip, and then I am going to bed. When I come back, you better be out of my sight and nowhere near the bedroom." She said through gritted teeth and marched towards the kitchen where the door to the backyard was. Chip followed her like a shadow.

The townhouse had a small deck with a small set of stairs to get to the yard. She collapsed on the last step and wrapped her arms around her legs. Mason didn't mean what he said; he couldn't have. He was probably still mad from last night. And the trip back to their hometown stirred up the grief from his parents' death and the horrific memories of the fire. He and Vicky had been close when she died. He just needed to grieve, and he'd be okay.

An icy wind blew through her hair. The same icy wind she'd been feeling for a while. Suddenly, Chip stood at attention, facing the back fence. An unprompted, low growl had all the hairs on her arm stand up. The same type of growling that he did mere minutes before Remi broke in. Her blood ran cold. She stood up, ready to run back up the stairs, and called her dog's name sternly. The dog stood defensively and continued growling into the dark. Celeste looked across the stairwell to see the weed whacker leaning against the concrete wall. She jumped over the last step and ran for the gardening tool.

"I wouldn't do that if I were you, Pet," a cool voice said from the middle of the yard.

CHAPTER 33

Celeste whirled around to see the Devil standing in her yard, his icy blue eyes practically glowing—the only part of him she could see under the moonless sky.

"Hello, Pet," Lucian purred. His voice was cool and even, like he was greeting an old friend.

"How did you find me?" Celeste whispered. Her heart dropped into her stomach. Still growling, Chip stalked over and took his place in front of her. Always protecting his owner.

He chuckled darkly. "I have my ways."

"No, please. I just got my life back," she pleaded.

Lucian stepped into the path of the floodlight. Her breath caught in her throat. He was sharply dressed in a black sport coat and black slacks. His facial hair was neatly trimmed, and a devilish grin slowly stretched upwards. A different kind of fire started to burn in her, and for a moment, she could see why she fell for him all those years ago; he was *godlike*. "May I remind you; your life is mine." His voice was dark and menacing. "It's time to go, Pet."

"No, I am not going anywhere with you," she snapped.

Lucian blinked and then lowered his eyes as he drank her in. The icy blues she used to call home were now replaced with blood-red irises. He strutted towards her, the only thing keeping him from being on top of her was her dog. His long arm reached across the remaining space and grabbed a hold of her tattooed arm. He stretched her arm out, tattoo facing up. His other hand waved over the starry sky. The L and wings mark she had covered up all those years ago appeared in new, bright red ink, breaking up her night sky.

"You bastard! That was expensive!" Celeste yelled harshly as she tugged her arm away from him. He let her go immediately. "You might own my soul, but you don't own *me*."

"Alice?" Mason's voice called from the deck. She glared at Lucian, then cranked her head to the deck. The steps creaked under Mason's weight. He paused halfway down the steps and locked eyes on the man. "I suggest you get away from my girlfriend," Mason threatened, his voice deeper and darker than she had ever heard it.

Lucian clicked his tongue and turned his attention back to her, as if Mason was merely a gnat. "Despite the cover up, my symbol is still on your wrist. Therefore, you belong to me," he snarled.

Mason continued down the steps, taking his place beside her. His hand pulled her left wrist to him, Lucian's tattoo glowing brightly against her cover up. His body stiffened as he took in the symbol. His gaze met hers briefly, eyes widened and lips parted slightly. He finally believed her.

Lucian towered over Mason by a good four or five inches. Mason looked him over, sizing up his opponent as if in battle. "Go inside, Alice."

"That will not be happening," Lucian growled darkly, sending a chill down her entire body. She flinched and took a step backwards, creating space between her and the Devil. "It's a pity the good die young."

"She is not going anywhere with you," Mason spoke with a deathly calm. Instinctively, he grabbed her arm and pushed her behind him. Her head peeked around Mason's shoulder.

Lucian arched an eyebrow. "You really think you can stop me from taking what is mine?"

"She is not yours. She's mine."

"Is she really? You call her yours, yet when you constantly call her by her sister's name," the Devil taunted Mason.

Celeste swallowed thickly, wondering how he heard that. Mason's hands balled up into fists. "Name your price, Lucian. I need more time. I just got my life back." Her voice was weak, almost not believing her own words.

Lucian clicked his tongue. "Too late for that. This was no fault but your own." A rope of blue fire shot out from his fingertips. The fire twisted around her wrist, and with an unearthly force pulled her towards him, knocking Mason over.

She yelped into the night and dug her shoes into the ground, just like she had last night, but her flip-flops did little to slow the forceful drag. Chip jumped into action, barking and growling like mad. Teeth snapping at Lucian. Lucian waved his hand, and red fire encapsulated Chip.

"No!" she screamed and flailed against the fire rope now wrapped around her wrist like an iron chain; she was stuck. "Don't touch him!" Her dog. Her fucking dog. The first thing that made her want to keep living after Lucian left. Chip was her baby; she loved him more than her own life. A war started within her. She'd spent every day worrying if it would be her last. She purposefully kept everyone at arm's length. Only Cate had been stubborn enough to break through every wall she put up. Tears rolled down her cheeks. Once she finally decided to live her life he came for her— and took her baby. This was the exact reason she knew better than to have gotten involved with Mason and Morgan. She should have fought harder with Mason about his determination to break the deal and move her to Philadelphia. She was an idiot to think she could break it.

The barks grew fainter and fainter until there was nothing. The fire receded, and to her surprise, there was no ash, no burned dog. Chip had just vanished. She killed her parents and her dog. Chip didn't deserve that outcome. She didn't deserve life, but she couldn't stop the tears.

The rope of fire slackened and fell away from her wrist. Lucian put her behind him protectively, just like Mason did earlier. She looked towards Mason, who had a steely, calm look on his face as he assessed his options.

"Take me instead," Mason demanded. Her breath caught in her chest. Her eyes widened with awe, despite their fight. He would still fight for her.

The Devil looked her boyfriend over like a lion watching his next meal. "You would sacrifice your life for hers?"

Mason swallowed and nodded his head slowly. "You tricked her into a deal. I am willingly offering myself for her."

Lucian arched his eyebrow as his hands raised in exasperation. "Do I look like I work in customer service? I do not do exchanges or refunds." Lucian turned to her. "Ready, Pet?"

Celeste opened her mouth to respond when she saw Mason's hands around Lucian's throat, fingers tightening against the ivory flesh of the Devil's neck.

Lucian's hands wrapped around her boyfriend's hands and pulled it off with supernatural force. Tendrils of smoke rose from Mason's wrists; Lucian was burning him. The Devil twisted his arm and forced him to the ground, effectively disabling him. To his credit, Mason did not yell or scream out in pain.

Mason tucked in his toes and bent into a squat, ready to pounce at a moment's notice. He stretched out his leg and kicked the Devil. Lucian fell backward, the back of his head hit the hard concrete with a sickening thud; stunning him momentarily. Mason straightened up and hovered a foot over Lucian's chest—Taunting him. Knowing he could step and crush Lucian's chest in had a sick smile growing on Mason's face. He turned to Celeste; eyes wild with adrenaline. "Alice, *Run.* Lock the door."

Without a moment's hesitation, she charged for the stairs. Behind her, a loud cracking noise caused her to yelp. She said a quick prayer that the sound belonged to Lucian. As she reached the first step, flames shot out from the wooden boards. The wood snapped and crackled as they ate away her chance for escape. Her head snapped to the side. The Basement. The glimmer of hope vanished. The door was locked from the outside. Her only other option was to run across the yard to the fence.

An arm wrapped around her neck, putting her into a headlock. It was just enough to allow her to keep breathing but one wrong move and she would be gone. He whirled her around to see Mason lying on the concrete walkway. A large pool of blood circled his head. Her body went limp in Lucian's headlock. Her knees buckled with the weight of her shock. Tears pricked her eyes. She did this; she killed her boyfriend, killed her dog, and killed her family. She deserved her place in Hell after all.

Lucian mumbled some words, and then blue fire erupted around them in a circle, the same way he left the beach house that final time. Thick smoke filtered in between them, almost separating them. She squeezed her eyes shut, not wanting to see how she was going to end. The fire engulfed them into total darkness. Pure terror fell out of her mouth as she screamed. Lucian dropped his arm from around her neck and pulled her into a comforting hold. Her head hit his muscular chest and his cinnamon, nutmeg, and clove sent filled her nose. What used to feel like home to her now increased the terror in her body. Her world went black.

CHAPTER 34

The crackling of the fire slowly diminished into nothing.

The concrete she had been standing on turned into something stone-like. Her body was still tensed and bracing for the worst. Her breath got stuck in her throat as she waited for death's final blow.

"You can open your eyes, Pet." Lucian's voice was softer than earlier. "You're safe here," he promised. If she didn't know any better, she would have thought it was genuine.

Slowly, she opened one eye, then the other. They were standing in a regal, medieval-looking room. The walls were made of smooth obsidian stone with fire-lit torches evenly spread out. The firelight was mostly absorbed by the black walls, giving her a dim, hazy view.

A large throne sat on one end of the room. Black twisted metal formed the frame, and rubies glinted along the top of the high-backed chair. The plush seat cushions were a deep blood red. Over the dark grey mosaic tile floor, a matching red runner stretched across the room from the throne to giant, dark, wooden double doors. It was too dark for her to see the designs that were carved into the wood.

This was Hell, but it didn't feel or look like how she had been taught. The temperature in the room wasn't hot at all. It was mild, like a calm summer day with no humidity. Her skin didn't bead up in a sweat. "This is Hell?" Her voice cracked with grief of Chip and Mason's death.

"No, this is my throne room. Hell is down a few levels." He smirked. His face fell for a moment, and he made a noise of remembrance. He dug into his suit pocket and pulled out a necklace. "Take this. You'll need it to get into where we're going."

A thin black rope with two knots for adjusting held a circular pendant. The pendant, dark blue and outlined in white, was a pattern of interlocking lines, a Celtic knot. Glaring, she snatched the necklace from his hands and slid it on.

"I'm just trying to keep you safe." He murmured as he walked to the main door. Two people pushed the door open and stood guard, waiting for Lucian to walk out. The firelight shined on their thin and fragile hair and glowed against translucent skin and sunken cheeks. They were weak and would fall over if she pushed them. Celeste followed hesitantly. She skidded to a stop in the middle of the doorway. The same tattoo she had was also branded on their sickly pale wrists. Lucian owned them just as he owned her. Their hollow, sunken black eyes met hers with a snarl. For people who looked to be on the verge of death, they had an attitude about them. Fear rushed through her blood and settled in her stomach; she didn't want to look in a mirror if she looked like that now.

"Come, Pet," Lucian ordered. "It's rude to stare."

She bent her head down ashamedly and ran after him. He led her through a maze of stairwells, hallways, and corridors, coming to a stop in front of a wood and iron door. A tall man with giant dark grey feather wings stood across from it with utter disgust written all over his face. His arms were crossed over his chest, and a blade was sheathed at his belt. A cold sweat broke out on her arms. He was just waiting to attack her too.

The Devil waved his hand over the lock, and it clicked. She swallowed thickly; she would never be safe from him. He pushed the door open and motioned for her to enter. Her eyes jumped from the open door to Lucian, to the Fallen Angel, and back again, her fast-food dinner on the verge of coming back up her throat.

Lucian, seeming to sense her fear, looked to the Fallen Angel. "Give us five minutes, please, Sam." The Fallen Angel didn't look at her as he bowed his head and stalked off. Lucian turned back to her. "Sam will not hurt you. He has been ordered to not touch you in any way unless you try to run. Then he is allowed to do what he needs to subdue you. If he touches you for any other reason, let me know, and he will be dealt with." No wonder the man looked disgusted, the bastard drew the short end of the stick and is now on babysitting duty.

Celeste wet her lips and then bit them as she looked back into the room. She felt a nudge in her back, encouraging her to go in. As she entered, a light flicked on, giving view to a small room, much like a hotel room: A bed against one wall, a bathroom on the other, and a small kitchenette across from the bathroom. Two sets of clothes sat on a circular dining table between the bed and the kitchen cabinets.

"You'll be staying here for tonight. There are pajamas and a set of clothes for tomorrow. They should be in your size. If anything doesn't fit, let Sam know."

"What's going to happen after tonight?" She asked as she turned towards him. A part of her wanted to prepare herself, the other just wanted to curl up in a ball and cry.

"Grand tour tomorrow. It's late, and I'd like to get some sleep. I will come get you in the morning," he tells her cooly. His eyes grazed over her face, the icy look in his eyes melted a fraction as he studied her. When their eyes met, he blinked and turned towards the door. She could have sworn she saw his cheeks redden. "Good night, Pet," he murmured and hurried out of the room. The lock on the door twisted itself; he'd locked her in here.

Goosebumps popped up on her skin, and she ran to the door and twisted the knob. To her surprise, the door opened. She tested the knob on the other side. She sighed with relief. Only the outside was locked to keep anyone from coming in. Anyone but Lucian. The Fallen Angel, Sam, was back in his post. His red eyes watched her, his head tilted curiously as if he were studying her.

An uncomfortable chill crept down her spine. She slammed the door and locked it again as a way to ease her anxiety. Celeste pressed her back against the door. Slowly she sank to her knees and started to sob. Chip was dead,

Mason was dead, she was in Hell, and it was all her fault. For the first time in years, she wished for a blade.

Celeste woke up the next morning, curled into a ball on the cold floor. She sat up and rubbed her eyes. Her cheeks were sticky with dried tears, and she already knew her eyes were bloodshot. Slowly, she got up and walked to the dining table where the clothes sat. There was nothing extravagant about them, just blue jeans and a dark blue blouse, both in her size. Behind the clothes was a bag of toiletries. She grabbed the bag and went to the bathroom.

The bathroom was small with just the necessities. She saw to her needs and got dressed. The bag of necessities consisted of a hairbrush, a ponytail holder, toothbrush and toothpaste, and a mini bar of soap. She might burn for the rest of eternity, but at least, she would be clean. Finally, she lifted her head to see her reflection and gasped.

She looked *nothing* like those Demons she saw last night. Her eyes were indeed bloodshot, but still blue, and her cheeks were flushed and blotchy from crying all night. Her thick blonde-highlighted hair was dirty and messy but not limp and thin. Her skin was the same light olive color as always. She was still *her.* She didn't know if that was a blessing or a curse.

She threw it into a ponytail and then splashed freezing cold water on her face. There was a knock on the main door, and her muscles stiffened. She waited with bated breath for him to welcome himself in. He did not. Instead, he knocked again and called her name. Celeste wiped her face with the towel on the counter. She took a deep breath and trudged over to greet the Devil. She opened the door to see Lucian standing in the doorway with his hands in his pockets. He was dressed nicely in an unbuttoned black suit jacket and a dark grey shirt, the first few buttons left undone. Behind him, she could see the feathered curve of bones—his wings. On his mop of black curls sat a black crown with rubies along the base and on the peaks. He looked like evil incarnate. It had to be a sin to look that good.

"Good morning, Pet. I wasn't sure if you would be awake."

She eyed the crown, then rolled her eyes. "Conceited much?"

"Fit for a King." He grinned, a playful look warming the ice in his eyes. He pulled out a granola bar from his pocket. "I don't know if you are hungry or not. It's not much, but we'll get breakfast later."

As if on cue, her stomach rumbled. Celeste snatched the granola bar from him and eyed the wrapper, looking to see any evidence of tampering. They were in Hell, after all. Why not poison its prisoners? "Breakfast? Demons eat? This is Hell, you would think you would starve them."

Lucian inhaled deeply; his lips twitched upwards. "You are not a Demon. Come on." He started walking away.

She remained rooted in the doorway. "What do you mean I'm not a Demon?"

"Come on, Pet. The sooner we get the tour done, the sooner we can get breakfast," he called, not looking back. She mocked him silently as she pocketed the granola bar.

She followed him down four flights of steps. The temperature increased with every floor they went down. A sheen of sweat broke out on her face. They entered a small alcove. It was as if she had time-traveled back to the medieval era, every hallway was stone and lit by torches. The firelight did little to deter the shadows lurking about. The darkness was thick enough to brush her against her arm. The heaviness in the room had her wanting to retreat into herself. "God, it's…" she started as they entered a small alcove. Words died in her throat as they skidded to a sudden stop at a balcony. Torturous screams filled the air, almost piercing her eardrums. She moved beside him and looked down. Thank God she didn't eat that granola bar.

Below them, a sea of gaunt-looking people stood in lines; their eyes bulged out of their sockets. Some of them were screaming, some were sobbing, and others were fighting. Men and women with various shades of black and grey feathered wings struck them with a baton and pushed them back into some semblance of a line.

"Jesus," she breathed, stunned at the atrocity of it. Medieval torture had to have been better than this.

"He is not allowed here," Lucian quipped dryly.

She swallowed hard. This was her fate, and now she didn't know what was worse: this or growing old with her family still alive. "What is this place?"

Lucian watched the people down below with feigned interest. "Soul intake. Each soul gets checked in and processed. From there, we look at their transgressions and assign them one of two places: The Pit or the Eternal Tombs."

Behind the lines were desks with other feather-winged creatures typing away at their computer screens. The souls at the front of the lines begged and screamed for forgiveness. Other gaunt-looking people, like the ones that stood at the door of the throne room, pushed and shoved souls into two separate directions before disappearing through one of two doors.

"Who are they?" Celeste asked and pointed to the gaunt looking people.

"Demons. People who sold me their souls. I call them my servants."

"I thought Demons were supposed to be powerful, evil creatures." Celeste studied the Demons.

"It depends on the role assigned, but I assumed you would know that it's not what's on the outside. It's what is on the inside that counts."

"What role will I be assigned to?" Fear crept into her stomach at the thought of becoming one of them. Absolute death would be a better fate than this.

He shook his head. "Like I said, you are not a Demon."

Lucian motioned her onward and led her around the corner. A glass breezeway bridge gave a three-sixty view of the souls below. The sounds of the screaming had been drowned out with the sound of rock music, talking, and laughing. The hallway was busy with Fallen Angels either walking from one end to the other or standing to the side in groups engaged in water cooler chat. As they entered the hallway, the talking and laughing silenced immediately. Some even stopped walking and moved to the side. Each one bowed their heads to Lucian then settled their red eyes on her. Some smiled the same twisted smile that Remi had back in the spring. She moved closer to Lucian in an attempt to shield herself from them.

"As you were!" he barked at them. All the angels fixed their postures and went about their day. He rolled his eyes and looked back at her. "You are safe here."

Celeste snorted. "Bullshit."

"That's a promise. They are under strict orders not to touch you without your enthusiastic consent. They also know the consequences of breaking that rule."

She shivered at the thought of the attack. Her eyebrows furrowed at the implication of having sex with these Fallen Angels. She had a boyfriend, for God's sake. *Had.* Celeste eyed him again. "Where are you taking me?"

"To Hell." He chuckled at his joke.

Her eyes once again found the souls below her feet. She knew better then to beg for forgiveness. There was no one to blame but herself for ending up here. With each step she took, she shut her emotions down, one by one, until only the comforting numbness remained.

CHAPTER 35

The next area he brought her to was a sharp contrast to what they had just walked through: modern and plain with white walls and metal flooring. It was devoid of people and eerily quiet. The calm quiet she knew all too well. Before them was a large metal door. Lucian pressed his hand into a black pad beside it, and a blue light ran down the length of his palm; just like a science fiction movie.

A loud buzzer sounded, and the door slid open. Immediately, they were bombarded with a wall of heat and humidity. Loud, guttural, and inhuman screams sliced through the stagnant air. Sounds of pure terror shredded into her and ravaged her eardrums. The rock concerts and loud music she loved had never prepared her for this level of screaming. She covered her ears and closed her eyes tightly. Hell, he didn't even have to kill her; her bleeding eardrums would do it for him.

Shutting off her emotions be damned. she did not want to go in. She would sell whatever she had left to avoid that. Her heart hammered, and her throat closed up, making her breaths quicker and shorter. Her legs turned to shaking jelly; she did not want to be tortured for eternity. This was not worth a few good years away from her parents. She didn't understand why he did this to her. He cared about her back then, or at least he had pretended to. The hatred for Lucian that had been festering in her belly for years cemented into disgust.

She needed out. *Now.*

A large hand clasped her shoulder. "Celeste. Look at me," Lucian yelled over the din.

She shook her head violently, and her knees gave out. She hit the metal floor with a sob. It was too much; she would not survive an eternity here. "The screaming…They're in pain! Stop it. Make it stop. Make it stop! Make it stop!" Her breath became shallow and no matter how much air she gulped down, she still couldn't breathe.

Lucian knelt beside her. "Celeste, look at me," he said to her again. His finger hooked under her chin and lifted her head. Her bleary eyes met concerned red ones.

"Do not touch me!" she screamed and batted him off with her elbow. She didn't dare to remove her hands from her ears.

With a roll of his eyes, he put one arm under her knees and the other one on her back and lifted her as if she weighed nothing. She squirmed in his arms, but he had an iron-clad grip on her. She thrashed her elbows in an attempt to hit him, but he dodged her swings. He didn't let her go until they were out of the room. He set her down on shaky feet. Her hands dropped and gripped his jacket like a crutch, the echo of the screams still rattling her eardrums.

"You're out. You are okay." His hands rested on her middle to keep her from falling. The smell of nutmeg seemed to put her body into automatic relaxation. It took some time for her shortened breaths to become longer and more normalized. "We'll go home. Okay?"

Her eyes narrowed into a glare. She knew he didn't mean Earth and she didn't care to know what his definition of home was. Objects of medieval torture hanging from the walls, a bed of sharp nails to lay on, or maybe a coffin came to mind. "This is not my home!" she yelled. In a fit of rage, her hand balled into a fist, and she hit him in the chest. And then whacked him again, and again. All the while, Lucian knelt beside her and took every hit without a word. "You took my home away from me. I can never go home." Her heart ached for Mason and Chip. God have mercy on their soul.

Lucian did not say another word, instead, once she could walk again, he led her away from hell and back towards the throne room. She followed him silently, wiping the tears from her face. He turned left at a stairwell and went upwards—not downwards into Hell. At the top of what felt like endless flights of stairs, fire-lit torches were replaced with overhead electric lights. The stone turned into beige-painted walls and smooth tile floors. In mere steps, they had traveled through time.

Lucian kept walking down the hallway until they stopped at a service elevator guarded by two Demons sitting behind a desk with a computer in front of them. Both bowed their heads to Lucian and pressed a button to summon the elevator.

To her left, they had bypassed lines of other souls. These souls were nothing like what she had seen down below. Some were hollow looking like the Demons, some had wings, and some looked like her. She heard some cries of grief, and heaviness hung in the air, but it was lighter than what she had just heard.

"Ladies first," Lucian instructed when the elevator opened for them. She stepped inside. There was no button to press. Once Lucian was in, the doors shut, and the elevator started moving as if it knew where to go.

She picked dirt out of her fingernails to keep herself from trying to find ways to kill him. in a broken voice, she asked, "Where are we going?"

"Elysian," his voice as cool as the Atlantic Ocean on a July Day.

She arched her brow as her face shot up to study him. "What?" He repeated the name. "I thought we were in Hell?" The elevator doors opened revealing a large flat area. The familiar midnight sky of earth felt lighter than the sky here, or lack of sky. No moon or glittering stars— just a heavy, all-consuming, empty void. Bright, stadium-like lights illuminated the immediate area around them. But even the bright lights failed to penetrate the darkness beyond the edge of the building, the black hole swallowed it up completely. Across from them near the edge, red cable cars shuttled people in and out of that impenetrable night sky. Demons opened and shut doors, helping people get in and out. Another pushed a button and the cable car squealed to life. There was a line of passengers waiting to board like it was some kind of amusement park ride.

"We were in Hell. This is a separate part of my domain."

Her brows furrowed. There was only Heaven and Hell in the Bible. "But you're the Devil. The Devil lives in Hell."

"If you hadn't noticed, it's really fucking hot down there. Besides, I'm more of a fall or winter person myself." Lucian smirked like he was proud of a secret only he knew. "Before Elysian, Fallen Angles, Nephilim, and Demons lived in Hell. Then, a few billion years ago, Micah kicked the Witches, Vampires, and shifters out of Heaven. They had nowhere to go so I created Elysian. The Supernatural version of Heaven."

"Who's Micah? He must have had good reason to keep them out of Heaven. They had to have been bad people in life. Only good people get into Heaven."

All noise around them came to a complete halt. Every pair of eyes turned to stare at them. "Shut your mouth before someone kills you where you stand," Lucian snarled. The name was like a curse to those around them. People—the Supernatural—had narrowed their eyes at her. Some of their faces twisted in disgust, others had a murderous rage written across their faces. She took a small step towards, and behind, Lucian. "The majority of them are not evil. They don't belong in Hell with those who do. So, I created a safe haven for them. All Witches, Vampires, Nephilim, and Shifters who have parted from their physical bodies remain here."

She eyed him, then the area around them. He had to be lying to her; that would be too nice of him. She straightened her posture, crossed her arms, and shot the Beings the same nasty stare she gave to the drunken creeps at the bar. Most bared their teeth while others looked impressed that she stood her ground. "What about Zombies and Ghosts?"

"Don't be ridiculous." He rolled his eyes and deadpanned, "Zombies aren't real, and Ghosts are stuck on Earth until they make their peace." His hand gently took her elbow, leading her to an open cable car. It was square, with windows sandwiched in between red metal. The word 'Charon' was written in black ink on the sides. Underneath the name was the silhouette of a skiff. "To get to Elysian, we have to ride a cable car. It goes extremely high into the air. So, close your eyes until I tell you to open them again," Lucian instructed her and guided her into the red cable car.

The inside of the car had a U-shaped bench with plush cushions. A small light on the ceiling emitted a soft glow bright enough to see him sitting across from her. Celeste turned her head to the window in an attempt to hide her shock. She forced herself to focus on the Supernatural move about on the loading dock. "How did you remember my fear of heights? Do you remember every little detail about your servants or something?" Her glance in his direction turned into locking eyes with the Devil. His red eyes were fixed on her like he was staring into her soul. She tried to look away, but something was keeping her attention on him.

"No, I don't know everything about my Demons, nor do I care to." He spoke with a coldness designed for enemies. His face softened, "You, my Pet, are unforgettable."

Celeste chomped on the bottom of her lip to keep herself from blushing. There was no way in hell she'd give him the satisfaction of an emotional response. Out of the corner of her eye, a woman with dark gray wings similar to Lucian's stood at the edge of the roof, stretched out her wings, and was airborne. Her eyes tracked the woman's graceful and easy movements until she was absorbed by the void.

"Fallen Angels and Nephilim fly to Hell and back," he mentioned.

"Is it far?"

"It's not walkable. Elysian is a separate place. And thanks to the Witches, there is a glamour over Hell so you can't see anything." Metal screeched and the car started moving.

"How do you know where you're going?" She looked out at the pitch-black sky.

"This is the only way between Hell and Elysian, so they'll end up there eventually. Newer Fallen Angels will stay close to the cable cars."

"What is below us?" She swallowed hard as her heart started to speed up.

"A lake filled with ravenous monsters," he said sarcastically. Bile rose in her throat. "I'm kidding, mostly. Below us is the River Phlegethon, but no monsters unless any water-based shifters want to ruin someone's day."

Her gulp was audible as she looked back into the dark abyss below them. Maybe if she was lucky, the cable would snap, and she would drown. At least it would be painless. Her lungs suddenly forgot how to function, and she was gasping for air.

From beside her, there was the soft crunch of velvet fabric. "Breathe, Celeste." His broad hand splayed across her back comfortingly.

"Get away from me." Her attempt at sounding intimidating came out as a weak, squeaky order. She took in a long, shaky breath and then slowly exhaled.

Lucian immediately lifted his hand off her and slid away to give her space. She repeated the breathing for what felt like hours. She wasn't sure how long they sat in that thick silence, but Lucian motioned to the window. She flinched as her eyes tracked the movement of his hands. "We're in Elysian."

CHAPTER 36

Celeste gazed out the window and gasped. Her fear subsided for just a moment. The darkness of Hell was replaced by a cloudless blue sky and morning bright yellow sun. Below was a pentagram land mass, each point separated from the middle by a clear blue river. Two lakes surrounded the left southwest point. The northern point had a little island to the west of it with a small lake. Surrounding the pentagram were rolling green and brown hills extending beyond the horizon. From above, Elysian was beautiful. But it had to be a mirage. Hell wasn't supposed to be beautiful. Hell was supposed to be a fiery pit. As soon as they touch down, the glamour will fade and she will be in a place similar to the castle they just left. The hair on her arms stood up again, and fear crept back into her as her stomach began to flip flop.

She turned her focus on Lucian, who was looking out the same window, deep in thought. He looked a little older than he did eight years ago. The jawline under his trimmed beard was sharp enough to cut and draw blood. His soft black hair was short with gentle curls but long enough to run her fingers through it.

His foot rested on the other knee, and his elbow was propped on the seat back. His thumb rested under his chin while the index finger crossed over his lips. The small bubble of attraction she had buried down all these years started to rise to the surface. It had only grown and matured as she had gotten older and more experienced. She cussed silently at herself for allowing those feelings to lie dormant. He ruined her life and took her away from her family—not once, but twice. The first time, it was warranted, but the second time, he was just being cruel.

Mason. A wave of guilt washed over her. She belonged to Mason; she *loved* Mason. Morgan had been hinting that the two would be married within a year. Two tops. She wanted Mason. She wanted Mason's last name and Mason's children. And now he was dead at her hands, just like her parents and sister—and *Chip*. She hadn't even let herself think about her dog. Acknowledging her dead dog would send her to the point of no return.

"You don't have to force yourself to stay upright; it'll just send you into another panic attack again," he kindly reminded her.

"I'm fine," she snapped, her eyes darting to the window.

Elysian got bigger as the cable car descended. Houses grew in size, and parks grew more detailed. Air whooshed out of her lungs once the cable car stopped. With a deep breath, she pushed off the seat to her feet. Her legs immediately gave out, and her hands flew out. Her palm flattened against the window, trying to find purchase. Lucian grabbed her by her waist to steady her.

"I don't need your help," she barked and swatted at his arms. He let go of her immediately. Celeste took a deep breath and lifted one shaky foot. She took a step with no issue. She exhaled, shifting her weight onto that leg. Confident, she lifted her foot to take another step when her knee gave out, and gravity pulled her down.

Lucian grabbed under her arm, yanked her up, and threw her arm around his neck. His other hand wrapped around her waist with a careful grip. The movement was so fast she barely had time to register what had happened. "There's no shame in asking for help."

Her face scrunched up as he helped her out of the car and onto land. He moved her out of the way of incoming Supernatural from the other cable cars so Celeste could regain her land legs. It took a few minutes to get her bearings. She let go of him once she was stable. "Why did you bring me here? To torment me?"

"I have more important things to do than waste my time tormenting you." His caring demeanor vanished and that icy cold look of his was back. This is your home now." Lucian said and walked down an asphalt-like path in between rolling green hills, leaving her behind. The giant city loomed below.

Her legs were too small to keep pace with his large strides. She was practically running to keep up with him and cussing him out mentally with every foul word she knew.

He continued to speak, "As you saw, the islands are separated by the river Styx. City Central, or Unity Square, is its own island in the middle. Due to turf wars and enemy lines, the city divided its living quarters up by species. Each bridge leads to a different area. Fallen Angels and Nephilim to the north, Witches to the east, Shifters to the southeast, Vampires to the west, and Demons to the southwest."

"I thought you said that this was supposed to be like Heaven. Isn't supposed to be all Kumbaya and shit?"

Lucian chuckled, a deep sound that went straight to her head. "That was the intention, but try telling a vampire and wolf to live next door to each other, and you'll wish you would have stayed in Hell."

An uneasy feeling piled up in her stomach again as they entered the city limits. Everything she knew was beginning to feel like a lie. Her faith, Heaven and Hell, and the idea of the Devil that she was raised to believe. The Devil was supposed to be filled with hate in his heart and loved to lead people to sin. He wasn't supposed to be kind to other creatures. Or be Goddamned devastatingly beautiful.

He continued, "Unity Square is where everyone mixes for shopping, drinking, theater, and day-to-day life."

She took in the two and three-story buildings, all of various shapes and colors, new and old. Mopeds, carts, bicycles, everything but cars rode up and down the streets. Gold-tinged leaves hung from trees lining the roadways and swayed in a cool, gentle breeze. It was a much-needed respite from the extreme heat of Hell.

Every passerby bowed their head to Lucian and mumbled a quick "Your Highness." Lucian acknowledged each one by name with a smile. Even as they kept walking, there was no shaking their lingering gazes. Sweat broke out on her forehead and arm from the skin-crawling attention.

Music began to fill their ears and soon the area around him. Lucian came to a stop by a circular stage where an orchestra was playing a bright, happy tune. Dozens of Beings, all humanlike, were standing or sitting on benches, listening and watching intently. Two women with thick black hair and gray wings passed by with cups of cold beverages and shopping bags. Across the street, a bar with open windows gave views to people cheering at a TV screen while others sat on patios eating, drinking, and talking with friends.

"Unbelievable," Celeste whispered to herself. It was like she stepped into any city on Earth.

Lucian beamed proudly and took in the sight. "It's one of the things I am most proud of. Once you get settled in, I'll show you around. Everything you could ever imagine, we have here. There are café, restaurants, bars and nightclubs. The marketplace has clothes and other gifts made by residents, not to mention art studios, theaters, libraries, and museums."

"How do they pay for that?"

"They don't." He shrugged. "Everything is free. The Demons work because I require them to and the Fallen help run Hell. As for the others, why spend an eternity doing work? Although some choose to do some kind of work to keep themselves busy for all eternity. I am able to provide my people with everything they need," he said as he led her north.

"What do they do then?"

"Hobbies. Some teach classes, some farm and raise animals on the outer rim, some design fashion, and some work on science and technology. It really depends on each person."

They crossed over a dark metal bridge. The lamp posts that lined the bridge displayed a banner with black feather wings. Over the bridge, a mountain loomed in the distance. Something in her gut told her that was where they were headed. Her feet were starting to ache from all the walking. She hadn't hiked this much in years.

At the base of the mountain, a set of steep steps mocked her. She wished for death as they made the climb. She was positive she would be in shape after a few months of climbing the stairs every day. The top was blocked by a tall iron gate.

Lucian pressed a series of buttons on a keypad. "72826. You'll want to remember that," he said as the gates swung open.

"What is this?" she asked breathlessly once the gates swung closed behind them.

"The homes of the royal court. More easily known as my friends," Lucian said and walked down a sidewalk. A giant stone wall blocked her view of any houses. The two turned a corner, and the stone fence gave way.

Red and orange-tinged trees lined the street, partially blocking the view of four houses arranged in a half-moon shape. Massive houses came into view as they walked further into the court. The first house on the left side was built from grey stone, matching the medieval décor of hell. Beside it was another, smaller cottage-type house like the one she and Cate lived in at the beach. It was white with a brown sloping roof. Ivy snaked around the windows and the door. Dozens of Rose bushes and flowers hugged the outside of the house. Across the street, a white-paneled colonial-style home stood tall and elegant. At the base of the court was a large red and black Victorian mansion.

Lucian walked up the front stone path mansion with a wraparound porch. The front door was black, with a long, thin window on either side. He dug in his pocket and pulled out two keys. He outstretched one silver key on a simple key chain with a small painting on it.

"*Starry Night*," Celeste breathed and took the key from him. As a child, she had been drawn to that painting long before she discovered her love for astronomy.

He unlocked the front door with his key. "I wasn't sure how you felt about art. But I took the liberty of assuming that you would like it." The door swung inward, and he motioned for her to enter.

"Why are you giving me this?" she asked, not moving from her spot.

"This is your new home, at least for the foreseeable future."

Her eyebrows knitted together. She recalled him saying the Demons lived in the southern end of Elysian. "I'm one of your Demons now, aren't I? Shouldn't I be living with them? What about that room I was in last night?"

"The room you were in is for people who are visiting temporarily who have business with me. Yes, the Demons live in the Demon District. But you are not a prisoner here, Celeste. I have not made you a Demon. Therefore, you would be out of place and in danger. You will live here with me for the time being. If, in time, you absolutely hate rooming with me, I will set you up with your own house on the block next to Thayne's," Lucian promised and nodded his head towards the colonial house next to them.

"Why not now?" she asked. There was nothing but time now.

"You need time to adjust to your new life, and like Hades, am I going to leave you to your own devices right now."

Celeste scoffed, "I can't die, even if I wanted to. I'm stuck here in this hell hole because of you."

He flinched. "Like I said, this is not Hell. It's Elysian."

"It's hell with another name."

Ice froze around his pupils. "This place is nothing like Hell. And one day, you'll thank me for saving your life."

"You didn't save me. You damned me and I'll never forgive you." Her words sliced where she wanted them to. His hands curled into fists, and Celeste stood bracing herself. Instead, he marched inside, leaving Celeste to fume on the porch.

CHAPTER 37

Entering the house had her entering a different time period again. Black hardwood floors were covered with cream area rugs. A curved staircase to the side led to a second level. On the left of the stairs was a glassless window. Peaking from the window was the top of a sofa. From what she could see, the white walls with black trim matched the foyer's walls. Large wrought-iron chandeliers hung from the ceiling. Old, Renaissance-inspired paintings adorned the walls. The painting closest to her was of a man with wings sitting on the ground, glaring outwards. She took a few steps closer to see the man in the picture was Lucian, the conceited bastard. A few green plants were scattered around the foyer giving just enough color from the constant neutrals. In the corner, a statue of an angel stood, watching over the front door, almost blessing anyone who stepped inside. The mansion even carried his cinnamon and nutmeg scent. Despite her own feelings about Hell, the Mansion smelt like home.

Lucian leaned against the iron railing by the stairs, watching her intently. A part of her wanted to be surprised by the darkness of the foyer, but she couldn't find it in herself to be surprised. She expected the Devil's home to be this dark and brooding. "Upstairs consists of the bedrooms. I have the biggest one at the end of the hall, marked with double doors. There are three other guest rooms, one of which will be yours. You can pick whichever room you want. Each one has a walk-in closet and a private bathroom. Upstairs, if you take an immediate left, it will lead to a sitting area, but it's unused. You are more than welcome to turn it into anything you want."

"You have indoor plumbing?" Celeste blurted out without thinking. Everything here was so *old*.

Lucian chuckled. "As you saw in the bedroom last night, Elysian is up to date on common amenities. What did you expect, more stone and torches?"

Celeste's eyes narrowed, and she curled her lips into a look of disgust, not wanting to give him the satisfaction. Smirking, Lucian pushed off the rail and began his grand tour.

"This is my favorite room. I tend to spend all my free time in here during the colder months. You are welcome to spend as much time in here as you like," he instructed her as he opened the only set of double wooden doors on the first floor. Inside, numerous tall bookshelves lined the walls. Each one was stuffed with books and other trinkets. A few individual shelves seemed to have better days. In the center of the room sat a large ornate desk. Behind it, a giant window framed the desk like a halo. Sunlight streamed onto the desk, illuminating everything in a holy glow.

To the right of the giant window and three bookcases down, a bay window with red plushy cushions invited her to sit. The view of the city below was picturesque. There was not a tree in sight as far as she could see. It was a far cry from the small window at Mason's townhouse. The view alone gave her the perfect place to gaze at the heavens.

You're a long way from Heaven, the voice in her head reminded her.

Ashamed, she turned her head away from the window. On the other side of the room, a grand piano stood, ready to be played. The black bench matched the glossy color of the piano and had a velvet cushion on top. On the piano were two music sheets—one blank and one half-filled.

"I didn't know you played piano," she stated. Not that she knew much about him anyway.

"I've had an eternity to try a lot of things. The piano is my favorite instrument.

Her eyebrow arched. "Do you play other instruments?"

"Guitar and the drums."

A hint of a smile danced on her lips as she glanced over at him. "What about the fiddle?"

Lucian laughed loudly, a true, gleeful laugh. Amusement sparkled in his eyes as he gave her a flirty grin and a wink. "Only when visiting Georgia."

A laugh escaped her lips before she even realized what the sound was. Lucian's eyes sparkled at the sound. "It's incredible in here," she whispered, breathless. "I never could have imagined something like this in Hell."

Another small, proud smile stretched over his lips. "Thank you. I've spent a lot of time and money to make this room comfortable. Come on." He nodded his head in the direction of the main doors, then turned his back, walking out. Celeste followed him to another door at the end of the hall.

"What's in there?" she asked.

"My sex dungeon," Lucian said with a cool evenness, like he was naming another kitchen or a bedroom. She swallowed hard and then brought her fingers to her lips. Her fingernails picked at the skin, a habit she hadn't done in a long time. Nausea rolled into her stomach like a giant wave. *That* was why he was letting her live here. *That* is why he said he didn't make her a Demon. She was going to be his sex toy for all eternity. The two never even kissed when they were…whatever they had been. Their…relationship had been one-sided, with her giving more than he did. Had he just been biding his time all these years? Celeste whipped her head around to see Lucian smirking, his eyes dark.

"Did it spark your imagination, Pet?" he purred. Her throat went dry, and heat flooded her cheeks in embarrassment. The thought of him naked in her bed *had* flashed briefly through her head. Guilt began to gnaw at her stomach; she had a boyfriend whom she loved very much. *Had* a boyfriend, she reminded herself.

"Why would you have a sex dungeon? On second thought, don't answer that. You're Satan. Of course, you would have a sex dungeon."

Lucian chuckled darkly and turned the knob and pushed the door open. Darkened stairs showed the way. "You can go in." He said, making it seem like she had the option of not seeing what torture objects she'd be subjected to later. Celeste hesitated before slowly walking down the steps, gripping onto the railing for dear life. At the bottom of the steps, her fingers brushed against a light switch. She closed her eyes as she flicked on the light. Slowly blinking her eyes open, she took in the room.

It was a home gym.

The room was light-colored and modern looking with various machines, punching bags, and weights. One corner even had ballet bars and a stereo.

She sighed with relief and whipped her head back to him. His head tipped back, roaring with that deep familiar laughter she once loved to hear. There was nothing sinister in the laugh, just pure joy and amusement.

Celeste balled her hand into a fist, calculating her chances of living if she punched him. "Asshole!"

"You should have seen your face!" he said between laughs. "You really believed me!"

"Of course, I did!" she yelled. Her fists relaxed and open palms waved around. "I'm supposed to be one of your fucking Demons, yet I don't look as sickly as they do. And, you're letting me stay here with you. When you said you had a sex dungeon. I thought you were gonna use me as your sex doll for all eternity!" Her voice wavered as hot tears pricked at her eyes. She used so many men the last eight years. Him using her would be the atonement for her sins.

Lucian's laughter faded immediately at the words *use me*. Like the flip of a switch, his whole demeanor went dark and gruff. "I don't need an in-house whore. I'm perfectly capable of finding a willing participant to bring to my bed." He turned his back on her and went back upstairs. She shut off the lights and hurried behind him.

He strolled towards the back of the house to the sliding glass doors. Lucian slid them open and stepped out onto a screened-in section of his wrapped-around porch. Couches, rugs, a small firepit, and a television adorned this small section.

Celeste stormed past him and opened the door that separated the outside from this cozy nook. Looking straight ahead, Sunlight glinted off the rooftops of the city below. A low fence and bushes with blooming flowers kept the backyard from falling into whatever lay between the city and this hill. At one end of the yard was an Olympic-sized swimming pool. The area surrounding the pool was stone, like an extra-large patio. A hot tub sat feet from the top end of the pool. Eight black and red lounge chairs were spread evenly around the edges. On the other end of the large patio, a new-looking stainless-steel grill shined against the sun. The grill was paired with a large white table and chairs that matched the lounges. The backyard was its own kind of heaven. All it needed was sand and she would be in Heaven. She slowly walked deeper into the backyard. The stone ended, and soft, bright, green grass took its place. A soccer goal was placed at the other end of the yard with a soccer ball just waiting to be kicked in.

Something rubbery and spiky squeaked beneath her foot. She gasped and brought her knee up to her chest. Hiding in the semi-tall grass was a blue spiked dog toy. Almost immediately, two dogs emerged from the corner. One muscular, long-legged, and covered in short black fur ran in front of a familiar chocolate-colored dog.

"Oh my God, Chip!" Celeste shrieked. Fresh tears immediately streamed down her face. She watched Lucian kill him, yet here he was. More questions filled her head, but she shoved them aside. Right now, she would hug, kiss, and love her dog. Chip whipped his head in her direction and pivoted towards her, full speed ahead. Celeste dropped to her knees and let the Lab pummel her to the ground. She giggled at the onslaught of wet, slobbery licks. "What are you doing here?" she asked him as if he could respond. He barked in response. She turned her head to Lucian. "You killed him last night."

Lucian walked over to them. The other dog, Celeste now recognized as a Pit Bull, stood close to his side. "I didn't kill him. I'm not a monster. I don't kill animals. I wanted to make this transition easy for you. Not to mention, Roxie has been hounding me for a playmate." He gave her a soft smile and petted the Pit Bull's head. Roxie nuzzled into his palm.

"How?" She gently pushed Chip away so she could sit up.

Lucian knelt beside her, his hand resting on the back of the Pit Bull. "That necklace I gave you is a Celtic knot, which symbolizes eternal life, but this one is special as it possesses magic. Humans, living or dead, aren't allowed here, only the souls of the departed supernatural Beings and living animals. That necklace hides the parts of you that make you Human and alerts the others that you belong here and not in Hell. You cannot take that necklace off. Ever."

"Or what?" The question came off a bit more sarcastic than she intended. Her free hand rubbed the slightly raised surface of the knot. She sold her soul.

There was no reason for her to be alive or in this limbo he had her in.

"You'll be dead by sunrise if the Fallen Angels and demons don't try to assault you or the vampires don't drain you of your blood first."

An ice-cold shiver ran down her back. Remi flashed in her mind and her stomach knotted up. "So? I'm already dead inside anyway. You killed that part of me when I was eighteen. And to top it all off, I'm already in Hell. Where am I going to go? It sure as hell won't be Heaven." She winced at the words. She had already angered him enough today. He was probably out of patience with her, and if she pushed, she feared he would snap.

Lucian was quiet and his Adam's apple bobbed as he swallowed. Whatever anger that simmered within him did not explode. He spoke quietly and calmly, not giving in to her anger or her need to battle it out with words. "You already went through a Hell most would not come back from. You deserve this place as much as the Supernatural. But because you are Human, I needed a way to allow you access here."

Celeste was quiet. Her old life had been her own form of Hell, but hearing it come from someone else brought tears back to her eyes. Words stuck to her dry throat. The two sat in the heavy silence of that comment and let it settle among them. Lucian threw the spiky ball across the yard, and watched as the two dogs ran after it.

"Most of your stuff was brought here and put into the first bedroom on the right, but feel free to take any of the other rooms if you like one of them more," Lucian rasped as he stood up.

She stayed seated in the yard, her head spinning rapidly. God, he was infuriating. He gave her a roof over her head and the ability to live *almost* like she had. He had brought Chip here for her, for Heaven's sake. And most importantly, she was not in that screaming pit of horrors. Yet, he took her from her family, from her *life*. She wanted to scream and yell in frustration, but deep down, she couldn't, *wouldn't*.

"Thank you," she said quietly. "Although I'm still pissed at you."

Lucian smirked. The half-crooked smile flipped her stomach. "I think there's a fan club you could join."

"Hilarious."

He motioned her up. "I promised you breakfast. Then you can come back and unpack or whatever you need to do."

"What's for breakfast? Babies?" Celeste asked sarcastically.

"You won't know the difference; they taste like chicken." Lucian deadpanned as he walked towards the door. Celeste's jaw dropped. He turned around to see her shocked state and laughed. "Kidding, I told you; I'm not a monster. Now hurry up, I'm starving."

CHAPTER 38

To the side of the mansion was a driveway she hadn't noticed before. Lucian climbed into a black golf cart-type vehicle.

"Seriously?" Celeste raised an eyebrow as she eyed the cart before climbing into the passenger seat.

"It's how you'll get around. There's also a moped." Lucian pointed to a garage that stood apart from the house. He backed the cart out of the driveway and drove back towards Unity Square.

"Why do you have them? You have wings."

"Again, they're for *you*. Fallen Angels and Nephilim have wings and, therefore, fly. Witches have broomsticks.

Demons, Vampires, and Shifters without wings use carts, mopeds, bikes, skateboards… You get the idea," Lucian told her.

Celeste leaned back into the seat. "You guys really rely on stereotypes here with the Witches and brooms."

Another bright laugh escaped his lips. "The stereotype led them to try it, and they loved it. So don't rain on their parade. They'll hex you, and I know from personal experience that is not fun." Lucian drove the cart over the bridge and entered the main city. Beings of all shapes and sizes bustled about. Yet every single one managed to stop and turn their heads to see the two of them in the cart, all wanting a glimpse of the King of Hell and his new Human roommate. She kept her eyes downcast, staring intently at her jeans.

Celeste watched various people—Beings— walk up and down the sidewalk from her chair in some café's patio. Everyone looked so normal. Some walked by with earbuds or headphones, some talked on cell phones, while others were in groups laughing and joking. *All of them were enjoying themselves.*

She picked apart her cheese omelet instead of eating it. The terror of seeing Hell and the grief she felt over Mason had ruined her appetite. She wondered if one of the neighbors had found his lifeless body yet. Her stomach growled loudly, protesting her grief. Celeste bit her lip. "I don't understand how everyone is so happy here. We're in Hell."

Lucian's eyebrow shot up as if he hadn't explained it to her twenty times already. "*Elysian,* Pet. Most of the souls here were killed unjustly. They don't deserve fire and brimstone just because of who they are."

"But you're the *Devil*," she sneered, reinforcing the idea of what the Devil was.

"I am." Lucian nodded his head, taking a sip of his coffee. "Someone has to take care of the outcasts because it certainly isn't going to be my brother."

"Well, aren't you just the Patron Saint of kindness." Sarcasm dripped from her lips like acid. She set her fork down, giving up on eating.

The corner of his mouth pulled upwards. "I was a good little Angel until the Fall."

She turned her head back to the busy city street. Everyone she locked eyes with stared at her in a mix of emotions, ranging from anger to awe. She had been here all of five minutes and Beings already hated her. Great.

"Ignore them. The people here aren't used to seeing me out here without my family."

Grief and anger struck her like someone plucking a guitar string. Her face steeled into a neutral but cold position. "Your family? You have a family? People *love* you? How is that possible? Not even God loves you."

Her words struck him where she wanted them. His lips thinned, and his blue eyes grew icy. "*Yes*, I have a family. You'll meet them in due time. I think you'll get along with them very well."

"You took me from my family but expect me to get along with yours? I want nothing to do with them or you."

Lucian sat his fork down on the plate. It clinked softly against the glass. "He was not your family, Celeste. That fight was clear enough."

She leaned back, startled. How much of her and Mason's last fight did he hear? She squared her shoulders and blinked back the tears of last night. Her eyes narrowed, laser-focused on him. "You are not my family either."

"Eternity is a long time to suffer alone. And you've already suffered enough."

Celeste looked down at her plate of untouched food. She deserved every ounce of isolation. Now that she had Chip back, she could do it. "You should have made me a Demon. As you said, I've already been through Hell. I'm not worth the trouble of keeping alive."

Lucian leaned forward and whispered, his voice like cold death, "Don't get me wrong, Pet, I can still make you a Demon and make you cater to my every whim. I could have taken away your free will and made you get on your knees for me any time I wanted. I could have made you a Demon and left you to fend for yourself in the Demon District where they would eat you alive and destroy every scrap of dignity you have left. I'm sure you remember the feelings of worthlessness from your youth." Lucian stood up abruptly. "Come." Celeste shivered but remained seated and glared at him.

"Let's go see what their life is like and then maybe you'll thank me."

CHAPTER 39

The golf cart sped down the street faster than she could ever imagine. The flags on the light poles along the bridge bore the same symbol that was on her wrist. The Demon District, he called it, looked abandoned. The further in he drove, the more decrepit it became. Windows were either falling out or boarded up, and doors were hanging on by a hinge or rested against the front of houses. The ground was littered with dirt and garbage.

A woman's bloodcurdling scream pierced the air. For a moment, she thought she was back in Hell. Lucian slammed on the brakes and threw his arm sideways to keep her from falling out. The cart screeched in protest as it slowed to a stop. Just ahead of them, a male Demon disappeared around the corner.

"Stay here," He ordered through his teeth as he stepped out of the cart. His wings furled out to full length. Celeste knew they were large but seeing the wings expand well past both ends of the golf cart had her shrinking in her seat. Lucian took to the sky like a hawk. He circled the area and hunted his prey. Watching him fly was like watching a Ballerina in action. His wings flapped to a beat only they heard. His body moved through the air with an angelic grace.

The terror in the woman's screams snapped her attention back to ground level. Celeste jumped out of the Cart and ran to the noise. As she turned the street corner, the male Demon had one arm around a sickly pale young woman's neck, locking her in place. She was kicking and screaming but getting nowhere. The Demon's other hand covered her mouth and nose with a dirty white cloth. Her red eyes closed, and her body instantly went limp in his arms.

The asphalt shook and cracked as Lucian landed. The Demon, finally realizing he wasn't alone, dropped the woman and let her fall in a heap on the ground. Lucian's stretched-out wings made him look taller, and the red eyes screamed *Do not fuck with me*. The demon's face dropped, and the fear that had filled the woman transferred to him. Lucian rose slowly to his full height. A dark snarl echoed through the street. The vile Demon took off in the other direction. Lucian pulled out his phone and barked an order to someone as he knelt by the woman.

Almost immediately, three Fallen Angels flew in over their head, plucked the Demon off the ground like birds collecting their prey, and took off back into the air. The

Demon's legs dangled in the air, screaming louder than the woman as he was carried off into the horizon.

Celeste paced outside of Elysian Coven Injury Clinic. She didn't even see the point of Elysian even having a hospital since everyone in here was dead, but Lucian said It mostly tended to Fallen Angels injured on the job and Demons like the woman. He also claimed it included a vet clinic for legitimate pets. She had barely stopped the moving car before Lucian had picked up the woman and hurried inside the building. She couldn't bring herself to follow them in. Hell, she hadn't stepped into a doctor's office since she had worked her shift at her parent's practice the Friday before their death. So, she stayed out here and paced from one end of the sidewalk to the other.

When he emerged from the building, his face was solemn. Celeste stopped mid-pace and ran over to him. "Will she be okay?" Celeste croaked out.

Lucian nodded his head and led her to a bench. "Yes. Demons are already dead, but that doesn't stop them from getting severely hurt. What happened back there is a regular occurrence in the Demon District. Female Demons get drugged, raped, and brutalized every day. The males go to battle with each other constantly."

Celeste stared at a crack in the concrete. The Demon District felt like a fate worse than Hell. "Then do something about it. You said it yourself; Elysian is supposed to be a Heaven for the Supernatural. It's supposed to be safe."

His eyes avoided her gaze, keeping them on the hospital doors. Beings in scrubs walked in and out of the automatic doors. "The ones that act out are the ones who were already vile to begin with. Not everyone who sold their soul to me are like you. The ones who made deals with less evil intentions, like yourself, are the ones who are hurt and attacked. I have Fallen patrolling the area, but they can't be everywhere at once. It's the only place crime runs rampant here. The Demons aren't allowed anywhere but here or at their job location, where they are heavily watched. The rest of Elysian is safe. That is why I can't have you living there."

Celeste fiddled with the necklace, the pendant resting on her bottom lip. She wasn't that good. If she had been a good person, Mason would be alive, and Cate wouldn't have run away. "Maybe it's what I deserve."

"No," he whispered breathlessly and placed a gentle hand on her knee. She turned her head to see his blue eyes gazing at her softly. "You are good, Celeste. Better than any Human or Angel I know."

Drained, Celeste went straight upstairs to the first room on the right as he instructed. The events of the day had her overwhelmed and full of grief. She opened the door and gasped. The walls were painted a sage green, her favorite color. Two windows on either side of the king-sized bed gave a beautiful view of the backyard and the rest of Elysian. The bed was already made with the constellation comforter she had left at the beach house. Tucked into the comforter was a plush blue crab. A sad laugh escaped her lips as she walked over and plucked it from the bed. Days after Cate moved into the cottage, Celeste invited her to the boardwalk with a few other waitresses. The two had bonded over whack-a-mole and blew through Celeste's just-earned tip money to win two giant crabs. She hugged it, wishing it was her best friend. "I fucked up, Cate." She whispered.

She sunk into the bed and scanned the room. Across one wall and to the side of the bed, a book on a small, relatively empty bookshelf caught her eye. She immediately recognized the pink sparkles over a green cover—it was her Bible. Her lips cracked into a smile, and the laugh that followed sounded foreign. Oh, the irony of it. She was in Hell, and her Bible sat on the shelf, mocking her, reminding her of what she'd lost. Lucian had to have put it there to spite her. There was no saving her now. She was too far gone to be redeemed.

Boxes of her stuff were spread out in the room with writing on them. To the right of the room were two doors. One was open, revealing a large bathroom. The clothing boxes were next to the other, most likely a closet, and her wall décor was in a box against the opposite wall. A flat-screen television was attached to the wall across from her bed. Much to her dismay, it felt a little like home. Lucian infuriated her. He did nice things for her yet took her away from the only thing that mattered.

Celeste fell back on the bed. Above her, glow-in-the-dark stars were arranged in various constellations. Her sister had glow-in-the-dark stars on her ceiling and glow-in-the-dark butterflies on her wall as a child. Celeste did not, of course, but she had wanted them desperately. It had been a passing conversation between her and Lucian eight years ago; she didn't know what to make of the gesture.

The cracked laughter turned into sobs. She missed Mason, Morgan, and the girls. She missed her life on Earth. She missed Cate and the beach; she'd never see the beach again, and the only one she had to blame was herself.

Later that night, she wandered to the backyard. The cool late summer night invited her to relax in one of the lounge chairs by the pool. Her head tilted to the clear, starry sky. Unlike Mason's townhouse—her townhouse—there were no trees blocking her view. Moonlight shined brightly on the patio. It was the clear, calm kind of night where planets could be spotted with a little help. Her heartstrings pulled with grief for her lost telescope.

"Penny for your thoughts?" Lucian's honeyed voice halted her imaginary travel through the cosmos and brought her back down to Hell. He was dressed more casually now in ripped blue jeans and a black shirt featuring a rock band they used to bond over. *This* was the Lucian she remembered. The suit and tie *royal* from earlier was just as foreign to her as the reality of him being the Devil. In his hands was a mug of tea and a saucer. She muttered a thank you and took it. From the base of the saucer, a copper coin shined up at her. The tag on the string declared not only that it was pomegranate tea but her favorite brand. Bastard.

With a huff, Celeste set the saucer and the mug on a small end table beside her. She picked up the penny and toyed with it, rubbing the cool copper between her fingers. It had been ages since she thought about their little game. She had made it a point to forget everything that made her fall in love with him eight years ago.

Uninvited, Lucian made him comfortable in the seat next to hers, "Still waiting for that thought, Pet," he said as he took a sip from a glass of whiskey he had brought out for himself.

Celeste shrugged, turning her attention back to the sky with a small smile. "The night sky is almost as beautiful here as it is on Earth."

His soft voice was full of nostalgia, "You used to spend almost every night out on the beach, lying on a towel and watching the night sky." He paused, almost like he was reminiscing the worst days of her life, "Remember the night we met? You had pointed out a couple of constellations that we could see despite all the lights from the bar."

A ghost of a smile danced at her lips. That life-altering night was burned into her brain. She couldn't forget it even if she wanted to. It was the beginning of her end. "After you stole my soul, astronomy became more than just exploring space; it was the only time I'd ever see Heaven."

Lucian stared into the night sky. She took his silence as regret. "Heaven isn't all it's cracked up to be."

"Says the Angel who got kicked out," she snapped a bit too harshly. From her peripheral, Lucian recoiled, almost like the statement hurt him. Yet, from what she knew, the Devil had been all too happy to leave Heaven.

He scoffed, then fell into a moment of silence "I noticed your telescope wasn't with your things." Her head snapped towards him.

"You went through my things?" She didn't have her telescope when he last saw her.

"The Beings I ordered to pack your things mentioned extra telescope tools but no telescope."

Her eyes shifted down to her hands, to the penny still tightly pressed between her fingers. It had been seventy-two hours since she lost it, but it felt like an eternity. "It got stolen."

"I can get you a telescope if you want," he offered.

The sincerity in his voice poked and scratched her nerves. Her face turned sour. "I don't need anything from you."

Lucian turned his head, his eyes glowing like stars in the moonlight. "We were friends at one time, Pet. And, if memory serves me correctly, you loved me." His voice was light, and she could not tell if he was teasing her or not.

"That was a different life. And you never said you loved me back. It was just a one-sided, silly little schoolgirl crush." *Alice* fell in love with him. *Celeste* hated him with every ounce of her being. Now, she wasn't sure who she was. She spent the last 8 years as confident but soulless Celeste. Over the last few weeks, with Mason's help, shy and religious Alice had begun to resurface. "You painted the room, put those stars on the ceiling, and brought my stuff here. You think you know me, but you don't."

His eyes scanned her face. Suddenly, she felt naked without her heavy make-up and piercings. "Do you even know who you are?"

The million-dollar question. Mason was confident that she was Alice Delco, the lost girl from his past and his sister's best friend. Celeste was Lucian's; he came up with the name and gave her a new life. Alice was an abused girl whose dreams were bigger than the world. Celeste was the hardened woman who let her dreams crash and burn around her like a meteor strike. There was no denying that the last eight years were the happiest she'd ever had. The abuse she faced day in and day out had died alongside her family, and she hadn't found solace in a razor blade in seven years. Her skin twitched at the memory.

She loved the Wards and Cate. She loved the life she'd carved out in Ocean City. She loved Alice's dream of working for NASA. For Celeste to have achieved Alice's dream of going to college and working for NASA would have been the best way to use her 'new life' as Lucian had called it. But that's all it would have been—a dream.

Realistically, Alice would have gone to medical school, become a doctor, and worked the rest of her life at the family practice. She would have been forced to marry some doctor her parents picked and settled down with two kids and a white picket fence. A life she neither wanted nor would have chosen for herself. If she had become what they wanted her to be, would the abuse have stopped, or would Alice's husband have picked up where her family left off? Would she have continued to find comfort in the blade?

Finally, she spoke, her voice a deadly calm. "Doesn't matter anymore."

CHAPTER 40

D*o you know who you are?* The question haunted her day in and day out. Celeste had no desire to leave her room after that night. If she saw Lucian, she'd have to give him an answer. Instead, her days and nights were spent in a blurry cycle of sleeping, waking up in a cold sweat, and crying. Her nightmares rotated between the fire, Mason lying on the walkway in a pool of blood, and seeing that female Demon get drugged. She knew in her heart that she should have been in that woman's place, but for some Godforsaken reason, she was not. Maybe God was still watching out for her even in this hellhole.

When sleep evaded her, and she couldn't get the images out of her head, but there were no tears of grief left to cry, she watched the television that hung on the wall. To her surprise, the television was hooked up to the same streaming services she had on Earth.

Lucian, to no avail, tried to get her to talk. Like clockwork, at every meal time he would knock on her door and call her name. He took her silence as an answer, but not before telling her he left food at her door. Most of the time, the food went untouched.

Once the cheesy romantic dramas she and Cate used to watch failed to be the distraction they had once been, she decided to unpack the boxes in the room finally. Since she would be stuck here forever, she might as well make herself at home. She'd made her peace with this fate a long time ago, but that was before Mason put hope back into her heart.

"Pet," Lucian purred from the other side of the door one afternoon as she put her clothes away in the closet.

She groaned; her fingers curled into claws. She hated that damned nickname. It was just another reminder that he owned her. "Fuck off."

"We're having dinner tonight with my family. I'm cooking."

The claws air scratched at the door and she made a face. Like Hell if she'd break bread with his *family*. They were probably nothing but murderers, rapists, and thieves. "I'll pass."

There was an impatient huff from the other side of the door. "This is not a prison and your room is not a cell. You can be mad at me all you want but stop punishing yourself and eat for once." Celeste stared at the door, waiting for him to open it. He'd done it before, but only to let Chip or Roxie in when they waited outside. Otherwise, he left her alone in solitary confinement. But she was trapped in Hell. This *was* her prison, isolating herself and denying herself food *was* her sentence. She had to atone for her sins somehow.

Lucian took her silence as an answer and spoke in a harsher voice, one he used to make her follow orders, "You can either come down at dinner time civilly, or I will carry you down there and tie you to a chair. Your choice," he threatened; his voice cold as ice. She silently mocked him and kept decorating. There was no way in hell she would associate with Beings the Devil cared about.

Laughter and heavy rock beats echoed through the house to the point even turning up the volume on her television did little to drown it out. That damned dinner was going to happen whether she wanted to join or not. Giving up, she padded downstairs and immediately inhaled the scent of ham and mashed potatoes. Joyful and pleasant laughter greeted her and crawled under her skin. This was *Hell*, for God's sake, and they were *laughing*. Then again, they all probably got their kicks swapping murder stories. Celeste inhaled, stepped into the square archway, and looked into the massive kitchen.

The floor was white tile paired with espresso-brown tiled walls. All the appliances were stainless steel and looked to be top-of-the-line. The pots and pans sitting on the stove looked a little worn and dented from one too many crashes on the floor. A dark green tea kettle sat to the side where tea boxes were stacked up. On the far end of the counter was a coffee machine.

In the back of the room was a large, dark cherry table already set with dishes and utensils. Next to that was a small bookshelf of cookbooks. A speaker sat on the bookshelf thumping with the bass of the song.

A large, dark cherry kitchen island sat in the middle of the kitchen with high bar stool chairs around one side. Two men sat at the island, laughing at a joke she didn't hear. Lucian stood in front of the stove; lip curled in concentration as he scooped up a spoonful of red glaze. A tan dish towel was thrown haphazardly over one of his wings like it had been tossed there by one of the others.

A deep throat clearing had Lucian snapping his head over to the doorway. His blue eyes lit up, just like they used to when he saw her. His smile was just as bright. "Celeste! Hope you're hungry. Do you still like ham and mashed potatoes?" Lucian asked. Celeste nodded, shocked that he remembered her favorite meal. On the counter beside him sat steaming bowls of green beans, sauerkraut, and her absolute favorite—macaroni and cheese.

"I figured you'd have *servants* cook for you," she sneered.

"Used to," One of the men said. The one with coppery hair turned towards her and gave her a friendly smile. The first truly friendly face she had seen here. His face fell for a brief moment as if he recognized her. He looked to be Lucian's age, with wide chocolate-brown eyes and wavy hair that reminded her of AJ. An ache grew in her heart. She could only pray that AJ would forgive her for abandoning her and her mother again. Despite the similarity, nothing about him seemed familiar. Behind him were large, black, feathery wings with the tips tinged white. "Eight years ago, he decided he liked cooking. He cooks all the time when we are together. We always have a family dinner at least once a month. It had been on hold until you got used to life here." He took a sip of clear liquid from his glass.

Celeste's eyes shifted back to Lucian. He put the spoon back in the glaze jar casually, like he wasn't paying attention to the conversation. Lucian had been a terrible cook when they met. The nights she was left alone at home, she taught him how to make her favorite meals. He had caught on quickly and became a pro at her favorite dishes. Had that been another thing he lied about? How could a man be billions of years old and not know how to cook?

"You could introduce yourself, idiot." Lucian lightly scolded the man. There was no ill will in the name-calling, just like it was between her and Cate. The man gave her a boyish smile as he got up from the chair and walked over to Celeste. Sitting down, he looked like any other lanky twenty-something. On his feet, he seemed to be Mason's height and extremely toned. His large wings splayed out and pulled back in loosely, making him look even more menacing. His young and ornery face was a juxtaposition to the rest of his body. Celeste took a giant step back into the hallway to keep distance between them.

"I'm Thayne. I don't bite, I promise. Unless you're into that." He winked at her, causing her cheeks to flush. A soft growl echoed through the room. Thayne turned his head to Lucian, eyes wide and eyebrow arched. A silent conversation passed between the other. A fierce, protective look simmered in Lucian's eyes. The look of a man staking his claim. Pig.

When Thayne turned his attention back to her, his smile seemed even brighter than before. He held his hand out for hers. Hesitantly, she reached out to take his hand. Before she could blink, he grabbed her and pulled her into a hug. Her body locked up and went rigid. Her face was smashed against his chest and there was no choice but to inhale a comforting pine and vanilla scent. Nothing about him immediately set off alarm bells. Not that her internal alarm system worked anyway.

"For the love of all things unholy, Thayne, let her go before she suffocates to death. You're off the clock for Hades' sake." a voice she barely recognized spoke with a hint of amusement. Thayne let her go with a soft apology and a sheepish smile. Behind him, the second man sat watching—studying her with a predatory gaze. He was slightly older than both Thayne and Lucian yet oddly familiar. His shiny black hair stopped just below his ears. His red, rounded eyes bore into hers. His wings were full of pitch-black feathers like Lucian's.

A lightbulb went off. "Don? What are you doing here?" she gasped. *England, my ass.*

He opened his mouth the speak just as the front door opened.

"Sorry, Bea blew up her fucking cauldron *again*. A hundred years and-" A female voice cut off abruptly. The voice was as familiar to her as her dog's barks. Celeste's heart dropped into her stomach. "Cate?"

Cate stopped frozen in the doorway, jacket half off, looking like a deer caught in headlights. The woman hadn't been expecting her to be here. The two locked eyes, and Cate gave her a weak smile. Cate's eyes glazed over with tears. "Hey, Celly." She breathed.

Celeste's eyebrows furrowed and her throat went dry. She couldn't fathom why they would be here. Cate a *living* Witch. Yes, she admitted that she knew Fallen Angels. She just didn't specify which ones. All this time, she worried about her own deal and Cate had her own deal with him.

Anger flooded her bloodstream; Lucian had his hooks in everyone.

"What did you do?" Celeste gritted through her teeth as her eyes narrowed at Lucian, arms crossed over her chest. He could have her life but not Cate's. Cate was a better person than she would ever be.

Lucian hesitated before speaking, choosing his words carefully. "Don is one of my best friends. He is also the Angel in charge of Hell."

"Satan is supposed to rule Hell."

"I delegate." He nods his head. "Cate is the Queen of all Witches and leader of the Elysian Coven. She is what AJ and Breanna are to you." Lucian reintroduced them. His tone was level but filled with caution like he was trying to carefully detonate a bomb.

Celeste swallowed hard and blinked back tears. Cate had been her best friend in her new life. She had trusted Cate with her life. For the last eight years, she played Celeste like a fiddle. Lucian had sent Cate to be her friend to keep tabs on her. *She lied.* Celeste crossed her arms, rage filling her core. "He's your *family* and you didn't think to say anything? Especially after I told you what he did to me?" Celeste asked, her voice went up an octave with each word.

"It's complicated, Celly," Cate said with guilt written all over her face.

"Did you know what he did to me before we met?"

"We can discuss this later. I'm starving, let's eat. Are you hungry?" Cate walked into the kitchen shoving off the last sleeve of her jacket and draping it around a chair. Cate embraced Don and exchanged a quick, sweet kiss.

Pure fiery rage broke through the surface. The last time this insurmountable rage broke free was eight years ago, and it was directed at Lucian. Her hand curled into a tight fist like she had when she attempted to punch Lucian. Even she knew better than to punch a Witch.

"No, we will discuss this *now*." Each syllable was more pronounced than the one before.

Don shifted in his seat as his wings flared out, one curling around Cate like he was shielding her from the incoming bomb blast. Lucian, in turn, started towards Celeste. The wing closest to her stretched out to cover her. She raised her hand to stop him, and to her surprise, he stopped a few feet away, and the black wing pulled back. He'd let her fight her own battle. Thayne took a defensive position in the middle; his wings stretched out as if to put a physical barrier between the four like he was playing referee.

Cate shook Don's wing off, letting it slide off her shoulder. "Yes, I knew. But Celle—"

Celeste snarled. Eight years. *Eight years* she struggled with the thoughts of him coming back, and yet, he was watching her the whole time. "So, you were his spy? He ordered you to spy on me, right? You came back here to give him a report about me, didn't you? Is this where you went when you left without a word?"

Cate's eyes glazed over. The two girls have had their squabbles but they were nothing like this.

"Cate went up to Earth of her own accord. I did not send her to you," Lucian defended her friend.

"Fuck off, Lucian," she spat at the Devil.

Cate steeled herself and spoke with a cool, steady voice, "I was not a spy for him. He told us about you. He was worried about you, with your depression and self-harm. From what he told us about your personality, I thought we'd get along, so I wanted to meet you and be friends. I don't have a lot of girl friends."

"Because you were too busy fucking them," Celeste shot back. Don growled defensively as his red eyes narrowed in on her. His chair screeched against the floor and tipped over as he shot up. He charged towards her, snarling. He looked every bit of a Demon from Hell. A slight gasp escaped her, standing before her now was her father, ready to strike. Her muscles tensed and locked her into place.

Lucian matched Don by charging towards him, wings flaring into a straight line. Thayne pulled both girls behind him. White tipped wings covered both of them to keep them from getting hurt in the crossfire. Plates clattered to the floor and glasses shattered. Celeste flinched at the noise and looked away, catching the hurt in her friend's eyes. Good.

Cate steeled her face to make it seem like the comment rolled off her back, but it didn't. Celeste knew her words hit their mark. "You are my friend, just as Luce is."

Grunting came from the other side of the feathered wall. Clipped, unintelligible words were muffled just enough to keep the girls from hearing it. The ticking timebomb that sat like heavy weight in her heart finally exploded.

"Best friends don't lie to each other! They don't hide the fact they're a fucking Witch and only reveal it after they get attacked by *their* kind." Celeste sneered towards the Fallen Angels. "You tricked me from the start. You lied to me to get me to trust you. You took advantage of my vulnerabilities and became someone I trusted. *You* took me away from my family. Mason is *dead!* Yes, Lucian killed him, but his blood is on your fucking hands. He would still be alive had it not been for you! Fuck you. You are dead to me."

Celeste knew she hit the jugular, but she no longer cared. Cate's turquoise eyes started to glow. She spoke with an even, icy tone, "You are the one who went crawling to him. Not me."

Lucian controlled every aspect of Celeste's life; her friends, her house, her past and future, and her soul. She despised him just as much as she hated Cate. Without another word, she turned on her heel and stormed out of the kitchen.

The anger reared its ugly head again as she slammed the door with the same force her father would use. Her shoulders shook as she heaved tearless sobs and sank to the floor. Every damn time she began to feel loved, happy, and wanted, she was given another reason that proved to her she was always meant to be alone.

You are worthless. Not even God could love you.

Every time this happened, her mind brought her right back towards the dark loneliness that had been festering in her soul for years. It was a deep dark abyss that never truly went away. Only the mass of it changed throughout the years.

Her eyes locked on the bathroom that had been fully stocked upon her arrival. Robotically, she got up and depressed the door lock quietly. She turned on the speaker and cranked the heavy music up loud and greeted an old friend.

CHAPTER 41

Licks of blue hellfire singed Lucian's palm. He had one arm pressed tightly to Don's throat while the other covered his mouth to keep the fire inside Don's mouth. Let the man burn for all he cared. Lucian's teeth were barred, ready to tear him apart. The Angel of Hell had intimidated Celeste, had made an attempt to hurt her. After he explicitly told Don to play nice. The absolute terror in her eyes had sent him into a rage.

"Lucian, enough." A distant voice echoed through the ringing in his ears. Large arms wrapped tightly around his middle and dragged him away from the Angel of Death. Thayne brought him across the kitchen to where Celeste had just stood. Her vanilla scent tinged with sea breeze still lingered in the air. The fire burning in his soul fizzled out and the dark tunnel surrounding his vision faded away immediately.

Across the room, Don coughed, gasping for air. Cate held a glass of water to his ashen lips and forced him to drink to kill the fire in his throat. Tendrils of smoke slipped from his mouth. Don leaned against the counter, heaving while Cate rubbed his back.

"Did you really kill Mason?" Cate croaked. Although her dislike of Mason had been obvious from the start. Celeste's words seemed to have cut her like a knife.

"If he was dead, he would be in Hell already, and it's been weeks." Lucian sighed and walked back to the island. He bent down and picked up the towel that fell from his wing and balled it up. He threw it angrily at the cabinet door, hitting it with a soft *thunk*. The itch to punch something gnawed at him. "I told you eight years ago that interfering with Celeste's life was a bad idea, and you went up there anyway."

The young Witch spun around to face him; turquoise eyes glowing. "Do *not* blame me for this. I am not the one who dragged her here."

"You asked me to! Once you told me that you were worried Mason would kill her, I put a detail on her, and one of the Demons said he brought her back to Elizabethtown; he saw Mason yank her out of the car. They spoke with a Pastor; He mentioned the name Micah. It was now or never." Although there were plenty of men named Micah, he wasn't going to take the chance that it wasn't his pain-in-the-ass adversary. He would rather face his Father's true wrath than have Celeste come into contact with Micah.

"We told you not to get involved in the life of a stupid, little Human," Don reminded him.

"Cate got more involved in her life than I did."

"Cate wouldn't have gone up there if *you* hadn't gotten attached. All because of your Goddamned savior complex. She's just a worthless Human. She's not worth the time of day."

A demonic growl rumbled through the kitchen as fire roared to life out of his fingertips. Lucian charged at his friend, throwing him up against the refrigerator. The doors caved inwards from the force. Photos, magnets, and pictures clattered to the ground by their feet. His hands balled Don's shirt up by his throat and pressed his fist into his throat, cutting off some air. Celeste was not a worthless Human. Misguided, maybe. Troubled, definitely. But not *worthless*.

Don's fist connected to Lucian's nose with a sickening crunch. White-hot pain radiated from the point of impact. Lucian let go of the Fallen Angel and put a hand to his nose. Don rubbed his throat and narrowed his wild, blood red eyes onto Lucian. He stepped forward to the King of Hell, grabbed his head, and slammed it into the counter. Pain seared through Lucian's head, and his vision dimmed.

"ENOUGH." Thayne's voice was deep and loud enough to rattle what was left of the silverware on the dining table. The Witch pulled Don away to the other side of the kitchen, whispering something to him, her hands pressed to his chest.

"I specifically warned Cate how Celeste gets when people lie to her. How do you think I ended up in the position I'm in? I should have never let it get that far. I should have never allowed you to go up to Earth."

"You don't have a say in the matter," Cate argued.

"Yes, I do, as your King. And most importantly, I promised your mother I'd take care of you. I don't break my promises."

"That was over three hundred years ago! Celeste is my best friend! You don't know what it's like not having one person you can talk to about anything and everything. You three have always had each other. I see your sister once in a blue moon, and I have Don on a good day when we don't want to rip each other's throats out, but even then, I can't talk about certain things with him. I can't tell you and Thayne everything because you've known me since I was an infant and are friends with my mother. Celeste would go to bat for me like you three would for each other."

Deep down, he knew the friendship was good for both of the girls. Cate did more for Celeste than he ever could. "I'm sorry," Lucian apologized with a heavy sigh. "Celeste hasn't forgiven me yet, but maybe she will forgive you. She just needs more time to adjust."

"Good thing she has an eternity," Thayne quipped, earning a glare from the other three. He grinned cheekily, unfazed.

"If you two are done with your pissing contest, I would like to go home." Cate glanced between the men. Both of them nodded once. Cate helped herself to an unbroken plate of food and left with it. Don followed suit quietly.

Thayne picked up a shattered plate off the floor. "That was fun," he said as he tossed it and any other shards he could pick up. The dogs finally felt safe enough to run in and eat what scraps they could get away with.

"Don't you have somewhere else to be?" Lucian snapped as he forced his nose back into place. He shuddered from the pain. Thayne was his oldest friend and used it to be a pain in his ass. Don had followed Lucian when he left Heaven, had been his general in the rebellion, and they grew to be good friends. Lucian allocated parts of his job to even the playing field between the three men, but at the end of the day, Don was his subordinate.

Thayne smirked. "Nope," emphasizing the 'p' before digging into what remained of the mashed potatoes. "I got all night."

Lucian's eyes rolled to the back of his head as he walked over to the dented refrigerator. He wouldn't dare tell Thayne, but he was glad for the company. Despite his new house guest, the house had felt lonelier than ever. It was like the life had been leached from every room of the house. Even Roxie chose to spend time with the Human and not him, leaving him completely alone.

He pulled an ice pack from the freezer and a shaken beer from the dented-in door. All the items that had been on the door shelves had either fallen onto other shelves or onto the floor with a loud crash when the door opened. He picked everything back up, tossing them back onto the shelves, and shut it. At least it still worked. He looked at the nearly empty kitchen table.

Tonight was the first time he'd seen Celeste since the day he brought her here. He thought having her see others and meet his friends might help her be more open to coming out of her room. This disastrous night set back any hope of progress of getting her to see that Elysian wasn't a bad place after all, that she could be just as happy here as she was on Earth.

CHAPTER 42

The next morning, Celeste left her room later than normal with the hope that Lucian would have already left for the day doing Devil knows what. Last night's blood loss left her with a throbbing headache. Much to her chagrin, freshly brewed coffee greeted her at the doorway of the kitchen. Lucian was perched at the island with a mug next to his black laptop. He was sharply dressed in navy blue button-down and grey slacks. His muscles nearly straining the seams of his sleeves. Celeste internally cursed at herself when she considered the thought of placing a hand on the bulging biceps. God, Mason dressed similarly for school, but he couldn't pull it off as well as the Devil did. Chip and Roxie were curled up by the feet of the stool. Whatever mess Lucian and Don made had been cleaned; it was like that fight never happened.

Lucian saw her from the corner of his eye. His jaw dropped slightly. "The Pit is going to freeze over. What have I done to deserve your presence today?" She raised her middle finger at him in response as she walked to the coffee pot. Sitting next to it was a chipped sage green mug. Had he been setting a mug out for her every morning since she got here?

She opened the cabinets near the coffee pot. Sleek black and red mugs lined the shelf as well as a couple of different colors. They looked to have been gifted to him. But none of them were green. A quick flash of irritation flashed through her. The chipped rim made it feel less like a coincidence. As she turned the mug over, a pink-colored 'C' initial caught her eye. This was *her* sage green mug that she had left at the beach house.

Celeste whirled around to face the Devil. "How did you get this?"

He ignored her at first, finishing his typing, and finally looked up at her. The side of his nose was black and blue. A small, satisfied smile appeared on her face. She would have to thank whoever ruined that perfectly beautiful face of his. "I had Cate collect your belongings from the beach house and Mason's so you would feel more at home here. That's how I knew about your missing telescope. And if you cared, it's why Chip has all his toys."

Celeste grimaced and stared back down at the mug. Cate had packed her stuff up and brought it here. She did that out of kindness, and in return, Celeste yelled at her. Guilt swam in her stomach, suppressing her ability to eat breakfast. Her raw and red arm twitched and burned underneath her long-sleeved shirt.

You ungrateful bitch.

You don't deserve kindness.

She shoved the guilt into a deep corner of her gut. "This isn't my home."

Lucian exhaled loudly, nose flaring as he ran a hand through his hair. "This is your home now. Cate brought your things here because you are her best friend. Although you could have fooled us with how last night went." His voice dripped with obvious disappointment.

Celeste turned back to face the counter, suddenly feeling small. He was belittling her, just like her father did; the same tone and everything. She held her breath, waiting for the shock of his hands pulling her to turn around. Waiting for his yelling face mere inches from hers. But it didn't come. She turned her head slightly to see him still at the island, softly clacking away at the keyboard.

Silently, she walked to the severely dented fridge door. Her eyebrow arched; seriously, she'd have to thank whoever kicked Lucian's ass. She grabbed the bottle of creamer from inside and shut the door, her eyes catching various photos haphazardly placed about. The photos spanned decades, centuries even. Old children's artwork on yellowed paper with names and dates from centuries past mixed with newer ones. Pictures of Lucian with his friends from various decades. Her eyes trailed over Lucian, Thayne, and Don with long poofy hair, looking like they belonged in one of her favorite bands from the eighties, the three and Cate in a grunge outfit from the nineties, and Lucian and a blonde girl who vaguely resembled him. Both were dressed in black skinny jeans, tight black top, and studded boots with matching studded jewelry. The

Devil looked sinful in his black rocker clothes and shaggy hair. She loved punk rock music, but she and Vicky were forbidden to listen to it at home or even wear black nail polish.

Vicky.

"My parents." She breathed in and turned on her heels to him. "And Vicky. Are they… They're here, right?"

"Yes, in Hell," he murmured softly. "Your parents are in the Eternal Tombs. Your sister is in the Pit."

"Which is worse?" Celeste shocked herself at the nature of her question; as if one was more deserving of fire and brimstone than the other.

"The Eternal Tombs."

"I want to see them," she told him, trying to keep her voice even. The screams of pain, agony, and grief rang loudly in her ears. This time she would be prepared for the sounds of torture.

Lucian closed the laptop softly, giving her his undivided attention. "Do you think you can handle it?" There was nothing harsh implied in his soft voice. It was just as if he cared about her mental well-being. For a moment, she wondered if he knew she'd relapsed after seven years last night.

Celeste considered the question for a moment. His concern wasn't important as people had faked their concern for her for years. "Yes."

He stared at her for a few unwavering seconds. She almost changed her mind when he stood up with a sigh and said, "Back to Hell we go."

CHAPTER 43

Over the next few hours, Celeste poured all her thoughts into preparing herself to see her family and to see Hell again, to the point that she was too distracted to even panic about the ride over. It didn't even register to her that they were outside the metal doors to the Pit, as Lucian called it, until he handed her black earplugs and instructed her to put them in.

Squeezing her eyes shut, she braced herself for the screams as the doors opened. She was greeted with silence. The earplugs blocked out all the screams. Her shoulders slowly moved away from her ears, and she opened her eyes. They walked onto a large metal grated platform, the metal was slightly warm beneath their shoes, like sand on a sunny late morning.

Under the large platform, A large, football stadium-sized crater sank into the ground in the center. Licks of red, yellow, and orange fire danced above the Pit. She tried to peer inside, but he kept her along the back wall, not allowing her the chance to investigate the crater. "I'm not in the mood to deal with another one of your panic attacks today." He yelled loud enough for her to hear.

Fallen Angels patrolled the area armed to the teeth with a variety of daggers and swords. All of them bowed to Lucian as they walked by, scoffing at her in the process. Not to mention all of them seemed unfazed about the heat of the Pit. The sweltering heat formed a sheen of sweat on her arms, causing her irritated skin to burn.

Lucian guided her with a hand on the small of her back to another metal door that opened to an elevator. An electric shock coursed through her from the touch, and her heart skipped a beat. *He killed Mason. He took you away from him and Morgan.* She reminded herself. She could not allow those old feelings to surface.

Cold air blasted them as they stepped into the elevator. Once the doors shut, they were immediately moving upwards. Lucian motioned for her to take out the earbuds. Celeste braced for the wail of screams as she took one out, but it was silent.

"Soundproof," he informed her.

"How does it not bother you?" Celeste took the other earbud out and slid them into the pocket of her jeans.

He shrugged. "It's just background noise now. You'll get used to it." The elevator doors opened to a technical marvel. Another instant change from medieval to futuristic. Fallen Angels sat by various machines and screens. Floor-to-ceiling windows allowed optimum viewing of the crater below. One of the windows had a door handle and, beyond that, a fence to keep the Fallen from falling in. A side door was ajar.

Celeste followed him to the window and gazed into the Pit. Her stomach flipped when she couldn't see the bottom; it was just a black abyss. The rocky-sloped walls made it so no one could climb out. It had to be hundreds of feet deep. Numerous levels with flat surfaces circled the black void in the center. People—souls and Fallen Angels alike—moved like ants. Spurts of fire had the tiny specks of millions of souls hopping around trying to avoid the flames, but the flames seemed to follow them and engulf them. Tiny, winged figures walked through the fire like it was nothing.

"This is the Pit, what you Humans call Hell," Lucian said from beside her.

It was just as she was taught: a giant pit of fire and eternal suffering. A shadowy figure appeared in the corner of her eye, scaring her half to death. She jumped to the side and right into Lucian. His arm instinctively wrapped around her waist, holding her steady, keeping her pressed towards him and away from danger. A wave of calm washed over her; like her body was telling her mind she was *safe* in the Devil's arms.

Don's red eyes raked over her menacingly. He had been so protective of Cate that she had thought he was going to kill her last night.

It would have been better if he had.

Lucian gave a warning glance in his direction. "Don oversees all the souls down there and the Fallen who monitor the Pit."

"Every soul here at the moment is subjected to hellfire and torture methods deemed inhumane." Don grinned darkly, like he gets off on the torture. Her heart dropped into her stomach. This monster was the same man who ate breakfast with her, Cate, and Mason. The same man that made goo-goo eyes at Cate in the hot tub. Maybe Cate was better off dating only women.

"At the moment?" Celeste croaked, her throat going dry. There were only two options, Heaven and Hell.

"Every soul down there is able to reincarnate once they have learned their lesson. How and when that will be is up to them. At the end of their next life, if the soul the soul can prove they saw the error of their ways, they'll move up to heaven. Otherwise, back into the Pit they go. The Eternal Tombs are for the worst of the worst: Hitler, Ted Bundy and other serial killers, politicians who think they can control women and their bodies... They will never be able to reincarnate and try to make it to Heaven. They spout my Father's word, but they interpret it all wrong." Lucian spat the last two sentences.

Never in a million years did she take the Devil for a feminist. The explanation brought an odd sense of comfort to her. The corner of her mouth pulled upwards with the satisfaction that they were only blowing hot air. "Some churches say gays will end up here. Do they? What about animals?"

"All animals go to Heaven. Roxie and Chip will both go there when they pass. I've had many a pet in my time, and they don't come back here once their time is done. As for Humans, my Father doesn't care if a man loves another man. He cares about how you treat others. People seem to forget that. The extremists love quoting the Bible without even reading it, or they pick and choose what passages to believe in and which ones to ignore. 'Whoever claims to love God yet hates a brother or sister is a liar. For whoever does not love their brother and sister, whom they have seen, cannot love God, whom they have not seen.'" Lucian quoted with a voice that made it sound sinful, unholy, yet beautiful. She wouldn't mind if he quoted the Bible to her for the rest of eternity.

"First John." Celeste recalled automatically. All those countless hours studying the bible as a child actually paid off.

Lucian gave her a proud smile. "Very good, Pet."

Celeste agreed softly. "I didn't know Satan read the Bible."

"Celeste, my dear, I was there when it was written. It did take me a few millennia to finally read it, however." Lucian chuckled.

"I'm surprised you didn't burst into flames." She smiled softly. Lucian, with amusement in his eyes and a crooked smile, held up his hand. Blue fire roared to life at his fingertips. He wiggled them at her, fire dancing in the air between them. A lick of it brushed her cheek, tickling her instead of burning. A shameful, girlish giggle escaped her lips. It was the first time she had laughed since she was brought here. His dazzling smile grew wider at the sound. That same damn smile that made her fall in love with him. Her heart fluttered as a flame softly caressed her cheek once more before extinguishing.

"How do you know if a soul is destined for Hell or Heaven?" she asked curiously, glancing back down at the Pit.

"Auras. The darker the aura, the more likely they'll end up here," Don spoke up. She jumped slightly, forgetting he was there. The fabric of his suit jacket brushed up against the newly reopened cuts on her shoulder. She took in a sharp breath and winced just enough for the two Fallen Angels to notice. She did not dare look at the Devil, so she focused her eyes on the Pit. "Auras can change over time, but when Kingdom comes, the dark auras come here. Brighter auras go to Heaven."

"How do auras change?" she asked.

"Good acts and treating everyone with respect, even those you do not see eye to eye with, will make a Human's aura brighter. Bad acts, disrespecting others, abuse of others, and lawbreaking will darken the aura," Don explained.

Celeste furrowed her eyebrows. Although she personally thought it was based on how good of a person they are, some voices who preach loudly and confidently say differently. "But the Bible says—"

"The Bible also says you can't eat pork or any sea creatures that don't have scales. Yet, people do. It tells men to marry their sister-in-law if their brother dies before they make an heir. And He commands everyone to love each other the way He does and to not judge others, and yet men kill women all the time, take their rights away, and treat them like property. Wars are started because one nation views another as less than, People judge others based on material wealth. People invalidate the gays, the trans, and the non-binaries. Many do not believe in science, and let's not forget how they preach that the solution to curing depression, anxiety, and other mental disorders is to 'pray it away.'" The Devil ranted, growing more irate with every word. 'Praying it away' was her parents famous last words.

"Humans think they know everything about Heaven and Hell. But they know nothing," Don scoffed, crossing his arms.

"To this day, I still don't understand how and why my Father loves humans the way he does." Lucian's voice dripped with disgust. "Humans put a lot of pressure on other Humans for no damned reason. At the end of the day, the only ones they have to prove themselves to is whatever higher power they believe in and me." He smirked at the end, as if he was a God himself.

"But I'm Human," she mumbled as she looked up at him.

Lucian flinched like he had forgotten about her humanity for a moment. He paused. "You are the exception. Anyway, the only person my Father hates is me," Lucian continued, shrugging his shoulders at the end. "The Bible also says not to cut yourself either." Celeste pressed her arms tighter to her sides and stared at her shoes as guilt crept into her. "But you believe in and love my Father and his grace. And according to Lutheranism, that's good enough for Him. If you hadn't made your deal, you would have ended up there."

Celeste's jaw hit the floor. She had always hoped for that. Yet, even before the deal was made, it always felt out of reach. Her family had repeatedly told her that she was not destined for Heaven because she wasn't perfect and didn't obey the Word like her parents did.

"How can you be so sure?" Celeste breathed.

"Your aura." His ice-blue eyes settled into her stormy ocean ones. "It's iridescent. I have not seen one as bright as yours in all my existence." Lucian's eyes seemed to pierce her soul, open it, and see everything inside it.

"I'm not a good person," she said softly, looking back at her shoes.

Lucian's fingers gently tilted her chin, forcing her to look back at him, the ice melting into the baby blues she loved so much. "You are everything that is good in this world." The world faded away as she looked at him. There was such sincerity in his voice. If she had been anyone else, she would have believed him. A spark in her chest seemed to ignite itself.

Celeste broke the gaze and faced the window again as she wiped a tear away.

He's lying to you. Her mind reminded her. *All he's ever done is lie to you.*

She was as worthless as the Demons he enslaved. She didn't deserve Heaven and the goodness that lived there. She exhaled, setting her attention back to the spurts of blue hellfire. "You said Vicky was down there?"

"Yes, somewhere."

"Would you like to see her?" Don offered, reminding them that he was still in the room.

Lucian gave his friend a wary look. "I don't think—"

"How?" Celeste cut him off.

With a sly smile, Don summoned her to the side room. His name was etched onto a gold plate on the door. The smaller office was a scaled-down version of the main room. Numerous televisions were bolted along one wall, each one with a different view of Hell, and the floor-to-ceiling windows continued in here. He sat at the computer and motioned for her to stand beside him. Lucian leaned against the doorway, his eyes simmering with a dark rage.

Don typed away on the keyboard. "Here." He pointed to the computer screen.

What the camera showed horrified her. Vicky was lifeless. Her once full and vibrant blonde hair was now ashen, stringy, and limp. Black and purple bruises were splattered over her sickly pale skin. Her busted lip was crusted with dried blood. Her lively brown eyes were now sunken in, lifeless and vacant. The outer parts of her eyes were tinged in matching black and purple, and her nose was crooked. She stood like she was in line for slaughter.

"What did you do to her?" she asked, covering her mouth with her hand. This was the price for her freedom.

"What happens to every soul down there." Don leaned back in his chair with his hands behind his head and grinned darkly. "Payback."

"She's all beat up. Even our father only left us with bruises we could cover with makeup."

"It's different down here. My team is trained to bend and break the soul by any means necessary."

Celeste swallowed hard as she stared at the screen. Vicky's mouth opened in a silent scream as blue fire engulfed her for what felt like an entire minute. Unlike the others dancing around her to escape the flames, she allowed them to swallow her up. The older sister she had once loved was broken and lifeless. Vicky had given up. "Does she look like this every day?"

"They all look like that after a month or two." Don shrugged.

"Turn it off," Lucian ordered Don, watching the same thing they were on another monitor.

She narrowed her eyes at Lucian. "You allow this?"

Lucian had a solemn look on his face, "Celeste, you need to under—" He was cut off by motion in the monitors. A breathless curse finished off his sentence.

A Fallen Angel stepped into view of the camera and in front of Vicky. In his hand was some heavy-looking object. The Angel gripped the object tightly and raised it above his head. Vicky didn't even flinch. She made no movement of recognition as he swung at her. Celeste watched in horror as the blunt object collided with Vicky's temple. Vicky's limp body went flying across the rocky platform, falling to the ground lifelessly in a limp pile of bones.

Bile rose in the back of her throat. *She* did this. Celeste sentenced her sister to an eternity of being beaten, bruised, and Devil knows what else. For eight years, her sister had endured this while Celeste spent her time partying and living happily at the beach. She took off out of the room. A female Fallen Angel pointed her to another door she had not seen earlier. Celeste opened it and slammed the door shut. It was a bathroom, and Celeste flung herself headfirst to the toilet.

"I'm sorry you had to see that," Lucian apologized once they were in the cable car back to Elysian. He sat across from her, watching her every move intently. As if at any moment, she'd throw herself against the door and fall to her death.

"Do my parents look like that?" she croaked. Her eyes focused on the hem of her shirt.

The hesitation gave her the answer she needed. "Similar, they are each locked away in their own personal Hell."

A small, twisted smile appeared on her lips. That she could live with. She hated them. Hated everything they were and everything they did to her. "Why are they locked away and not my sister?"

"For what they did to you. Vicky was also a child when you were being abused, so for that alone, I gave her the chance to redeem herself. But your parents will *never* have the chance to hurt someone again."

"You allow your Fallen Angels to do that to Vicky, to everyone down there?"

Lucian swallowed, his hands smoothing out any bumps on his slacks by his knees. "Yes. I'm not proud, but I'm not sorry about it either. I will never apologize for their punishments."

Celeste gripped the velvet seat cushion, "Why did you make it like that? Medieval décor aside, why did you make a separate area for the worst of the worst? Are they also jumping from flame to flame?"

"Because torture and fire aren't enough of a punishment for their earthly actions. They are stuck living their own personal Hell."

Celeste sat and pondered it. "Like, is Hitler surrounded by Jews?"

Lucian smiled darkly; he enjoyed inflicting pain on humans as much as Don did. Although he hid it better, it was clear he got off on it, and it made her sick. She hated herself even more for having loved him, "I can't give you all my secrets, Pet, but I will say Karma's a bitch."

She shivered from the thought. "Why do they get their own personal Hells and not just locked in a room with fires and being tortured like the souls in the Pit?"

"Stereotypes." He chuckled lightly at his own joke. "Hell is not just a place. Hell is in your head. A place is just a place until your mind gives it meaning. Hell is what your mind determines it to be. That is why Humans say, 'that sounds like Hell' when hearing about an unpleasant situation or place. On the other end, when people find a place or situation they enjoy, they say, 'that sounds like Heaven.' It changes with each person."

"So, your Hell is a city? Since you live here." Celeste glanced down at the city looming in the distance, her stomach twisting into a knot.

"No, Pet," A tired look shot in her direction, "As I've told you several times now, Elysian is a sanctuary. For the Fallen who could not stand Heaven any longer, for the Vampires and Shifters and Witches who were outcasted simply for what they are. For the Nephilim, because they did not ask to be born, they were just dealt an ugly hand. Children should never be blamed for the failures of their parents."

The words poured into her like ice water. He sounded so sure of himself and his opinion that she had to turn her head away from him or else he'd see the rogue tear ready to spill. He was so genuine to the supernatural yet so malicious towards humans like her. She did not deserve to be here; she deserved to be in the Pit with her sister.

No one wants you here. You will never be wanted.

"Hell, as you were taught," he continued, "is how I wanted it to be perceived by Humans; fiery, hot, and awful. The souls who come into Hell are so evil they deserve to suffer for what they did to their peers." Lucian smoothed out a wrinkle on his suit pants.

"What is your Hell?" Celeste asked cautiously.

Lucian was silent for a moment. He stared just past her out the window. "Vulnerability. I hate being vulnerable or being in a position where I have to be." His eyes glazed over; he was miles away from this cable car in Hell.

"That's not really a place."

"Being vulnerable is Hell. To be completely open with someone in hopes they won't one day turn against you. *That* is Hell. It took me years to learn I could trust Don and another friend of mine. Every day, I feared that I told them too much about me: my fears, my secrets, and the things I love. I had opened up to two ex-girlfriends and my own blood, and they all used it against me."

A cold chill went down her spine. Maybe they were more alike than she wanted them to be. Vulnerability was a foreign concept, one not allowed in her household. Any sign of weakness was used against her. She had let herself be vulnerable with Lucian, and now she paid the price.

CHAPTER 44

The room was dark. Quick spurts of orange fire acted like a strobe light. Lucian, Don, and 2 other dark-winged men punched, choked, and kicked Victoria, knocking her to her knees. Bloodcurdling screams of torture reverberated off the rocky walls of the Pit, searing her eardrums. The sickening crack of bones followed. Black boots grounded into her body as if squashing a bug.

"Alice!" Vicky groaned out. Her frail broken arms reached for her younger sister through a small wall of fire to her. Lucian and Don turned around to face her. Their eyes were red and hungry for blood. Don unsheathed a blade from his side. Fire glinted off the cool, sharp metal. Her fingers twitched, itching for the chance to grab it and use it on herself. Oblivion would be better than seeing this.

"*Celeste!*" a distant voice screamed for her. The sound wrapped around her heart and tugged, trying to pull her away, but her feet remained cemented into the ground.

"Alice! Help me!" Vicky moaned. "Why won't you help me?" The Fallen Angels turned back to Vicky. Deeming her not important, Don turned and knelt by her sister. The knife pointed at her sister's eye.

"*Celeste!*" the other voice frantically called out again. Her heart pulled sideways. "*Move,*" *it* told her

"I…I can't." Celeste croaked. She couldn't save her sister. She didn't want to. Vicky never saved her.

"You're my sister, you're supposed to help me! Why won't you help me?" Vicky cried, her lifeless brown eyes pleading with her. Celeste lowered her eyes to her shoes just as blood splattered around her feet. She caused *this*. Her sister was tortured daily because of *her*. She was no better than her father. Waves of guilt filled every vein, artery, and her lungs in an attempt to drown her. Maybe tonight, she'd let it consume her and become what she was always meant to be; nothing.

"*Celeste!*" The voice screamed again. Closer. The Pit started shaking violently. Bits of rock shot across her vision, and dust clouded her sister, obscuring her from view. Through the dust cloud, Vicky's arm hit the ground with a hard thunk.

"*Celeste!*" Her eyes flew open as she bolted upright. She panted as her head whipped around the room. She was *not* in the Pit but in her bedroom in Elysian. Her bedside table light was on. The soft yellow light shone on Lucian. He sat on his knees on her bed, eyes wild with worry and his hair a mess, his hand gripping her shoulder tightly. He was shirtless, of course. Her eyes scanned him from his head to the defined muscles of his abs to the top of his boxers. *Everything Vicky goes through is because you fell in love with him. You are a good-for-nothing whore.*

Forcing her eyes away from him, she settled on Chip and Roxie. Both dogs were now awake at the edge of the bed, concern plastered on their faces. Her television was still blasting the show she had been watching when she fell asleep.

"You're okay. You are safe. It was just a bad dream. Again." He lifted his hand off her shoulder and tucked a strand of hair behind her ear.

Celeste's face dropped into her hands, and she scrubbed her face viciously. This had been a nightly occurrence since she went back to Hell weeks ago. She no longer woke up refreshed, just more tired than the day before. She did her best to evade sleep with copious amounts of coffee, energy drinks and the constant booming of her television, but her body still failed her.

You are a failure.

Celeste inhaled deeply, held her breath, and then exhaled slowly. She repeated the movement until she was calm.

"Do you want to talk about it?" he asked softly for the umpteenth time.

She wanted to talk—*needed* to talk about what she saw. Just...not to him. She wanted to talk to her friends and Mason. She *needed* her friends. Morgan and Mason knew her family and would sympathize with her. Cate never judged her and never made her feel like her feelings weren't valid. But Mason was dead, Morgan was on Earth, and she blew up her relationship with Cate.

You brought this upon yourself, idiot.

Lucian took her silence for an answer. "Well, when you're ready, I'll be down the hall." The corner of his mouth turned upward in a sad half-smile. He walked out, leaving the door cracked, unsure if Roxie would stay with her or go to sleep with her owner. Roxie tended to stay with Celeste most nights.

All of this is your fault.

Nothing she did made things better. Everything was worse because of her.

You are an ungrateful bitch.

Her sister was tortured every day while she complained about being here with Lucian. She had her own bedroom and bathroom; she had her dog, for God's sake. Vicky had nothing.

Mason is dead because of you.

If she had just stuck to her guns and not gotten involved, he would be alive.

It should be you in the Pit. You should be the one getting tortured.

Hot, angry tears pricked at her eyes as she marched into the bathroom. The now dry silver razor blade was waiting for her on the counter on top of a hand towel, clean after last night's use on her upper arm. She slid off her cotton shorts and took a seat on the cold white tiled floor. Her back pressed against the bathtub as she stretched out her right leg. She picked up the small sharp object with her left hand.

The razor grazed her thigh lightly at first; small red beads bubbled up to the surface. She went over the line again, and again, sticky blood smearing across her thigh. The thoughts and images of her sister oozed away with the blood that appeared. A twisted smile splayed on her lips. With each slice across, she washed away her own sins. The noise in her head began to quiet down, and all of her emotions faded until all that remained was the slight euphoric pain from the razor opening her skin.

CHAPTER 45

Lucian woke up to the next best thing to morning sex—wet-nose dog kisses.

"Good morning, baby. How's my girl?" He scratched the dog's fluffy ears and paused mid-scratch. Roxie didn't have fluffy ears. His eyes flew open to see Celeste's dog, Chip, licking him awake.

His bedroom door was ajar, as it used to be before Celeste moved in so Roxie could roam as she pleased. Now, it was to get to Celeste quicker when she had her nightmares.

Chip pressed his nose to Lucian's cheek while whimpering and pawing at him. Lucian sat up and examined her dog. "What's wrong, bud?" He asked without expecting an answer and scrubbed his cheek. His fingers brushed against something wet and sticky. The hair on the back of his neck stood up as ice ran down his back. *Blood.* His eyes darted back to the dog. Chip's nose was dripping with blood. The two locked eyes for what felt like minutes before Chip barked and dashed out of the room, not bothering to wait for him. Lucian grabbed a shirt from the floor and slid it on as he ran to Celeste's room.

His heart hammered wildly against his chest, and his body began to shake. She wasn't in her bed. He skidded to a stop in the doorway of her bathroom. His Human was slumped against the bathtub. Her right thigh was covered in blood. The now red razor was on the red-stained tile floor beside her.

His heart dropped into the pit of his stomach like the first drop of a roller coaster. Bile rose in his throat. There was so much blood. "Celeste!" His voice cracked as he hurried over to her. He pressed two fingers to her neck to check and cursed loudly. Lucian gathered the Human into his arms like she weighed nothing and took off for next door.

He all but kicked Cate's front door down, screaming her name.

The Witch stopped halfway on the steps, tightening her robe. "Lucian, what's—holy shit. What happened? What did you do?" Cate hurried down the steps to them.

"She's bleeding out, and her pulse is weak; what the fuck does it look like? Save her!" Lucian stomped past Cate, towards the dining room table. He laid Celeste on top, ignoring the loud crashing noises from the items he shoved off the table.

"Rip your shirt in half and tie it around her thighs like a tourniquet, it'll staunch any more blood from coming out," she instructed Lucian as she examined her friend. He quickly shed his shirt and followed orders. "Béatrice!" Cate yelled for her daughter as she pulled off Celeste's long-sleeved shirt to look for any more bleeding. Lucian wanted to vomit right there.

Celeste's upper arm was bandaged tightly with blood-soaked gauze. Her key tattoo on her right wrist was shredded into nothing. Celeste had tried to *cut it out*. He could barely make out what it was. It was only when a mangled sob fell from Cate's lips that he knew it was the match to Cate's key. Undoing the gauze only added to his never-ending nightmare; her right arm was a mix of new cuts crusted with dried blood and white and pink healed scars from years of self-inflicted pain. Both of her shoulders were red with irritation. Lowering his eyes, her right hip had the word *mistake* carved out in white scars. The left hip was a mix of white and pink scars. Only her calves and left shin were untouched. Her right shin bore one single pink scar that was big enough to pass off as a childhood accident.

"I swear to Hades, Celeste," he hissed weakly. His heart shattered into a million pieces. He'd known it was bad—Hades, he'd helped her bandage her lower arm some nights. But *this*. This he never expected. A cold, murderous rage seeped into his bloodstream; he'd burn the world and kill anyone who was the reason for those cuts. Her parents were already suffering in the Tombs, and Vicky was being tortured daily. Mason was next once he could get his hands on him. Lucian knew some of the cuts were due to him and he would throw himself in the Pit over many millennia as his penance if she asked him to.

"Mom. What's going on—who's that?" a small voice called from the hallway. He lifted his head to see Bea's dark blue-black eyes staring at Celeste in horror. The girl was still in her pajamas; he couldn't recall if Cate was in hers. Hades, he didn't even know what time it was.

"I need you to go back upstairs and call your grandmother. Tell her to get to my house immediately with her healing kit. Then come back with mine, it's in my practice room."

All color drained from the teenager's face as she stared in horror. "Is she dying?"

"Now, Béatrice!"

Lucian stared down at his Human; her iridescent aura was fading quickly. "She'll be okay. Go upstairs and do what your mother asked, please, Honey." The words were unconvincing. Bea would see right through it; she was more intelligent than any of them gave her credit for. But Celeste would be okay. There was no other option. Her soul belonged to him, dead or alive. Although, he preferred her as she was.

What felt like an eternity later, Cate's mother came barreling into the dining room with her suitcase of herbs and potions. Her face and hair were windblown from the flight over. She set the suitcase on the floor and assessed Celeste's body. Her aura flickered out with every breath. If they didn't save her soon; he'd toss both witches into the Pit. "What happened, Luce?" She asked in a faint British accent.

He sat by Celeste's head, absentmindedly stroking her hair, untangling the knots in her loose curls. His eyes never left her closed ones. "She went too deep, Hest. I…I don't know how much blood she lost. I don't know how long she'd been lying there. I was asleep, and she could have been calling for me, and I wouldn't have heard her." Guilt, thick and heavy, poured from his mouth. His throat closed up and all breath had left his lungs. He should have never left her after her nightmare. He should have stayed with her until she fell back asleep. His eyes lifted towards Hester. Behind her, standing proud yet with a face of misery, was Thayne.

Thayne and that fucking scythe in his hands.

Lucian's blood began to bubble at the sight of his friend. At everything his friend was. "Get. Out," He hissed, slowly rising to his feet. his wings flared out to the ends of the room, a tactic he used for scaring humans. Thayne was not a human and had never been afraid of Lucian or his wrath.

"Lucian-—" Thayne started.

"Get. Out," Lucian repeated, baring his teeth. Red clouded his vision.

Thayne gripped the scythe tighter and swallowed. His own wings flared out in challenge. A few pictures and wall décor crashed to the ground. Both of them got a quick, dirty look from Cate. "I don't want to do this."

"Then don't."

"I wish I could make that decision, but I can't. I'm not God!" Thayne hissed. "You think leading your girlfriend to the afterlife is something I want to do?"

Lucian looked down at His human and brushed a finger down her cheek. She looked like she was sleeping. It was the only time he ever saw her truly relax. The Angel of Death hovered over Celeste's feet. Conflict moved back and forth over his face.

"Both of you—outside, upstairs, somewhere. I don't care where, just not here." Hester scolded the boys. "Neither one of you is helping her by bickering like children. Lucian opened his mouth to speak but Cate spoke first.

"Do you know what blood type she is?" she asked as she prepared an ointment. Hester's hand stretched out over Celeste's thigh. She was mumbling something in Latin, too low for him to hear. A white healing light grew from her palm.

Lucian shook his head. His eyes never left Celeste's face.

Cate sighed, "If you hadn't found her when you did, she would have exsanguinated. Lucian, go to the Vampire Lair and get as many bags of angel blood as they will give you.

"Angel blood?" Lucian finally broke his stare and pinned it on Cate. Angel blood had healing properties to help them heal faster after injury. A little angel blood, maybe a bag at the most would fix Celeste up immediately. To give her multiple bags would turn her blood and kill her.

"There's no time for you to ask questions. She's *dying*. Just. go. Thayne, go get me any angel blood the injury clinic has stored and an IV stand."

Thayne opened his mouth to protest, but the turquoise glow in Cate's eyes convinced him otherwise. Angel of Death or not, he was going to get that IV bag.

Lucian leaned down to Celeste's ear. "I need you to fight. You are not one of my servants but it is still an order nonetheless. You are not allowed to die on me," He hoped for some small movement, some acknowledgment, but she remained a barely breathing corpse.

Vampires looked to the sky as his shadow blocked the sun, creating an ominous dark cloud across the street. Although he was King of Elysian, he rarely came to the Vampire Lair. Each section had its own head who made the day-to-day decisions for them. Leaving him to put his energy into the bigger issues at hand.

The sidewalk cracked as he landed. Nearby vampires stumbled as the ground shook. Two fell flat on their backs from Lucian pulling them down with him, not paying attention to where he was landing. Normally, he'd help a Being when they were down, but Celeste was dying. He ran into the Blood bank, ignoring the protests and yells from passersby.

In the heart of the Vampire Lair, the Elysian Blood Bank was a black, gothic-looking building that housed all the blood for Elysian. It was mostly filled with human blood because it was a food source for the vampires, but it also housed concentrated amounts of Angel blood for safekeeping. A bag of angel blood to a vampire was equivalent to a nice vintage champagne. He raced up the front steps, pushing and shoving his way inside. A young vampire woman sat behind a long counter that stretched along the back wall.

"Angel blood. *Now.* As much as you can give me," Lucian demanded of the Vampire.

The woman glanced up from her magazine and raised an eyebrow. Bright golden eyes checked him out with a hunger he hadn't seen from a woman in billions of years. Not since Abby. Her eyes landed on below his waist. He followed her gaze and groaned. He was dressed only in his boxers. He had been in such a rush to help Celeste he forgot to put on pants, and his shirt was tied around Celeste's leg.

Shadows rolled out of his palms. The opaque cloud concealed his lower half. He was still a sight to behold, but at least with the shadows, he had *that* part covered.

The woman flung her magazine onto her desk, crossed her arms, and leaned forward. "With all due respect, Your Majesty, the blood is for the vampires. We don't care if the Witches want to practice blood magic. They can use their own."

Lucian's nostrils flared. Today was not the day to start an argument with him. The front doors to the Blood bank slammed open, and a cold breeze filled the room. "My people told me a Fallen Angel fell from the sky, I never would have thought it was you, King Lucian." The cool, sultry voice of Elysian vampire leader, Isolde boomed through the room. She approached him, eyeing him; a cruel smile stretched onto her face, and her fangs elongated, shining against her dark skin.

"Isolde." He bowed his head slightly in a sign of respect. "I'm sorry for dropping in like this, it's a bit of an emergency. I need any and all angel blood you have."

Isolde's deep brown eyes trailed him from head to toe, lingering on his mid-section and the circle of shadows.

"You know, angel blood is special and we hardly have any to spare. It's a rarity as it is. Unfortunately, we don't have any to spare for your people." She smirked as if she didn't have a few Fallen Angel Males at her disposal on any given day.

Lucian shook his head, "It's for Lady Celeste."

Isolde's face fell into shock. "You want my blood supply for a stupid Human?"

Lucian narrowed his red eyes at the vampire. Fire sparked at his fingertips, and his wings stretched out to full length, making him look menacing. "She is a member of the royal court, and you will give her the proper respect."

"Oh Lucian, don't be brash. She doesn't really need it. Why are you even keeping her alive? I heard she's supposed to be one of your demons. She's not going anywhere."

His nostrils flared. His history with Isolde was as ancient as she was. Yet he still hadn't learned to not let her get under his skin. "She's more valuable to me alive than dead."

"All humans are more valuable alive. But this is Elysian, there is no need for a human life here."

"Yes, well, Father's plan and all that." He shrugged, not entirely convinced why he needed her alive anyway.

Isolde's smirk faded, and her head tilted to the side, "How important is this girl to you, King Lucian?"

"She's a friend."

"You have lots of friends and I've never seen or heard you showing up demanding blood in only your boxers. Not even when your Witch of a niece was dying."

Lucian grounded his teeth. He had failed Bea. He owned up to it and had been forgiven. Celeste was worth life. The world was an infinitely better place with her in it. Yet, he took her away from her world and brought her here. "If any more Fallen Angels act out of line, you have my word that you can drain them of their blood before I dole out the final punishment."

"That could be centuries!" Isolde argued.

"Once lady Celeste is healed, I promise, I will come by every other month and you can draw my blood until you get back to the number of bags you had in storage."

"Why can't the human just use yours if you are offering it to me?"

"That would take too much time. She's dying and I need blood *now*."

The vampire leader considered it. "Give the King any angel we have on hand." She ordered. The worker disappeared for a moment and came back with a cardboard box filled with blood bags.

"She must mean a lot to you." Isolde shoved the cardboard box at him. Lucian didn't bother to waste precious moments to answer the question. He ran out, barely clearing the main doors before he took off into the sky.

CHAPTER 46

The dining room-turned-operating room was a mess.
Dirty glass vials and bowls were strewn about haphazardly.
Bits of leaves, roots, dirt, and blood covered Cate's cream
rug. Celeste looked like a corpse; All color had drained
from Celeste's face. The blood had been wiped from her
body, and her thigh was stitched up with several rows of
sutures. A red wire poked out of the inside of her right
arm.

For a moment, his eyes fooled him. The box of
blood crashed to the ground and Hellfire roared to life at
the stillness of her. He had been too late. Thayne must
have gotten his slimy hands on her. "Thayne!" He roared,
his voice a deep, dark threat, "I'll kill you, you son of a
Bitch!"

Hester ran into the room, "Put your flames away for Creation's sake. She's alive—barely. What took you so long? Cate had to give her some of Bea's blood just to keep her heart pumping. The elder Witch snatched a bag from the box and glided around Celeste. His eyes concentrated on her chest for the rise and fall of breath. If he blinked, he would miss it. There was no sign of life in her. Even her faint aura winked in and out. "Take her upstairs to my old room. We'll lay her there as she goes through the transfusion."

Lucian picked Celeste up gently, and carried her carefully up the stairs and down the hall, making sure to not yank her IV out. Thayne had come out from another part of the house and helped carry the box of blood and the IV hook, keeping pace with the Devil.

Hester pulled the bed sheets down and Lucian laid her into the bed. Thayne hung a blood bag on the stand and took steps back to the doorway, clear of Lucian's path. Hester pulled the blankets up around Celeste like she used to for Cate and Bea. "We've done all we can for her. Go home and put clothes on. I love you, but I do not want to see all of you."

Lucian laughed wearily. His muscles collapsed into a chair that Thayne had quietly slid over to Celeste's bedside. His fingers brushed a section of hair behind her ear and caressed her cheek. She looked so peaceful and serene, a juxtaposition from the thoughts in her mind.

"I know what it's like to hate yourself, but how does someone hate themselves so much to inflict physical pain on themselves?"

Hester sat on the arm of the chair and wrapped her arms around his neck in a hug. Her head rested on top of his. There was nothing romantic in the gesture; the two had always been nothing more than friends. She had sold her soul for magic, wanting to help her family in the plague. However, she fell short, losing her first husband and her sons, Cate's older brothers. He admired her for that, and for that reason, he never collected his debt. Hester quickly became one of the most powerful witches in existence, third to Cate and Bea. The two had remained close since. "The mind is a scary place; a thousand different reasons for one action."

"But she's so good and kind. She doesn't deserve this. Her family failed her, Mason failed her, *I* failed her," he croaked. He wouldn't dare to admit failure to anyone other than Hester. He was a King and a leader; failure is not an option.

"You saved her life."

"Everything I've done has been for her. I got her out of that house, I brought her here to get her away from Mason, I left her alone when she asked. Yet she fights me tooth and nail. She started cutting herself again. I thought she was, but I was afraid to confront her about it." He paused to watch Celeste's chest rise and fall with breath. He didn't realize how much he needed that constant confirmation. "I almost killed her."

Hester sighed deeply and rested her head on top of his. "You are doing things that *you* think will help her. From what I gathered from Cate about her parents and her boyfriend, she knew her parents were abusive. But with Mason, she can't see it. Mason is a childhood friend, a crush. He's familiar. To her, Mason is a safe person because of her friendship with his sister. Mason and his sister represent everything she wants and never had. You gave her something she didn't know she needed. And there's the guilt she's harbored concerning the night her family died about leaving her friends. She felt obligated to return to them, to make things right on her terms.

"Not to mention, in romantic situations, people tend to mirror the relationships their parents had. Her parents did not have a good relationship and that is all she knows. Look at my daughter and that prick." Her tone sharpened with every word. Cate and Don's relationship was complicated, but unlike her mother, Cate chooses Don time and time again. "Mason was probably the first man in her life to show her any bit of kindness, and she clung to it. In her teenage dreams, she made him out to be her hero, her white knight, and if that were to change, her worldview would crumble."

"What about her cutting? I know why she did it before. I saw the cuts, I even cleaned some of them, but I guess I never really *saw* the scars. I had no idea it was that bad. Why would she relapse? Cate said she stopped."

"You forcefully took her away from her parents, forcefully took her from her lover then you made it seem like you killed him. Every time you waltz back into her life, it's violent. The abuse she suffered already made her insecure, depressed, and anxious, and you aren't helping that. You and Don let her watch Victoria get beaten, for Creation's sake. Not to mention she's religious. Everything you are is the antithesis of everything she believes in. For years, she thought she would go to Heaven once her human life was over, and then you tell her she'll never see it because she made a deal with you despite not knowing who you are. She feels like she has to punish herself. She also lashes out on herself because the world has taught her that her emotions and feelings don't matter. It's safer for her to hurt herself than to express her emotions and be retaliated against."

An anvil fell onto his shoulders. He'd willingly spend a thousand years in the Pit for every single cut that she made because of him. He'd carry the pain for her if she'd just ask.

A flash of light caught his eye. Her iridescent aura flickered brighter for a moment. Good. Celeste was going to live. She was beautiful, of course, but most importantly, she was good, kind, and resilient—all the things he was not. Earth was a darker place now that she was in Elysian, but Elysian was a brighter and better place with her presence. Now, he just needed her to see how worthy of life she is. He made a silent promise to spend eternity showing her how valuable she was to the people in her life, how much she enriched his life and Cate's, and how she was *worth* everything good and holy in the world. Even if it killed him.

CHAPTER 47

Celeste woke up feeling like she had been hit with a thousand bricks. Her thigh and arm burned and itched like never before. Her soul ached with an exhaustive heaviness. She opened her eyes and looked around the unfamiliar area. It was dark, save for the floor lamp in the corner emitting a soft yellow light.

"Am I dead?" she thought aloud.

"No. Fortunately for us, and especially me, I didn't have to use my scythe on you," a deep male voice said in a light tone. She shot up with a start and pulled up a fistful of the sheet to cover her as if she were naked in bed. The world spun with her movement. "Easy, easy, easy, you're safe."

Thayne appeared next to her. He was the last person she expected to find in this room. She sunk into the headboard; the support of the wooden frame helped the world straighten out. "Thayne? What are you doing here? Where am I?"

"You're at Cate's house," He helped himself to a seat on the edge of the bed beside her legs, facing her. "I want to know why you're obsessed with me," he asked her, the hint of a smile on his face. Her eyebrow arched in confusion. "Angel of Death, remember?"

She nodded slowly in acknowledgment, still not understanding why she was in Cate's house and why he was in this room with her. "But you just said I'm not dead."

"You're not. You just like to flirt with death a lot. You almost died from cutting yourself." He glanced down to her blanket-covered leg. Celeste tossed the blanket to the side. She was in a new pair of grey shorts, revealing a fully bandaged right thigh. Her left hand felt up her right wrist up to her shoulder, patting the bandages underneath her old pink *Blue Marlin* shirt. That life felt like a million years ago. "This isn't the first time you've almost died, y'know. This is what, the fifth time you've gone that deep? And your third attempt?"

She quickly covered her thigh up, her eyes fixating on the ivory blanket, unable to meet his eyes. God, she was so stupid; this was the first time she'd cut *that* deep in years. The last time had been before Lucian walked into her life. "How did you know that?" Her demanding tone was shaky at best. First, Lucian walked into her life unannounced, then, Cate became her friend right after Lucian left, and now, Thayne knew everything about her. She was a gnat trapped in their web long before she ever knew any of them existed.

"When Humans die, I'm the first one they see. When they're dying, I'm in the corner with my scythe, waiting. I've come to take you to Heaven five times. Five times I've stood in the corner fighting with myself about separating you from your human body." The pain and grief in his eyes were palpable. He was genuinely upset, and he barely knew her.

"I don't remember seeing you."

"Humans don't see Angels unless we want them to see us. But I was there many-a-nights. Sometimes staying long after you pulled through the night."

That realization she had after visiting the first church had been right. God really had abandoned her. In those moments when it was just her and a razor blade, or her and her thoughts, she never felt *truly* alone. She assumed that God had been there with her, but it was death. Death—Thayne—had walked beside her during her darkest points in the last decade. Thayne, *not* God, was keeping her alive. He broke from his job duties to keep her alive and was willing to do it again.

Maybe she really did deserve to be in Hell. "Why didn't you say something when Lucian introduced us?"

"I didn't know it was *you* Lucian talked about all the time. He never referred to you by name either. I had no reason to put the pieces together until then, and after the way you yelled at Cate, I wasn't going to say anything."

Celeste scrubbed her hands over her face, rubbing the heels into her eyeballs until she saw color. She was no better than the people who raised her. She never wanted people to be afraid to say anything to her for fear of her reaction. "Why didn't you just use your scythe on me…when I was growing up?" She'd wished for death often as a teenager and it had been mere steps away. How fucking poetic.

"You still had fight in you then. You didn't know it or feel it, but you did," he said simply, then exhaled, his demeanor changing. His hand ran through his copper curls and tugged on them. "Yesterday, you didn't fight. Even as a teenager, your body fought to keep you alive despite your mind trying to kill you. But yesterday, you just…gave up."

Guilty tears rose to the surface. "I wasn't trying to kill myself, but I wouldn't have cared if I died," she whispered weakly. "I just wanted the voices to stop. I wanted to stop feeling so much at once. Cutting numbs everything. The voices and the thoughts stop, and I don't have to feel any emotions," she blurted out to him as she wiped a tear from her eyes. The guilt and depression she kept buried down found their way to the forefront. "I don't like emotions; I don't like feeling. All I feel is…anger."

"What or who are you angry at?"

Hot tears spilled over onto her cheeks. "God, Jesus, Lucian. I'm angry at Cate and Don. I'm angry at my sister. I'm angry at my parents. I'm angry with myself. I'm angry for the way I grew up. I'm angry no one did anything to help me; people just stood there. I have nowhere for this anger to go, and when it becomes too overwhelming, I lash out. Usually on myself because it's the only option. And while I'm cutting, time stops. The voices stop. Everything just *stops*."

Thayne put a comforting hand on her left knee. "Emotions make you Human," he said lowly. Tears welled up in his deep brown eyes.

"A part of me doesn't want to be Human. A part of me just wants to end it." She admitted thoughts she had never spoken aloud before. There was something comforting about Thayne that the weak part of her seemed to cling to.

The severity of her words seemed to slice through Thayne. His face seemed to come undone. "Don't say that. You don't mean that."

Celeste shrugged and brought her pendant to her mouth, running it in between her lips. The constant texture of the smooth base and the slightly raised Celtic knot kept her from slipping back into her thoughts. "Not like I could do it; I'd still be stuck here. He should have just made me the Demon I was supposed to be." Her voice was weak and shaky. Being a Demon is what she deserved. She didn't deserve to wake up in this bed with her thigh and arm stitched up. She didn't deserve to be *alive*. She made it a point to not look in Thayne's direction. The disappointment in his eyes only added to the guilt she felt about her secret coming out.

"Those Demons are monsters, and you are not," Thayne told her softly. His finger gently wiped away runaway tears.

She scoffed, jerking her head away from him. She didn't deserve his kindness. "I am a monster, it's all I've ever been."

"Lucian, Don, and I have dealt with our fair share of monsters. You are the farthest thing from one. You might be holier than the three of us put together." His chuckle at the end was sad and forced. A sad and unsuccessful attempt at bringing a smile to her face.

"Did he put you up to this?"

The Angel of Death sighed deeply. "Does it matter? We just want to help you."

We. Together. The words sounded good. But words are just words until there are actions to back them up. "I don't think I can be helped," Celeste whispered, her heart breaking into a thousand pieces.

"Can't or won't?" he asked a bit too sharply.

Celeste sighed and shrugged her shoulders. "I've always been this broken."

"Doesn't mean you have to stay that way. Cate said you were really happy at the beach. You stopped cutting."

The words Mason had once told her filtered through her mind. "At the beach, I got to be someone else. I pretended to be someone else. Someone who used men like people used me. I got to be a bitch to people without facing the repercussions. When Mason came back, he reminded me who I really was." Mason constantly applauded her for *being like you used to be*. Lucian said the name change would give her a new start so she decided to become someone else. But his coming back only proved she couldn't outrun her past. She would never outrun who she really was.

"There's no reason you can't merge the two and be happy," he suggested.

She shrugged again. "I don't know who I am anymore. I've always played a part. I played a different role with my parents, with Mason, and with Cate." To her parents, she was the dutiful, pious daughter. One that did what they said despite the vitriol they spewed at her. To Cate, she was the fun girl who danced on bar tables, brought guys to their knees, and made the best damn strawberry Daiquiris in town. To Mason, she was a damsel in distress who craved love from the one man who knew why she was so fucked up.

Lucian knows the real you. You opened up your soul to him. Yeah, he stole it for his own selfish gains, but he knows *you.*

"Well, you have all the time to figure it out. If it takes you fifty years, then it takes you fifty years. I think it took Lucian, a hundred years to find himself. None of us would judge you. Contrary to your belief, we *do* care about you."

"Lucian doesn't." The words were out before she could even register then.

"He cares more than you know." He snapped, defensively.

If he had cared about her, he would have never taken her soul. He wouldn't have killed Mason. "If he did, I wouldn't be here."

Thayne shifted uncomfortably. His face twisted with uncertainty. His eyes darted back and forth, like he was having a conversation with himself. The silence grew tense and had her itching to get away from him to be alone. He spoke softly with a slight waver in his voice. "When I got here, to…to collect you, he threatened me. He would have sliced me to shreds with my own scythe if I touched you. The man flew to get you blood in just his fucking boxers. When he got back, he thought you were dead and the first thing he did was scream that he was going to kill me. He did not want to leave you until you woke up. Hester had to force him to go home to put on some clothes. Then he came back here and sat with you for *hours*. I relieved him about two hours ago."

The image of Lucian flying in nothing but his boxers had her body stirring awake. But him doing that for her was impossible.

"I doubt he did all that. I'm not special. I'm a Human, and he hates Humans."

"He's killed three of our own before because they laid a hand on you. He risked a rebellion for you."

Celeste's eyebrows furrowed. He never mentioned a rebellion or gloated about a lack of said rebellion to make her feel like she owed him. "What do you mean?"

The Angel of Death sighed and considered his words carefully. It was as if he had been sworn to secrecy. "Lucian, Don, and I came to help you and Cate the night Remi and his friends attacked you. Later, he tortured and killed them as punishment. It was a nightmare here in the weeks following. Once they were nothing but smoke, he went back to check on you and Cate. His only concern was your safety. His only concern since the day he met you has been your safety. So don't say for a moment he doesn't care about you."

Her eyes glanced down at the blanket staring a hole right to her cuts. There was nothing left to give. Lucian already had her soul, and now she owed him again, and for what? There was no point to living down here. There was no point in being *alive*. "He had no reason to do that. He already has my soul. I saw Vicky and how awful she looked. *I* did that. *I* caused that. If I had never met Lucian, Vicky wouldn't be in the Pit tortured every day. If I never went back to Mason, he'd be alive. It's all my fault. *Everything* is my fault. That's why I relapsed. I needed to stop the thoughts in my head. I needed the quiet. The pain felt *good*, and it was what I deserved. That is why I started cutting when I was thirteen. I was the reason for my parents' unhappy marriage. I was the reason why my father hated my mother. When I cut, it releases all this anger inside me, and it calms my mind. It's the least I can do to make up for everyone I hurt." Hot tears streamed down her face.

Thayne placed both hands over her cheeks. They weren't as big as Lucian's, but they were still strong yet gentle. She couldn't help but lean her head into his hands. A heavy weight seemed to leave her mind and absorb into him. His thumbs wiped tears from under her eyes. His chocolate eyes glistened. "Nothing is your fault. You didn't do anything wrong. You are not responsible for the actions or emotions of others. You deserve to be happy. I haven't met a single person who has gone through what you have and *lived*."

She squeezed her eyes shut, tears still fighting their way out. She shook her head. "I'm not living, not really. I've always been dead inside."

"Well," Thayne wetted his lips, "Maybe it's time to find something to live for."

CHAPTER 48

If Celeste was enemy number one to herself, stairs were enemy number two. Every step down had her leg muscles tensing up. Excruciating pain radiated from her thigh making her groan every time she put the slightest amount of weight on it. The thrill of the cut only lasted so long and all she was left with was more hatred, and pain. Her hand squeezed the life out of Thayne's arm, almost snapping it in half.

"You know, everyone could have just come to you. You almost *died*. Lucian would be more than happy to carry you around if you ask." Thayne said lightly. Celeste forced a smile. She'd worked through the pain before, she'd deal with it now.

The house smelled of jasmine and bergamot, just like the candles Cate would burn at home. Photographs spanning decades and beautiful artwork lined the off-white walls. The home felt so well loved and lived in, similar to how the beach mansion was after the girls remodeled it. Thayne guided her to the family room, never more than two steps away.

Cate was sitting on a black leather couch with an identical but slightly older woman. Both had that old Hollywood glamour look that Celeste envied deeply. Don's back was to her, eyes trained on the medium-sized television in front of them. Absent among the group was Lucian. So much for caring.

Thayne cleared his throat and a mischievous grin spread across his face. "She has risen!" The room's collective gaze shifted from the television to Celeste.

Cate jumped up from the couch, grinning from ear to ear as she made a beeline for her. She all but tackled her friend, causing Celeste to stumble backwards. Thayne put his hand on her back to steady her. Celeste embraced her friend as tightly as she could. She hadn't realized how much she missed being hugged or touched. The last time she embraced anyone had been that quick hug from Thayne during that disastrous dinner.

"Please, be gentle. I literally just got her walking," Thayne lightly scolded the girl. Cate batted him away with her hand. He laughed as he took her place on the couch.

"How do you feel?" Cate asked her as she pulled away, giving her a sad smile. Her turquoise eyes were glistening with tears.

"Like shit," Celeste answered honestly.

"Good." Cate nodded like Celeste deserved to look awful, which she did. "You look like shit too."

A mix of sob and laughter escaped Celeste as she embraced Cate again, hugging her as close to her body as she could. "I'm sorry," she rasped out. "I'm sorry for what I said to you. I didn't mean it. I felt betrayed because you are my best friend and didn't tell me the truth. No one tells me the truth anymore, not you, not Mason, not Lucian. And then you left without a note or a goodbye. I was angry, and I took it out on you. I'm sorry." She never wanted to hurt her friends. Hell, she worried more and cared more about Cate and Morgan than she did herself.

Cate squeezed her tightly before letting go. "I'm sorry I lied to you. I never wanted to hurt you. I wanted to keep you safe. I knew how things ended between you and Lucian, and I knew you were going to react badly, so I kept it hidden. You need to know that Lucian did not send me to spy on you. Ever since he met you, he's worried and cared about you so much that I felt like you were already one of us. I was excited at the thought of having a new friend in the group. Especially a girl who wasn't related to either me or Lucian."

Celeste wiped a tear from her face. She still found it hard to believe Lucian cared about a silly little mortal like herself. She held out her pinky finger. "No more secrets."

The Witch immediately hooked her pinky finger around her friend's and giggled sadly. "No more secrets after tonight, promise." Cate smiled softly. "But there are two people I want you to meet." She turned to face the woman on the couch. "Celly, this is my mother, Hester. She knows all about you and helped save your life. Mother, this is my best friend, Celeste."

Hester was older than the rest of them by two decades or so. Even so, she had an immortal beauty about her. Both shared bright turquoise eyes and dark mahogany red curls. The only difference was the few silver streaks that highlighted Hester's hair.

"I'm so glad to finally meet you!" Hester stood up, hurried over to the girls, and embraced Celeste. The hug was warm, genuine, and motherly. She could not remember a time when her mother hugged her like that.

Celeste froze in her spot, unsure of what to do. Then, slowly, she wrapped her arms around Hester. "It's nice to meet you too," she said, her voice barely above an awkward whisper. "And thank you, for helping me." Her eyes locked with Cate's and pleaded for help. A mother's embrace was not a concept she understood.

Thankfully, Cate placed a hand on her mother's shoulder. "Mother, do you think you could make that spaghetti I love? You make the sauce better than I can, and I'm sure Celle is starving."

Hester caught the hint and let Celeste go. She agreed happily, telling Celeste it would be the best pasta dish she'd ever have.

"Follow me," Cate instructed and tilted her head in the direction of her back door. Celeste followed her outside onto a medium-sized deck. The night air was chilly and smelled of Autumn. She wasn't a fan of Fall, but the air always smelt like new beginnings. Maybe this was a season of new beginnings for her.

One side of the small yard had a small soccer goal with fairy lights overhead, giving that portion of the yard enough light to see.

Lucian was guarding the goal, bent down in a defensive position. His hands were out, and he was barking out orders. His voice lacked the harshness it had when he yelled at the Demons. The more she listened, the more she realized he was coaching someone.

A teenage girl kicked a soccer ball, zig-zagging across the yard towards Lucian. She got within what could be considered the box and kicked. The ball curved left, and Lucian caught it with both hands

"That's not fair! The goal is small," the girl yelled with a faint French accent.

"Exactly, you've got to narrow in your sight. Hit the ball where you want it to go." Lucian made a hand gesture and kicked the ball back to her.

The girl put her hands on her hips. "I want to make it hit you right in the—"

"Béatrice Hélène Lefai!" Cate shouted the girl's name in a perfect French accent, effectively cutting her off. Celeste coughed back a laugh; Lucian needed a good kick in the balls. The girl clearly was close enough to him to even speak like that. Béatrice flailed her arms in frustration. "He's been doing this all night, Maman!"

Cate waved the girl towards them. As she got closer, Celeste could see dark reddish brown flyaway hairs pasted onto Béatrice's forehead with sweat. She had Cate's face shape with rounded black-blue eyes. Her skin was not as ghostly pale as her mother's, flushed cheeks aside. It was reminiscent of Don's creamy beige skin. Black wings that almost blended in with the night framed her body. The girl was stunning, just like Cate.

Cate picked a blade of grass from her daughter's shirt. "Celle, this is my daughter, Béatrice."

"*Be-ya*," the girl corrected Cate with an eye roll. "Please call me Bea. Béatrice and *Bee* are *so* last century." Cate pouted defensively, clearly not in love with the nickname.

Celeste's throat went dry and the word cracked on her tongue. Her eyes nearly bugged out of her skull.

Daughter. Cate never mentioned a daughter… Cate didn't even look old enough to have a child, let alone a teenager. "Daughter?" The word sounded foreign to her. She couldn't begin to imagine her best friend, who used to dance on tables drunk, had once been responsible for an half-Angel, half-Witch child.

"You asked for no more secrets," Cate reminded her.

"Bea is a Nephilim," Lucian added in, sneaking up on the group.

"Béatrice, go inside and help Mémé. Tell her to pull in any of the boys and *help* her, please," Cate instructed her daughter. Bea opened her mouth to protest, but Lucian hurried her inside, leaving the two girls alone.

Celeste turned to Cate. "Anything else? Are you secretly the fucking Queen of Sheba too?"

"No, just Queen of the Witches." Cate grinned cheekily; the playful smile Celeste knew by heart. Cate had truly forgiven her. The wide smile soon fell and her eyes glazed over. "She's not my only daughter. I have another girl, Winnie, but she's a story for another day."

"But you're a Witch. How is she a Nephilim? That's the product of an Angel and a human."

"All Witches are human, with the exception of myself and at one point, my mother. In addition to being a Witch, she's part demi-goddess, and part Fallen Angel."

"Goddess?" Celeste choked on the word. I mean the teenager, her mother and her grandmother were all beautiful woman, but *goddess.* "Like Greek and Roman gods? They're real?"

"Of course they're real Celle. Luce's father is not the only god in existence. *I* am a demi-goddess. Queen goes over better with the supernatural and with humans like yourself. My father is-*was*-a god. But that's also a story for another day," Cate said sharply, effectively shutting down that avenue of conversation.

"And Winnie?"

"half Demi-goddess, half Witch." A painful sigh escaped her. "She was more human than I wanted to admit for many years."

"Who is her father?"

"Which one? Winnie and Bea have different fathers. Winnie's *sperm donor* was a good for nothing warlock," the words spewed venomously from Cate's lips. A flare of anger flashed through Celeste's own heart. Cate had been burned by that man and something just as awful happened to their daughter. A dark part of Celeste's heart wanted to rip the man to shreds, but she was sure Lucian had already finished the job. Or Cate ripped him to shreds, she was feisty and confidant enough to ruin a man. Hell, Celeste has seen all five feet three inches of Cate humiliate a six-foot man at work just for cat calling the two of them "Bea's father is Don."

Celeste whipped her head towards the interior of the house fast enough to crack her neck. "Him? The asshole Angel of Hell?" Her jaw fell to the ground. Celeste was going to be sick. There was no kindness in that man. "But you like women. Did he hurt you? Did he force you to have his child? What about Winnie's father force you? When I'm better, I'll kick both their asses." She knew it would be a futile attempt, but the sentiment was there.

Cate laughed softly and gave her friend a sad smile. "I love both men and women. I prefer women and unfortunately, him. My relationship with Don is…complicated. We have been on and off since the mid-eighteen hundreds. He's not my favorite person in the world, but he's better than Winnie's father. He's also the only man I've ever been with that knows how to use his dick." Cate busted out laughing at Celeste's scrunched-up nose. Evil incarnate, she realized, wasn't Lucian, it was Don. "We loved each other once. Bea was a result of that love, although he thinks she was a mistake."

"What?" Celeste breathed. More hatred for Don festered in her. He was no better than her own father. She barely knew AJ and Bri and she loved them more than she'd ever loved anyone. And although she just met her other best friend's child, love for Bea and for Winnie, wherever she was, already began to swell in her chest. All four of those girls were family. She could never look at them with the same disgust and anger her parents had worn whenever they looked in her direction.

"Don and Bea can't be in the same room together without arguing. But they have created some kind of truce with each other since you almost bled to death on my dining table."

Celeste looked sheepishly at her feet. "I'm sorry. I really am."

"I'm just thankful Luce found you in time.

The back door slid open. "Maman! Miss Celeste! Dinner is ready!" Bea called for them before disappearing back into the interior.

"Come on, I'm sure you're starving." Cate motioned towards the house and walked inside. Celeste stayed rooted into the deck. She wasn't hungry, still riding the emotional numbness of her self-harm. Instead, her arms crossed over her chest and she watched the commotion inside. The *Family* moving about.

On the other side of the glass, Bea was laughing and squirming as Thayne jokingly put her into a headlock and rubbed his fist in her hair. Lucian, casually leaned against the kitchen counter. His feathery wings were gently crushed against the wood and marble counter. His large hands shoved into his pants pockets. His hair was damp and shone in the light. Ropes of muscle snaked up his arm and hid under his tight t-shirt. Those arms had carried her limp body from her bathroom to Cate's house. Those arms *saved* her-*again*. A wide smile stretched across his face as he spoke to Hester, but his eyes were red. Not the Demon red she'd seen on him and Don, but blood shot. Under his eyes were two dark and puffy crescents.

Don pulled out a tray from the oven and Hester stirred the pot once more. Everyone in that room looked so happy to be there. They looked like they *belonged* there. Thayne, the embodiment of death, teased the little girl as a brother would, and the Angel and King of Hell spoke to each other, their eyes glinting with happiness. There was so much darkness and death in her, the mortal and child of God, yet there was so much light and *life* here. She didn't understand where she went wrong.

Celeste ate dinner between Lucian and Thayne. Lucian was relaxed as he ate. One of his wings curved around her back. The feathers lightly brushed against the back of her arms, sending an electric pulse through her. Celeste couldn't shake the twinge in her lower abdomen, and willed her cheeks from turning red. Throughout the meal, she watched the group laugh, talk, and joke like any normal dinner with friends or family, and for a moment, she felt like she belonged there. Maybe she could belong there.

Maybe, Hell wasn't as bad as she had been taught.

CHAPTER 49

Every step towards the mansion had her thigh barking at her in protest. Celeste and Lucian barely made off of Cate's front steps before he scooped her into his arms bridal style.

"Lucian," She groaned, but was too weak to fight his grip, "Please put me down. You know I don't like being carried."

"At your pace, you'll be thirty before we get home and the dogs are waiting for their nightly game of fetch." Lucian quipped. To his credit, he walked her instead of flying the short distance to his mansion.

"You play fetch with Chip?"

"No, I just force him to watch Roxie play." Sarcasm oozed from him, "Yes. Every morning and night. You would know if you left your room." His eyes slid over to hers.

Celeste's nostrils flared. "You're awfully snippy for someone who sat by my bedside for hours wishing I woke up."

His face soured, "A 'gee, thank you, Lucian, for saving my life' would be nice."

"I don't want to fight, Lucian." Celeste sighed, looking down at her hands. The jury was still out on if she was thankful.

The rest of the short walk was quiet and void of small talk. For the first time since she got here, the voices in her head were quiet too.

"Are Bea and Hester dead?" she asked quietly as they entered the house.

"Yes," he replied curtly.

"And Winnie?" A slight, barely noticeable nod was his answer. The girl's death must have been painful on all of them.

"How did they die?"

"Winne was the only Witch they hung in Salem. Hester and Bea were murdered by Micah." He spat the name like venom on his lips.

"How old was Winnie?"

"Nine."

"Jesus," She breathed. "She was a baby." She paused for a moment. "If Hester and Bea are here, then where is Winnie?"

"We don't know. As a Witch, her soul belongs in Elysian. We have plenty of other Witch children as well as

Shifter and Vampire Children. We suspect Micah has something to do with it."

"Who is Micah?" She was entering dark waters, but she needed to know who this man was and why he killed Cate's family. She had just met Hester and Bea hours ago, but she was already added him to the list of people she'd rip to shreds for causing Cate pain.

Lucian carried her into his library, setting her in one of the plush chairs in front of his desk. "Short answer—*the* head Archangel you know and love. Long answer—Micah is responsible for the murder of Nephilim and innocent children, and the displacement of all Elysian's residents. He is the reason women have to fight to have control over their bodies. He's the reason certain Christians treat the Jewish like absolute shit. He is the reason people discriminate against others who do not look like them. He fed Humans all kinds of bullshit about God's word and what it means to live and walk in His footsteps. He has caused holy wars in the past just to see people suffer and beg for mercy."

A cold chill ran down her spine. There was no way they were talking about the same Archangel. "That can't be right. He's God's *favorite*. Angels are supposed to be good. How can he be so mean and still be an Angel? Isn't that your job?"

Lucian chuckled darkly as he walked over to his desk. From one of the drawers, he pulled out a small canvas. His face softened as he stared at it. He looked *homesick*. Celeste stretched out her legs and let out a loud groan. Her thigh throbbed with its own heartbeat. Keeping it tucked in only seemed to make it throb more. Lucian gently placed the small canvas in her hands.

There was no frame and the corners were rounded and smooth, worn out from frequent holding. The oil paint was old, faded, and cracked from time. Two small boys, no older than eight stood on the ends next to a man and a woman. In the woman's arms was a younger girl, maybe five with comically large white wings. Her eyes traveled right to the pale boy on the left with his shock of, thick, wavy black hair and large black wings behind him. The ornery look in those unmistakably bright blue eyes and boyish smile in the painting was an exact match to the man in front of her.

"You were so cute." A mischievous smile grew on her face, "What happened?" Lucian chuckled and sat beside her in the other chair.

The other boy was his exact opposite: blonde hair, glowing skin, and large white feathered wings. His wide, golden eyes looked familiar, but it couldn't be who she thought it was. This boy was an Angel.

The little girl had blonde hair, white wings and Lucian's bright blue eyes. The older woman was beautiful. Her pale skin was a sharp contrast to her long, curly black hair. She shared the same eyes as the blonde boy. The man next to Lucian was golden like the other two kids but with Lucian and the girl's blue eyes.

"Mind you, billions of years had passed between when we were that small and when oil paints were created, but Da Vinci did a fantastic job with the descriptions I gave him. It's how I remember him, when we were that age."

"That's Micah? *The* Archangel? The same one we were just talking about?" Her brain refused to consider the possibility that this sweet and innocent-looking boy was the same man that grew up to murder innocent people.

"Yes, Micah is my brother. My twin brother, to be exact. Fraternal, so lucky for you and me, I got all the attractive genes." He smirked. Her mouth gaped open. She'd had enough bombs for one day and felt like she needed a strong drink. "Thank Mother for that."

"Thank Mother? Don't you mean thank God?"

"No. I would never thank my Father for anything. He doesn't deserve it."

Her head tilted to the side. She looked at the painting again. "Were your parents Angels too?"

"My mother, Aurora," he pointed to the beautiful woman, "was the goddess of Dawn."

"Cate said she and Bea were also part goddess. And that the Roman and Greek gods are real. They're supposed to be stories. The first commandment—"

"You shall have no other gods before Me." Lucian let out a shaky laugh. "Clearly, there has to be other gods out there, or else there'd be no reason for the commandment. He thought He could control them too. Only one was blindly in love and followed Him. And she ended up dead."

"Your mother?" she confirmed. He gave her a slight nod.

The realization turned her blood ice cold. "Your biological father is God." She pointed to the older man in the painting. "*That is God?*" The painting fell into her lap. That man was the beginning and the end of all things; the reason for her parent's hate. That was the man she put her faith in. That was the man she thought she felt nearby after she had taken a blade to her skin. He wasn't just a feeling or a name or a presence. God was *real.* Lucian wasn't just God's favorite angel. He *was* God's legitimate son. Celeste swallowed thickly. "But the Bible says no one has seen him. And he told Moses that no one would see him and live."

"Well of course. People wouldn't fear him if he looked like an equal." Lucian paused briefly. "God was a wonderful father. He was incredibly warm and loving when I was growing up. He adored me, my siblings and my mother. Although he had a temper that could put any Italian to shame. But think about it, Genesis quotes him as saying 'let us make man in our image, in our Likness'. So logistically, he has to look humanlike."

Even in the painting, God's eyes seemed to cut right into her soul, just like Lucian. "So, you're related to Jesus too?"

Lucian knelt beside her, his arm resting on the chair. "More or less, unfortunately. I don't have any issues with the guy on a personal level but his birth is a sore subject or me and my sister. Sure, it was immaculate conception but he is still my father's son. Gabby," He pointed to the little girl in the photo, "and I had difficulty coming to terms with the fact that father still produced a child with someone that wasn't our mother. He adored my mother. It was one of those once-in-a-lifetime, all-consuming loves that you could only dream of finding for yourself." Lucian bit the inside of his cheek. "Although my parents would never admit it, I was father's favorite and Gabby was our mother's. Mother made sure we knew she loved us all." He smiled softly. Grief tinged his words at the memories of his mother. "I loved her more than anything in the world.

Before her brain could stop her, her hand laid over Lucian's, and she gave it a light squeeze. She did not mourn her mother but grief was universal. His arm stiffened at the touch, then relaxed. Her fingers curled into his, and he squeezed her hand back. "What happened to your mother?"

Lucian inhaled deeply, and his eyes fluttered shut. His body began to shake, the memory unpleasant enough to cause a physical reaction in an otherwise cool, calm, and collected man. When he opened his eyes, he was far away from his study in Elysian. "Micah had her killed during the rebellion."

"If she's dead, then where is she? Wouldn't she be here with you?"

"Although impossible without the proper equipment, Angels and gods can be destroyed. Micah turned her into nothing more than a pile of ash. Gabby and I tossed her ashes into the sky, and they began to glow. What remains of our mother is what you Humans call the aurora borealis." He turned his face away from her. Whatever was going through his head and on his face, he did not want her to see it.

Being vulnerable is Hell.

Words failed to form on her tongue. Celeste gave his hand a comforting squeeze. His other hand found the top of hers, encasing it between his. Her head rested on the top of his head. The closeness was all she could offer him. Talking about his mother seemed too painful for him so she shifted the conversation.

"Why did you rebel? If God was as loving to you as you claim. Why would you go against him?"

"I was young—twenty or so. When I was fourteen or fifteen, I became one of my father's guards. It was fun at first, but I was his firstborn son, I thought I should have been learning how to do his job so I could eventually take over. He didn't like that. He usurped so much power from others, but Heaven forbid I try to do the same." Lucian shrugged, "Upon my…*departure*, Micah became His favorite. He has been doing everything I fought—and lost for. The only reason he gets away with it is because he frames it as being done in the name of our father and not my brother. I know that what my Father wanted for the Humans is not what Micah has been doing. Your parents, despite the torture they put you through, were Micah's unwilling victims," Lucian explained softly, treating her with kid gloves.

Celeste's mouth went dry. Everything she had been raised on started crumbling around her. As a child, she knew in her heart that the comforting presence that continuously surrounded her had been God. But when the depression overtook her, no matter how hard she prayed, the presence had disappeared. The comfort she had found in prayer had transformed itself into the shape of a razor blade. And all along, that presence had been Thayne, not God like her heart told her it was. "Where's God? Where is our Father?"

Lucian exhaled deeply and was silent for a moment. "I don't know." His voice was deep and gravelly. "I haven't seen Him since I rebelled. But after seeing what your parents put you through, I think He's gone. I don't know if Micah killed him or imprisoned him. What I do know is that your faith keeps you with Him. I see a lot of my father's goodness in you. I've always admired that about you." His hand lifted and tucked a piece of hair behind her ear.

"He abandoned me a long time ago." Her faith was all she had growing up. Her parents made her live for God, and it was all a waste. She blinked back hot, angry tears. "Why would He leave me?" Her voice—and heart— broke.

He looked at her sadly and wiped the tears from her face. "I don't know, Pet. I wish I had the answers for you."

CHAPTER 50

The Devil watched the minutes tick by slowly. Another sleepless night to add to an already sleepless two months. Celeste's lifeless form on her bathroom floor haunted his dreams. The sight of her limp body on the floor in a pool of her own blood was etched into his eyelids.

There was so much blood: blood on her and blood on the floor. He retiled the bathroom the day after the incident. It had been 14 billion years since he last prayed to his Father, yet as he retiled, he found himself, on his knees in the bathroom, *praying* that she would live.

If and when he did manage to fall asleep, he woke up in a cold sweat and all but flew to her room to make sure she made it through another night. Only then could he breathe.

She made a good show of being fine during the day. He couldn't speak to the nighttime hours after she retreated into her bedroom. His every thought was consumed by her; making sure she was safe, looking for any sign of her cutting again, looking for any sign she was given too much angel blood and her blood was poisoning her. He knew he couldn't be with her all hours of the day. She wasn't his; he didn't have the privilege of her every waking moment.

After she came home, their friends made it a point to keep Celeste occupied and out of her head. Most days were spent with Cate, Hester, and Bea. Usually, she spent the majority of her time on the screened-in porch, either watching some television show with Thayne or by herself with both Chip and Roxie by her feet. If only the dogs could guard her from the inside demons instead of the outside ones. However, she thought she was alone, the light would leave her eyes. The corners of her mouth tilted downward. Sometimes, he would spot her Bible in her lap.

The truth of her God seemed to wreck her more than losing her time on Earth. He tried his best to get a snarky comment out of her but to no avail. She was just so *quiet*. He could see the pain on her face every time she feigned happiness when speaking to any of them; even Chip couldn't bring a smile to her face anymore. Sometimes, when she happened to join him in the study, with her nose in her Bible or another book, he would see her hand wipe away a silent tear.

It took all of his willpower to not charge up to Heaven and find the answers for her. Doing so would start a holy war. Sure, wars had been fought for less, and he could force his kind to fight that war. But he'd already risked his kingdom twice for her. A third time could mean his own demise—and ultimately hers.

What he had said about his Father wasn't an exact lie. Based on events over the last few millennia, he was convinced his father had abandoned the humans he once adored. However, whether that was due to Micah or not, he didn't know. Lucian just knew he couldn't break her again; couldn't be the reason she'd slice her skin open again. Not now, not ever. Her faith meant the world to her. It kept her relatively together, so he would do his damnedest to keep her believing. He cursed whatever karma he had that made him fond of a devout Christian.

The clock on his nightstand ticked mockingly. Fuck it. He tossed the covers off and climbed out of bed. He quietly padded down the hallway to her room. Each step caused his heart to beat faster than the next.

The first time he saw she wasn't asleep in her bed, his heart stopped altogether and dropped into his stomach. He'd hurried to the bathroom, prepared to see her dead on the floor in a puddle of blood. But the bathroom had been empty. He turned to the stairs, slid down the railing, and searched the house frantically. He had found her sleeping peacefully in the screened-in porch. The space heater was on, keeping the area warm despite the cold Elysian winter air just on the other side of the screens. The TV was flashing with some show that she'd fallen asleep to. Chip was curled up on the couch by her feet and Roxie against the couch on a blanket Celeste must have put on the wooden floor for her. He breathed out a sigh of relief and covered her up with the blanket. Even in sleep, her face had that sad, broken look. He hadn't seen her sleep peacefully since the night she went back to the beach house.

The Devil slowly opened her door. Thank Mother, Celeste was in her bed. He watched the rise and fall of her chest and exhaled the breath he'd been holding, closing the door.

By dawn's light, he was wide awake and dressed in grey sweatpants and a sweatshirt. Celeste wouldn't be up for hours, but he still went downstairs to make breakfast for them. Just like he had the morning after the fire, and the morning after Celeste's first night in Elysian, he made her chocolate chip pancakes. He wrapped up her plate in tinfoil with her name on it and set it in the refrigerator, just like he did with every other uneaten breakfast he made her. She'd warm it up when she was ready. He took his plate and mug of coffee to the screened-in porch. He turned on a small heater next to the table.

Aside from his study, he loved this little portion of the porch. He and his family could sit outside at night no matter the weather and watch soccer games on the television attached to the wooden porch frame in the corner. It was an eyesore to the Victorian exterior of his house, but no one would see it but them.

The dogs followed him outside, barking to be let out into the freezing cold air of his backyard. He obliged them, opening the door, and they took off into the grass. The two were only out long enough to see to their needs before begging to come back in.

He ate his breakfast on the couch and watched the sun rise over the horizon of Elysian. The city down below looked beautiful, washed in the pink and orange of the sunrise. Heaven was beautiful, but Elysian was beyond compare.

Chip trotted up to him holding a neon blue tennis ball. He set the ball in front of Lucian's feet and nudged him with his wet, cold nose.

"But it's cold." Lucian complained, "You literally went out and came right back in." Chip stamped his feet in a huff. "Alright. Alright. Only because I like you." He chuckled, setting his dish beside him on the couch. He picked up the ball and followed Chip out into the freezing cold. His wings pressed tight to his body to keep in what was left of his body heat.

He wasn't sure how much time had elapsed while playing fetch with the dogs, but it was long enough for his extremities to go numb and for Celeste to appear on the other couch with her plate of pancakes.

Lucian threw the ball once more before making his way over to Celeste. She looked tired, eyes red and face puffy. Lucian ran a hand through his hair and wiped away a bead of sweat. "I have to run some errands. You should come with me." Celeste set down her plate of barely eaten food. Her ocean eyes looked him up and down taking in every inch of his body. He winked playfully. "See something you like?"

Her nose scrunched up cutely. Hades, he could watch her do that for hours. "Where are you going?"

"The school."

She cocked her head in confusion. "What school?"

"The Nephilim school."

"Why?"

"Why don't you come with me?" he answered her with a question.

She seemed to consider it. He held his breath. He would enjoy her company, and it would be good for her to meet them. Hades, it would be great just to get her out of this house. "I don't really think I have a choice anymore, do I? Being on suicide watch and everything?"

Lucian looked out towards the grass. He would have preferred her to come of her own volition and for his own sanity.

She finished her breakfast in silence. "I wasn't trying to kill myself. Dead or alive, I'd still be here."

"I know," he said gravely and ran a hand through his hair. Human or Demon, it wouldn't have mattered in the grand scheme of things. A Demon's soul was broken, diluted, and missing. But her humanity was her strength, her soul made her who she was. It was hanging on by a thread, so he would do anything and everything to keep her humanity and soul intact. "I don't know if that's a blessing or a curse for you."

Celeste exhaled deeply, setting her plate on the coffee table. "I don't know anymore either."

The Nephilim school was on an island directly next to Armaros, connected by a cobblestone bridge. A stately wrought-iron gate greeted them. They approached a small booth. Inside, a shaggy-haired, college-age kid with giant wings smiled and waved Lucian through. A windy, long, tree-lined path gave way to a traditional college campus. Red-bricked dorms surrounded a large, ancient building in the center. Ropes of ivy snaked up the brick walls of each building.

Like everything Celeste had seen so far, she was surprised to see how modern the inside of the center building was. The first floor was bright and open. Benches were filled with young, winged children talking animatedly with each other. Immediately by the door was a receptionist's desk with a middle-aged woman with slightly warm-looking skin. The slight color did little to hide the look of a Demon. Her black eyes confirmed her fate.

"Hello, Mari. Sorry we're late," he apologized politely with a bright smile.

"I'm not the one you have to apologize to. Who's your friend?" The older woman asked. Her soulless eyes still maintained some kindness. She looked like a sickly grandmother, but one who would have loved her grandchildren unconditionally.

Lucian held his hand to Celeste. "This is my friend, Lady Celeste. I wanted to show her around." Celeste's eyebrow arched. He shot her a *later* look in return. "Celeste, this is Marigold, she is head of the Nephilim school. She makes sure all the kids have activities to do and makes sure any lessons they take would actually be valuable to kids."

The woman gave Celeste another warm smile. The sweet look made Celeste stare down at her feet, uncomfortable with maternal kindness. "Well, welcome, dear. If there's anything I can get you, let me know."

Celeste thanked her and followed Lucian down the hallway. The Devil took long strides, almost rushing to their next destination. She grabbed a fistful of his shirt and forced him back towards her. "Lady?" she hissed.

Lucian slowed his pace. "You are a part of my court.

"What do you mean *part of your court?*" the shock had her voice lifting an octave.

He shrugged in a matter-of-fact way. "I'm King of Hell. Cate is Queen of the Witches. Bea is a princess as would Winnie if she was here. Don, who is my second, and Thayne are Lords. Hester is Cate's second in command so she is a Lady. I may not be your friend, but you are mine. You are also Cate's best friend so it would be natural to make you a lady here in Elysian. Also, having the title lets everyone know that you belong here in Elysian and not in Hell with the other humans." He continued his strides, entering a stairwell and descending down towards the basement.

"That's why Remi called Cate *your Highness*," Celeste said out loud to herself, the connections she had missed earlier in the year were snapping into place. Lucian made a noise of agreement. "*Lady* makes me seem important."

"You *are* important." His head turned to face her as he spoke. The two stared at each other for a moment. Lucian's eyes held so much sincerity that it was impossible for her to think he was lying. "One day, we'll prove it to you." He promised as he opened the door for her.

The basement was like a portal to another life. For a moment, she had stepped into her old elementary school. White floor tiles, and white bricked walls covered with brightly colored flyers. Classroom doors had name plates and decorations. Some rooms were filled with young, winged kids around tables doing some activities. Other rooms had older children hovering around easels.

"How do you feel about kids?" he asked calmly as if he were asking about the weather.

She skidded to a stop. "Excuse me?" Her thoughts started to spiral. She knew he was being too nice to her.

He just told her that he considered her a friend. That Bastard. He only saved her humanity because he wanted something from her.

Lucian turned to look at her and stopped walking. "Do you like children?"

"If you're asking me to bear the spawns of Satan, fuck that." Her arms crossed over her chest. She would never have his child. She would yank the necklace off before she ever went to bed with him.

Lucian put a hand on his stomach and tipped his head back. A clear bright laugh emanated from him like he used to when they would joke around. "No. Not *our* children, Pet. But children in general. Do you like them?" he asked a third time.

"I love my nieces, but I never really gave my own much thought once you took my soul. I didn't want to bring children into a world where I could have abandoned them at any time." Guilt flashed in his eyes. He turned around and continued walking. "I started to consider having children again after Mason and I got back together. As a teenager, I had Mason's and my children's names picked out. Also, I would never have kids with you. I'd rather die."

An unsuspecting, low growl came from his direction, but he said nothing. He made a left down another hallway. She followed a few paces behind him, staring a hole into his back. He led her towards a room with glass walls. Inside the room, a giant mass of winged toddlers collectively gasped before they stormed the door.

CHAPTER 51

The three-winged adults inside struggled to keep the fifty or so toddlers at bay. The children varied in height, weight, and race, but they all shared similar dark, feathery wings. Lucian smiled brightly and opened the door to screams of "Luci!"

He knelt to their level and enveloped as many as he could into his arms. He even greeted all of them by name. After the greetings, he moved more easily into the room. He picked up one bronze-haired boy who remained seated on the couch with a pouty face and crossed arms. Lucian bounced him lightly, trying to comfort him.

"Who are you?" a girl with a round face, striking blue eyes, and black hair asked, pointing at Celeste. She looked like Lucian; a lot like him.

He looked over at her and motioned her into the room. She took a few tiny steps into the room and gave them a small wave and a forced smile. "This is my friend Miss Celeste. Can you say hello?" he asked them. A chorus of hellos erupted from the children. The smile she pasted on her face faltered when she remembered what Lucian had told her. All of these children were dead. They were just *babies*. Babies with their whole life ahead of them. Her breakfast crept back into her throat. Lucian gave her a sad smile paired with an understanding and sympathetic look. "Find a spot. I'm going to read a story to them." He took a seat in a rocking chair in the front of the room; the boy curled up on his lap. The Devil picked up the book that was already on the end table.

Celeste found a spot in the back of the classroom against the wall with the other adults. Lucian dove into a rhyming storybook. His sweet voice fluctuated for each character. The children hung onto his every word.

When he set the finished book down beside him, the kids rioted, chanting for one more. Lucian tried to reason with them kindly, talking to them like they were friends.

Celeste rubbed her face furiously. Everything he did pissed her off. A real Devil would not read toddlers a book, let alone hug each one and address them by name. After a tough negotiation; Lucian folded immediately. He read one more story with the same enthusiasm as the first one. When it was done, he set it down and made his rounds of goodbye hugs. The gentleness he had with them was unlike any other. Celeste's heart tugged, against her better judgment.

"The one you picked up looked like a smaller version of Thayne," Celeste commented as they entered the stairwell to go back to the first floor. "and that little girl looked just like you."

"Because Thayne is his father. And Micah is the girl's father. Told you I got the good genes."

She stopped in her tracks. "What do you mean?"

"When two people get drunk, sometimes better judgment goes out the window, and they decide to—"

"I know how babies are made, idiot." She cut him off with a sharp look. "What I mean is why is Thayne's son here and not with Thayne? Does he not know?"

"Do you know the story of the Nephilim?"

It took her a moment to recall it. It had been ages since she thought about biblical history. "They are giants, created from the sons of God and the daughters of Men."

He made a noise of agreement, "There was a group of male Angels called Watchers. Aptly named, they watched the Humans. The Watchers showed the Humans a thing or two about the world my Father created for them and spent considerable time with them. Then the Watchers fell in love with the Human women, and nine months later, half-human-half-angels were born."

They waved goodbye to Mari and walked outside.

"So was Thayne a Watcher?"

"No. While yes, the Watchers joined me in the rebellion. Once they left Heaven, they introduced the other Fallen Angels to Human women. The Fallen loved the new freedom brought by not following my Father. They could walk on Earth, do what they want, who they want, when they want. Many of the Fallen Angels have children they don't know about."

He led her opposite of their cart, towards a grassy common area filled with kids and teenagers. "But if the Fallen live on the other side of the bridge, why don't they know they have kids like 500 feet away?"

"There are all sorts of different reasons. One, they raped a woman, and either do not care about the repercussions or have no desire to be a parent for all eternity. Two, they don't remember who they sleep with, so they claim deniability. Three, most of the Fallen hate children and want nothing to do with them. And four, those who don't know they reproduced, don't know their child was murdered. As for the female Fallen Angels, the majority of them don't desire to be a parent and will abandon the child somewhere on earth. The adult Nephilim are a hit or miss with their biological families. Not many are as loved as Bea is."

Celeste's heart broke. She knew first-hand how it felt to be unwanted. They stopped by a tree in a courtyard, away from listening ears. "How can you be friends with Thayne and Don if they raped a woman or went on a sex spree? Don and Bea can't even be in the same room together! How can you even look at him?"

Lucian shoved his hands into the pockets of his jeans as he leaned against the tree trunk. "It wasn't easy. Both of them have been my friends since before the Fall. Thayne and I grew up together. I trust him more than anyone with my life. As for Don, his relationship with Cate is complicated, and not my story to tell. But he made it very clear he didn't want Bea and I can't change him. I can't force him to change."

Her eyes narrowed, "You are the King of Hell. You can do whatever you want."

Lucian looked past her shoulder, giving the impression he was looking at her. "I have some power over him as a former Archangel but not enough to force him to be a father to a child he never wanted."

She crossed her arms over her chest. "My father raised me, and it was very obvious he didn't want me."

"And look at how you turned out," Lucian snapped a bit too harshly. She flinched and pulled back from him. He gave her an apologetic look. "You have to understand, not everyone is like your parents. Not everyone feels the need to fake a perfect, godly family when they're miserable. Yes, Cate was devastated and hurt, and Bea was hurt when she found out, but it's been over a hundred years. That's a very long time to hold a grudge."

Her face twisted in confusion. "They forgave him?"

"It was hurting Cate. Bea had already been dead 70 years or so. She wanted her mother to be happy."

Celeste bit the inside of her cheek. She felt like an immature teenager. A sixteen-year-old child could forgive the actions of her parents, and yet, Celeste could never and would never forgive her parents and her sister. She couldn't imagine having to see them for all eternity, knowing she couldn't die or get away from them. They were a cable car ride away and it still felt too close.

The two were silent for some time. They leaned against the tree and watched a group of preteens throw a football around. "Do you have children here, that you know of?" she asked softly. She blurted out the question, dreading the answer.

Lucian shook his head. "Human women aren't my type. But even then…I could never take advantage of a woman like that. I did, however, raise Bea. The early nineteen hundreds were not a great time for single mothers, so I spent the majority of my time with Cate and Bea on Earth, acting as Cate's brother. When she started talking, Bea used to call me Dad. It broke my heart and Cate's."

Celeste took in the information and watched the various groups of Nephilim. The younger ones chased each other in a game of freeze tag while other groups of the same age sat together, talking, laughing, and playing card games.

"You did all this for them?" Celeste said, breathlessly. All of them were happy; she could not see one ounce of grief in any of them for their situation. If they could find happiness and make the best of a shitty situation, maybe she could as well.

Lucian smiled like a proud father. "They didn't ask to be born, and they most certainly did not ask to be killed by Micah for what they are. They should be able to be free and have fun."

She looked at a group of high schoolers sitting in a circle, cheering about who knows what. "How does Micah find the Nephilim? They look like humans."

"The presence of magical abilities usually but also, every Nephilim has a mark on or around their shoulder blade in the shape of a wing. Once they have a suspected Nephilim in their grasp, they check their back. If the birthmark is there, they are killed on the spot."

"But if they are half angels, why didn't they go to Heaven?"

"Micah believes Nephilim are dangerous. Nephilim are not giants like the Book of Enoch says they are. That was just Micah's propaganda to turn people against them. The Nephilim adults have strong magical abilities and Micah is terrified of that. He fears they could bring him down. That's why he tries to kill them early on in their lives because the magic takes time to develop and make itself known to the child. Bea is especially lethal because she is part goddess, Witch, and Angel. Bea could destroy worlds with the snap of her fingers if she ever wanted to."

"Do they lose their power when they die?"

"Not at all, but Micah thinks they do. So, it's our secret. Mother forbid Micah attacks Hell, all the Nephilim take classes to hone their abilities."

A shiver ran down her spine. Bea could have used that power to get back at her father. But she chose to put her grudge aside for her mother.

Celeste wanted to throw up. They were just children. Her God loved children. "Micah is vile," she commented as she rubbed her arms, wiping away invisible dirt.

Lucian laughed bitterly. "If you only knew. But there's a price for being the favorite. The power goes straight to the head."

"You would know, right?" He laughed loudly again, eyes glimmering. The laugh was contagious enough for the corner of her mouth to turn upwards for a brief second. She exhaled deeply. If God was here, He could have stopped Micah. With everything she'd heard, He must have been gone for centuries. "Did you bring me here to prove to me God's not around?"

He looked at his tennis shoes. "No," he whispered, lifting his head back up. The icy blue eyes melted into a pool of silent grief. "You are broken enough. I wanted you to know you are not alone. The Nephilim were all let down by someone they love. You may be a Human, but you have a lot in common with the Nephilim. I thought introducing you to their world would bring you some comfort. I know they would love you. I know you hate me; you've made it very clear." Celeste winced. "But you are here for an eternity, and I wanted you to know there are people out here who would accept you and like you for who you are."

She looked back at the courtyard. Everyone there was unwanted. Unwanted by their fathers, possibly their mothers, and their God. Yet here they are: happy, smiling, and surrounded by love from their friends. They were dead, but they were thriving. Maybe she could too.

CHAPTER 52

The ride home was silent. She couldn't get her mind off the Nephilim, how the children seemed to make peace with their fate, and how she, an adult, couldn't.

You're pathetic.

It wasn't until they reached the front door to the mansion that she was able to pull out of her thoughts. A tall brown package leaning against the wall caught her attention. Next to it, a smaller square white box. A huge, dazzling grin appeared on Lucian's face. "Fantastic. It has your name on it."

Celeste moved out of his shadow. There, scribbled in black marker was her name on the brown package. Whoever wrote it clearly didn't like her. "I didn't order anything. I didn't even know Hell had a postal Service. What is it?"

"We have messenger angels." He shrugged. A sparkle danced in his eyes, "I don't know, let's go find out." Lucian handed her the small white box and carefully picked the tall one and walked around the porch to the back yard. Metal shifted around in Lucian's box and glass shifted in hers. He set the box down on the patio table and whipped out his knife from his back pocket. "I'd let you open it, but then I'd have to give you a knife," he admitted sadly. His lips flattened as he glanced at her. She wanted to take offense but could find it in her. He was absolutely right, putting a knife in her hand was asking for trouble. The blood behind her scars throbbed in agreement. The silver blade glowed blue as it swiveled open; like it was saying hello.

The tape split in one quick, graceful glide. Her eyes traveled to the blade; her skin itched seeing how nicely it slid through the tape. Blood leaked down creamy skin. Her mouth parted open with a sharp intake of breath.

"Celeste," he called her back gently.

Her eyes blinked and flickered to Lucian. His icy eyes jolted her out of her fantasy. When she glanced back to the box, that's all it was again—a box. She peered inside and gasped. Instinctively, her hands wrapped around the metal tube and pulled it out of the box.

"Oh my God, my telescope!" she exclaimed, eyes watering with happiness for the first time in months. She sat the telescope on the table and ran her hands down the length of it, inspecting every inch. There were some scratches and dents on the tube and on the legs, but it looked relatively okay. An enormous weight lifted off her chest. It was her telescope. Her baby. The night she lost it;

she'd lost a piece of herself— the piece that made selling her soul worth it. She hugged the telescope tightly, squealing. She was complete again.

"The focal piece was missing, and the eyepiece was broken. The white box has different eyepieces and a new focal lens for you." He sliced open the white box and folded up his blade, stuffing it back into his pocket. Safely away from her.

"How did you…Where did you find it? Mason said it was stolen."

"I had my servants go and look for it. They found it in a storage room at a university nearby. Unfortunately, they couldn't find your journal and your pens. I'm sorry."

An odd wave of peace overcame her. It was as if her heart and soul were starting to settle down. Now that she had her telescope maybe she could be content to live out eternity here. "You didn't have to do this."

"I wanted to." He smiled softly. His eyes showed the same kindness she saw when she first met him. "I wanted you to feel at home here. You deserve to spend eternity doing what you love."

Her heart stretched in different directions. *This* was the Lucian she met years ago. Kind, thoughtful, considerate Lucian. *This* was the Lucian she fell in love with. *This* was the Lucian she knew before he told her he was the King of Hell. Her heart and mind did not want to accept it. She wanted to keep hating him; he still lied and unknowingly took her soul away from her.

He called you a mistake.

She exhaled slowly, the bricks stacked back up around her heart. "Why do you care?" she asked him. "Why have you been so nice to me? You told me I was a mistake."

Lucian's eyes glazed over in grief. Pain and guilt washed over him. His Adam's apple bobbed. "You are my friend, Celeste. And I care about you, even though you love to hate me. I haven't slept in months for fear if I do, your dog is going to wake me up with blood all over his nose again. I don't breathe until I hear you leave your room to and I know you're alive. Every morning I'm terrified you'd cut too deep the night before and bled out."

Celeste chewed on her bottom lip and stared a hole into the ground. She'd guessed he was behind the missing sharp kitchen utensils, but she didn't know about him not sleeping. God, she felt awful, he worried so much about her and she never really cared if she woke up the next day or not.

He continued, "You have made it more than obvious that you hate it here. But you don't need to suffer or torture yourself. Eternity is a long time to hate yourself, to hate others."

An icy cold wave washed over her, clearing the angry filter that had covered her eyes for the last eight years. The Lucian she knew was standing right in front of her. He had been there the whole time. It was easier to deny the truth than to accept that the Devil wasn't as evil as she had been told.

"Why did you befriend me back then? Was I just another charity case to you like the Nephilim?" She wiped a runaway tear from her eye. The words came out sharper than she wanted them to. That damn mouth of hers was going to get her killed. That was just another reason why she cut: to control her emotions, to keep herself from lashing out at others. Lucian's goodwill would only last so long.

Lucian's body recoiled away from her and a part of her felt guilty for asking. "I was alive when the stars were created. My mother's sister was the goddess of the moon and they had been incredibly close. After my parents got together, it was obvious she missed her sister and would spend many a night under the moon and stars. When I heard you talking to your friend in that bar line about the constellations, it reminded me of the stories my mother used to tell me and my siblings. I love soaring through the sky and the feel of the wind blowing through my feathers. I loved looking down and seeing the beautiful world my father created but I never saw it like you did; I never cared to."

The corner of Celeste's mouth turned upwards. Lucian had interrupted her conversation with Morgan to correct her on the mythology behind the Andromeda constellation. Lucian, tall, dark, and handsome with bright, icy blue eyes and a dazzling smile had captured her heart. From that night, until the day after she sold her soul, Celeste had been in love with him. "Then you unconsciously pushed up your sleeve, and I saw the red marks on your arm. Believe it or not, I do care about those who have been mistreated, Human or not. That alone led me to believe that the world had been cruel to you. Yes, I felt the need to be kind to you. You needed a friend that gave a damn about you. You were dealt a shitty hand, and despite everything you've been through, you've remained pure at heart. You've remained good. Most people who've been through what you have don't stay that way. If I didn't know any better, I'd say you are an old soul."

Except, her heart *wasn't* pure and she *wasn't* good. She refused to see Lucian as anything other than the villain of her religion when all he had ever done was *show* her who he was. She judged him and his family. Back at the beach, she toyed with the hearts of men who didn't deserve it. She was nothing but a hypocrite and a mistake. Hot tears welled up and fell down her cheeks. "I'm not a good person, Lucian. I judged you for what you're supposed to represent and not what you *are*. Not to mention, I fight you tooth and nail about everything. I accused Cate of being your spy when all she's ever done is be a true friend to me. I made a deal to kill my family. Mason is dead and My sister is tortured and raped every day by *your* Angels! *I did that.* It's my fault! Everything is my fault. That's why I started cutting again! I needed to stop the voices in my head but I also needed to atone for my sins. I don't deserve your kindness or Cate's or anyone else's. I deserve to be rotting in the Pit. I should have just bled out on the bathroom floor. I am to blame for *everything*," her composure cracked. Every emotion and feeling she had shoved into a deep dark place in her mind exploded. A sob ripped out her and she covered her face with her hands. Her knees hit the hard, cold ground with a thud.

Lucian knelt in front of her. "Look at me," He pleaded softly. His warm, slightly calloused hands gently pulled hers from her face. She opened her eyes and stared right into the melted ice of his eyes. It was the same soft baby blues that had watched her grieve her home. The same eyes she used to see whenever he looked at her. She'd hated the color blue until that moment. Her parents always called out her blue eyes and how different, how *ugly* she was. But his blue eyes were kind and beautiful. Maybe blue eyes weren't all that bad.

"Celle, listen to me very carefully," he ordered in a quiet, yet demanding, voice. It was a calmness that demanded to be heard *and* felt. She leaned into his hands and sniffled. "That deal *saved* your life. If you had stayed there, in that house, you would've been dead either by your own hands or theirs." It pained her to admit he was right. "The world would be a darker place if you were dead. *You* did not kill your family, Celeste. *I did.* I told you no one was going to get hurt. *I* made plans to have your family forget you existed, but when I saw them, the *Devil* took over. I was furious with them. They were supposed to protect you and love you, but instead, they tried to kill that bright light of yours. They used my Father against you. They made you feel like you were going against Him and that you didn't love Him when that was not the case. The love you have for my Father is not out of moral obligation or to get your parents to love you. It's a rare, pure love, which is more than they had. Their deaths are *never* on you. Their deaths are on me." Lucian gently took her hand and placed it over his heart with his over hers. Celeste willed herself to focus on the gentle throb of his heartbeat to calm herself down and to keep herself from retreating into the darkest parts of her mind.

For eight years, she blamed herself. Her chest heaved as she tried to suppress the sobs. Despite her best efforts, sobs continued to escape her with force. Lucian sat down in the grass, pulling her to his chest. Her body fit perfectly into him, like two puzzle pieces finally clicking together. His wings cocooned around them to comfort her. They slowly started to rock back and forth in a soothing motion.

Eight years of guilt, shame, and hatred heaved out of her body with each sob. A huge weight was lifted off her chest.

"I'm sorry I let you carry that burden for so many years. It was never yours to carry. I hope you, eventually, can find it in yourself to forgive me," Lucian said softly in her ear.

Everything stuck with her. Words, emotions, and pain. Eight years was a long time to suffer and make her cold. She had forgiven Cate. She could forgive him.

CHAPTER 53

"**A**nd what did I do? I blubbered like a fucking baby!"

Celeste summarized the moment she and Lucian shared last week with Cate as she took a bite of hot pepperoni pizza. She winced and fanned her hands at her open mouth, breathing through the heat of the marinara sauce. "Fuck, this is hot as Hell. Literally." The slice dropped onto the plate on the side table. The girls were having a long overdue girl's night. The last time they did, they had been attacked by Remi. She shoved the thought aside. Tonight was for pizza, drinking, and stargazing.

Cate laughed and took a sip of her coconut rum and pineapple juice drink. "It's a start. I think you two can finally move past everything and be friends again. I thought the tension between my mother, daughter, and her father was thick, the tension between the two of you was unbearable. All I want is my family to be able to be near one another without starting another Holy War." She smiled weakly. "Right Chip?" The Lab barked as if he was agreeing with her.

Lucian and Celeste had come to a truce. Over the last week, they were kinder to each other. Talking, joking, and laughing like they used to. The two now shared all their meals together. She made an effort to eat more than she had over the last few months. There was a long road ahead of them but it was a start.

Celeste took a sip of her drink and walked over to her telescope. Having it back practically raised her from the dead. Every cloudless night, she was outside until the bitter cold caused her blood to turn to ice. "I love that we're not fighting anymore but all those old feelings are coming up, and I *cannot* have those feelings again. We may not be *at* each other's throats anymore, but I can't stop thinking of being *down* his throat! It's wrong. Mason's not even cold in the ground yet."

"You're better off without Mason. He clearly couldn't see you for who you are now," Cate stated, biting into her pizza slice. Her foot kicked a tennis ball across the yard for the dogs to chase.

Celeste winced. Mason was the love of her life. "You're not supposed to speak ill of the dead."

Cate exhaled loudly. Gone was her best friend; and in its place was a mother ready to lecture her child. Celeste's skin crawled at the look, and she threw back the rest of her drink in one gulp. "He changed you." Cate gestured to her clothes.

Celeste looked down at her light blue flared jeans, a light pink sweater, and booties. A far cry from her staple of skinny jeans, black blouses, and skater shoes. The outfit was reminiscent of something Vicky would wear. "What's wrong with it?"

"It's not you. And what happened to your nose ring and eyebrow piercing? Remember how happy you were when you got your nose done? And now it's probably closed up."

She had been over the moon to get her nose pierced. Cate had driven her to the tattoo shop and held her hand as the needle pierced her nostril. She sighed and waved a hand. She grew out of them. People were allowed to grow out of things. "I was rebelling. I was free from my parents, and I went a little crazy. I'm twenty-six now. I had to grow up sometime." Chip bounded back towards them with the tennis ball in his mouth and Roxie not far behind. He made a beeline to Celeste. She wrangled the ball from him and threw it back across the yard.

"And your hair… You never wanted highlights when I suggested it, but now I'm glad you didn't. You don't look good as a blonde." Cate admitted, causing Celeste to run a hand through her curls. The blonde highlights had grown out, leaving her hair an ugly half-blonde-half-brown. Cate bit her lip. "I'm just saying, you can do better than someone who is going to change you."

"Like who? Lucian?" Celeste spat. Cate shrugged her shoulders like she had considered the idea. She shook her head wildly and waved her hands. Hell would freeze over before she let herself fall back in love with the Devil. "No. Absolutely not. No chance in Hell. Sure, we're fine now but he still lied to me."

"I lied to you."

"I never loved you like I loved Lucian." Celeste walked back to the patio table where their food was growing cold. She took a seat in a chair and refilled her almost empty drink. Chip followed her, wanting her to throw the tennis ball again. She waved him off. "Go play with Roxie." She whispered to him. Roxie was curled up into a lounge chair.

"Everyone has different sides. Lucian has two different sides: the demonic side, which is terrifying and makes everyone afraid for their lives, and the side we all see every day. The man who loves his family and will go to the ends of the earth for them and for others. Thayne has different sides; he is kind to those he takes to Heaven and awful to the ones on their way to Hell. And I have two different sides. Your sister did, and so did you. You played the part your parents wanted you to be around them, then you were yourself when you were alone or with me or with Lucian. Lucian is nice to you because he cares about you."

Celeste sighed and waved her hand dismissively. It stabbed at her pride to admit that Lucian did care about her. He always had, even when she didn't deserve it. Her mind had trouble reconciling the fact that he lied to her yet had only been himself around her. "I liked it better when you got drunk on bar tables with me. I don't like this reasonable mom friend shit." Her tone light and joking.

Cate laughed; the noise was contagious enough to crack a smile of her own. "We'll go drunkenly dance on tables one day down in the Block." The Block was a strip of nightclubs and bars towards the southern end of Unity Square.

The screen door clanked open and the dogs erupted into a chorus of barks. "What are my favorite heathens up to?" Lucian's voice boomed loudly, hitting her ears as if he was beside her. Her body tensed up at the word. Her mother used it as a threat day after day. Lucian's light tone was a stark contrast to her parents. She had to remind herself repeatedly it was Lucian talking, not her mom. He pulled the patio chair beside her out and sat down. His blue soccer jersey was soaked and stuck to his body like a second skin. Black curls were matted to his forehead and his body heaved from the exercise. He wiped his forehead with a damp towel. His finger pointed to the firepit not too far from them. Fire roared to life. Her arms tingled slightly, warming her just enough to be comfortable in the early march night air. He gave them a playful smile as he started to take off his cleats and shin guards.

"World domination," Cate deadpanned, smirking as she stood up. "I need to get going. Bea went on a date with a boy from her spell-casting class and should be getting home by now. I need to make sure there's no funny business." The two girls embraced quickly.

"What? No goodbye hug for me?" Lucian teased lightly, making himself busy with a left-over slice of pizza.

"You stink." Cate wrinkled her nose and went into the house, letting herself out the front door.

The two were quiet for a moment. The awkward silence had faded into a comfortable quiet that she enjoyed. Lucian devoured the slice like it was his last supper.

"How was your game?" Celeste asked.

He set the slice down on a napkin and picked up his water bottle. "My team lost. Fucking Shifters." Lucian grumbled before finishing off his water. The bottle crushed easily in his hand.

"How? You have wings, just fly across the field."

"That's cheating, my dear. I'm not that evil." He smirked, his eyes crinkling at the corners.

Celeste chuckled and shook her head. "Remember when we used to play at the field in PA?" In the warmer months before the fire, she would tell her parents she and Morgan were going to the park near their house when she was really meeting up at the park across town to play soccer with him.

His lips curved upwards at the memory. "I used to kick your ass."

Celeste scoffed, "Like Hell! I was way better than you! You were old and rusty," she teased, although she could not remember who won those scrimmages.

"Maybe I let you win." He shrugged his shoulders innocently. The mischievous glint in his eyes said otherwise.

After everything she'd seen of him, he probably did let her win. "I was on Varsity all four years of High School! If anything, I let *you* win!" the corner of her lip curled into a smirk. Although new to their current relationship, the friendly banter was reminiscent of a past that maybe wasn't all *that* bad.

"Sounds like we'll have to have a rematch. See who the better player is." He grinned. He reached down to pet both Chip and Roxie who had settled by his feet and not hers for once.

The smirk on her face fell into a frown. He would win the rematch regardless. She hadn't been able to pick up a soccer ball since before the fire without feeling nauseous from the memories. "Maybe."

"You are a fantastic player. The Nephilim team would love to have you. I can introduce you to Eloa, she runs their team."

Celeste shook her head. She had just started to feel like she belonged among Lucian and his friends; There was no way in Hell she'd make a fool of herself in front of the Nephilim. As a human, she was already an outsider in Elysian, she wasn't about to drive the point home.

The two sat in a brief, comfortable silence, taking in the clear, pleasant evening. "What's going on in the heavens tonight?" Lucian asked softly. Their heads tilted simultaneously towards the night sky. It wasn't the same sky she fell in love with, but Lucian had created a great copy when he created Elysian.

"I'm just looking at constellations. I've missed them."

Lucian glanced over at the telescope in the yard. "May I?"

"If you'd like."

The Devil got up from the chair and walked to the telescope. He bent down to the eyepiece. "Tell me what I'm looking at."

She hesitated and stared at him, mouth agape. He *asked* her to use her telescope. He *asked* her to teach him about what he was seeing. Months ago, when she tried to do this with Mason, he made her feel like she was wasting his time with something silly. She walked on the balls of feet; afraid that any loud noise would scare him away. She spoke softly to him from a foot away, "If you look straight, you'll see the Little Dipper. To the bottom left of that is Draco. Below Draco's tail is the Big Dipper."

Lucian seemed to hang onto her every word. A smile crept up his face, growing wider by the second until it stretched past his eyes. "This is incredible."

"It's beautiful. The sky is so vast, and there's so much out there that we don't know about. When I'm looking up at it, I feel like a part of something for once." Her head tilted upwards. "I love seeing meteor showers and eclipses. But stargazing is unbelievable. It's so fascinating how, despite how dark the sky is, the stars always find a way to shine." Her eyes came back down to see Lucian staring at her, his face inches from hers.

"You are the brightest light in the darkness," he whispered, tucking a loose strand of hair behind her ear.

Celeste's cheeks flushed; his breath was hot on her neck. She started to lean into him when Mason's face flashed through her mind. She jerked her head away and stepped backward, giving them both some room. The slightly cold air was a welcome feeling on her face.

Lucian blinked and pulled away. "I'm going to shower and then I'll be back to stargaze with you."

She blinked and shifted her eyes to him. Her mouth opened slightly in shock. Mason would have told her no or found another excuse to spend a night between the sheets. "You don't have to. I know it's boring."

"Not at all. It reminds me of some better times." He smiled softly, his eyes glazed over. He must have spent many a night outside with his mom, watching the night sky.

Celeste immediately fixed herself a new drink, pouring the rest of the bottle of rum into the glass, filling it almost to the rim.

True to his word, he came back outside about an hour later with a glass filled with an amber liquid, and a plate full of cookies.

"Really, Lucian, you don't need to stay out here with me. I'm okay here by myself. It's just the backyard. It's not like I'm trespassing in a park."

Lucian offered her a chocolate chip cookie like it was a peace offering. It was one of Hester's homemade cookies Cate had brought over earlier. "I want to, Pet. Surprisingly, due to my wings, I love the sky. Although I prefer the blue sky of day as opposed to the black sky of night." He chuckled softly, a somber look quickly fell over his face. "When I was about eight or so, my mom was in a bad mood and I thought that if I flew high enough, I'd touch the stars and could bring one back down to her. I had flown higher than I ever had before when my father met me and stopped me."

"That didn't really happen, did it?" Celeste laughed, picturing a smaller version of a determined Lucian flying up into the sky.

"I have no reason to lie about my childhood. But I also can recognize that I was eight and an idiot. I had no idea what space was or how the sky worked outside of my father creating it with the help of my mother and her siblings."

"Do you miss Heaven?"

He shrugged. "I mostly miss my mother. I do miss the dad my father was to me as a kid. I miss my sister, although I do see her once in a while. I miss those warm nights when my parents and my siblings would sit in the backyard on a quilt, and we'd listen to my mother talk about the constellations. Hades, I miss the person my twin was when we were children." Lucian inhaled deeply and let go slowly. He blinked a few times, sneakily blinking back any tears that threatened to fall. Suddenly and without warning, she finally saw the Lucian she met all those years ago, the one she had fallen in love with. He'd been right beside her the whole time.

CHAPTER 54

His half of the soccer field was void of Lucian's defense.

All but two were still trying to catch up to Celeste. He'd known she was an incredibly skilled player, but he also didn't realize how *slow* his teammates were. Yesterday, he finally convinced her to come out and play in a pick-up game with him in Kore Gardens Park. Nephilim adults, Celeste, and Bea, played against his Fallen Angels. It was more of a scrimmage than a game. And, it was clear his team needed the practice. Watching his team lag behind her, he saw they needed more. He groaned internally at the thought of more suicide drills.

Despite Bea's insistence, the Nephilim initially hesitated to let Celeste play. However, once they watched her steal the ball from a Fallen twice her size and assisted

Bea with the first goal of the game, they quickly changed their tune. By the looks of it, she would have a starting position on their team by the end of the day.

Celeste's ponytail swung violently back and forth as she dribbled the ball down the field. The mid-March wind blew small strands of flyaway hair into her eyes, but that did not stop her from narrowing in on her target: him. Ocean blue eyes locked on him and a slow, devilish grin grew slowly upon Celeste's beautiful face, threatening to bring him down. Lucian mimicked her smile—challenge. He bent his knees and hunched into a defensive position.

He pulsed on the balls of his feet, ready to block the ball to keep her from scoring, *again*. Celeste dribbled it towards him then kicked it to a Nephilim to her right. His body moved instinctively as he tracked the Nephilim. He entered the circle, and Lucian stepped out of the goal, smirking. Fortunately for him, the man was a fast runner but never great at scoring. Anytime he tried to score, he'd kick the ball to wide and miss the goal. The man pulled his leg bag to kick it towards the goal but the ball went rolling towards Celeste. She had snuck up behind Lucian, on the left side of the goal he had left wide open.

Lucian pivoted and jumped towards the other side of the goal to block her shot. His fingers tipped the ball which did little to slow the ball's movement into the goal. He heard the swish of the net as he landed on his side with a hard thud onto the grass.

Celeste, unable to slow herself down, tripped over him. He rolled onto his back and shot his hands out to catch her. His hands gripped her hips to steady her. Her body came crashing down on his, knocking the air from his lungs. Lucian felt his body tense at the feel of her on him, like two puzzle pieces clicking together. It was a position that he had dreamt of recently, although fewer clothes were involved. Her ponytail dangled and brushed against his stubble, and they were both breathing heavily. Her Celtic necklace popped out from underneath her shirt and whacked his chin. It dangled in between them, the only wall to keep him from lifting up and kissing her. The rest of the world faded out, and he only saw Celeste. Her cheeks were flushed from the exercise, and her blue eyes sparkled with a happiness he rarely gets to see. Happiness was so beautiful on her. He would do anything to keep that look on her face.

They stared at each other for another minute or more, he wasn't counting. Lucian gave her a purely male smile. "If you wanted me to fuck you, you could have just asked. It would have been a better workout." He smirked. He felt his pants straining, and Celeste tensed in his arms. She blinked and looked away before lifting herself off of him, placing both knees on the grass between his legs. Her cheeks flushed a deeper red from his comment. His heart was racing from the gaze she did not dare break.

"You shouldn't have been in my way," Celeste retorted and finally broke their staring contest.

"You shouldn't have been so sneaky with that shot! And they say I'm the Devil." Lucian joked.

He helped her stand, her hand in his larger ones. Her hand was sweaty, but soft and seemed to fit into his perfectly. Once she was up, she didn't pull her hand away and he didn't either. One sudden movement and Celeste would retreat into her shell. Their publicly private moment was interrupted by the shrill voice of his assistant Mindy, "Your Highness…There's a visitor in the throne room."

Lucian blinked, bringing him back to the soccer field, and turned his head to Mindy. "Tell them I'm busy. It's not even half-time."

"Samael and I delayed the Archangel and his…friend as long as possible, but they demand to see you and they won't leave without seeing you…and the human." Mindy stared at him, pure terror in her eyes.

Lucian cocked his head; Mindy was not afraid of anyone or anything. She has crushed the hearts of many Elysian men with her haughty looks and holier-than-thou attitude. He knew the unexpected guest couldn't have been Gabby, as she never entered Elysian through the proper channels anyway. Archangel Raffaello hadn't been seen in thirty years or more, not that he ever deigned to visit Hell anyway.

Micah. Lucian closed his eyes and swore. Not only was that damn boy alive, but by some unholy miracle, he'd gotten through to the head Angel in charge.

"Thank you, Mindy. Tell him we will be with him shortly," he said through gritted teeth. Mindy nodded her head and dismissed herself without a word.

Lucian excused himself and Celeste from the rest of the game. His fingers wrapped around her forearm and almost dragged her off the field.

"What's going on? Where are you taking me?" Celeste questioned. Her arm jerked back to shake him off but his fingers sunk tighter into her skin.

"You got what you wanted. Your *boyfriend* managed to find a loophole." Red tinted his vision as his blood began to boil. Death trailed his twin more than it did him and he'd be *damned* if Celeste ended up dead because of Micah.

It was a flurry of activity as soon as they got home. Cate, Don, and Thayne were waiting for them inside the foyer. Cate was dressed in a long black chemise and a purple overlay with a white stitch design down the sides where purple strings were tied in a crisscross pattern. A black and purple crystal-thorned crown adorned her head. Don was dressed in a similar Medieval style. It was the standard uniform for people directly in and adjacent to his court: a slightly loose black tunic, black pants, black socks, and black boots. The only exception was Thayne. Due to his still active connection to Heaven, the black tunic was swapped for a white one. Both were armed to the teeth with weapons strapped to their sides. Although hidden from view, he knew Don had a sword sheathed down his back between his wings.

"Go get cleaned up. Cate will help you dress," he calmly ordered Celeste. Cate pulled her upstairs before she could even protest.

Lucian hurried into his room, Don and Thayne following like lost puppies. They waited in Lucian's bedroom while he hopped in the shower. He walked back into the bedroom with just his black pants on. Any privacy between the three of them had evaporated billions of years ago.

"I wonder how the boy got to Micah." Don thought aloud.

"Fallen Angels love their gossip. And some are known for mixing with Angels on Earth. News of a human in Elysian is bound to be a hot topic." Thayne commented. Being a busybody helped break up the monotony of eternal life. He and Don pretended to be above the gossip, but when alone, they were no better than teenage girls. "You have nothing to worry about, Luce; you're much better looking than the human," Thayne said with a smile.

The Devil shot his best friend a sly smile as he buttoned up his red tunic. It was a far cry from his form-fitting suit, but even he had a role to play in Micah's game. "I was never worried." He walked over to his dresser where his crown sat on a small pillow. His fingers wrapped around the cool metal and placed it on top of his head. In an instant, the blue-eyed, kind, and just ruler of Elysian disappeared, and instead, the red-eyed King of Hell and Angel of Darkness and Torture stared back at him in the mirror. At least he earned his position as King, unlike his twin brother who just stole power whenever he saw fit.

"I'm not in love with Celeste. Never have been. We're just friends." He scolded his friends as he pulled out a wooden box made of oak from the top drawer. A thick layer of dust laid atop it. He brushed it off with the towel from his shower. The box was old and worn, but the crown inside was still in pristine condition.

"Whatever you say, boss. But we're pretty good at reading people. It's kind of our job. You're in love with a Human." Don told him, "You wouldn't be the first or the last angel to do so."

Examples A and B were sitting right on his bed. However, Lucian was *not* in love with the Human. He couldn't be in love with something that he hated. And no one would love him back. Right before he was cast out of Heaven, Micah and their Father vowed that no soul alive would ever love the Devil at the cost of salvation. Sure, he was loved by his friends, but in Micah's eyes, they weren't souls; they were barely people. But any feelings Lucian felt towards another woman since Abby were just lust. Pure fucking lust. His feelings for Celeste were…complicated.

The Angel of Death raised an eyebrow. "We all heard you growl when I flirted with her at dinner months ago. That was a—"

"I am not in love with Celeste." He repeated sternly, cutting Thayne off. "She's incredibly intelligent, kind, and yes, she is gorgeous, but I'm not in love with her." Lucian tightly gripped the sides of the box.

"Then why are you giving her that?" Don asked him, amused.

Lucian twisted the box in his hands slowly and carefully, thinking about the day he received it and the meaning behind it. "Because as of right now, she is still mine," he ended the conversation and marched out of the room.

The short walk to Celeste's room felt miles long. His footsteps were soundless from loud screaming rock music blaring from Celeste's room. A growing smile stretched from ear to ear, a girl after his own heart. Lucian stopped in his tracks. He loved rock music, but he absolutely *hated* screamo. *She* liked it. He tolerated it because it made her smile. He rolled his shoulders back and picked up his head. He was *not* in love with her, and he *hated* screamo music. Lucian took a deep breath and knocked on the door. The sound was absorbed in the screaming. He closed his eyes and turned the knob. The door opened, and his eardrums shattered.

When he opened his eyes, Celeste was sitting at her vanity in a medieval-style red dress with black lace trim. The large, flowy sleeves went past her fingertips. The red complemented her complexion beautifully. Thank Mother for Cate buying that for Celeste years ago to go to some

Renaissance festival. Cate stood behind her and combed through Celeste's long damp hair. The ends of her hair were already starting to curl. Lucian leaned against the door, not wanting to frighten them, and watched the two girls sing along. Cate was nodding her head to the beat.

Despite the circumstances, Cate needed the girl time. Cate loved doing make-up and hair so it was almost a distraction. The last time she saw Micah was when he killed Bea. Archangels are immortal but she had dreamt of tearing him apart limb from limb since. They all did in the aftermath of Bea's death. Cate didn't smile again until the 1980's.

Cate separated Celeste's hair into sections and began braiding. She must have seen him from the corner of her eye because she screamed at the speaker to shut off the music.

The thumping bass stopped but Lucian's ears rang loudly. If he had been Human, he probably would have gone deaf from the noise. But he'd take the ringing over that racket any day. "How do you stand that shit?" he asked and pushed off the door frame. The spicy sweet scent of Cinnamon and clove wafted around him. The culprit was a half-used candle burning on her dresser.

The bedroom was now a far cry from the lifeless yet well-preserved bedroom of some historic house. Now it looked as if someone actually lived here; Clothes were scattered around the floor, looking like they had fallen from the bed or been thrown from the chair of her vanity. One shin guard was by the door and another across the room. Her cleats were on opposite sides of the room. Paperback books with half-naked men on the cover and half-colored sketches of constellations and planets covered every inch of her desk by the door. Despite her words, she looked at home here.

"How do you stand yourself?" Celeste shot back, unable to hide her smirk. The two were getting along better now. They still teased each other to no end, but at least now, hatred no longer laced her words. Cate grinned coyly but kept her focus on Celeste's braid.

"I mean, what's not to like?" Lucian smirked as he looked down at himself and gestured to himself with his hands. Celeste rolled her eyes with a laugh. The bright, wide smile on her face took his breath away. Lucian blinked and turned his attention to the box in his hands. It suddenly felt a hundred times heavier.

He was not *in love with her.*

The Devil took a seat on the corner of the bed and set the box behind him, away from view.

"Why do we need to dress like we're heading to a Renaissance Faire?" Celeste asked.

"You've seen what Hell looks like. We have to play a part when the Angels are here. I can't have Hell look like a medieval torture chamber, and we look like we own a Fortune 500 company."

Cate tied off the braid. It went straight around the back of Celeste's head and over her shoulder. Cate did a great job on her hair, but he liked it better when it was long and wild with her curls. Lucian silently chastised himself, she could do whatever she wanted with her hair.

"What is my part?" Celeste looked at him through the mirror.

"You will not mention a single word about Elysian to Micah. Micah has no idea that the Supernatural are here living a peaceful life. Understood?"

Celeste nodded her head. The Nephilim were at stake. Her friends were at stake. Micah could take it all away if he knew. Lucian would put up a hell of a fight for it, but Micah always gets what Micah wants.

"I can't do her make up if she's talking to you." Cate shooed him out so she could do her friend's makeup.

"Alright, Alright, I'm going." Lucian grabbed the now three-ton box and walked to the two girls. "You'll be wearing this." He handed the box to Celeste.

Celeste's eyebrows furrowed inquisitively but accepted it. She gently opened the lid. Inside was a black tiara. Onyx gems were inlaid into the base and the intricate whorls. Large rubies capped each point of the tiara. A more feminine version of his crown. The jewels still shined like they were regularly polished.

"Lucian, it's beautiful," Celeste murmured as she picked it up. Her black-painted fingertips lightly traced over the gems. "I can't take this. It's too nice."

"It's a family heirloom. I would be honored if you wore it today."

Cate gasped, her hand covering her mouth. "Are you sure?"

"Sure about what?" Celeste asked, looking at them through the mirror.

Lucian nodded his head once and went downstairs, leaving them to finish up. Don and Thayne were waiting in the foyer. Don threw a ball down the hall. Loud click-clacks scratched against the floor. Chip barked, and the click clacks started again, growing louder as they entered the foyer, Roxie appeared first with the ball in her mouth.

"Good girl, Roxie!" Don bent down and wrangled the ball from the Pit Bull's mouth, tossing it back down the hall. The dogs took off again, shoving each other into the wall.

"I have priceless stuff in that hallway. You break it, and I'll throw your ass in the Pit," Lucian scolded as he fixed his sleeves and watched Roxie run back to Don with the tennis ball.

Don smirked and wrangled the ball out of Roxie's mouth before tossing it again. "I'd like to see you try."

"How'd Celle take the tiara?" Thayne asked.

Lucian shrugged. "I didn't tell her the significance. Cate asked if I was sure."

"Are you?" Don asked him from the floor as he scratched behind Chip's ears.

Lucian opened his mouth to speak, but Thayne whacked him in the chest and nodded to the stairs.

All three men looked up, mouths agape, but his eyes only found Celeste. The deepness of the blood-red dress juxtaposed her sparkling, radiant aura. She was both light and dark. Her face makeup was soft and natural, but her eyes were dark. The heavy eyeliner drew him to her ocean-blue eyes. Her lips were red as blood. Her Celtic necklace sat comfortably on her large breasts. His pants strained at the thought of holding them in his hands. In a heartbeat, he had gotten so absorbed by the thought that he didn't even notice the black choker and ruby earrings until the sunlight from the windows caused them to sparkle and demand attention. The jewels on the tiara sparkled from the sunlight. The woman staring back at him wasn't his Celeste; It was a Queen. He watched her walk down the steps and at that moment, he knew he wasn't going to let her go without a fight.

Thayne wolf whistled. "Damn, Celle. You look—" He got cut off with a jab to the stomach by Don.

"Stunning." Lucian was breathless. "You look stunning."

Celeste's blush almost matched the color of her dress, and she focused her eyes on her fabric. Her fingers toyed with the skirt part of her dress. "Thank you."

Lucian held out his arm for her. Celeste stared at it hesitantly for a moment before quickly descending the stairs and taking it. They looked every part of the regal rulers he wanted Micah to see.

"What am I? Chopped liver?" Cate teased as she descended the stairs to them.

"You look beautiful too, Cate," Thayne added in with his charming smile. Cate rolled her eyes as Don pulled her in for a kiss.

Outside, the group split up. Thayne and Don took to the sky with the wind beneath their wings. Cate took off with her black and purple broom. Lucian walked Celeste to her cart.

As they got to the cable cars, every Being in a one-mile radius seemed to stop what they were doing and stare at the two of them. Some bowed to them while others murmured to their companions, restarting the rumor mill. He muttered under his breath and sent threatening looks in their direction.

"Why are they looking at me like that?" she asked him once they were alone in the cable car.

"Because you're beautiful."

Celeste's cheeks went red. He turned his head to look out the window. He could not let himself linger on her or let his imagination run away with him. He needed to focus on Micah, on keeping Celeste safe. For the first time since she almost bled out, he prayed.

CHAPTER 55

Celeste entered the throne room through a back door with everyone else. All of them took their places like they were about to perform on a stage. Cate led her to a spot along the stone wall, away from Lucian and the throne that loomed over them.

"I'm going to be directly across from you. If at any point you don't know what to say or do, look at me. Okay?" Cate instructed. Celeste nodded slightly and gulped. Lucian took his seat on the throne, with Don standing to his right. Thayne stood tall near Celeste. His red eyes slid over to hers. He shot her a reassuring smile. Her heart was moments from exploding from her chest.

Everything felt *wrong*. The room closed in on her, and the air was stuffy. Her breaths started to come in short pants. The little air that did fill her lungs felt polluted. Cate would say it was the energy of the room. She spread her fingers wide and wiped them down the length of her dress. Her stomach turned and her skin started to feel clammy. She was going to throw up if she didn't leave *now*.

"Celle, look at me." Lucian's low voice said from in front of her. She lifted her head to see her blue-eyed Lucian suddenly standing before her. His wings stretched around them to block her from view of the others. "Good. Take a deep breath. Everything is going to be fine." She shook her head violently as her body heaved. Her lungs couldn't get enough air. Lucian put a hand on each shoulder.

"I'm not going to let Micah hurt you." The Devil promised. "Breathe with me." Lucian inhaled loudly to get her to follow. She gulped down as much air as she could. He exhaled loudly, inviting her to follow suit. She followed his lead as they went through multiple rounds of breathing. Once she was calm, he kissed the top of her head and stepped away. He blinked, red eyes returning, and sat back down on his throne.

Her eyes scanned Lucian from crown to toe. Gone again was the man she had gotten to know. In his place was something truly evil. His bright red eyes bore into the door like he was burning a hole through it. Tendrils of shadows she'd never seen before seemed to emanate from him.

Don looked every bit the Angel of Hell. His wings stretched out wide, making him look a few inches taller than he was. His wrist rested over one of his swords, ready to unsheathe it at a moment's notice. A ghost of a twisted smile hovered on his lips. He was ready and itching for a fight.

She looked to Cate who was mouthing a silent spell or prayer. Her eyes were closed tightly, and her hands were balled into fists. Cate was about to be face to face with the man who murdered her daughter. Celeste bounced on the balls of her feet, ready to run over and hug her best friend. A newfound anger filled her heart as she thought of Bea. Sweet, happy Bea, who only hours ago, cheered wildly for her on the soccer field.

She turned her head to Thayne. His hand came up and slowly gestured downwards, signaling to her to calm down. She dug her heels into the stone floor and inhaled deeply. He looked poised and ready to play referee. His wings were also stretched out, making him look larger than he was. But instead of a look of evil on his face, his red eyes were soft, and he gave her a reassuring smile.

"Bring him in. And tell him to remember his place," Lucian spat to a Demon. His back was pressed against the back of the throne. He appeared calm, yet annoyed with the disruption of his day. A hint of his anger floated just beneath the surface.

The Demon bowed to Lucian and signaled to the others at the door. The two Demons she saw the first day opened the throne room doors. Two men immediately marched in.

Much like the oil painting Lucian showed her, Micah was a carbon copy of the Devil, except with less printer ink. They had the same hairstyle, ending just before their ears. The only difference between them was the lack of stubble on Micah's slightly fuller face. While Lucian was shadows, darkness, and fire, Micah was everything glowing and gold. The man was wearing an all-white suit to match his white feathered wings. Above his head, a halo of pure daylight. Celeste's mouth parted in shock; she'd seen him before...

Her eyes traveled to the man next to him, and she gasped.

Mason.

Her knees grew weak and she wobbled but managed to keep herself upright. Her heart stopped beating. Celeste wanted to cry out with joy. He looked the same, but there was something off about him she couldn't quite put a finger on. He looked older than his 32 years. His dirty blonde hair was longer than the last time she saw him, ending at the nape of his neck. Deep dark circles rimmed his dull hazel eyes. A beard had grown on his normally clean-shaven face. She could not hide the smile growing on her face at seeing him. He was here. He came for her.

Mason's tanned skin and hazel eyes looked rather bland compared to the striking beauty of Lucian and his twin. He stood tall, trying to make himself bigger like he was trying to be the Alpha male. But it fell flat in comparison to the Angels. Lucian just exuded that energy in everything he did. Mason's eyes found hers, and a flash of lust appeared and disappeared quickly. In its place was the same beaming smile that made her fall in love with him.

"Well, well, well, to what do I owe the displeasure? Micah, have you forgotten you are not welcome here? Does Daddy know where you are?" Lucian's mocking voice was icy and deadly.

A sick smile grew on Micah's face. "You seem to have forgotten your own place, brother. I don't have time for this inane chit-chat. I'll just get to the point. Rumors have been going on for years that you've taken a Human lover. I was not surprised, knowing the kind of company you keep." A few animalistic growls echoed in the room. "But then I heard you forced a Human woman into a deal," Micah said smugly, putting his arms behind his back. "Even a Fallen Angel knows you can't force a Human against their own will."

Lucian looked around the room, hands flailing. "You tell me, Micah. Does it look like I've taken a lover, a *queen* to rule beside me?"

Micah sized him up and smirked. "You and I both know that means nothing. You Fallen Angels love your whores. Am I correct, Thayne? Abaddon? By the way, Abaddon, how is your *daughter*? Béatrice, *wasn't* it?"

Don made no acknowledgment of the bait dangled in front of him. The pent-up rage simmering inside Cate exploded and she screamed, "You bastard! How *dare* you speak her name!" The pain in her voice had Celeste's own heart breaking. Cate ran to Don's side, tears streaming down her cheeks as she unsheathed one of Don's blades from his side. It looked similar to the one Lucian kept in his boot. "I should have struck you down years ago."

"Cate, no." Lucian ordered. His voice was even and commanding, a tone she never heard him use with his family but it was no use. Cate raised the blade above her head and charged towards Micah. As she brought the blade down towards him, Micah raised his palm. A blast of powerful, pure white light came out. Far brighter than the light Cate summoned that night at the cottage. The blast sent Cate airborne and backward. Her back and head hit the wall with a sickening crack. Her body slid to the ground into a lifeless heap, the blade clattering against the stone.

Celeste's mouth opened, but no sound came out. A dark mass—shadows—emanated from Lucian's palm, making a beeline toward her. They encroached on her, forcing her flesh against the wall. A wisp of a shadow brushed against her face and settled on her lips like a gag, effectively silencing her. Another wisp wrapped around her wrists like handcuffs. Her eyes slid to Lucian. Concern flashed on Lucian's face, but he remained unmoving. She then turned her attention to Thayne, silently pleading with him to get Lucian to release her, but he gave a slight shake of the head, telling her to keep still. Don remained unmoving, not bothering to check on the mother of his child.

"I wouldn't be so quick to judge, brother. Despite our…estranged relationship, I have managed to keep *your* indiscretions at bay. You wouldn't want your Angels finding out about them, would you?" Lucian shot back hotly.

Holy fire flickered in Micah's eyes. Celeste swallowed hard. Any fire he spewed would be far worse than Lucian's. "This man tells me you kidnapped his girlfriend, forced her into a deal under duress, and attempted to kill him.

"I never forced anyone into a deal. You know Humans never want to take responsibility for their actions."

Micah put an arm around Mason's shoulders, grabbing the back of his neck. Mason didn't flinch. He was stone-faced and frozen; trancelike. "Knowing you, I am very much inclined to believe him."

Lucian looked Mason up and down before staring menacingly into Mason's eyes. Mason stood tall and didn't blink. "I can assure you I don't know what you're talking about."

"Where is Alice Delco, Lucian?" Micah's voice boomed loudly.

"I don't know who that is." Lucian kept his face neutral.

"Then who's the beautiful girl to my left?" Micah demanded with an edge of annoyance. Micah's face twisted into a smile as his eyes focused on her. She wished the shadows covered her fully; the hunger in his eyes made her stomach roll.

"She's Cate's second in command," Thayne said immediately. Celeste's eyes met Thayne's, and she gave him a small, thankful nod.

Micah huffed and rolled his eyes. "I wasn't born yesterday, you imbeciles. I know all of our Father's children. I know that is Alice Delco. No wonder He gave you this position. You just love to trick people and lead them away from our Father."

"You do that all on your own." The Devil's voice dripped with venom.

"You see, Lucian, Mason here tells me you singled her out many years ago. You took her out on dates as a minor. You tricked her into selling her soul for the deaths of her parents and sister," Micah recapped as he walked closer to her.

Lucian's jaw clenched. "What else did he say?"

"That you took advantage of a young, vulnerable minor."

"I do not pursue minors," Lucian spoke with a deathly calm. "That is a priest's job. And it's obvious she is not an altar boy."

Micah, now red in the face, stopped a few feet away from her and snapped his head back to Lucian. "Then why is she here, Lucian? The 'deal' you struck is invalid as she didn't know what she was getting herself into. Therefore, it must be lifted. You wouldn't want Father to get word of you trapping one of His children." Micah clicked his tongue as he studied Celeste. His pearly white teeth gleamed as he smiled at her. His golden eyes studied every piece of her body, from toe to crown. He took a moment to stare at the tiara before moving on. Goosebumps pebbled up on her arms. The hungry look in his eye was worse than Remi's.

Her eyes shifted over to Mason. She was so close to him yet so far. He remained frozen in the center of the room. Their eyes met, but there was no warmth there. He looked at her like a prized possession. Lucian owned her soul yet never looked at her like the way Mason was now.

Micah's hand caressed her cheek. Her head jerked back from his icy cold touch and ricocheted off the stone. It was far from the lukewarm feel of Mason's hand or the fiery warmth of Lucian. "My, my, Lucian, she's turned into a beautiful woman. I can see why you'd want to lock her down here. The tiara was a nice distraction, but you are destined to be alone. We both know that," Micah hissed.

The Twins growled. Lucian shot out of his throne and stalked towards his brother. Micah held out his palm, and Lucian froze like an invisible wall was blocking him from moving any farther.

The shadow gag and cuffs dissipated. Suddenly free, Celeste ran toward Mason and threw her arms around his neck. Her touch pulled Mason out of whatever frozen state he had been in. Mason's arms wrapped around her waist and pulled her tightly into his chest. His head leaned down, and he kissed her urgently. "I told you I'd find a way to get you," he whispered. She kissed him back with the same sense of urgency and longing. Her hands cradled his face. The feeling of his skin under her fingertips made her cry out in joy. He looked alive. or was he an angel? Her saving grace. No matter, he came for her, just like he promised.

"Nobody leaves Hell without my permission. Not only that, she still bears my mark." More ropes of shadow snaked around her and wrapped around her left arm. A supernatural force jerked it away from Mason and pulled it straight into the air for everyone to see Lucian's bright red mark on her wrist. The tattoo glowed like a beacon in the dark. Pain shot up her arm. Her tattoo, which hadn't burned in months, exploded in white hot pain. She chomped down on her lip to keep from screaming but that didn't stop the tears from forming. Mason growled and tightened his grip on her waist.

"She is a child of the Lord, Lucian, tricked and deceived by you. You would not know it, but our Father has plans for her. The word of the Lord is binding. It's no longer up to you," Micah retorted.

Lucian licked his lips, a lion about to devour his prey, and straightened out. His wings flared. "And where is our Father, Micah? He's been gone for a few millennia."

"He's busy, taking care of His people."

The Devil smirked and rolled his eyes, then they landed on her. The shadows receded and gravity pulled her arm down. The pain vanished just as quickly as it had appeared. "Celeste, my dear, do you wish to leave Hell? Has your stay here been as bad as they want you to believe?"

Five pairs of eyes landed on her. Her mouth suddenly went dry. Both of her worlds were right in front of her. Her eyes looked to Cate, who was still unconscious, but thankfully, her chest rose and fell slowly with breath. Her best friend. The one who helped her grieve and start anew. She slid her eyes to Thayne. It had been him that had walked beside her growing up. He risked his position and life for her. She wouldn't let that be in vain.

Then her eyes fell on Lucian, now back on his throne. The Devil, despite his role, took care of her. He saved her life and tried to help her with her depression. They finally repaired their friendship. Most importantly, he kept her alive, kept her Human. Humans weren't allowed in Elysian anyway. How much time did she have down here before one of his Demons or Fallen Angels killed her, or a vampire drained her of her blood? Also, her old feelings were resurfacing, and she needed to get away. Her heart belonged to Mason and would never, *never* belong to the Devil again.

She turned to Mason, and guilt filled her belly. She had finally accepted his death and started to move on. She'd grieved for him, and all the while, he never gave up. Even in his death, he kept his promise of helping her. She owed him her life. Mason's eyebrow arched in confusion on why she had not answered yet. His being here meant that God knew her; God was not missing. He had not abandoned her as she had previously thought. He heard her prayers. Lucian had deceived her again. God was there all along.

"I don't belong here, Lucian. I'm Human, I belong on Earth." Her voice was low, almost mumbling. Her hands began to toy with her dress again.

Lucian leaned back. His face was void of all emotions. Celeste wasn't sure which was worse for her at the end of the day, him angry or him not showing any emotion at all "Even if I *wanted* to free her, she would not be free from Hell's clutches. She will forever be consumed by her personal demons until they eat her alive. If my Pet wants out of Hell so badly, she will have to conquer her demons. If she can, she can leave. If she fails, she will stay here—as will the boy."

CHAPTER 56

Mason's nails dug deeper into her skin. She knew those crescent-shaped marks would now be etched into her waist just as her self-harm scars were. She opened her mouth to protest; Mason's attempts to save her would not go down in vain.

Micah narrowed his eyes at Lucian. "Absolutely not. She has already suffered enough."

"I cannot let her just walk out. I'd have a riot on my hands! And I'm sure Father would not want to hear about an uprising of the undead."

"Father would not care if you lost your throne. You are a disgrace. Look at the way you mock him. It's pathetic."

"At least I didn't steal his job," Lucian snapped.

"I did not come here to bicker with you, Lucian. Release Alice Delco."

"I said I would, but she has to accept the challenge."

"Absolutely not—"

"I'll do it." She cut Micah off. She gave the Angel an apologetic look before turning her attention back to the King of Hell. Lucian smirked. "Perfect. You," He snapped and shouted at the Demons by the door. "Show my *brother* and his friend to the best room we have."

"The girl comes with us," Micah demanded.

Lucian's eyes narrowed. "No."

"Lucian, please." She pleaded with him.

She gave Lucian a pleading glance. The Devil's lips pursed and he waved them off. "You have an hour."

The Demons led them to a room closer to the Pit and far, far away from the cable cars to Elysian. The faint moans, groans, and cries for help from the souls in Hell had the hair on her arms standing up. She hated being over here, and Lucian knew it. They may be friends, but there was no escaping that sinister side of him. Micah walked in front, followed by Mason, and then her. Her hands clasped his shirt as if keeping him in her line of vision because if he disappeared, her brain would tell her it had all been an illusion. His hand stretched out behind him for her to grab onto. She took it with both hands and gave it a light squeeze. *He was real.*

One of the Demons opened a door and rudely gestured for them to go inside. It was similar to the room Lucian had her sleep in her first night here. The apartment was bigger than the one she had stayed in. It had two bedrooms, a living room, and a slightly bigger kitchen.

Celeste kicked the door closed behind her. Mason didn't waste any time in pressing her back against the door. His lips pressed onto hers with ferocity. She kissed him back with a need she'd shoved down for months. Her hands found their normal spot in his hair.

"I'm so sorry, I'm so sorry he killed you," she said breathlessly when they came up for air.

"I'm not dead." He pressed another kiss to her lips.

Celeste froze. "What? But I-"

Mason continued. "Neighbors heard the commotion and called the cops. Luckily, I only had a concussion." He kissed her lips again.

She lightly pushed him away. He fought a little but only backed up enough for them to talk. "You came for me," she whispered, her finger tracing the side of his face.

"Of course, I did." Mason gave her a weak smile and kissed her again and again. He trailed down her cheek, jaw, and neck.

Micah coughed, and Celeste shoved Mason away from her and stared a hole into the ground; Purposely not meeting Micah's gaze. "I think it's time we had a conversation." He ordered them to the small, round kitchen table. Heat flushed her cheeks like she was a teenager getting caught by her parents.

Mason kissed her forehead. "Later," he whispered and winked. They took their spots at the round table, not letting go of each other.

Micah smiled softly at her. "I don't know if you remember me, Alice. The last time I saw you, you were a child."

Celeste gave a slight nod. "I remember you, Pastor Micah. I didn't know you were *the Archangel*, though," she admitted. He had hidden the secret well. Just like Lucian. His eyes and smile still look the same as they did years ago.

"Of course, I couldn't tell you or anyone. Exposing who I really am would not be handled well by the people. Besides, I'd rather have my Father receive the praise for the work I do when I help His children."

She looked over to Mason. "If you're not dead, how did you find him?"

"Pastor Louis promised he would call Pastor Micah, remember? He came through. It just took a while. He's a hard person to get ahold of," Mason told her. She made a mental note to thank Pastor Louis when she got back to Earth.

"Where did you go?" she asked him. "You disappeared when I was twelve. Did you know about the fire?"

"I was needed in a different part of the world at that point. I serve my Father, and wherever He wants me, I go. As for the fire, I found out not long after. I'm so terribly sorry for your loss. Your father was a true servant of the Lord. I cared about him and your family deeply."

Celeste chewed her lip. She debated about whether she should lie or be honest. "I'm not."

"*Alice*," Mason hissed.

"They were your family. How could you want them dead?" Micah asked, astonished she could even say such a thing.

Her nostrils flared. "I never wanted them to *die*. I unknowingly told the Devil I would sell my soul to get away from them. I didn't know that would have meant *death*, but my life improved when they were no longer here."

"They were good people! Vicky was a good person!" Mason exclaimed hotly.

Celeste's eyes narrowed and slid over to him. "Vicky did nothing to protect me. She was my sister, and she let them hurt me."

"Vicky was abused too, Ali. You forget that," Mason growled.

Celeste leaned back in shock. Her arms crossed over her chest. "I'm sorry. Are you trying to save her or me?"

Mason was quiet for a moment, anger flashing in his eyes. "I'm just saying…Vicky didn't deserve to die. Your parents were a little much, but you would have gotten out. We still could have had a life together." Mason tried to backtrack.

"You and me, or you and Vicky?" she snapped. Seeds of doubt were starting to plant themselves in her brain.

There was a pause before he spoke again. "You and me." He pressed a kiss to her hand and she pulled it away.

"There would *not* have been a you and me or a you and Vicky. My father ruled with an iron fist! At the time of Vicky's death, she was dating her professor, and my parents didn't approve of you since you weren't a doctor and were an agnostic. Besides, you still would have married that Tori woman because you still would have been in the military. Not to mention, you never saw me as anything more than Morgan's friend until that night at the beach when you didn't know I was Alice." Her fist hit the table with a loud bang. The rush she felt after hitting the table was soon replaced with guilt.

"I know a lot more about your family than you think I do," Mason whispered, voice tight with emotion.

Micah put a hand up between them, silencing them. "Now, now, no need to start an argument. It's been an interesting day for all of us." Micah leaned back in his seat, "Now, Alice—"

"Celeste," Celeste cut him off with force. "My name is Celeste."

Mason kicked her leg under the table. It was the same movement her sister would make when she and her father would strike up an argument at dinner. It was a sign to stop talking. She glared at Mason.

Micah continued, "Did *he* give you that name?" Inferring Lucian.

"Yes, but only because I couldn't come up with anything I liked."

"But your *God*-given name is Alice, correct?" Micah asked her. She nodded in agreement. "Then you *are* Alice. Lucian can't take that away from you." There was a tone of finality in his voice. Her identity was not up for debate. "Mason told me a lot about your situation. But I want you to tell me: what was the relationship between you and Lucian? Start at the beginning and be very detailed about what you remember."

Celeste took a deep breath and then started at the beginning. She began with the abuse she suffered at the hands of her parents all the way to when Lucian came and got her from Mason's townhouse. "Did you know? Did you suspect the abuse? You were my father's friend."

Micah shook his head. "I didn't see anything. You and Vicky were lovely children. There was nothing that looked awry. It wasn't until Raffaello came to Pastor Louis and me during one of the memorials alleging abuse from when you were a child. I denied it; I saw no signs.

"Who is that?" she asked him. "I don't know a Raffaello."

"Another Archangel. There are three of us. Me, Gabriella, and Raffaello. Micah nodded. "He seemed to know you." Micah looked at her carefully and hummed, "Interesting."

Celeste's head tilted. Knowing one Archangel was a coincidence. Having two Archangels intertwined in her life was not a coincidence. Her eyes slid over to Mason and he just shrugged his shoulders.

Our father has plans for her. Micah had told Lucian a little bit ago.

Maybe God was around, He *had* to be to guide Mason to Micah and save her. Maybe He had some great plan for her. And whatever the plan was, it wasn't doing her any good being stuck down here. There was no choice but to do whatever it took to get out of Hell. Even if it meant coming face-to-face with her demons.

CHAPTER 57

"**A**re you a fucking idiot?" Thayne growled as he wore holes into the carpet of Don's office looking over the Pit. "She's finally healing."

"How can you be so *stupid?* They will kill her," Cate yelled angrily from Don's office chair as she held an ice pack on the back of her head. He thanked what lucky stars he had to see her awake, but wished she was still unconscious for this conversation.

The crack of her head against the stone made him want to finish the job for her. But doing so would have started a Holy War. Forcing his people to fight on behalf of a slight to his family would be cause for his removal as King. Lucian leaned against the window, staring at the Pit.

Souls were running in their futile attempts at escaping the eternal fire.

"She doesn't belong here," Lucian restated Celeste's earlier statement. "She's not truly happy here. She will *never* be truly happy here. Regardless, you've seen her aura. This is not a place for a soul like hers." He'd seen the way Celeste looked at the Human; it was forever burned into his retinas. Abby used to gaze at him like that—like he hung the moon. Lilli had faked it and he had fallen for it like an idiot.

"No Demon or Human is happy here! It's Hell! You should have just killed her in that fire or better yet, let her bleed out on that bathroom floor. She would have done the job for you but no, *you* went off the rails with this girl. She's just a stupid fucking Human," Don snarled.

In a heartbeat, Lucian charged Don from his spot next to Cate and threw him against the wall. Bits of paint and drywall floated around them. Both of them bared their teeth, and Lucian's hands were clasped around the Angel of Hell's throat. His fingertips burned with fire. The smell of burning flesh hit his nostrils, only encouraging him to squeeze tighter.

"Lucian!" Cate and Thayne yelled. Thayne pulled Lucian off of him and pushed him back towards the other side of the room.

"Pull yourself together," Thayne growled.

Don gasped for air and rubbed at his throat. "This…is why you don't get attached… to Human women."

"No, you just fuck 'em and leave them to carry your child," Cate bit out, crossing her arms. Lucian could sense power straining at her fingertips, ready to strike Don. "Mind you, she is my best friend. Lucian, you need to go get her and tell her that this little *challenge* you are planning is over. She needs to stay here. She's not safe with them."

Lucian rubbed his face with his hands. "You keep saying that, but you won't give me any evidence to prove it. Why shouldn't I let her go to her precious lover and the leader of Heaven? All she ever wanted was to go to Heaven. Even the souls down here get a second chance, and they don't even deserve it." He points to the Pit.

Cate inhaled deeply and closed her eyes. Her fingers pinched the bridge of her nose. "Because she's not getting into Heaven."

All three men stopped in their tracks. "What do you mean she's not *getting into Heaven?*" Lucian asked through gritted teeth.

"She has the mark of the Nephilim on her back," Cate said lowly and stared at a picture frame on Don's desk.

Thayne swore and walked towards the window, needing to look away from them. Don closed his eyes and exhaled tiredly.

The words sent Lucian into a tailspin, enough to make him physically ill. She may have unknowingly entered into a deal with the devil. But he unknowingly damned her soul. Now with Micah involved, there was no getting into Heaven for her. There was only Elysian— the place she was desperate to leave. Celeste wouldn't survive the challenges he ordered her to undergo. But at least she would be here, where she belonged.

CHAPTER 58

Lucian barged into the guest room to the three of them sitting at the table speaking in hushed tones.

"Ever heard of knocking, Lucian?" Micah sighed from his seat at the table.

"My castle, my rules," Lucian smirked. His eyes immediately ran over Celeste from top to bottom. She was tightly wrapped in the young man's arms. Don wasn't lying about Mason's dark aura. The space surrounding Mason was darker than anything he'd ever seen before. It was like looking at a black hole. Every light and noise in the room was absorbed into Mason. Even Celeste's iridescent aura seemed to get sucked in, growing darker by the second. How Micah saw past it, he didn't know. "Celeste." Lucian held out his hand for her.

"Absolutely not. She's staying with me." Mason tightened his grip on Celeste, rage etched onto his face. It was the look of a man holding tight to his property. The dark look in his eyes sent a chill down Lucian's spine. If Mason was anything but a Human, he would have given Lucian a run for his money.

Celeste cupped Mason's face in her hand, forcing him to look at her. His muscles didn't relax or soften at her touch. Even with all the fights Cate and Don have had over the years, and even in the years they were not actively seeing each other, Don always relaxed in Cate's arms. Even he remembered the way his own body reacted to Lilli's or Abby's touch, and it's been over a millennium since he'd relaxed into the arms of some female he loved. "Mase, It's okay. I'll be okay. Lucian won't hurt me." She gave Mason a small goodbye kiss. Her innocent kiss turned into a male staking his claim. He kissed her roughly, enough to elicit a little moan. A smile tugged on Mason's lips like he was proving a point that she belonged to him. Immediately after her little moan, she pulled away. Her cheeks turned bright red with embarrassment. She got up from the table and walked past Lucian to the hallway, keeping her eyes focused on the floor.

"We will see you bright and early tomorrow." Lucian bid them goodbye with a wink.

Lucian stared out the cable car window, thinking of all the ways tomorrow could go wrong. Or worse.

"Did you know Mason survived?" Celeste asked him, wringing her hands.

"I would have known had he died. His name never appeared on any register."

"That doesn't mean anything. He would have gone to Heaven."

He shook his head and bit his lip, debating on telling her the truth. "His aura is pitch black. He's a walking abyss. There's not a chance he's going to Heaven."

Celeste shook her head violently. "You're lying."

"I promised you no more lies. I make good on my promises."

"He's a good person. He got Micah involved and came here for me. An evil person wouldn't do that for someone they love."

"They would if they considered you their property."

Celeste scoffed. "I'm not his property. I'm not anyone's property." She grounded out and crossed her arms over her chest. Lucian sighed and sent waves of red-hot pain by her tattoo. She hissed in pain and covered her tattoo with her other hand. "I cut myself because I felt so guilty over his death. I couldn't leave my bed for *weeks*."

Lucian flinched. He thought he was doing right by her to think him dead. She needed to stop mourning her drab Human and her life. He didn't have a good reason to give her. "I wanted you to move on. You were going to be here forever. It wasn't going to do you any good to hold on to hope. Hope destroys people."

She scoffed and shook her head in disbelief. "I had a right to know, Lucian. He's my boyfriend."

"He's a son of a bitch," Lucian snapped. Anger bubbled at the surface. He swallowed it down. The look on her face eight years ago when he called her a mistake never left his mind. He had been angry and lost his temper with her. He had been just as bad as her parents that day, and since then, he vowed that she would never see him angry.

"And so are you!" Her face set angrily on him.

"I'm the fucking Devil; it comes with the territory."

"At least he was able to find a way for me to break this damn curse! I've asked, no, I've *begged* you several times, and you told me no. At least he cares."

The rage he tried to keep back escaped him before he could reel it in. "*I* saved your life not once, but *twice*. I risked rebellions for you. *I* found your telescope that he didn't bother to go searching for. Don't you *dare* say I don't care about you! I am trying to keep you safe. At least I've never called you Vicky to your face." He heard that fight that night and saw her reaction from the window. It hadn't been the first time Mason called her by her sister's name.

Her guard snapped up; her steely gaze was now impenetrable. Fire and anger flared, almost causing her eyes to glow. He had seen that only once before. The day after the fire, when she went to punch him. "And was burning me part of your plan to keep me safe?"

Lucian sat up straighter. "What are you talking about?"

Her arms crossed. "Every time I got within arm's reach of a man or brought them into my bed, I got this searing pain in my arm where your damn tattoo is imprinted. It burned constantly with Mason. Was that your idea of keeping me safe or keeping tabs on me?"

His head tilted and his eyes fell on her wrist. He was powerful, but he couldn't inflict pain on someone he wasn't around. He's only used his power to inflict pain on her three times. Once, the day after the fire when he forced her to eat breakfast, and the second time, earlier today in the throne room, and the last time just moments ago. It pained him to do so each time, and he *never* would have caused her pain for bringing men into her life. She could do what and who she wanted. That was the whole point of her deal.

"I…uh," A coldness settled in the cable car; all warmth and friendliness between them had evaporated. Fine, if she needed someone to blame, he'd rather it be him than for her to blame herself. "I just wanted you to be safe. That's all I ever wanted."

Celeste chewed on her bottom lip and shook her head in disbelief. The silence was painful for him. He could begrudgingly handle the depression silence, but the angry silence was enough to make him want to throw the cable car doors open and fly the rest of the way home.

"What is the significance of the tiara?" she asked as the doors opened. Lucian's heart dropped into his stomach. He didn't think she would actually ask about it. His brain quickly came up with several different ways the conversation could go. He looked down at her as they walked to her cart and decided on honesty.

"It was my mother's. After I rebelled and before she was killed, she gave me her crown for me to give to my future queen."

More silence. He stole a few glances in her direction on the drive home. Shock and fear were evident in her eyes.

"We are not in love," she reminded him after a few moments.

No, they were not in love. He was certainly *not* in love with her. "You were in love with me eight years ago."

"That was a mistake. I don't love you; I love Mason."

"Micah knew what the crown meant. I had to make statement." It had been effective. He saw the way Micah's eyes lingered on the tiara and the way his lips twisted in disgust. Lucian took a gamble on it and won.

"What statement was that?" Her voice dripped with irritation.

He typed in the code to the gate to get into their neighborhood. The keypad buzzed and the iron gates started moving. "A reminder that you belong here with me, with your friends, with your family. And to prove a point. You are better off here. And I knew it would piss Micah off."

Celeste took off the crown and held it in her hands, gripping it tightly. "Is that why I had to live with you? To play your loving wife?" she hissed.

"No." Lucian was damned to walk alone. But he would be lying if he said he didn't love having her in his house. Just knowing she was there made the place feel more alive. Waking up alone was one thing, but waking up alone in an empty house was another. "Having you live with me was purely for you to adjust to life here."

Celeste shifted uncomfortably in her seat. Their house came into view, and he could tell she was itching to put as much space between them as she could. "Did you ever love me?"

Lucian clenched his jaw. "You don't know what love is."

"Bullshit. I—"

"You loved everything I embodied," he cut her off. "The freedom I had to do whatever I wanted, whenever I wanted. You craved that. You loved the fact that you got to be yourself around me. You were so broken, Celeste. You were incapable of love—of truly loving. You clung to any taste of hope and freedom and savored it. Real love isn't saving you. The only person who can save you is you. At the time, you needed someone who really gave a fuck about you. Caring and romantic love, although similar, are not the same. I cared about you more than Morgan or Mason do. Cate cares more than them. Thayne cares. I gave you an out. They knew you were cutting. They knew the abuse you suffered as children, yet they didn't try to get adults to intervene." Lucian pulled into his driveway and kept his focus in front of him. From the corner of his eye, he saw Celeste's face turn bright red. She was a ticking time bomb.

"You liar! They care about me. They love me!"

"They love *Alice*. Not you." He turned off the cart.

Celeste jumped out of the cart. "Alice and Celeste are the same fucking person!"

"Are they? Because you keep flipping it whenever one fits the convenience of others," he snapped roughly.

Celeste wiped a tear from her eye. "Fuck you, Lucian. Just when I thought we were getting along, you do something that makes me hate being around you. I hate you!"

"Hate me all you want. I don't care. I got you out of that shithole, you got your goddamn freedom. You still have it here, even though you clearly don't see it."

"I'll have my freedom when I get to walk out of here with Mason and Micah. He may be an ass, but at least he'll help those who believe in and love God. You just want to take me away from Him! That's what the Devil does!" Celeste spat the same rhetoric she had when she first got here. In just over an hour, Micah already had her brainwashed again. Months of hard work—gone in an instant.

CHAPTER 59

The entry to Charon's loomed over her like a giant monster waiting to swallow her up. Another sleepless night led her here. Celeste couldn't sleep knowing her very alive boyfriend was in Hell and she wasn't with him. She slipped out of the house without a word and wasn't noticed by the dogs. A cable car waiting for her as if they were expecting her. High in the distance, small blinks of lights of cable cars disappeared into Hell. Her stomach flipped; it was too high up. She hated being inside that damn cage. It made her nauseous and that was with Lucian sitting with her. Bile rose in her throat at the thought of her going in the car by herself.

The Demon holding the door for her glared at her.

It's too high.

You can't do it.

The car wire is going to snap, and you'll fall to your death.

Her mind raced. She took one step backward to leave. The Demon, angry with her for taking this long, stormed around her and pushed her into the car. Celeste flung her hands out and caught the padded bench.

The door slammed and the lock clicked loudly. This was it. Celeste collected herself and sat down. With her eyes squeezed shut, she began to breathe. *In, hold, out. In, hold, out.* She repeated the movement. Her body jerked, and she squealed as the car began moving. Her hands were white-knuckled on the edge of the seat. Her heart raced wildly in her chest. The breathing pattern she learned from Cate years ago was no longer helping. She tried to picture Mason; his boyish smile and friendly eyes. Her dirty-blonde hero was almost within reach.

The car screeched to a stop, and the door flew open. She opened one eye, then the other. She was back in Hell.

"Come on, *Lady*. We're not getting any younger here," a different Demon attendant snarled at her. She held tightly to the top of the bench as she stood up. One wobbly step after another, she made it out of the gondola without the demon pulling her out by her arm.

She found her way down to Hell and walked down the various hallways, each one the same as the last. How the hell was she supposed to find Mason? The place was a maze of hallways and dead ends.

On her first pass through Hell, she wound up on the balcony where she and Lucian had watched all the grieving Human souls beg and scream for redemption and for their savior. Unlike the first time, Celeste didn't feel anything for them. Lucian said they all deserved their place and Micah had every reason to keep them from entering Heaven.

Celeste ducked her head and kept walking. After turn-after-turn, she kept seeing the same four walls. Finally on her next turn, she saw the Fallen Angel Samael, from her first night there, standing guard.

The Fallen Angel didn't acknowledge her, although she would not put it past him to report her movements back to Lucian. She ignored him and knocked on the door. She didn't hear any movement from inside, and no one came to the door. Why isn't anyone coming to the door?

They're asleep.

Samael probably hurt Mason.

Why is he there? He's gonna tell Lucian.

Celeste knocked once more. If she got no response, she would go back to the mansion. After a few moments of silence, she turned her back and started walking down the hall.

Someone whisper-yelled her old name. Celeste skidded to a stop, and pivoted around to see Mason's head sticking out from the doorway. Her lips stretched into a wide smile, and she hurried back. She barely made it inside before he slammed the door and locked her in between the door and himself. Her back pressed into the cool wood; both of his hands pressed against the door on either side of her head. His head tilted downwards, and he kissed her with a desire and urgency she had never felt before. A fire lit in her belly. She missed him—missed this.

Celeste's hands balled up his tank top and tugged him closer, until he was practically on top of her, eliminating whatever space remained between them. She opened her lips to let him in, and he immediately took control of her mouth and tongue. He tasted of Heaven and sin, and she wanted—needed—more.

Heaven. Shit. Micah.

"Mase." She called his name. His mouth was on her jaw, kissing a line down to her neck. She called his name again and got no verbal response. Her stomach was coiling into a knot. "Mason, stop," she demanded. It wasn't until she found the strength to push him away that he stopped.

"What?" Mason asked as he was shoved away, his eyes wild with lust.

Celeste bit her lip. She needed him, just not in earshot of an Archangel. "There's an Archangel in the next room, *the Archangel.* We can't do this. We're not married!" she hissed.

"That never stopped us before!" Mason argued, leaning back down to kiss her.

She blocked his kiss with her hand. "There wasn't an Angel in the next room that could hear us!"

"Then we'll pray for forgiveness tomorrow." Mason held his hand out for hers. Celeste's eyes darted from the closed bedroom door to Mason.

"Since we're in Hell…" Celeste took his hand.

Mason led her into his room, shut the door, and locked it. She waited for him at the end of his bed, fidgeting with her hands. She had forgotten to account for Mason sharing an apartment with Micah. Mason met her at the edge of the bed and immediately pulled her into his arms. His fingers lightly dragged under her shirt and up her body, feeling every inch of her.

Celeste's eyes fluttered shut, and she tilted her head back. His touch sent electric chills through her. Mason's hands traveled back down to the hem of her shirt and began pulling it up. Her hands covered his and she gently pulled his hands and her shirt down. The last people to see her with all her cuts were Cate and Hester when they brought her back from death's door. Since then, Celeste had worn nothing but long-sleeved shirts, sweatshirts, and pants to keep her scars covered.

"*Alice.*" Mason let out a breathy groan. "He's asleep. He can't hear us."

"No, it's not that. I…uh…" she faded, wetting her lips. She hated herself, letting her needs get the better of her. "I started cutting again. It's bad."

Mason put some space between them, examining her, as if he could see through her clothes. Clothes or not, she was already bare in front of him. "Because of him?" Lucian had saved her life, but Mason wouldn't have wanted to hear that. She shook her head. "We'll talk about it later." Mason continued, not seeming to be phased by her revelation, or not wanting to bother with it. She let go of his hands, raising hers to help him take her shirt off.

Her boyfriend breathed out an expletive as he bundled the shirt and tossed it aside. She wasn't sure if it was from her being braless or from the plethora of red, pink, and white cuts of varying sizes up and down her right arm, and the peaks of scarred tissue of others on her hips.

His hands immediately cupped her breasts and squeezed. "I've missed you so much," he breathed as he gently pushed her back on the bed. To her surprise, the bed was surprisingly soft and comfortable. Maybe Hell wasn't so bad…

Mason climbed above her, one hand gripping the headboard. With his other hand, his finger and thumb pinching her now hard nipple. His mouth engulfed the other, his tongue running over it in quick swipes and teeth lightly pulling at the peak. Celeste called his name in a low throaty moan. Mason lifted his head with a loud wet pop. He winked at her before tending to the other with his mouth.

"Tease." Celeste tried to push his head down to where she needed him. He responded by pressing his lower half against her, increasing the friction. She could feel his bulge against her thigh.

"Mase," she moaned.

"Patience, dear," he mumbled, giving her nipple one last flick with his tongue.

He slid her pants and underwear off with ease. She gasped from the cold air, but it was not cold for long, as Mason slid one finger in, then another, fingers curling upwards and pumping in and out of her slowly. The coil in her stomach grew tighter and tighter.

He didn't bother with the rest of the foreplay. Mason quickly shed his boxers and wasted no time entering her. She took in all of him and moaned as he pounded into her. He grabbed onto her hips so tightly she was sure it would leave a mark tomorrow. She lifted her hips upwards to take him deeper. The coil in her sprung loose as she came with his name on her lips. She saw stars as her body wracked with her orgasm. His grunts and breaths and thrusts quickened as his release followed moments after. His thrusts slowed as he rode it out and came to a stop. He collapsed next to her, still inside her, not bothering to pull out. The two panted and gazed at each other with wide, loving eyes.

For the first time in months, she fell asleep in his arms. She hadn't realized how much she missed sleeping beside someone else; how much she loved it. She believed in Heaven, but also, in that moment, realized that Heaven was in the arms of someone she loved and who loved her back.

503

CHAPTER 60

The lovebirds were jolted awake with a shake of the bed and a sudden cold draft. Celeste's eyes snapped open, to see a red-eyed Lucian with the blanket in his hands. With a shriek, tried to cover herself with her hands. Mason sat up and put their pillows in front of her to help cover her up.

"What the hell?" Celeste spat.

"Get dressed. It's time for your first task," Lucian said through gritted teeth. His

"Ever heard of knocking?" Mason snapped.

"My castle. I can go where I please. You have five minutes." Lucian snarled and turned his back on them and marched to the doorway. Mason and Celeste scrambled for their clothes.

Once dressed, on their way out the main door, Mason made a point to bump shoulders with Lucian, but the Devil, who was taller and more muscular than Mason, remained as unmoving as a mountain.

Celeste shot Lucian a dirty look as she walked by him. "You're a bastard, you know that?"

Lucian pushed off the wall with a wink and a devilish grin. "That's what happens when you play with fire. You get burned."

✵

The hallway Lucian brought them to was similar to every other hallway in the godforsaken place. She wasn't quite sure where in Hell they were. Lucian and Don led the way. She and Mason walked hand in hand behind them, shooting daggers at the back of Lucian's head. Micah brought up the rear, looking bored to death.

What made this area different from what she had seen before were the dozens of names engraved on gold plaques on stone doors that were sealed with padlocks. These rooms had to be soundproof as she didn't hear any screaming or crying like she did near the Pit.

Lucian stopped them between two doors. The names on the doors had her heart sinking. The hair on the back of her neck stood up as she broke into a cold sweat. Her head whipped over to Lucian. He stared at the doors, purposely not meeting her gaze.

"The first demons our dear Celeste will face are the people who got her into this little predicament. Her parents." He pulled a key from his pocket and opened the padlock. The door opened with a loud, eerie creak like something from a horror film. A cold chill ran down her spine.

Micah scoffed. "You cannot be serious, Lucian."

Lucian shrugged, looking just as bored as Micah. "They are the reason we're here right now. They are the reason she sold her soul. If she wants her soul back, she has to stand up to her parents without breaking down like she always did."

Her blood went ice cold. This was not just some ordinary hallway. This was the Eternal Tombs Lucian had talked about. Celeste shook her head violently. There was no way she'd go in and see them. Seeing Vicky almost killed her. This *would* kill her. "No, I can't go in there, Lucian!"

"Do you want your soul back or do you want to stay here forever?" he snapped as he unlocked the first door and pushed the door open. Celeste stared into the dark abyss that was her mother's tomb. There was no sound coming out, no screaming or yelling or prayers for salvation. Just deafening silence. Her mother was in there somewhere. A woman she hadn't seen for years, a woman she hated with every fiber of her being.

Celeste took a step back, hitting hard muscle. Her head twisted to see Don standing behind her, wings stretched out, cutting off her view of Mason and Micah. Any chance of her escaping just evaporated.

Celeste took a step backward. She lifted her head to look at him, pleading with him silently. His red eyes stared back at her, unmoving and unwavering.

Lucian grabbed the back of her shirt and dragged her towards the open room. Tick tock."

Celeste screamed and pleaded for him to let her go. She dug her heels into the stone, but he was stronger than her. Her fingers tightly gripped the doorframe. Her nails bit into the stone so hard she thought her nails might break. It only slowed him down a fraction. Don peeled her fingers off the stone one by one as the Devil all but tossed her into the room like a discarded toy. She lost her balance and fell to her knees on the floor.

Light vanished with the slam of the door and a click of a lock. Celeste screamed and turned around to go towards the door, but everything around her was as dark as nighttime in the deep forest. "Get me out of here, Lucian. I swear to God—"

"Alice?" a disembodied voice said weakly. It was familiar enough to cut her off. Adrenaline rushed through her body. She knew that voice and knew it well. She hated that voice, yet this voice was fragile, broken.

"Mom?" Celeste called out.

A flash of bright white light illuminated the room, blinding her. When her eyes readjusted, she found herself in her childhood living room. The familiar green plaid couches and worn blue pillows faced a small television. On each side of the television were bookshelves full of medical, history, and Christianity books.

Her mother was curled into a ball on the floor in the corner of the room. Her head rested on her bony knees rocking back and forth. Her clothes were tattered and worn with blood stains. Her once blonde, then dyed brown hair was now light gray, and her ashen skin was covered in wrinkles and black and purple bruises. Her mother lifted her head. Celeste's hands flew to her mouth. Thank God she hadn't eaten dinner or breakfast. Two black holes replaced her mother's naturally brown eyes

"Mom?" Celeste gasped.

"Alice. Oh, sweetheart. My Alice. My sweet, sweet Alice." her mother gasped, her mouth wide in a smile. Her arms reached for her daughter. Celeste gasped, horrified. Sounds were emanating out of her mother's mouth, but her tongue was missing. Celeste's blood went cold, and she took a step backward. She wasn't sure how her mother was talking. There had to be a Witch behind it. She just prayed it wasn't Cate's doing.

She looked worse than Vicky did. Celeste scanned the room again, the old family room familiar yet foreign. Lucian had explained the Eternal Tombs as a room with the individual's personal Hell. The realization caused her throat to dry up. Her mother's Hell was the same one she lived while she was alive.

Her mother tried to stand up but her body was too weak. Celeste swallowed hard and watched her mother struggle. Against her better judgment, she hurried to help her up.

"Oh, my baby, my sweet, sweet girl." her mother asked as they made their way onto the couch. Celeste opened her mouth to speak, but words would not come out. She wasn't sure she even wanted to say. "Where is your sister?" her mother continued as they sat down.

Her sister's deadened face flashed through her eyes. "I don't know," Celeste croaked out.

"Where have you been? It's been years since I've seen you. You're all grown up." Her mother continued. Celeste still didn't know how to react or respond. She sank into the couch, shrinking herself. Did she know how long she'd been here? The black holes in her mother's head stared directly into Celeste's eyes. This was worse than any Halloween decoration she'd ever seen. Even without her eyes, Celeste could see that look of disapproval and disappointment that she had gotten so used to seeing. "Why did you leave me?"

Shame started forming like a giant in her heart. "I had to." Her eyes focused on everything but her mother.

"First your sister, then you. How could you forget the woman who raised you? The woman who took care of you? You two were supposed to take over the business. Instead, your father had to sell it. We built that practice for you and Vicky. We paid for your education, and this is how you girls repaid us? By leaving us?"

Celeste raised an eyebrow. Vicky was the good child; the loved and wanted child. "What happened to Vicky?"

She caught a glimpse of her reflection in the mirror on the other side of the room. In an attempt to put as much space between her and her mother, Celeste hurried over to it and stared at her reflection. The woman who stared back at her was much older. Dark brown hair streaked with gray. Wrinkles and laugh lines on her face. The small holes where her eyebrow, cartilage, and nose piercings used to be were long gone. She looked down at her arms. Her right arm was covered in faded white scars while her left arm was free of her night sky tattoo. This is what she would have looked like had she not been tricked into making that damn deal.

"She's a whore who threw away her life," her mother sneered, her voice stronger, back to how she remembered.

"Vicky got into medical school," Celeste said, remembering. At the time of the fire, Vicky was weeks away from starting at Johns Hopkins University Medical School.

"She dropped out," her mother snarled. "That cad across the street got her pregnant. She dropped out, and they moved to California. Left her old mother here to wither and die."

Celeste whirled around; her eyes wide. "Mason?" Dread sank into her like an anchor. This had to be some alternate reality. Sure, Mason had taken Vicky to prom and had mistaken her for Vicky and assumed she liked the same things Vicky did. At the beach, he seemed hurt when she told him Vicky was dating her professor. Time and time again, he defended Vicky when they argued about her. But Mason loved *her*. Mason came *for her*.

"Yes! The Wards! They were never any good, but we couldn't tear the both of you away from them. They were our neighbors, so we had to pretend to be friendly. They were nothing but heathens!" her mother hissed. Celeste's jaw hit the floor. Her parents were always nice to the Wards. They wouldn't have let Celeste go on vacations with the Wards if they didn't trust them. "We raised you both with the Lord and yet you both are going to Hell." her mother said. If she wasn't already on edge, she would have laughed. Maybe her mother didn't know where she was.

"What the hell did I do?" she asked as she walked back towards the couch. Her mother let out a broken laugh.

"You moved to Houston after you went behind our backs and disobeyed us by getting a degree in Astronomy," her mother hissed.

"It's still a science," Celeste said defiantly, feeling like a child again.

"Sure. But we paid for a medical degree. God created the sky, the stars, and the planets. What else was there to know?"

Celeste closed her eyes and took a deep breath. "I never wanted to be a doctor. I wanted to study the universe, creation."

"God created the world. Everything is because of Him."

"If everything is because of Him, then why study medicine? Isn't life or death God's will?" Celeste snapped at her mother.

Her mother glared at her. "God's work, our hands."

"Oh, so now we're playing God?" A broken, pathetic laugh escaped her lips, *"God,* the way you two act, you would think we were Catholic!"

"Maybe that's where we went wrong with you both," her mother grumbled.

Celeste chomped down on her lip to keep from yelling. "Where's Dad?" she finally asked after a few deep breaths, her voice thick with emotion.

"Heart attack. He was so upset and hurt by you and Vicky. How you went against him, went against God. You knew better, Alice. This is all your fault," her mother said tightly.

Rage boiled beneath her skin. This is what Lucian wanted her to do. Eighteen-year-old Alice would have apologized to stop the argument. Twenty-six-year-old Celeste wanted to fight. She balled up her fists and whispered, "It's not my fault."

"What?" her mother asked. Celeste flinched at the tone. It was her mother's way of saying *Excuse me?* Or *I'm going to have you repeat what you said, and this time, it better be what I want you to say.*

"It's not my fault." Celeste raised her shaky voice.

"Of course, it is, you stupid girl! If you had just done what you were told—"

"No!" Celeste yelled, silencing her mother. "No. I did what made *me* happy. A scientist is just as good as a doctor! I never wanted to be a doctor. That was not my dream."

"Do not yell at me. I am your mother, damn it. It didn't have to be your dream. It was your duty as a member of this family. We gave you food, clothes, and shelter. We paid for all of your activities. We didn't have to let you play soccer or join scouts, but we did. We paid for college. It's how you were going to pay us back," her mother spoke with a deathly calm. If they weren't in Hell and her mother wasn't already dead, Celeste would be wishing she was dead.

"No! No, that's not how that works!" Celeste exclaimed, irritation lacing every word. She marched around the couch to face her mother despite her body telling her to run and hide. But no more. No more hiding. She was done. "I was your child! You were supposed to love me unconditionally! You were supposed to feed, clothe, and shelter me because it was your job. You and Dad chose to be parents. I didn't ask to be born! I did not ask for any of this."

Her mother laughed hysterically like Celeste had told the funniest joke she had ever heard. "You think I wanted you? All the pain and suffering I dealt with was because of you! You were just a mistake. An unwanted mistake. Therefore, you owed it to us to do what we told you to do."

Celeste stood a little straighter like Lucian did when he wanted to appear more menacing. "I will not apologize for who I am, for who I chose to be. I'm not sorry I left. In fact, I'm glad I left this hell-hole because no matter what I did, it would never have been enough for you.

Even if I became a doctor and took over the practice, it wouldn't have been enough. You would have found something to complain about. I hate you. I hate him. I hate Vicky. I want to be done with all of you. You will no longer have a hold on me. For *years*, I used to be sorry that Lucian killed you and damned you here, but you haven't changed one bit. I'm not sorry Lucian killed you. I'm glad he did."

Her mother crossed her arms over her chest and gave Celeste her famous look, looking down her nose with a tight mouth. Even without her eyes, she could see the disappointment. "I never loved you."

Celeste rolled her shoulders back to keep them from dropping. Her mother's words punched her in the gut. She knew it was true, but knowing it and hearing it were two different things. Her lips thinned into a tight line. She spoke through gritted teeth, "I know. The feeling is mutual."

The same bright flash of light from earlier went through the room. The bright light faded. Her old living room faded before her eyes. From afar, she saw a small reddish, orange glow. *Fire. Hell.* She made a beeline for the light like it was a closing door and she was about to be trapped again. The light framed a black door, and she pushed it open.

She stepped into the light and let out a sigh of relief. She was free. Celeste looked around eagerly, hoping to find Mason waiting for her with open arms.

"So glad you could join us here today, Alice."

CHAPTER 61

"No," Celeste breathed. She wasn't out. Mason, Lucian, Micah, and Don weren't there.

She wasn't even in Hell. Instead, she was in a courtroom. Not just *in* the room, she was standing next to a solid oak witness stand. To her right was the judge—a grandfather type in a black robe. He gestured for her to sit down. "It's okay Miss Delco."

Celeste took a hesitant step, her feet like lead as they hit the wood harder than she wanted. Her whole body was shaking by the time she sat down.

At the defense table was her father. He looked a little younger than when she last saw him. He was healthy, full of color, and unlike her mother, had both eyes. The murderous rage in his brown eyes still had her whimpering and wanting to run away to anywhere but here. It was a look she was very familiar with; a hand to her face or a twist of her arm always followed it.

Her legs pulsed, ready to jump and run when a nicely dressed man in front of her held out his hand. "You're okay, Alice. He's not going to hurt you." She slowly sat back down on the old chair, the wooden seat creaking with her weight. "Do you mind if I ask you a few questions, Alice?" the man, an attorney asked her softly, treating her with kid gloves. She looked over at the defense table. Her father sat with another well-dressed man with a beak nose and narrow eyes.

Past the table, in the front row of the viewing section were Mr. and Mrs. Ward. Next to them were Grammy and her mother's siblings. It had been so long since she had seen them that she had almost forgotten what they looked like. God, what she would do to be able to hug her grandmother and her aunts.

Celeste nodded her head slightly. He gave her a small smile and continued. "Where were you when your mother was murdered?"

"What?" Celeste breathed in shock and looked to the side of the room where she entered. She just saw her mother. There was no way she could have been killed, considering her father had dropped dead of a heart attack...

The door she pushed through had disappeared into the ether. This was her father's Hell. His Hell was his murder trial.

"Do you remember where you were when your mother was murdered?" The lawyer repeated kindly. The man had nice eyes and a comforting smile. He appeared trustworthy.

Celeste twisted uncomfortably in her seat. "In my room, in the basement." She wasn't sure if it was the right answer, but it was the most likely answer. She never spent more time than she had to in any other room.

"Did you hear anything at the time?" the lawyer asked.

"Fighting. They always fight," she stated.

"Do you know what they were fighting about?"

She shrugged. That was the million-dollar question. "I'm not sure. Could have been anything, from work to me and Vicky to people in the community."

The lawyer nodded. "Did they fight a lot?"

"All day. Every day. They'd argue constantly, and it usually ended with him hitting her. Or us."

The lawyer glanced at the jury and back to her. "Did he hit you?"

"Objection, Relevance," the beak nosed attorney from her dad's table interjected.

"Sir, Mr. Hines seems to have forgotten that in addition to this murder trial, Dr. Delco is also on trial for three counts of abuse. Two counts of abuse of a minor and one count of domestic abuse."

"Overruled. You may continue, Mr. Jones," the judge said.

Mr. Jones, the prosecutor, looked back at Celeste and nodded for her to continue. She glanced at her father and took a deep breath. "Every other day, it seems. Some weeks more than others."

"Did you ever talk to anyone about it?"

Celeste nodded her head. "My best friend, Morgan Ward."

"Yes, we spoke to Miss Ward earlier today," he reminded the jury.

Her father jumped up from his table and pointed at her, but there was only a stub. His hand was gone. What did Lucian do to her parents? "You imbecile! How could you betray me like that? After everything I did for you. I didn't have to take care of you but I did! And you betray your own family! Look at what you did, Alice. *You* tore this family apart. *You* killed your mother!"

Murmurs erupted in the room as her father charged toward her.

The judge slammed his gavel down three times. "Mr. Hines, control your client!"

Celeste froze in her seat. Her father's brown eyes were wild and crazy—and familiar. She knew better than to move. It would only make the hit worse. Mr. Jones stood in front of the witness box with his arms out and his back to her to protect her. Officers descended on her father, knocking him to the ground.

"Get him out of here," the judge ordered with a slam of his gavel.

The officers cuffed him and dragged him out of the courtroom through a separate door.

Once things quieted down, Mr. Jones looked over at her. "Are you okay, Alice? Do you need a break?" Celeste stared at the door her father had just been carried out of, unable to focus on anything else. The officers only prolonged the inevitable. "He's not going to hurt you anymore, Alice."

"He'll kill me," Celeste whispered robotically. She had said it numerous times before but in a twisted way of joking. She was completely serious this time.

"You're safe now, Alice," the attorney promised.

She shook her head no. She was never going to be safe unless he was dead.

"He killed my mother. He won't stop at just her. It'll be me next, and then maybe Vicky."

"Objection! Accusatory," Mr. Hines yelled.

"Sustained. The jury will disregard." The judge hit the gavel.

"Your Honor, may I request a recess?" Mr. Jones asked.

The judge agreed and hit the gavel again. The jury was taken away, and the people in the viewing gallery all began to stand up and converse among themselves. Mr. Jones led Celeste to the gallery where her extended family sat.

Her grandmother opened her arms and embraced her. The hug was warm and affectionate and everything she never received from her parents and her sister. The floodgates opened and she sobbed into her grandmother's chest. The rest of her extended family circled them, reassuring her she was going to be okay.

When the judge called the room back to order. Celeste was back on the stand, and her father was back in his chair, this time with his arms tied around his back.

"Now, Miss Alice. Can you tell the jury what your father would do to you?"

Celeste looked over at the jury. They were all staring at her dead in the eye. She wrung her hands. The courtroom was silent. Now, for the first time, she could tell the world everything she had been too afraid to say.

"He would hit me and smack me in the mouth for defending myself. I wasn't allowed to go play with the other kids. He would yell and throw things at me if I came home with a B plus. He threw things at me a lot: pens, shoes, books, and the like. He would constantly tell me I was a disappointment to the family. Told me daily that I was never supposed to be born. He called us heathens if we didn't go to church or if we didn't pray enough." Celeste sat up a little straighter. A heavy load had been lifted off her shoulders.

"Objection, Hearsay," Mr. Hines called out.

"It's her testimony to the abuse she suffered," Mr. Jones fought back.

"Overruled."

Mr. Jones gave her a solemn nod. "How was he with your mother?"

"The same."

"Thank you, Alice. No further questions." Mr. Jones walked back to his table in front of her grandparents and sat down.

"Mr. Hines?" The judge called her father's attorney to ask her questions.

The man stood up and fixed his suit jacket. His eyes narrowed on hers like lasers.

"Miss Delco, you were diagnosed with Major Depressive Disorder, General Anxiety, and Social Anxiety?"

Celeste leaned back in her chair. Her parents never took her to a psychiatrist, so she had never been formally diagnosed, but it didn't take a rocket scientist to see she what she was struggling with.

"Objection, your honor. Relevance?" Mr. Jones spoke up.

"Goes to her credibility, your honor."

"Sustained."

Celeste looked between the three adults. "I guess."

"You know what a lie is, correct?"

Celeste tilted her head. She was twenty-six years old. "Obviously," Celeste spat.

"Teenagers." Mr. Hines shook his head and chuckled. Celeste glared at him; she was about seven years removed from being a teenager. In her mother's Hell, she was much older than that. But, if her grandparents were in the viewing area, then she had to be at least fourteen. "And you know the consequences?"

"You go to Hell. What does this have to do with anything?" Celeste asked, and then it hit her. "You think I'm lying?"

"You said it, not me," Mr. Hines said.

"Objection, question?"

"Move it along, counselor," the judge ordered grumpily.

Mr. Hines shoved his hands in his pants pocket. "Your father has worked hard to provide for you and your sister. Why would you ruin it with lies?"

Mr. Jones opened his mouth to object, but Celeste had had enough.

She shot up in anger, the chair she sat in clattering to the ground. "I'm not lying! Why would I lie about him hurting us? I had to make up lies to cover up the abuse because I was afraid of him! When teachers and peers asked me about the bruises, I deflected and said I fell riding my bike or fell down the stairs. I played the happy daughter. I was *never* happy. I wouldn't know happiness if it hit me in the fucking face!"

She went silent for a moment, her words hitting her ears. She had been lying to herself all this time. If she had been forcing it, had she truly been happy those eight years at the beach?

"That's enough, Miss Delco," The judge told her sternly.

"No!" she yelled at the judge. He raised an eyebrow and leaned back into his chair. She couldn't have cared less about the consequences of talking back to a judge, but he made no effort to stop her. "He deserves to be in jail. I'm not safe with him. I wasn't safe at home. My mother let the abuse go on because he abused her too. I saw it. Not that night but other nights. I watched his fists collide with her face over and over and over. I saw the belt marks on her back. I knew where they were from because they matched the ones on me! But when it came to me, the bruises and cuts were always darker and deeper than on my mother. He preached the Bible but never followed it, never understood it. It was only a matter of time before he killed one of us. I just assumed he was going to kill me first," Celeste finished. Her face dropped at the last sentence. She had always thought it and knew in her gut if anyone were to die at his hand, it would have been her, but she had never uttered those words out loud. More tears sprung to her eyes. She needed out. Now.

"No further questions, Your Honor. I forgot the mentally ill are prone to outbursts."

"Mr. Hines! Don't think I won't put you in contempt," the judge snarled and turned to Celeste. His face softened with pity. "You are dismissed, Miss Delco."

Celeste took off from the witness stand. She ran to the court doors and flung them open, hoping to be back in Hell. To her chagrin, it was an empty courthouse hallway.

"Get me out of here Lucian! I'm done. I did what you wanted me to do! Just get me *out*!" she yelled into thin air. Tears streamed down her face.

To her left was a door labeled *stairway*. She pushed the door open and ran down the never-ending steps. Every time she would slow down thinking she had put enough distance between her and her father, she felt his eyes burning holes on her back. His menacing voice echoed in her head.

I'm going to kill you, you brat!

A door appeared at the end of the next flight of stairs. Her hands wrapped around the handle and turned. She pushed the door open to reveal…nothing. It was another black abyss, but she didn't care. She ran headfirst into the darkness; her only solace was the solid ground at her feet.

Her foot caught on something. She stumbled and fell *hard* on her knees. A spotlight came up above her. She turned her head to see the dead body of her mother, bloodied, and bruised. Celeste screamed in terror as she scrambled away.

"Lucian!" she screamed at the top of her lungs, hoping he would hear her. "This isn't funny, you sick bastard. Let me out!"

Radio silence.

"This isn't a fairytale, girl. No one is going to save you." Her father's angry voice was icy and deadly.

The only one who can save you is you. Lucian told her that the last time they were alone.

Her father's disembodied voice continued. "You stupid bitch. You ruined our lives."

"No! You ruined it yourself," Celeste yelled back as she quickly backed away from the body.

Something moved in the dark just on the edge of the spotlight. It shifted and grew until her father's shiny black shoe stepped into the light. Her father stood beside her mother's body, glaring at her with dead and soulless black eyes. He never had a soul to begin with.

"Your mother was nothing but a whore, Vicky was an accident, and you were nothing but a mistake. My only regret is that it's your mother lying on the ground and not you."

Something metal clanged beside her. She patted the ground frantically until her hand landed on something cold and small. Grasping the metal with both hands, she rubbed it, feeling the object for any indicators of what it could be. Pain, blissful pain, sliced through her hand as a blue glowing blade popped out.

Her father stepped over her mother's body. Her fingers ran down the cool length of the blade, the sharpness was familiar to her. "Go ahead." He smirked, "Maybe you'll finally go deep enough, and we will be rid of you."

A switch flipped in her. Celeste stood up and faced her father. Her fingers gripped the base of the blade tightly in her left hand.

"You are a disgrace to the Delco name."

"No," she whispered with a cool evenness. A deathly calm that she only felt when she was numb. "You are."

Celeste drove the blade into his heart.

CHAPTER 62

A red flower of blood bloomed on his white shirt. Her father stumbled backward and his shoe hit her mother. He lost his balance and went backward, landing on her.

A blurry orange-yellow light appeared in the corner of her eye. She wouldn't fall for that again.

"Celle," a softer male voice called out. *Thayne.* She looked back at her father's now unmoving body. Thayne stepped into the spotlight, walking over to her father, and plucked the blade from his chest. He wiped the blood off with a clean portion of her father's shirt. He mumbled something under his breath as he closed the blade and slid it into his pants pocket. "Are you okay?"

Her heart caught in her throat. This was real. For eight years, she believed she killed her father in that fire, and now she actually did. His blood was finally on her hands. Her eyes remained focused on her father. She was no better than him or Lucian. "I killed him."

"No, you didn't. He was already dead. You knocked his soul out for a few hours. You're safe now. This is over," Thayne kicked her father's side for good measure and held out his hand. Her arms were anchored to her side. Her feet were cement blocks glued to the ground.

Thayne heaved a sigh and walked over to her. He picked her up with no complaints and carried her out of the room into the fiery light of Hell. Everything was a blur as he carried her to the guest apartment that Micah and Mason were staying in. Thayne sat her on the couch and knelt in front of her with his wing curved in to block Lucian, Micah, and Mason from her view.

Celeste felt like an emotionless zombie. She stared blankly at Thayne's white-tipped feathers, not able to register any voices or arguments from the men.

"Celle," a female voice called her.

"Cate," Celeste croaked, snapping out of her zombie-like state. All the emotions flooded back. She broke into a new round of sobs. Thayne pulled his wing back enough to let Cate onto the couch. The Witch sat beside her and pulled her into the tightest hug she could muster.

Cate shushed her. "They won't hurt you anymore. I promise you."

Celeste shook her head. "I stabbed him."

"I know."

"It felt good, at first," Celeste croaked.

"I know, honey," Cate whispered, rubbing her hand up and down on her friend's back. "I know."

"I wanna go home."

"We're going home. Do you think you can walk?"

Celeste shrugged but stood up. Her weight shifted on each leg as she took slow steps. Cate kept close to her right, Thayne on her left.

Mason hurried ahead of them and blocked the door. "No. Absolutely not. I'm not letting her out of my sight again."

"Calm down, lover boy. She'll be safe with me," Cate snapped.

"I can't trust you," Mason bit out.

The Witch rolled her eyes. "I lived with her for almost eight years. She is my best friend and my family. Get out of my way, or I will put you out of my way."

Mason's eyes shifted between the two girls and lingered on Thayne. "No, she stays with me."

Cate didn't bother with a response. She held her free hand up towards Mason then jerked it to the side. Mason, being controlled by another force, was pushed out of the way. He couldn't get his feet under him, and he fell to the ground.

✳

Cate's house smelt like ham and macaroni and cheese. Hester and Bea were cooking in Cate's kitchen as Celeste was led to the living room couch. To her surprise, Chip was lounging on top of the couch waiting for her. The corner of her mouth turned upward as she reached her hand out. He tilted his head into her palm like normal. He was always there when she needed him.

Everything felt so calm and normal in Cate's house, yet she had just gone through Hell. Celeste curled up on the couch alone with a hand on Chip's head.

"I can't believe he would stoop that low," Thayne hissed lowly from the kitchen. Celeste strained her ear to listen to their conversation. Her muscles stiffened automatically; the same way she reacted when she heard her parents whispering about her or her sister.

"That is not like him. Lucian would never do something like that to someone he cares about," Hester spoke in the same hushed tone.

"He better hope to Creation I don't throw him into his Eternal Tomb," Cate threatened with the same lowered voice. Celeste turned her head towards the kitchen. She couldn't see them talking and they had no idea she could hear them.

"And he wanted to throw me into the Pit for showing her the live stream of her sister," Don hissed.

"Is Aunt Celle going to be okay?" Bea asked her mother.

"No," Cate sighed. "Cell is not going to survive this. She is gonna relapse again. I just know it." Fuck. Cate knew her too well. Her wrist throbbed with the urge to slice it open.

"Lucian had turned the wall into a one-way mirror. All of us, Mason, Micah, Lucian, Don, and I could see everything. The way she looked at Don's Angel Killer, she was considering cutting or worse." Celeste closed her eyes, remembering the feel of the blade. It had been euphoric. Her skin was still tingling with the need to slice it open. She wished she still had it.

"I can't believe you jumped Don to get his blade to give to Celle. If Don doesn't kill you later, Lucian surely will." Cate told him.

Thayne scoffed, "I couldn't give her mine. It's built into my scythe. I wasn't about to stand there and allow her father to put his hands on her."

An uncomfortable dread filled her stomach. They all watched her father try to attack her. They just stood there and watched. Yet only Thayne came and rescued her after she had stabbed her father.

She must have fallen asleep because she jumped when she felt a hand brush the hair behind her ear. Her eyes shot open, and jumped awake. Thayne sat on the coffee table in front of her holding a plate. "You should eat."

"Not hungry," she whispered.

"Okay. Let me rephrase: *we* are going to eat. I heard you haven't eaten since yesterday's breakfast," Thayne said, his voice losing a little bit of the warmth she had come to know and adore.

Her face scrunched up. He was right. Yesterday, she and Lucian ate breakfast and then went to that soccer game. She never left her bedroom again until she went to see Mason. God, yesterday felt a million miles away. "Fuck you. Leave me alone."

She waited for a smart remark, but none came.

"Celle, I'm not leaving until you eat something," his voice softened. Celeste looked at the plate of food in his hands; it wasn't much by any means. He thought ahead. It wasn't even her favorite food that Cate's mother had cooked when she walked in.

Thayne grabbed a peanut butter-dipped apple slice and held it out to her like a parent spoon-feeding their child. "I can make train noises. Bea got a kick out of that when she was a baby. Cate didn't have these issues; she was just a bottomless pit."

"Hey!" Cate and Bea yelled from the kitchen. Hester laughed.

The corner of her mouth lifted for a fraction of a second. She lifted her head and opened her mouth. Thayne placed the apple slice in her mouth. "Good girl."

"There, you can leave now." Celeste scowled with a mouth full of peanut butter and apple.

"I lied. You're stuck with me." Thayne grinned and took an apple slice from the plate, eating one himself in solidarity.

"You don't have to do this Thayne. I'll deal," Celeste told him. She would be okay. *Eventually*. It wasn't the first time she'd had to battle her parents. But it was the first time she fought back instead of shrinking, and it was the first time she stabbed her father.

"Doesn't mean you have to handle it alone." Thayne gave her a comforting smile and held out another peanut butter apple slice. Celeste smiled weakly and took it as a silent oath, confirming what she had already known deep down but didn't want to admit since they were Lucian's friends.

She was loved by them. They were her friends too. These people looked out for her and cared for her. They sided with her against him when it called for it, despite their loyalty to Lucian. They loved her for who she was. True happiness, she realized, was here, with her true friends.

Sleep evaded her for most of the night. With what little sleep she did manage, her parents haunted her, their words repeated over and over like a broken record:

You ruined our lives.

You think I wanted you?

You were just a mistake. An unwanted mistake.

You are a disgrace to the Delco name.

She hated herself with every fiber of her being. She was not worth saving. She left the guest room, the same room she woke up in after the accident, quiet as a mouse, she wandered into the kitchen. She quietly searched through Cate's drawers until she found a small but sharp knife.

Celeste stood in front of the kitchen sink, the knife hovering over her right arm near her elbow crease. She took a deep breath and drew the knife across her flesh. Blood pebbled up to the surface, and a weightless feeling overcame her. Feeling lighter, she repeated the movement.

"What are you doing?" a male voice questioned her in the dark, startling her.

The knife clattered into the sink. She winced, hoping it didn't wake anyone up. Her left hand covered the fresh cuts on her arm. She had lost track of time. Her arm was red, and blood dripped down into the sink. Instead of one deep cut, she had made dozens of medium-sized slices into her arm. "Where the hell did you come from?" she asked.

"I was coming down for a midnight snack. What are *you* doing?" His chocolate eyes softened. She quickly averted his gaze, staring at the sink, not wanting to see the disappointment.

"Celeste..." He trailed off, his voice breaking. "Why?"

"The voices, the thoughts. I needed them to stop. I needed to feel something other than anger and grief."

He stepped away to the bathroom off the hallway. He came back with bandages and began cleaning her arm up. Just like Lucian, Thayne wasn't gentle, he cleaned her arm with a bit of force and frustration that he couldn't express verbally. "You did the hardest thing anyone could ever do and *won*. You are the strongest person I know. We are here for *you*. *We love you*. But we can't help you if you don't talk to us about what you need."

She'd always had to fight for herself. She had never had a person to lean on. Time and time again, she picked herself off the ground. Having a support system had never been a possibility until now. "I'm exhausted. Physically, mentally, emotionally. I don't know how much longer I can do this."

"I know," he whispered. "Then rest. I'll be right here."

True to his word, he never left her side. He became the sibling she never had. In the days following, none of her friends ever left her side. Bea slept on the floor with Chip, and Hester on the other couch with her daughter. Thayne slept in a recliner chair pulled up beside Celeste. After Thayne caught her cutting, Cate would always conveniently end up in the bathroom with her, usually sitting on the counter talking, much like they used to when they lived together at the cottage. Personal space had evaporated two years into their friendship. Every time she went into the kitchen to look for the knives, someone was always there ready to make her any food she wanted, effectively keeping her out of the kitchen. Hester doted on her and fussed over her like a true mother. Celeste didn't know how to thank her. Hell, She didn't know how to thank any of them for what they did for her. She wasn't sure if there was a way to thank them.

CHAPTER 63

Lucian waited a few long, agonizing days before going to see Celeste. Any earlier and the Witches might have hexed him. They still could if they so desired. He deserved it and would take any punishment willingly, but he needed to see Celeste first. He landed on Cate's lawn and hurried to the door. His fingers wrapped around the knob and an electric shock jolted through his palm and up his arm. He cursed as he jerked his hand away, shaking it out. He tried it again, only to feel the same electric shock. He let his hand hover over the knob and let his magic unlock the door. But no click of the lock came. Cate put a damn ward on the doorknob. He cursed and banged on the door with his fist. Hester opened the door, a murderous, glowing rage in her own turquoise eyes.

"Hest, how is she?" Lucian asked. He needed to see her with his own eyes. He didn't expect Celeste to react like she did in her parents' Hells. Then again, he didn't know what to expect either. Hester responded by reaching her hand out and slapping him across the face. His cheek stung as he brought a hand to the side of his face. "Fuck, Hester. I came to check on her!"

The crone took a step outside and shut the front door. "Absolutely not. Cate is ready to hex you, Thayne is ready to lock you up in a Tomb, and Bea's confused and angry but would be a willing accomplice to them all! You're lucky you got me at the door and not one of them," Hester scolded him. He was over a foot taller than her and yet she knew exactly how to make him feel small. "How *dare* you make that poor girl relive her trauma like that! You preach about how you want to help people who are like her, yet you did not have an issue letting her face her abusers. She stabbed her father, for Creation's sake!" Hester yelled; her finger jabbed painfully into his chest.

The heat of blue flames emanated from his fingertips, but he willed them back as best he could. An accidental burning would only fuel her anger more. "She's stronger for it now. She stood up for herself against the people who controlled every facet of her life. Her fear of them was holding her back all these years later. She could have never done that before, and now she can let them go! I wouldn't have done that if it wasn't in her best interest. She needs to learn how to stand up for herself, or else Micah and Mason will trample on all the progress she's made. They are already starting to re-brainwash her," Lucian tried to explain to Hester.

Hester shook her head, flabbergasted at him. "No Lucian, all it did was traumatize her. Thayne caught her cutting again. Now Cate and Thayne will not leave her side, and I had to hide all the sharp objects.

Lucian felt like he just got punched in the gut. She relapsed because of him, again. "Can I see her?" Lucian asked softly.

Hester's eyes narrowed. "No, Lucian, you can't. You are my oldest friend and Godfather of my daughter and granddaughters, so I say this with all the love in the world. You fucked up and I don't know if any of them will forgive you." Hester opened the door and walked inside. Lucian followed behind her only to run into it. The lock clicking was deafening. Even after his other screw ups, he had never been locked out of Cate's house.

Lucian stared at the door like it was going to magically reopen. Regret washed through him. He really fit his title as the Devil today. Only a bastard would do what he did. He probably belonged in his own Tomb for a few decades. Celeste started cutting again because of him. Maybe she was better off on earth, without him. Maybe in sixty years, they can try again.

Celeste wasn't sure if a week or a month had gone by, but it was warmer now than that fateful day. In Cate's backyard, she, Bea and Thayne were playing 2-on-1 soccer—Bea and Celeste against Thayne. Hester was curled up in a lounge chair on Cate's patio scribbling in a puzzle book with Chip by her side and Cate was tending to her garden. The backyard was not as fancy, nor as big as Lucian's backyard. But like everything else in Cate's house, it was cozy and well loved.

The sliding doors to the backyard opened as Celeste kicked the ball past Thayne and into the small rectangular goal. Heavy footfalls on the porch halted her celebratory cheer. All heads turned towards the patio.

Don stood tall, hands resting on his hips. His normal look of disgust had softened into a look of uncertainty. "It has been demanded that Celeste return to Hell for the next task."

"Absolutely not," Hester said defensively as she shut her puzzle book. "You tell that son of a Bitch—"

Cate stood up from her spot in the garden and wiped the sweat away with a gloved hand, leaving a trail of dirt on her forehead. "What's wrong?" she yelled and walked towards the deck.

"Orders from Lucian and Micah. It's time for her to go back," Don repeated.

"No. I'm not ready. I can't go through that again," Celeste pleaded to Don. The healing cuts on her arm started to itch. She'd rather open up the wounds than go back.

"It's been a month. I've put it off as long as I could. They pulled rank on me. Fucking Archangels," Don grumbled. "The Human thinks we've kidnapped you *again*. He wants proof of life."

Mason. Over the last month, she hadn't thought about him once. Guilt crawled into her like a tick, sucking out all the good feelings that had just started to seep back in. "I'm the worst girlfriend ever. I didn't even think about him being over there."

"To Hell with him. You needed to worry about yourself," Thayne reminded her.

"Yeah, but if I survive the tasks, I could go home. To Earth," Celeste said. "I could have been home by now."

"But your home is here." Bea stated. Concern furrowed her brows.

"I love you guys and I don't know how I could ever repay you, but I don't belong here. I'm not a Demon or a Fallen Angel or a Witch or even a Nephilim. I'm a Human." From the corner of her eyes, she saw Thayne and Cate exchange a brief, knowing glance. "And Micah said God has some plan for me. I need to go back to earth and figure it out.

"You can pay us back by staying here with us," Bea said nastily. The anger in her voice made Celeste do a double take. In the few months she had gotten to know the mild-tempered teenager, the most negative emotion she had seen from the girl was frustration when her soccer team lost.

"I don't see why I can't come visit."

"If the Human will let you," Cate muttered and turned up her nose.

"It's not up to him. It's my decision." She embraced Hester, Cate, and Thayne. Bea began crying uncontrollably. Cate wrapped her daughter in her arms and comforted her.

Bea shook off her mother and tearfully ran towards Don. She threw herself on her father and buried her head into his chest. "Daddy, please! I don't ask you for anything, but please, don't let her go! Celle belongs here with us." she begged him.

Don's eyes widened, looking immediately at Cate for help. Both Cate and Hester's eyes bulged out of their sockets and mouths agape. Don mouthed, "What do I do?" to Cate.

She shrugged and then mouthed, "Hug her back." It was obvious this was the first time Bea had hugged her father.

His eyes shifted back to his daughter. Hesitantly, he put one awkward hand around her and patted her back. He looked back to Cate, eyes pleading for direction. Despite the sheer awkwardness of the hug, it was the nicest thing she'd seen from him since she arrived in Hell. "I can't, Béatrice. I have my orders." His voice was a mix of soft and brisk. Half fatherly, half stern. Compared to Celeste's father, Don was a saint.

Bea tightened her grip and shook her head, begging him to get Lucian and Micah to change their minds. Cate walked over to them and pulled her daughter off of Don. Bea was sobbing. Seeing Bea sob and fight her leaving squeezed at Celeste's heart. She couldn't wrap her head around the fact the people standing there would miss her. She had not realized how much of an effect she had on them in the few short months she spent here.

Unlike the last time, she actually got to say goodbye to the people that she loved. She hugged each of them all tightly and made promises to see them again. It was a goodbye to her family that Lucian denied her the first time.

As she got to Don, the two just stared at each other, neither one feeling comfortable enough to share a hug. He held his hand towards the door. "Let's go."

Don led her deep into the halls of Hell. Celeste was certain she had only seen a small amount of this castle.

Hell was bigger than she could have ever anticipated. Every hallway looked like the one before. She had no idea how Don could just walk around and automatically know where he was going. The deafening sounds of the screaming were the only clue she was close to the Pit. He stopped in front of large metal doors. She was thankful for the small break from walking. The warm temperature of Hell, added with the many steps she'd had to take made her want to die. She wiped the sheen of sweat off her face and panted. God, she needed water, but ice water was probably in limited supply in Hell. Don turned to faced her. His round, beady red eyes met hers and held her gaze. There was some kind of control he had over her, she couldn't look away if she tried. He demanded to be seen and heard.

"I'm sorry for the way I acted towards you. It's obvious I don't like Humans nor do I trust them. I've been watching over Hell for billions of years, and they all look and act the same. I always assumed you were just another evil Human. But I see the effect you have had on Cate and on her daughter. You mean a great deal to them. You are a good Human—the only one I know. Therefore, you didn't deserve my hatred. After what you just went through, you have my deepest respect."

Celeste stared blankly at him. "Thank you?" she stated as an awkward question.

Don nodded his head once, turned back around, and walked through the metal doors. She followed him into the Pit.

Unlike the times Lucian brought her into hell, it was quieter than she anticipated. The moans and screams she learned to associate with Hell seemed to have been absorbed into the stone walls. He led her to a tall, but small gated platform above the souls walking into the Pit.

The Pit from this viewpoint looked much like everything else—Rocky, dim, and dark with a doorway only big enough to let one person in at a time.

The heat of the Pit was heavy and unbearable. The hallway was miserable but this was far worse. Sweat dripped down her skin the moment she walked in. Wisps of fire appeared around them in odd intervals. There was no way to tell when the next blaze would appear.

Lucian, Micah, and Mason waited for them on a metal platform. Her blood boiled at the sight of the Devil. An urge to punch him in the groin and make him cry was overwhelming. She wanted him to feel pain for once.

Mason laid eyes on her and sighed with relief. He rushed over to her and pulled her against him. "Oh, thank *God*. Are you okay? Did they hurt you?" he asked, kissing her lips between questions. His growing beard tickled her skin.

"That boy across the street got her pregnant. She dropped out, and they moved to California. Left her old mother here to wither and die." Her mother's voice entered her head. Celeste pushed him away. That would be the first thing she would bring up when they got Earthside.

"Are you okay? Did they hurt you?" Mason repeated as he ran a hand down her shoulder and arm. She winced as his fingers brushed over her still healing cuts.

Celeste shook her head as she pulled away. "I'm fine. My friends would never hurt me."

"They're not your friends, Alice," Mason sneered.

She opened her mouth to protest but was cut off by Lucian. "As I said, she's alive and fine. Let's get on with the next task." Celeste shifted her eyes to him. His icy eyes were awash with mixed emotions. "Welcome back. Now, I have installed temporary stairs in the Pit. The only way you can make your way out of Hell is to climb them and get to the top."

Celeste looked around at the rocky interior. She knew they were far beneath the surface of Hell but didn't know how far it was.

"How far below are we?"

"There's like nine circles," Mason stated.

Lucian snorted. "More like 900. Although, Dante was a great influence. Very inspiring work."

900 sets of stairs between her and freedom. 900 sets of stairs between her and Earth.

"I can't climb 900 levels. No one can do that." She shook her head. He was setting her up to fail.

"If they want their freedom, they can. And because I'm feeling gracious, I am allowing Mason to go with you for company. Hell can be a very lonely place," Lucian announced.

Mason put his hands on her shoulder and gave her a reassuring squeeze. "We'll make it out of this in no time." His military training had prepared him for things like this.

"And you two will be provided weapons. You'll need them against the souls. You can temporarily stun and paralyze the souls with these, just like Celeste did her father last month."

Celeste flinched. She barely made it out alive after the ordeal with her father, hurting other souls… that would damn her here and all of this would be for nothing.

Don came forward and shoved a sheathed blade into Mason's chest. Mase grunted and narrowed his eyes on Don. The Angel of Hell ignored him completely and gently placed another blade sheathed in leather into her hands.

"This is mine. It's called an Angel Killer, but it will still help you in there. It's the same one Thayne threw you when you...confronted your father. But it's mine, I'd like it back. Just like you did with your father, stab any soul that comes near you. It'll paralyze them and they will appear like they just dropped dead. Don't worry, they were already dead to begin with. But I wouldn't linger too long. Souls only stay down for so long." He instructed her and quietly explained how to use the knife while tying the sheath around the belt of her dress. Mason watched Don help her suspiciously as he tied his.

"I need to speak with Mason, alone," Micah told Lucian. Mason kissed Celeste's cheek and went over to Micah. The two walked to the other edge of the platform to confer with one another.

Lucian took Mason's place beside her. He shifted his weight back and forth on his feet. "Celeste," Lucian called her name. She could hear the pain in his voice. Good.

"It's quieter here," she commented, interrupting whatever he wanted to say.

"I had everything muffled for you. I need to talk to you. I want to—"

"Go fuck yourself." Celeste turned her back to him. She put her focus on Don and asked to see more basic moves that she could use. Lucian attempted to assist Don, but Celeste kept pushing him away.

"He's ready," Micah announced loudly. Both of them walked back to join the group.

Mason beelined for Celeste and gripped her hand tightly. He placed a quick kiss to the top of her hand. If they got through this, they would be able to go home. She wasn't ready to face her demons again, but she had no choice. Her only solace this time was that she was not alone.

543

CHAPTER 64

The Pit was enormous, hot, and pitch black. They could barely see a foot in front of them. Large beads of sweat dripped down Celeste's face, and she wished desperately that she could have worn modern clothing and not the medieval-inspired shin-length dress she was instructed to wear.

Inconsistent bursts of fire lit their path. Mason led the way, one hand gripped hers tightly, and the other held the knife. Souls identical to Vicky; ashen and lifeless, clawed at them. They screamed and begged for help, but Celeste could barely hear them through whatever magic Lucian used to muffle the noise. She elbowed some off of her, but Mason did most of the work. He sliced and pierced the souls gripping onto them. One by one, they fell to the side, giving a clear path to where they had been. The slain stared at her with their haunted, deadened eyes.

Celeste waited with bated breath for the bursts of fire like she had seen try to swallow up Vicky, but none came for them. It was like the fire purposely avoided them. She wasn't sure how much time had passed since they started. All she knew was that her knees were aching. Mason ducked inside a small nook to shield them from the souls. There was just enough room for the two of them. He lifted her chin and pressed his lips to hers, giving her a long, sweet kiss.

"Are you okay, really?" he asked again.

"I'm…better," she told him honestly.

Bright orange light filled the nook. Fire had shot up from the ground at the entrance of the nook. They braced for the incoming burn of the fire, but there was no burning sensation, just an uncomfortable heat.

This repeated constantly. Every time they paused more than a minute to catch their breath; hellfire erupted between them. So, the two had no choice but to keep walking and climbing. The stairs were the only place where the souls couldn't reach them. Souls clawed at it, but some type of magic kept them from climbing. Mason took the stairs two at a time. Celeste was behind him.

Anytime the souls clamored at them, Mason would pierce and slice them away. Celeste's knife stayed in the sheath Don gave her, and she never made a motion to grab it. She couldn't get her father's lifeless face out of her head. There was little to no light down here. The bursts of fire allowed them to see just ahead of them. Mason led her around the second level, hoping it was the same as the previous. Bits of rock and dust kicked up and Mason stumbled backwards, arms flung out to stop her from walking.

"What's wrong?" Celeste shrieked. Mason pushed her back and took a few steps backward.

He pointed to where he just stood. "The level breaks off. I would have fallen back to the bottom." She peered around him to see a black hole. A burst of flame suddenly appeared and glancing up, the ceiling also had a black hole. Any trip or stumble on the upper levels and she'd fall to her death.

He gently pushed her backward, keeping as much space between them and the edge as possible to keep it in view but not fall in.

Celeste wasn't sure how much time had passed. It felt like they had been there for days, but at the same time, only minutes passed. She also lost count of the levels. Each one as bleak, dark, and dingy as the one before.

She looked up to the sky, thinking she would see the tower that held that room Lucian brought her to, but all she saw was an abyss. There was no way... she saw the souls in here months ago. They were the size of ants, but she saw them. Lucian must have put a ceiling over them. She scoffed; this was a sick joke. They were never getting out.

"Fuck!" she yelled in frustration. She dropped to her knees, letting the hellfire consume her. She willed herself to get used to the feeling since this was all she would ever have again.

Mason turned his head and walked in place to keep the fires at bay. "What's wrong?"

Celeste let out another frustrated noise. "We're stuck here! We're not getting out! Lucian tricked us! Look up, there's nothing there! The last time I was here, I could see into the Pit. I saw the souls. I saw them getting tortured."

Mason looked at the sky and then at the dip below them. "That son of a bitch," he growled. "He was never going to let you go."

"Let go?" a small voice asked. The sound froze Celeste's muscles. She knew that voice. Envied that voice. *Despised* that voice with every fiber of her being.

Vicky stood before them. She looked just like she had the day Don showed Celeste that video feed. Her eyes were empty and dead. Her blonde hair was limp and stringy. She was a shell of the beauty queen she used to be.

"Alice." Vicky gave her a weak smile. Her empty eyes looked to Mason. Celeste saw the slightest sparkle of life in her eyes when she looked at him. "Mason."

"Vicky," they said in unison.

"Why are you here?" Vicky tilted her head towards Mason.

"To save your sister," Mason told her. He could not take his eyes off of her. "You're here..." He slowly walked towards her.

"Why? She sent me here." Vicky's voice picked up strength and turned dark. "She killed me, Mase. Did you know that? I'm here, where she should be." Her dead eyes locked on Celeste in a cold, hard stare. Her head cocked to the side. "Why did you kill me?"

"Mase, she's lying. I didn't kill her," Celeste squeaked, her voice light and shaky. Her shoulders hunched inwards in an attempt to make her small and invisible again. "You deserve to be here."

"Alice," Mason scolded her. Vicky's now black eyes settled on her younger sister. An inhuman, guttural, scream emerged from her mouth. Gone was Vicky, her sister, and lifeless form of the Pit. In its place was Vicky, a Demon.

Celeste unsheathed the Angel Killer and pointed it at her sister. "I did nothing to you!" Vicky skidded to a stop and recoiled; fear shone in her eyes. Don or his cronies must have used this on her often.

"You didn't stick up for me! You let Dad hurt me, not to mention you threw me under the bus too many times to count!" Celeste walked towards Vicky. The blue glowing blade was still pointed at her heart.

"I had to save myself, Alice. You weren't the only one getting hurt!" Vicky defended herself.

"He used to beat the shit out of me. He hurt you, yes, but nothing like what he did to me and Mom," Celeste yelled. Tears blurred her vision.

"Dad was worse on you than me because you're not his kid!" Vicky yelled back.

Celeste's muscles stiffened. "You're lying." Vicky had been cruel in life and clearly it hasn't changed.

"I'm not. He didn't like me because I was born when they were about to finish med school, and they cared more about not disrupting their education than they did me. Dad hated you because you're not his!"

Celeste shook her head. Vicky lied all the time. Lied to her parents about her faith, lied about going out on dates, but something like this…lying about this would have been downright spiteful. "There's no way. Dad never let Mom out of his sight. There would have never been time for an affair."

Vicky continued. "Mom cheated. She had an affair with an attending at the hospital she worked at in Philly. Dad wanted her to follow him into family medicine, but she wanted to be a surgeon. So, she went against him and started her surgical residency. Dad was pissed and that's when he started abusing her. In public, Dad acted like they were happily married, but at home, it was the same as what you and I grew up with. The only one who knew they were having issues was an attending. One day, after he beat her, she took me and left. We spent almost a year with that doctor. According to mom's sister, Jane, the day before the divorce was finalized, Mom and Dad reconciled. Barely nine months later, you showed up."

Celeste took a step towards her sister with the knife, but Mason stopped her. He grabbed her wrist. His eyes pleaded with her to lower her blade. She only raised it higher, aiming right for Vicky's throat.

Vicky continued. "Aunt Jane said that Dad forced her to end her residency and go into family medicine with him so he could keep an eye on her. She's the reason we weren't allowed to go anywhere. Dad liked control and having us all together so he could keep an eye on us. How did you not see it? You didn't look like us. You're the only one with blue eyes and brown hair! Mom resented you because she had to give up her surgical residency. Dad resented you because you reminded him of the attending. You ruined the family. You were a mistake. You were never supposed to be born."

Your mother was nothing but a whore, Vicky was an accident, and you were nothing but a mistake. Her father had told her.

You think I wanted you? All the pain and suffering I dealt with was because of you! You were just a mistake. An unwanted mistake. Her mother said.

Celeste shook her head. "You're lying." Her parents were lying and she was lying. They were just trying to get into her head and make her hate herself.

"I'm not. Aunt Jane told me one Thanksgiving when I was sixteen. That's why we stopped seeing her."

Tears welled up in her eyes. No matter what Celeste could have done, she would have never been loved by her father. She spent years trying to get him to love her. She knew then it was a waste of time, but some part of her had held on to hope.

"I tried to protect you when you were a toddler. But he wouldn't listen. I gave up. Mom said it was better that way."

"Fuck you, Vicky. *Fuck* you," Celeste rasped. Warm tears stained her cheeks.

"I…I'm sorry." Vicky said with as much warmth as a damned soul could muster.

"Sorry? You're *sorry*? That's all you can say? He beat me almost every day. They called me names! They yelled at me when I got a B on a test or paper. They grounded me for no reason. They made my life miserable."

"He did the same thing to me, Alice. You're not the only one who suffered."

Celeste let out a groan of frustration and screamed hysterically, "I was ready to die at eleven. Eleven, Vicky!" She lifted her free hand to wipe the tears away. "I tried it, twice, and I failed. God! I wish it hadn't failed."

"I wish it hadn't either," Vicky whispered. Celeste's eyes lifted. Anger and rage bubbled at the surface.

"You don't mean that, Vicky." Mason tried to diffuse the situation.

"Yeah, I do. Mom and I would have been better off that way." Vicky bit her lip, and her head hung down in shame. "I'm sorry you went through all that. I'm sorry I was a terrible sister to you. *I'm sorry* I listened to them and not you. If I could change the past, I would. I would have done more. We were all stuck playing the same stupid game. Please forgive me." Vicky pleaded with her sister.

Celeste sheathed the blade. A fire burned through her veins hotter than what Lucian had to scorch the souls. "I'm glad you're dead."

"Alice!" Mason scolded sternly. Vicky looked at her sister, shock, and guilt all over her face.

"I'm glad you're dead. I'm glad Mom and Dad are dead. I'm happy now. I am safe! I have people who love me, and I can do what makes me happy. I hope you burn in here forever." Celeste spit on her sister and stalked away.

CHAPTER 65

The other side of the rocky level they were on was not far enough away from her boyfriend and sister. Anger raged within her, but for once, she didn't want to turn it inward. She wanted people to pay. Every soul that clawed at her took on the appearance of her sister and her parents. With her knife at the ready, she slashed through any soul that came in her direction. With every soul that she took down, her anger slowly subsided. Paralyzed bodies lay around her in piles.

Panting, empty, and free, she drifted towards the giant hole in the center and peered into the dark, gaping crater. She picked up a rock and dropped it down the hole.

She waited silently for the clink. And waited and waited, letting blue hellfire envelop her, but no sound reached their ears. She swallowed hard; she was a long way from the bottom.

"*Do it,*" a voice whisper-moaned. It was not a voice she recognized. Celeste turned her head to see a wounded soul at her feet. His dead, black eyes stared up at her.

"Do what?" Celeste whisper-yelled at him.

"*Jump,*" the soul croaked. Celeste would be lying to herself if she said she hadn't thought about it. "*You are already here.*" The soul repeated words she had said a few dozen times in the last few months.

"I'm trying to leave. If I can escape this place, I can go home. I don't want to jump. I don't want to die," Celeste told the soul.

"*You have nothing to live for,*" the soul moaned.

Celeste shook her head. Eight years ago, she would have jumped with no hesitation. Now, she had her family and her friends. "I have friends to live for."

"*They don't love you. You will always be alone. You were nothing but a mistake. Everyone thinks so.*"

"I know," she whispered. Both Mason and Lucian had told her that in the last year. Her family told her that daily for eighteen years. She believed it herself. Yes, she had friends, and people who loved her, but loneliness was her shadow. No matter what, she would end up alone, and she would die alone.

"*They'll move on. Everyone moves on.*" The soul kept going.

They did move on. Morgan was getting married and had children. Mason had been married before. If she died—really died—they would continue living their lives. This was all a game anyway. Lucian was never going to let her go anyway. He dangled her freedom in front of her like a cat with a stick toy. Her soul was already stuck here so who cared if she killed her physical self? Celeste looked downwards and took a deep breath. She lifted one foot to step off the cliff.

"Alice!" Mason's voice called for her. His eyes were in a panic.

Glancing over her shoulder, Mason was barreling towards her. She set her foot down and missed half of the cliff. The edge her heel had just landed on crumbled and caved inward. Her body weight shifted toward the middle of the Pit. A blood-curdling scream came from her and reverberated from the rocks as she fell into the Pit.

Death waited for her at the bottom, wherever the bottom was. She waited for the release of death and braced herself for the impact. Her brain seemed to detach itself from her body. For once, her mind was blissfully silent, ready for the eternal darkness, yet her body scrambled to save itself. Her hands flung out to the sides and waved frantically, trying to find a rock to grip onto. Something warm gripped her wrist, and she stopped falling. Her body dangled in the center of the Pit; her arm stretched to the limit above her head. Looking up, she saw Mason gripping her wrist tightly. His teeth bit into his lip, and his face was turning red as he tried to hoist her back up.

"Hold. On!" Mase gritted through his teeth. Her knife slipped out of her hand and fell further down into the Pit. She kept waiting to hear it clink onto the ground, but there was no sound. She put her other hand on top of his. He dug his body into the stone for support as he slowly pulled her up. Once her head cleared the cliff, she used her free hand to help her up. She saw a red and purple-faced Mason grunting as he pulled her over the edge and back to him.

Celeste collapsed onto the heated rock. Her heart thumped rapidly in her chest, ready to burst out. Mason sat up and pulled her into his lap. She didn't have the energy to fight him off. She just curled into him with her head on his shoulder. He let out a large sigh of relief.

"What the hell were you thinking?" Mason panted angrily as he buried his head into her hair.

Celeste frantically looked for the soul. The soul she had spoken to was no longer there. "The soul…He tricked me. He convinced me to jump," Celeste panted.

"And you listened? Are you an idiot?" Mason asked, stunned.

Her eyebrows furrowed, and she shifted her eyes to him. "I'm a mistake. I'll always be a mistake. You moved on once; you can do it again."

Mason pressed his forehead against hers. "No. Alice, I'm not doing that again. I don't want to live a life without you. You and me, okay? We're gonna get out of here and live a long and happy life."

Celeste pushed herself out of his lap and stood up. "No, Mase. It's hopeless. We're not getting out. We're stuck here. I told you that!"

"Micah will make sure we get out," Mason reassured her as he got up.

"Micah doesn't rule down here. It's Lucian. We're just stupid little Humans to him. He hates Humans. This is purely for his sick and twisted amusement." Celeste paced and waved her arms frantically.

"There's a way out," Mason whispered, shifting uncomfortably.

"No. No, there isn't," Celeste reminded him harshly.

Mason's lips pursed. "Do you trust me?"

Celeste nodded her head. "Yes, but…" She trailed off as Mason stepped towards her. His eyes darkened with every step, a murderous look on his face he'd never seen before. Her feet melted into the ground, and she couldn't lift them despite her efforts to move.

Run, you Idiot. Run.

Mason's hands outstretched towards her. "Close your eyes, love. It'll be okay. I promise. This will be over soon," he reassured her. Celeste yelped in terror. Her body screamed at her to flee, but her feet remained unmoving. She froze like she had so many times throughout her childhood.

Mason's rough hands wrapped around her throat and slowly squeezed. Breath disappeared from her lungs, and words died on her lips. Her hands clawed at Mason's hands. Mason was squeezing the life out of her. She was dying by the hands of her lover. This was slower than the jump, and she wasn't sure which was worse.

"It'll be over soon, Alice. I love you. I'm sorry," he repeated over and over. Her legs gave out, and then her arms went limp. The world around her dimmed. Mason went blurry and faded into nothing. Then she felt nothing.

CHAPTER 66

The scream pierced Lucian's eardrums. It wasn't Human or Supernatural. It was guttural, feral, and animalistic. Lucian barely registered that it was coming from him.

The bastard put his hands on Celeste. The bastard was killing her. He needed to die.

Lucian tried to stretch his wings; except they wouldn't stretch. They wouldn't even move. He was frozen in shock and fear. He couldn't pull her out. Micah would get word back to Heaven that he saved a soul. It would start a war. His reputation, his secrets, and his kingdom were at stake.

The iridescent aura around Celeste was fading quickly. To Hades with the war; She was worth more than that. He'd rather spend an eternity fighting a holy war in her name than permanently lose the brightest light in his world. "Abaddon!" he screamed.

They were in Hell's control room, watching the light in Celeste sputter out. The Angel of Hell took off through the open door and onto a small balcony. His wings stretched out as he dove into the pit without hesitation. "Get the Witch doctors. Now." He barked at Samael as he stared at the security camera unblinkingly.

Celeste's body went limp in Mason's arms. Crocodile tears trailed down the human's cheek as he laid Celeste on the ground. Her aura faded into nothing.

Thayne appeared at Lucian's side with his scythe. His eyes watched the screen in horror. "What did you do?"

You lost her.

Don landed on the other side of Celeste and scooped her up, paying no mind to Mason.

"No! Leave her. I'm saving her!" Mason yelled at the Angel.

Don scoffed. "You're killing her." Don flapped his wings and took off for the sky. Mason screamed for him to bring Celeste back.

Moments later, Don sprung from the Pit. He laid Celeste on the rocky top of the Pit, right near the elevator doors to the control room. Lucian's feet finally broke free of their cement blocks. He jumped over the balcony and flew down to them. He landed on Celeste's other side and pressed two fingers to her neck. A weak pulse, but she was still there. He could save her. He began going through the steps of CPR

Thayne followed after him and put a hand on his shoulder, pulling him away. "Lucian. Lucian, you need to let her go. You fucked up, badly."

He pushed Thayne away and began trying to resuscitate her. "Come on, Celle. Don't fucking die on me. I forbid it." Lucian said through his teeth. Celeste's aura flickered brightly once and faded out. Thayne walked over with his scythe, the curved edge glowing blue. "No!" His voice broke as he pushed Thayne away, trying to get the scythe far away from Celeste. Don stepped over her body, gripped the collar of Lucian's shirt, and dragged him away.

The curved edge swiped across Celeste. A flash of pure white light lit up the room, blinding them all. The light faded and Thayne was gone. All that remained of her was her corpse.

The Witch healers he'd ordered put her on a stretcher and took her away. Cate threw unintelligible words at Don before running after the stretcher. It was too late. Celeste was dead. She'd still remain here in Elysian since she was a Nephilim but her humanity made Celeste who she was. She'd never forgive him.

Micah flew down to them. "Get Mason out of there this instant," he demanded like nothing just happened, like they didn't just watch a murder. Lucian slowly twisted in his direction. In the heat of the moment, he had forgotten about Micah. His main concern had been Celeste. He had let his guard down. He let Micah see how he felt about her.

How he loved her.

Lucian stood up slowly and spread his wings. In a second, Lucian charged him and threw him against the rock wall. His arm was pressed to Micah's throat. Bits of stone fell to the floor from the impact. "You bastard.

That fucker murdered a Human. He doesn't deserve to get out," Lucian gritted out, pressing his arm into Micah's throat.

Micah wrapped his hand around Lucian's arm, speaking in parts. "You and I both know she is not fully Human. She had the mark of a Demon—your mark."

If he wasn't so distraught, he'd sigh with relief for the fact Micah didn't know she was a Nephilim. Lucian pressed more of his weight into Micah's throat. "No. I rescinded the deal."

Micah's gold eyes widened slightly as if he just realized the mistake he made. "You didn't tell me that."

"I didn't have to. I do not answer to you. He can stay there for all I care! He killed Celeste. He should get a sneak peek at his future. Sounds like God had some great plans for her!" Lucian roared before stalking off, saying his third prayer in a month and a half.

CHAPTER 67

Heaven was nothing like the way she was taught. For starters, she imagined that Heaven would be full of light. Here, the darkness was impenetrable. Celeste reached her hand out to feel for something or someone. But there was nothing. She was alone; just as she had anticipated.

Goosebumps rose on her arms, and her teeth chattered violently. Hell was blazing hot, and Elysian was comfortable. But this place, wherever she was, was pure ice.

"Hello?" she called out into the black abyss. The was no echo or reverberation from her voice. The deafening silence ate up her words. Celeste slowly lifted her foot and took a step, feeling for the ground that she could not see. Her foot collided with something hard. There was ground, and that was good enough for her. She slowly took more steps and kept walking. In the darkness, there was no way to tell where she was going. She wandered aimlessly while shouting for someone with no response. She yelled for Mason, Micah, Lucian, Cate, Don, and Thayne. Nothing.

God, how she detested silence like this. This was when the voices in her head were the loudest.

Where is everyone?

Where am I?

Why is it so cold?

Where's Lucian?

Lucian's not coming. He doesn't actually care about you. You are nothing to him.

Thayne and Cate don't care about you.

His friends. They are his friends. They don't care about you either. You are nothing to them.

No one actually cares about you. No one would give a shit if you die.

"Stop it!" she yelled into the abyss. These thoughts swam in her head night and day. They could only be stopped by nights looking out her telescope, loud heavy metal music, nights in with friends, or the drops of blood that came from her skin.

"Celeste!" a disembodied voice yelled in the darkness. Celeste's heart picked up.

"Thayne!" she yelled back. The shouting continued and grew louder and louder as they walked towards each other.

In the distance, she saw a grey spotlight. Within the spotlight was a winged silhouetted figure. Celeste broke out into a run. "Thayne!" she yelled. The figure turned around in her direction.

His arms opened for her, and she ran into them, throwing her arms around his neck. His arms wrapped around her, giving her a squeeze with a sigh of relief.

"Thank God," he said as he pressed a kiss to the top of her head before letting her go.

"Where am I?" she asked. Her voice started to break. She was so relieved to see someone she knew. She was no longer alone in this darkness.

"This is the void," he said lowly. "It's not Heaven, and it's not Hell. It is the in-between. A quiet place for those here to reflect, for those neither fully good nor bad. It's also for those to decide where they think they deserve to be, and it's for those on the line of life and death while they decide where to go."

"But I sold my soul to Lucian. I'm supposed to be a Demon in Hell."

Thayne put a hand a comforting hand on her shoulder. "He rescinded the bargain after what he made you go through with your parents."

"What?" Celeste let go of him and held up her left wrist. The 'L' in between the wings that Lucian tattooed on her eight years ago and most recently cut through her cover-up was gone. Her night sky tattoo was as clear, sharp, and vibrant as the week she had it done. "Why would he do that?"

"I can't answer that, Celle. You need to take that up with him."

"So, I'm dead, then?" she asked. For once, she dreaded the answer.

He shook his head. "You're in limbo right now."

"Why?" She should be dead; she could still feel Mason's hands wrapped around her throat. Her hands clamped around her throat and rubbed at it.

"Only you can figure that out," he countered vaguely. She cared for Thayne and her new friends, but she was ready to strangle him. "You can either go and rest, or you can go back to your body; back to your friends."

"What happens if I choose to die?" she asked slowly with an uncomfortable coolness.

"I lead you over there," he points to the left. A small white hole glowed like Sirius, the brightest star in the sky. "And you begin your eternity in the afterlife."

Heaven.

Thayne points to the opposite side of them, a similar small white glowing hole, "That leads you back to your body. Like you said, there's no reason for a Human to be in Elysian. Although Lucian, Cate, and I can come to visit, Hester and Bea will miss you a lot." His voice was steady, but she could hear the twinge of pain.

"How long do I have to decide?" Celeste asked.

"As long as you need. Sit."

Celeste slowly dropped to her knees and sat down on the ground. Thayne followed suit. One of his white-tipped wings stretched out and covered her for the warmth she desperately needed in this freezing place. Her head rested on his shoulder.

As a teenager, she would have chosen Heaven immediately. Back then, she felt like she didn't belong in the Human world. There was no reason to stay. She knew at eleven years old she no longer wanted to be a part of the world. Going to Heaven and being with the Angels sounded like, well, *Heaven.* A place she could finally be happy.

But in her twenties. She found a reason to stay even though she was damned. She had Cate and Chip. She reconnected with Morgan and Mason, and she got the family she had dreamt about. She was content until Lucian came to get her. But was that worth the pain and emotions she had to deal with and would continue to deal with? Paradise was right there at her fingertips.

"What is Heaven like? Is it set up like Hell?" she asked.

"It's a mix of Elysian and the Eternal Tombs, but much, much nicer."

Celeste pondered, going back and forth between the two. When she made her decision, he walked with her to the white light. The two fell into an easy step side by side as they laughed and reminisced over the short amount of time they had as friends. Time that neither one would take for granted. With each step, the light got a little bigger and brighter.

When they approached the white portal, he turned to face her. "Are you sure about this?"

"I've never been more sure about anything in my life," she smiled softly as she hugged him one last time. Arms and wings enclosed her in a bear hug.

"It's been an honor being your friend, Celeste." He gave her one last friendly squeeze. When she let go, her hand took his as she took one step inside the light. Her leg disappeared completely, then her arm, then half her body. His hand slipped from hers as she stepped completely through the portal.

CHAPTER 68

Light. Bright light. Celeste gasped loudly. Her eyes opened, and her body tensed, then quickly relaxed.

"Cate!" Lucian yelled and gazed down at Celeste. His face softened with relief. "Welcome back, Pet."

"Out of my way, Witches!" Cate's voice shrieked. The Witch came into eyesight moments later, coming to a complete stop in the doorway. Cate's eyes watered while she broke out into a smile. "Holy shit. You're back! I didn't think it would work!" Cate shrieked again. Her high-pitched voice went right through Celeste. She winced and sank into the bed.

"Easy. Don't scare her back to death," Lucian lectured before turning his attention back to her. "How do you feel?"

Celeste looked around the room. It was light blue with beach décor on the walls alongside what looked like medical equipment. Then she turned inward. There was a painful ache in her lungs with every breath. Her head felt fuzzy and too big for her body. "Like I got hit by a truck." Her voice was hoarse and low. She grimaced in pain and rubbed her throat. Lucian nodded. Cate barked orders to another woman.

"Everyone will be so relieved!" Cate smiled at the two of them.

"I'll let them know. I'll be back in a bit." He kissed the top of Celeste's hair and kissed Cate on the cheek before walking out.

Another Witch came in with some water. Celeste took it and downed it immediately. The woman said she'd come back with a pitcher and took her leave.

"I'm so glad you're alive," Cate said before taking a seat at the end of the bed, leaning against the footboard.

"What happened? Where are we?" Celeste croaked out. Her mind was drawing a total blank.

"Elysian Medical Center." Cate fidgeted with her hands uncomfortably. "What do you remember?"

Celeste closed her eyes. The memories started to play like a bad horror film. "Mason. We…we were in a burning room…the Pit. And he, he came at me. His hands." Celeste gently placed her hand around her throat, where Mason's fingers had squeezed the life out of her.

"And then what?" Cate asked.

"He…he strangled me." Celeste's voice wavered.

Cate nodded; her own face winced at the memory. "He killed you. Don rescued you. Healers brought you here. None of us knew if you'd come back or not. Thayne had reaped your soul…then he was gone. I did a life restoring spell but I wasn't sure it would have worked. We just...hoped."

Mason would have never taken a hand to her voluntarily. "Mason is good. He had to have been possessed or something. Maybe Micah told him to do it."

"No, he wasn't possessed. Mason is not who you think he is. Celeste, he is not good for you. Once a man puts a hand on you, he will not stop. You *know* this."

"Mason came here to save me. He wouldn't have killed me intentionally, I'm sure of it."

"The excuse Don *extracted* from Mason was that because you had Lucian's mark, if they killed you, they'd kill the demonic part of you, cleansing you and making you Human again."

"Lucian never made me a Demon."

"They didn't know that."

"Did they know that Lucian rescinded the deal?"

Cate shook her head. "No. No one did until after the fact."

"Where is he?" Celeste asked as she wiped a tear from her face. "Where's Mason?"

Cate sighed. "Lucian left him in the Pit."

"What? No, Lucian needs to get him out. It was an honest mistake."

Cate blinked and opened her mouth.

"Celle!" Thayne cheered with a wild smile as he walked in, effectively ending their conversation. Lucian, Don, Bea, and Hester followed him in with giant smiles. Bea ran to Celeste's bedside and squeezed her into a hug. The air whooshed out of her lungs from impact.

"Easy, Bea," Cate reminded her daughter. Bea let go of Celeste immediately and wiped a tear from her eye. "I can't believe you're alive."

"I guess it wasn't my time." Celeste smiled at the teenager.

"Thank God for that." Thayne grinned and ruffled Celeste's hair.

Her friends stayed until the nursing staff kicked all of them out for the night, except for Lucian. Lucian remained in the seat by her bed.

"When I was in the Pit. I couldn't see out of it. Did you put a cover on it to trick me into thinking I'd never get out?"

Lucian's eyes shifted over to her. There were deep bags under his eyes from lack of sleep. His fingers were pressed to his lips. It was his deep-thinking position. "It's just a glamour, to keep the souls from seeing up and rebelling. I should have warned you, I'm sorry."

The two fell into a comfortable silence. It was the kind of silence where she could just *be*. And no dark thoughts would surround her. "Thank you," Celeste said.

"For what?"

"Rescinding the deal."

His head nodded once. "It's the least I can do after…" Lucian paused, getting his words together. "I want to apologize."

"For all the shit you did to me." Her words came out harsher than she anticipated.

He grimaced. "Yes. I am sorry. I didn't think it would have affected you as it did. I should have known better; I *did* know better. Cate said you had done a lot to get over your family. But you were still holding on to them. I tried everything I could for you to move on from your past. You needed the closure I didn't allow you eight years ago." He stood up. "I hope now you'll be able to move on." The Devil kissed the top of her head and walked toward the door, pausing in the doorway. "For what it's worth, I'm glad your attempt failed. I'm thankful you're here. I'm glad to have met you, to have been your friend." He smiled weakly before ducking out the door.

She watched him leave. He had saved her life on more than one occasion, and she had been a dick to him, fighting with him every chance she got. "Lucian!" she yelled out after a beat. She tried to sit up again, but her body argued in protest. Her chest felt heavy, and her head felt like it would topple off her neck. She plopped back down with a frustrated sigh.

Lucian came back in a moment later. His eyes were frantic. "What's wrong? Does something hurt?"

"I need a penny."

Amusement sparkled in his eyes as a lazy smile spread across his face. His hand dug into his pocket for change as he strided back to her bedside. He pulled a copper coin out and pressed it into her palm. Her hand burned at the touch— a warm, comforting touch.

"I forgive you for what you did. I was never mad at you for getting me out of there. I was upset you lied to me. People have lied to me all my life. The truth is all I have. It's when people lie that I second-guess their words and their actions. I second-guess how much I mean to them, and then I'm left wondering if I'm actually wanted or not. So many people were nice to me out of pity, and that hurt more than flat-out hating me. I'd rather be hated for being me than have superficial relationships with those who feel bad for me. It's easier to handle people if I know they don't like me."

Lucian nodded and smoothed out her hair. His fingers gently trailed down her ear and her cheek. They hooked around her chin, and he lifted her head to meet his soft blue eyes. "You are wanted. You are *so* wanted, Celeste. You are loved, *so* very loved. That is the truth. I promise, you will be happy and loved and wanted for the rest of your days. And I promise, As I have for months, I will always tell you the truth."

Celeste smiled weakly and looked down at the thin blanket. She was tired of clinging to the past. The imaginary hand she had gripping her past loosened and let go. She was free to move on. "I appreciate that. Unless I'm having a bad day. If I tell you I need to be lied to for the rest of the day for my own sake, just do it. I'll handle the truth the next day."

"Deal," Lucian promised without hesitation.

"Does that mean I get your soul now? You just made a deal with me." Celeste grinned.

"You little Devil." Lucian tilted his head back and laughed. His beautiful smile touched his eyes. "You can have whatever you want."

CHAPTER 69

The afternoon she was released from the hospital, Lucian took her back to Hell. She felt better, but the finger bruises on her throat were still highly noticeable.

She said her goodbyes to Hester and Bea with the promise she would keep the new cell phone Lucian gave her to talk to them regularly. The rest of the group promised to visit her on Earth.

"Your stuff will be back at Mason's house by tonight. Dog included," Lucian said. He looked regal in his tight-fitting red tunic, black pants, and black crown. Her clothes were a far cry from the beautiful velvet dress he had put her in a while back.

Celeste grinned. "Thank you. I mean that. Especially Chip."

"He and Roxie were getting too close anyway. Roxie's not allowed to date."

"Chip's a good boy." Celeste laughed.

Lucian laughed, his smile faltering a little. "I hope we can be friends. I always considered you a friend. Even when you hated me."

Without thinking, she threw her arms around him. His arms pulled her into him, wings encasing them, giving them some privacy. "It's easier to be your friend than your enemy."

Celeste's head turned towards the throne room doors. Inside, Micah and Mason waited for her. She hadn't seen either of them since that day and wasn't sure what she would say to either of them. She wasn't looking forward to seeing Micah. If it hadn't been for him, Mason wouldn't have strangled her. But it was Mason's fingers that were outlined on her throat. She also dreaded the talking about Vicky.

"Celle," Lucian called her name, pulling her out of her thoughts. She glanced up at him, her eyes meeting his devil-red eyes. "You need to know I will never forgive him for what he did to you. If he ever lays a hand on you again, call me."

Celeste glanced down at the ground and then back up at him. She wrapped her arms around him in another hug, inhaling his cinnamon and clove scent for the last time. Lucian rested his head on hers and hugged her tightly. "Thank you for not giving up on me."

Lucian kissed the top of her head again and let go. "You are worth it." Celeste stared at the door to the throne room. She knew she needed to go, but she couldn't let herself open the door. "When you're ready, Celle," Lucian assured her.

Celeste took a deep breath and entered into the throne room with Lucian beside her. Don and Thayne stood on either side of the throne. Lucian took a seat, back pressed against the backrest of the chair.

Mason stood beside Micah. They were watching her carefully like she was under a microscope. Celeste walked over to them slowly, studying the both of them. Mason's own bruised eye scanned her up and down, his eyes lingered on deep purple finger marks around her throat like a necklace. His throat bobbed. Micah looked as put together as he did when they came to get her a month ago.

"Alice! Praise my Father, you are okay. I am so thankful everything turned out fine in the end." Micah broke the silence with a warm smile.

Celeste's glanced back to Lucian. He was staring at a spot above her on the ceiling.

"My name is Celeste. Alice is dead," Celeste mumbled.

Mason shook his head. Micah's smile faltered slightly before bouncing back. "I believe we went over this, Alice. But let us be off. I'm sure you have lots of things you would like to do with your new freedom." He looked at his watch. "I believe we may even have time to go to a late service."

As much as she liked the idea, she longed for home. She longed for the beach house she lived in. All she wanted to do was lie in her bed, throw open the window, and let the gentle roar of the waves lull her off to sleep. Mason held out his hand for her. His hands looked bigger than before, not a mark on them. Celeste glanced from Mason and Micah to Lucian and the boys. Lucian, Don, and Thayne glared at the Angel and her boyfriend. She looked back to Mason who smiled lovingly. Despite everything they had just gone through, he still had the same boyish smile she had fallen in love with all those years ago. She took in a breath and walked right into his arms.

His arms wrapped around her as he leaned down for a kiss. She tried to kiss him, but when she closed her eyes, all she saw was his hands reaching for her throat. His hands reached for her cheeks. The feel of cold hands jump-started her heart. Her breath picked up, and she pushed him away.

"It's okay. It's okay, you're safe," Mason reminded her, taking her hand in his. "I'm so glad to see you."

"I…Mase…" Celeste stuttered. She didn't know what to say to the man who almost killed her.

"We'll talk about it later," Mason whispered to her. "Let's go home." He wrapped his arms around her waist, keeping her tight against him.

Lucian sat on his throne, his fingers over his lips in thought. "As you've been told, Celeste has been freed. She may live on Earth for all of her days. May she live a long, healthy life full of love and happiness." His eyes shifted over to Mason. "And may you pray to my Father that He lets you in at the end of yours." The last part sounded more like a threat.

"Father will be pleased to hear about this," Micah said.

"Well, then, you better be a good boy and hurry home," Lucian snapped harshly.

Micah rolled his eyes and turned to face the two Humans with his hands out for them. "Come, my children."

Mason took hold of her hand, and the three left Hell in a circle of holy light. A third chance. One she can spend finding out God's plan for her and maybe even search for her real father. She prayed her third chance at life went better than the first two.

CHAPTER 70

Lucian watched Celeste's failed attempt to keep Mason at arm's length as they took Micah's hands and disappeared in a poof of white light. The Devil leaned back on his throne, his crown weighing more than it ever had.

"Why would you let her leave with them?" Don questioned the king, exasperated. "You're sending her home with her fucking killer. How could you be so stupid? This is also going to undermine the Demons. You'll have a riot on your hands." Lucian adored his surrogate brother, but as Lucian's second in command and the person in charge of Hell, Don didn't have a problem lecturing him on his decisions.

All Lucian wanted to do was hit the bar to drink away her memory and bring home some girl to cover the pomegranate and vanilla scent that coated his mansion.

"I did what I had to do. But this won't be the last we see of her. I'm not talking about the visits we promised her. She's going to be back in Elysian sooner rather than later."

"You ended the bargain. You're an idiot if you don't think Mason and Micah will keep her locked up," Don chastised. Celeste had made quite the impact on their friend group, and she would never know the full effect. But that's the thing about humanity. They don't know how much They'll be missed because They'll already be gone.

"We both know Celeste cannot be caged. When she's had enough, she'll walk. Her home is here with us. She doesn't realize that yet, and I'm not going to force her into anything she doesn't want. She needs to come to that decision herself. Hopefully, she's wiser now to see the cycle she's in and will be able to get out. That's why I did what I did. Mason's not above being a scaled-down version of her family. Beyond that, Micah didn't do this out of the goodness of his heart, nor did he do it out of duty for our Father. He wants something either from her or the boy. I don't know what he's up to yet, but Heaven is going to break loose, and Hell help us all."

Acknowledgments

I started writing this book in April of 2015 and it has gone through many, many, many revisions. I hope you, reader, enjoy it as much as I did writing it. Or, I hope it makes you feel less alone in the world.

I want to thank my friends, Taylor, Sarah, Sophie, Sydney and Jill for loving me when I barely wanted to love myself. True friends are rare and after 20+ years of struggling with friendships, I am so fortunate and lucky to have five girls I can call sisters and best friends. There are bits of all of you in here; I hope you find yourself! Taylor and Sarah, I couldn't have made it out of our teen years without you. Also, thanks to Sarah for being a fountain of knowledge of Christianity and filling in my blanks.

Thanks to Corey for being a sounding board as I start to look ahead to book two and beyond in terms of world-building.

About the Author

Haley Moreau has been writing since she was in the fourth grade. A passion that became a lifeline during her mental health struggles. She is a 2019 graduate of Towson University in Towson, Maryland, with 2 bachelor's degrees, one in Criminal Justice and the other in Psychology. In her free time, you can find her either reading a book, crafting or practicing yoga. You can find her on booktok and bookstagram at Slytherins.Library. and on Blue Sky @haleymoreau.bsky.social

www.ingramcontent.com/pod-product-compliance
Lightning Source LLC
Chambersburg PA
CBHW030326010826
48973CB00004B/890